# No Rest

## Alex Campbell Real Estate Mystery Novel

## Volume Three

# By Charles Chaplin
(no kidding)

**Binx
Publishing**

Seattle, WA

### The Legal Disclaimer

This is a work of fiction. Clinton is not a real city. Names, characters, places, incidents and events portrayed in this novel and the excerpt from the forth-coming novel are the product of the author's imagination and entirely fictional. Any resemblance to actual persons or animals, living or deceased, business establishments, places, locals or events is entirely coincidental. No legal advice is given or implied in this work of fiction. Real estate laws vary from state to state in the United States. If you have legal questions concerning real estate, you should consult a licensed attorney who is a member of the bar in your state that specializes in real estate law.

Published by Binx Publishing Seattle, WA

ISBN: 978-0-9852103-4-2

# Books by Charles Chaplin

## Fiction

**The Alex Campbell Real Estate Mystery Novel Series**

No-List Alex (1)

No Serenity (2)

No Rest (3)

Note: these titles can be read in any order.

## Nonfiction

**The Smarties Books: The Consumer's Insider Guides**

Home Buying For Smarties

Home Selling For Smarties

## WARNING:

With the second half of your connecting flight now delayed for three hours on the tarmac, you have obviously finished the second in the Alex Campbell Real Estate Mystery Novel series, <u>No Serenity</u>. Here's another installment of your airplane read to help you fill the motionless hours as your plane sits in tarmac limbo. At least you lost the blob with Doritos breath who sat next to you before you changed planes. Although the screaming baby in the seat behind you and the grandma seated next to you now (whose head is inching closer to resting on your shoulder as she snores up a storm) is no real consolation. Please remember, do not venture forth into this series unless you can handle the insanity of all humanity; i.e. this ain't no PC playground! The goal is to make you laugh at yourself and the world and no group gets a free pass. If this does not appeal, then please move along. There are hours of unwatched reality TV waiting for you.

### Musical Note

To hear the *lovely lady* instrumental tunes that Beverly is so fond of, you can have a listen on YouTube and some songs are featured on the Ultra-Lounge CD series. Enjoy!

# 1

The scaly and yellow fungus-covered toe nails were really gross! She's gotta be kidding me, a pedicure? Sure enough, the one un-pedicured foot was sitting up on the blue leather ottoman awaiting my attention. Resting on the floor was her other fat foot, completely scale free, oiled and shiny, the five toe nails painted a perfect dark pink. "Here's the pumice stone, I'll start soaking in this tub of water. Be a dear and pour some witch hazel in it for me."

What? "Ah, Mrs. Holzer I came over here to give you my listing presentation, remember today at 12:30 our appointment? It looks like your pedicure person only got one foot taken care of. I can leave and come back another time if this isn't convenient." I was feeling it was time to leave but for some reason I didn't see the door.

"Leave, what? My you must be kidding me! Stewart Vezano was just here from Rockside Realty and look at what a great job he did with my left foot." Mrs. Holzer, pulled her pale blue bath robe open a bit and fanned herself. She was a white haired, well over 75 year old woman. I thought she was interested in listing her house. I had all my comps prepared and was ready to review and tour her house. I still couldn't make out a door anywhere, odd. "Now come on Alex, opportunity knocks. Come over here and take care of my right foot for me, it really needs a good scrub." She patted the sofa cushion with her gnarly liver spotted hand. "Alex I'm waiting. Stewart sure had no problem cleaning up my left foot, now did he? He also gave me a wonderful listing presentation and you know if my right foot isn't taken care of to my satisfaction, I may just have to list with Stewart."

# CHARLES CHAPLIN

She has got to be kidding me? Was my bank account really in such dire need as to scrub her nasty foot? No, definitely not! It is time to get out of here, let Stewart the major kiss ass whore, have this one. I'm out! But where is the damn door? I can't..."

"Alex! Alex, come on over here now and let's get my foot all nice and pretty...."

Aghhhh! What the? What's that wet slimy thing on my face? Oh god! Whew, that was one awful nightmare, "Get off of me Clyde, you can see I'm awake! No need to try and French kiss me as well." Oh my god what a fucked up nightmare. Jeesh, and I usually don't recall my dreams, much less wake up in a cold sweat from a nightmare. I got out of my bed and stumbled into my small bathroom and proceeded to scrub my face. Time for coffee; definitely coffee. I walked into my open kitchen and living area, pulled up one of the steel and glass garage doors which is also the rear wall of my little cottage. I let Clyde, my reddish brown Benji movie look-a-like dog, run out onto the patio and into the fenced yard to check out his turf while I filled his stainless bowl with kibble. God, things have got to improve I thought as I filled the coffee pot with filtered water. The last listing I had got all screwed up due to a missing owner. (see Volume Two) The real estate market in Clinton is definitely slowing down, still not as bad as the rest of the nation but worrisome enough. Hence the nightmare, eeewe!

I'm Alex Campbell, just over 41 and I have been selling residential real estate in the mid-size city of Clinton going on almost five years now. Some days are better than others and the start to this one was not exactly auspicious. Why would I have a nightmare about some old woman and a listing appointment? No listing appointment like that was on my calendar. I poured my coffee and went to sit outside on my patio. The sound of the gurgling water was nice and soothing. I had finally managed to build a little water fall feature in the small stream that runs through my back yard. My 800 square foot 1919, gutted and rebuilt, arts and crafts bungalow is in an undiscovered/un-named neighborhood just south of downtown Clinton and my lot borders a greenbelt. Clyde was out at the far end of my back yard, scouting for his nemesis, the squirrels, in the large oak tree. I was sitting there contemplating nothing when my cell phone began to ring. I noted it was Wanda's number and picked up.

"Damn, just let that phone ring and ring before you pick up!" She barked in an annoyed tone. "Wake yo' butt up! Alex, you get yourself dressed and get over to my house and take that Ethel Kluntz OUT! And honey, I mean out and you are NOT to come back with her until you have SOLD her something and her moving day is set in stone. I'm telling you the truth, that woman is playing on my VERY last nerve today. You know she took out them curtains I had made for my refrigerator this morning and was starching them? Says, the creases are not sharp enough! Then, sounds like she gonna be emptying out all my kitchen cabinets and cleaning them. She wants to put down that shelf liner crap, talking 'bout how no kitchen can have clean cabinets without no shelf liner paper. Wanting to know if I want plain white liner or one of them patterned liners. I'm telling you Alex this here is no good! Not gonna do no more at all!"

# CHARLES CHAPLIN

Wanda had taken in Ethel Kluntz as an unexpected house guest almost two weeks ago. Ethel is the mother of my client Norman Kluntz and Wanda was the mortgage broker for his loan. He recently moved into his new split level house in Rosedale that I sold to him, along with his girlfriend Amy. Ethel had flown from Philadelphia to Clinton to surprise her son on his closing day. However, Norman failed to let Ethel know he had a girlfriend or that he was moving in with her. Things did not go well when Ethel discovered what the living situation was. Thus, Wanda inherited Ethel. As it turns out, Ethel has decided she is going to move to Clinton and I guess it has become my job to find her a new place to live. Either that or Wanda commits homicide in her own home. I tried to placate Wanda, "Good morning to you too Wanda. I can tell you are not having a very good morning. You sound as if you are feeling a bit stressed? I can understand that feeling Wanda. I know Ethel may be a bit frustrating but at least you have helped her out and…"

"Frustrating? Have you lost your white-ass mind? Damn fucking pain in my fat black ass is more like it! Oh NO, I ain't hearing none of your new pop shrink/Dr. Phil wanna-be crap. You just do like I say! Get your bony butt dressed and get over to my house and take Ethel out and SELL her a house TODAY! Got it? That is what you still do right, sell houses? Last time I checked that's what your business card had written on it, *real estate agent*. So get moving and sell damn it! Cause unless you get it done and fast, there's gonna be some serious shit going down at *Chateau* Wanda and none of it pretty or fun in a reality TV way neither."

4

# NO REST

"I hear you Wanda and I understand your frustration. You know I have a tour set up for her today and I'm rolling over there in an hour or so. I'll see what I can do."

"I already told you to cut out that shrink validation crap, now didn't I? You read anymore of them damn pop shrink books and we gonna have blows. Hell, if that boundary assertion book you read wasn't bad enough, and now it sounds like you readin' some phony care bear book. All I can say is bitch better be ready to look her ass off, 'cause she best be buying herself a house today!" With that Wanda hung up. Clearly she was annoyed and honestly I can't say I blame her. Ethel Kluntz is a tad controlling. That said, Ethel was cleaning up Wanda's house, overstepping her boundaries in the process perhaps, but Wanda's house sure was looking shiny and clean these days. Wanda was correct, I had started reading another psychology book. This mass market tome is all about acknowledging others' feelings and validating where they are. Yes, <u>Honoring Me, Honoring You: Creating We Synergy</u> would hopefully help me out as much as the previous book on boundaries I read, <u>Step on My #ick and I'll Slug You!</u>

I finished my coffee and proceeded to get dressed. I wanted to wear my cut-off khaki shorts, a tee shirt and Jesus sandals as Wanda calls them, (a.k.a. Birkenstocks). Especially with the summer just about over, it will not be too much longer that I can roam around in my favorite attire. However, today I had already scheduled a tour for Ethel to see a couple of listings at Seaview, the snotty seniors-only town just south of Clinton. As rigid as Seaview is I am surprised I did not receive a memorandum as to what constitutes acceptable real estate

5

attire when showing a listing at Seaview. They have a rule for absolutely everything. Well, since no memo was received, I had to use my best judgment. I figured blue jeans of any kind would scare the hell out of them, so I opted for stone colored and dry cleaner pressed chinos, socks, which I despise, brown slip-on shoes (slip-on being key when you are a real estate agent), and a brown belt to match, an effort on my part. I found one of my more conservative short sleeve plaid shirts, this one a pale yellow and blue (soothing Swedish flag colors). I then put on my navy summer blazer and called it good. This is as close to proper real estate attire as I could muster. I made sure Clyde was okay in the back yard, shut up my little ranch and went to pick up Ethel at Wanda's house.

# 2

Wanda lives in the Highmont, an old neighborhood that sits directly north and above downtown Clinton. It is situated on a very high hill and has some of the best views of downtown and Warner Sound of any neighborhood in Clinton. The Highmont was developed in the 1890s and for a brief period it was the premier neighborhood during Clinton's boom years as a shipping port. However with the advent of the car in daily life and the removal of the trolley system in the early 1930s, the Highmont lost its luster. It is now a predominantly black neighborhood with artists and free spirits thrown in. It was Clinton's version of Haight Ashbury back in the day and still has a few active communal living houses and brightly painted Victorians and clapboards are fairly common. Wanda's house blends right in. It is a bright turquoise, late 1920s, three bedroom bungalow with two eyelet windows up top. Wanda frequently repaints her front door when her moods change and it had recently been repainted a vivid orange. However, as I pulled up to the curb in my aging, two-door, blue Volvo, I noticed her front door was now a dark brown. That certainly was off-character as Wanda lives for bright colors in all parts of her life. I was about to get out when Ethel shot out the door.

"No need to come in Alex, I am right here. Just a second and let me lock this door, the paint is still wet so this is a bit tricky." Ethel called out from the front stoop. Down the front steps she came dressed in a pink cloth coat, sensible tan lace up shoes, a big black purse, her oversized blue glasses, secured with a chain, making her eyes appear a bit bugged. "*Oy*, my feet are already killing me and we haven't even started our tour." she said while getting in the car. I had learned from the last tour, that despite her over 70 age bracket, she did not like old school open the doors for women protocol. This was fine by me. It reminded me of the sixth grade when we had this new "women's lib" English teacher at our school who was making waves left and right. One of her axes to grind was boys holding or opening any doors for her. She would yell and scream if you did it, going off on some diatribe about how she was a grown woman and could open her own doors thank you very much and how it was her duty to make sure boys like us never babied women, etc.... If she saw you holding the door or helping carry books for a fellow student that happened to be a girl, she'd start to yell and immediately dash over and lecture you about patronizing women, grabbing the books out of your hands and thrusting them into the girl's.

At the time, it was considered good manners to hold the door for any elder, male of female. But for Ms. Autri that was not acceptable, "Ms." being her other major point of contention. If you dare said "Mrs." by mistake she'd yell out, "No I am sorry, my mother is not here!" Then if you slurred or made a mistake and said "Miss" all hell broke loose. You were in for a lecture on male chauvinistic pigs and how demeaning that title was; such an odd time period the early 1980s were. Nowadays people are so rude in general that Ms. Autri need not worry about anyone patronizing her by holding a door open for her, male or female. I'm sure she's just thrilled with the recent group of 20-something women who seem to favor baby talk, acting like helpless bimbos, and dressing to look like hookers, not to mention plastic surgery out the yin-yang. Yes, I'd love to hear her take on the "sisterhood" today. However, I am sure the sisterhood is now all amiss due to some enormous male conspiracy.

Junior high flashbacks aside, I was driving Ethel Kluntz to Seaview today. She had not liked any of the in-city condos I had previously shown her and then she decided it would be best if she could live in an age restricted community. The few in-city age restricted condos that I showed her, she did not like at all. So, this left us no other choice but the town of Seaview.

Seaview is situated about 30 minutes south of Clinton, actually it is directly south of the greenbelt that is at the back of my house's lot. Well, the old Sutton estate and land preserve lies in between but close enough. Seaview is a legally incorporated town that was built by developers starting in the early 1970s. Only developers could have come up with such an inaccurate town or housing complex name. The "sea" is nowhere close by. The correct name should have been Soundview but the developers probably thought "Sea" sounded more exotic and would boost the sales prices, who knows! It was designed to be an age restricted town. Originally the minimum age was 70 but at some point it was lowered to 62. In the 1960s some retirees had an informal seniors-only mobile home park on the land where Seaview is. From there, the developers entered the picture, smelled money, took over and expanded. There are no mobile homes anywhere near Seaview today.

The first phase was completed in 1973 and that includes the town part and the first two five-story "tower" buildings. Originally they were rental apartments but they converted to condominiums in the late 1970s. These tower condos have actual views of Warner Sound far below. The three other building phases (1984, 1995 and 2000) consist of some bungalow neighborhoods, another grouping of five-story towers (without water views), and a small assisted living condo complex. As long as you have the bank account, from age 62 to death, Seaview has got you covered. Seaview, the town, is legally incorporated and has its own mayor, city council, police force, utilities; it is its own gated fiefdom. It is probably easier to get through the White House's front gate than the front gate at Seaview.

To show a listing at Seaview entails some pre-planning. First, you must contact the listing agent as all units require appointments regardless if they are vacant or owner occupied. They also require the listing agent be present for all showings, a ludicrous stipulation, but one of their rules none-the-less. One could surmise they put this rule in place because they would prefer the owner to list with Seaview Realty which is the town's real estate office and exclusive representative for all units which are owned by the Seaview Care Corporation. That works out to over 70 percent. They allowed a third of the units constructed to be owned in full by the occupant with no legal stipulation to list with Seaview Realty. However, they still retain very strict co-op board control approval of anyone who is going to live in Seaview and even the independently owned units must pay a hefty fee to the Seaview Care Corporation before title is transferred. With two thirds of the units in Seaview, the corporation actually holds title and they are exclusively listed through Seaview Realty. Even with the independently owned units, a listing agent and seller must present the list price to the Board for approval, prior to listing the unit for sale. He or she must also make sure prospective buyers meet all of the rigid income and rule guidelines prior to having the seller sign off on any offers. In addition, once an offer is accepted by an independent seller in Seaview, this offer must be submitted to the Board for further review and final approval. All signed around purchase and sale agreements must also include an addendum which outlines this and several other laborious buyer/seller processes that are unique to Seaview. In short, listing or selling in Seaview is a major pain in the ass for a real estate agent. Hence, the majority of listings and sales go through the Seaview Realty office. They are notorious for treating "outside" agents such as myself with great scorn and seemingly do everything they can to persuade owners not to list with another brokerage besides Seaview Realty. In recent years, there has been pressure by the State Attorney General's office to force Seaview to open up its real estate, lest they be charged with running a monopoly or racketeering I suppose. Therefore, Seaview is now reluctantly more open to agents such as myself representing a buyer or allowing an owner in Seaview to have one of us "outsiders" represent them as sellers.

However, this "openness" can only go so far as one of the state's ex-governors currently resides in Seaview and was preceded by two ex-governors before him who passed away there. And the death turnover rate is exactly what Seaview Care Corporation is all about. They count on deaths and a controlled turnover rate to ensure their profits. Regardless of who sells or buys at Seaview, the Seaview Care Corporation is assured at least a 40 percent share of all profits. And 40 percent is the very least, the norm being somewhere around 60 percent and 100 percent for the actual corporate owned units. The fees they charge as a "citizen" moves from say a bungalow to the assisted living complex are quite steep. And if you make it to "God's final waiting room" (a.k.a. Seaview Sunrise Care) then they empty all of your bank accounts before your last gasp registers on the EKG monitor. Not to worry though, because once you have expired, they'll move you along to the Seaview Mortuary where those kind folks will fleece the remainder of your relatives' pennies to put you up in style in the exclusive Seaview Eternal Slumber Columbarium. Cremation is mandatory in Seaview; I guess bodies take up too much saleable real estate? The Seaview Care Corporation has it all figured out, you never need to leave the gated town. They have their own supermarket, gas station, car wash, dry cleaner, drugstore, hair salons, movie theatres, radio station, local cable access TV station, weekly newspaper, shopping mall, gym, spa, restaurants, clubs, golf course, it's all there and only for residents and their approved guests' use. It is all safe and secure and marked up at least 10 percent over "real world" retail prices.

Once I exited the interstate and pulled onto the Seaview access road, there was the colorful billboard sign all spick and span (per the rules, they probably wash it once a day) complete with drawings of boats bobbing in water and seagulls flying above, *City of Seaview, Where Rest and New Beginnings Await You and Tomorrow Starts Today!* Then in smaller print below the huge shiny logo *Incorporated 1973. All access strictly limited to member residents and their approved guests only.* Who knows, since my last visit a couple of years ago, maybe they've installed iris scans as part of their front gate, security shake down procedure.

# 3

There is one gate for Seaview residents which has a keycard swipe and personal entry code and then there is the visitor's gate. The guardhouse is built to look like a mini Swiss chalet and the gate is no ordinary wooden slat that slowly moves up and down. No, the gate is a heavy metal affair that moves across tracks and the only thing that could remotely smash through it would be a semi truck.

I pulled up and a guard in the Seaview uniform, green polo shirt and navy slacks, came up to the car. "Dave" as his name badge indicated was somewhere in his early 50s and outfitted with a microphone on his lapel, a stun gun in his belt holster along with an industrial grade flashlight, a ring of formidable looking keys and handcuffs hanging from his belt. He asked for both our i.d.'s and took them in the gate house. After a long wait, he reappeared with a clipboard. He gave me a map directing us to the visitor's parking lot and said the Seaview Realty representative would be waiting at the Visitor's Center to meet us. Dave noted my car's make and license plate number, gave me a laminated card to place on the driver's side of the dashboard and two laminated visitor badges on green lanyards for us to wear. He said we could get our i.d.'s back when we checked out and returned the visitor badges. Dave then gave us a semi frigid smile and said, "You two enjoy your visit to Seaview today. Make sure you obey the 15 mile an hour speed limit at all times until you have safely parked your vehicle in space number six in the visitor's lot. Sir, be sure you only park in that designated space, or you will be towed." With that said, the huge metal gate slowly slid open and we were off.

# NO REST

Why Dave even mentioned the speed limit is beyond me, as they have sizeable speed bumps in the road every 50 feet. It would be a miracle to get your vehicle anywhere over 10 miles per hour before you lurched over the next speed bump. The entry road is windy and extremely well manicured. Vivid green (chemically fed) Bermuda grass lines either side of the two lane road with carefully maintained birch trees planted alongside every 100 feet. Around the curve on the right is the Seaview Gas Company and Car Wash. Directly across on the left is the sign for the Visitor's Center and parking. The lot had about 10 cars in it and there were plenty of open spaces. At least eight of the parked cars were large boats like Wanda's late 1980s Lincoln Town Car. She would appreciate their car choices. I followed Mr. Gate Nazi's orders and made sure I found the space with the large number "6" painted on the shiny clean asphalt in day glow yellow. It appeared each parking space's sizable number was repainted every month and the asphalt was squeaky clean. The Visitor's Center building looks like a Disney version of a Swiss chalet Heidi would live in. And just like Disney, there was a good (I hope) witch waiting at the Center's front doors.

"Well hello there, you must be Alex Campbell with Winterfrost Real Estate and this must be Mrs. Ethel Kluntz?" This, from an immaculately dressed, pressed and coifed woman who was over 70, although it was hard to tell exactly how far over 70 because she had obviously had a face lift or two. Her gray hair was sprayed into an unmovable helmet which was styled to hide her face lift scars no doubt and accent her gold ball ear rings which perfectly covered her ear lobes. She wore a light pink dress with tan hose and matching pumps. Over her dress she was sporting a green blazer with gold buttons. The Seaview crest was sewn on the breast pocket and a small gold name badge was tacked on her blazer's left lapel next to a pinned-on pink rose. "I am Beverly Ann LeFaye, so nice to meet you all!" She said as she smiled a wide frosted pink lipstick smile, while conspicuously winking at both of us. "I am the exclusive Seaview Realty agent, Social Coordinator for Seaview Care Corporation, resident since 2000, and homeowners' association board president going on two years now. Welcome to Seaview! Won't you please come in and let's get better acquainted." This she said in her honey coated voice, as she held the glass door open for us.

She let us in the immaculate lobby which had an empty front desk with a large framed map of Seaview behind it. American, state, and Seaview flags hung limply on metal poles off to the side. She led us into a smaller office with a sofa and coffee table seating area. "I see you are on time for your appointment and that is always a plus mark in my book! I always say it is so important to adhere to one's planned schedule. Please do have a seat and won't you join me in some light refreshment? I just brewed this pot of coffee. I always think coffee is best when served fresh, now don't you agree? The vice president of our refreshment committee, Patti Giffin Lawford, made these delicious coconut macaroons for us to enjoy, so please do help your selves. I don't think one or two will hurt our waistlines too much, now do you Mrs. Kluntz?" She said as she politely tittered and indicated we should sit down on the pale blue upholstered colonial style sofa. "Now Mrs. Kluntz do you take cream or sugar in your coffee?" Beverly asked as we sat down. She picked up the silver tea pot from the silver service tray and started pouring coffee in three bone china cups with matching saucers and silver spoons. The green Seaview emblem was on the side of each cup. I suppose having coffee was mandatory, not that I really wanted a cup thank you very much. But when Mrs. Wholesome quizzed me as to my java preferences, I let her know cream and three lumps of sugar. "Oh my no, Mr. Campbell! I'm afraid three lumps is just too much. Why you wouldn't believe it now, but sugar habits such as those will just make your waistline balloon as you get older dear. How about some nice saccharine, I personally prefer saccharine." I nodded my head no. She sighed just a bit and then picked of the silver tongs and promptly dropped one lump in. "Let's just see how we do with one lump, I think you'll find it is much better that way especially with my fresh coffee." She said as she winked at me and handed me the cup and saucer.

"Oh, aren't these coconut macaroons delicious? I see Patti has perfected my recipe! The secret is to make sure the egg whites are not beaten too stiff. I'm going to tell stories out of school here, but I believe you are from out of the area Mrs. Kluntz? And Alex, you didn't grow up in Clinton, did you? I don't know your family name from around here so I doubt it. Anyway, I used to be the hostess for the much missed ladies show on Channel Four. These macaroons are one of my most popular recipes from way back." She smiled demurely while offering us the plate of coconut macaroons again.

While taking another one, I let her know how good they were and then went for bonus points by asking her to tell us more about her

17

TV career. Beverly coyly tilted her head to the side, her helmeted hair not moving a follicle, while she slowly stirred her coffee, "Oh my, well since you ask, I had the number one locally ranked TV show for years in Clinton. I started way back before you were even a glimmer in your parents' eyes and I was in my 20s. I was already pretty well known in these parts as I was the local and state pageant beauty queen. Gosh darn, I competed in the Miss America pageant but that tricky Miss North Carolina won that year!" she said while setting her cup and saucer down and winking at us. "I did however, gain a lot of knowledge about live TV from the pageant. Anyhow, I was a happily married, young housewife living in Clinton, when the producers at Channel Four just practically twisted my arm and had me fill in as the hostess of the local ladies home show. Of course it didn't hurt that my husband was a local television executive. I was only supposed to be the substitute hostess for a few weeks while Mary Anne Devail took some time off for health reasons. Poor thing wasn't well and it was a darn shame when she passed away. They never did find out exactly what her cause of death was. If you ask me, I always thought Mary Anne was just too enthusiastic and I don't think her poor heart could handle it. Anyhow, I hosted the award winning, *The Ladies Hour with Beverly Ann LeFaye* every weekday from 1964 all the way until 1979. It was so special and such a treat to help all the homemakers out there and learn new fun and interesting things! Of course by the late 1970s, all that women's liberation stuff just changed everything. I am sure you remember that now don't you Mrs. Kluntz? Aghh, anyhow they reformatted the show and changed the name to *Women Are Talking* and

18

moved the time slot to after the soaps. Gone were any helpful tips, crafts or recipes. They wanted me to talk to women guests about politics, world events and business. Oh it was so tedious and no real lady is interested in that sort of thing. By 1981, we were gone and an era ended. Then my dear husband passed away and gosh, I have just been flying solo ever since. I was lucky enough to become a Seaview resident in 2000. My but I have just gone on here!

Now, let's talk about Seaview and first off I will relate this to what we were just talking about. Seaview has its own mini broadcast station here on the grounds and our local cable access channel is piped into every unit here and also available on extended local access in Clinton. Anyhow, everything just comes full circle and I now host a live weekly show every Saturday night right here called, *What's Happening Seaview!* Isn't that a fresh and hip name? We might be gated and secure but we are up on things here at Seaview. We've dialed in the 4-1-1 as the young folks now say! Mrs. Kluntz you may be interested in attending a broadcast once you live here. The shows are taped live and open to Seaview residents and their select guests. I've tried to combine a bit of my old show with some of the old late night TV glamour that we all so sorely miss these days. We always just have a ball doing the show. There's so much local retired talent living right here in Seaview, that we only need to have two outsiders help us with the production. The rest we handle in-house as we like to say here. Well, Mrs. Kluntz, Ethel if I may, why don't you tell me a little about yourself and then we can all go take a look at the lovely units that are for sale. Why you could even start with your last name. That is such an unusual and interesting name." Beverly set her cup and saucer down again and smiled demurely with her frosted pink lips, her left hand patting her shellacked hair making sure it was all still in place, while she stared directly at Ethel.

Ethel set her coffee cup and saucer down and proceeded to fill Beverly in, "My husband, Herman Moishe Kluntz, passed away over 10 years ago; gawd rest his soul. I naturally took his name when we married in 1958. Not like these girls do today Beverly, you know keeping their own names and all. The hyphenated names, I mean what are their kids supposed to do with all of that? Where will it end I ask you? What, their children's children are going to hyphenate too and then we will just have long hyphenated names, *feh*! Not that I'm some orthodox from Philadelphia. I am Jewish Beverly and I like some of the old values but certainly not to the orthodox extreme. Now Alex might have told you about my son, Norman Kluntz, he works at Clinton Chem Labs. He is a well respected chemist there. His father and I worked our *tuchases* off to put him through Temple and then graduate school as well. So I ask you Beverly, how does this only son of mine thank me? He moves away from his widowed mother here to Clinton. And then what? After years of pleading with him to quit throwing away his hard earned money on rent, he finally decides to wise up and buy.

Oh you say, this is good. No! Not good. You know what this disrespectful son of mine goes and does Beverly? He goes and purchases a perfectly lovely split level home, in Rosedale right Alex? He purchases and I come out here to surprise him and what do I find?

20

What did I find Alex? I find my only son has taken up living in sin with a stripper! A common two-bit, *goyishe*, stripper Beverly! Have you ever? I mean I don't know if my heart can stand it. Clearly now I am not moving in with my Normie but I do feel the call to be nearby. Only his mother can talk sense back into him and I need to be here to do that. I am only thankful that his dear and loving father is no longer here to see what he has done. So we are here today Beverly to tour your units for sale. I am thinking an age restricted community with progressive care facilities is exactly what I need, I mean we aren't getting any younger now are we Beverly."

Beverly shifted in her chair a bit and sat up straighter. "My, Ethel that is quite a story! You know a number of our residents here also have similar problems with their misbehaving adult children. In fact, we even have a support group, Parents of Misbehaving Adult Children Who Should Know Better that meets on Tuesdays in the Meeting and Activities building. Oh and you, *at my age!* My goodness, you are a youngster here in Seaview terms! We are a bit different from other adult communities. Most are restrictive to age 55 and older and if there is a spouse, they need to be 50 or older. Well, Seaview is 62 and older and any spouse has to be 57 or older. We just feel our age policy keeps things, oh just so! Of course, many of the newer adult communities conform to the *Housing for Older Persons Act of 1995* and don't provide any real activities or senior related services. But that has never been the Seaview way. You'll see we have an enormous range of activities for our residents and there is the option to move on to the assisted care complex when the time comes.

Anyway, I heard you mention that you are of the Jewish faith Ethel? That is just wonderful and here at Seaview we are a diverse and accepting community. We have an interfaith chapel on site and each Saturday there is a Rabbi who comes in from Clinton and he does a Jewish service. I should introduce you to Herschel and Harriet Moshberger and let them fill you in on all things Jewish at Seaview. You know, each year, we even put out and light up a large plastic Menorah along with the big Christmas tree in the town square. Oh yes, I think you will find Seaview is quite the diverse and Jew accepting place to be! You strike me as a woman who values diversity Ethel, not like some of those adult communities in our more humid climes which are shall we say, Jewish exclusive. Now *that* would be boring, not to mention petty, don't you agree? I am sure we can find you just the perfect place to call home here and you can start living your new life and who knows, maybe even reform that wayward son of yours! Now, let's go outside and get in the touring cart and take a look at the wonderful homes that are for sale!"

# 4

Into the golf cart we went. At Seaview they encourage residents to purchase or lease golf carts to use when getting around town. While cars are not illegal, the endless speed bumps and low speed limit do not exactly encourage one to drive. Beverly informed us they also have their own minivan buses that regularly run in between all of the Seaview hot spots which are free for residents and guests to use. The cart Beverly drove, was an open air electric cart with three rows of seats, akin to the carts they use at places like Disney Land to conduct tours. This cart was painted the Seaview green and sported a mini Seaview flag on the front antenna. Beverly put Ethel in the front with her and had me ride in the middle row. There was no doubt who was taking control of this tour. Beverly picked up the two-way radio microphone while backing up the cart, "Rover One to base, leaving for agent tour, over." Then one of Dave's cohorts at the base gave her a clipped, "ten-four, over" response.

Beverly looked back at me and winked, "You can see we take security very seriously here at Seaview Mrs. Kluntz, the base office always knows where all the carts are at all times." With that she hit the pedal and we sped off out of the parking lot. Next to all the streets are designated cart paths and next to them are designated walking paths, neither with the obnoxious speed bumps. It was clear Beverly's cart was going faster than the 15 mile an hour speed limit as she whizzed down the cart motorway, whisking us through Seaview's town center and over to the original water view towers. "Now these are the original towers constructed in 1973 and we have two showings here for you today. The first unit we will be touring is Alana and Alvin Ford's place which they have chosen to list with a Miss Tiger Conley. This is a ground floor, one bedroom unit. The Fords are going to be moving to an assisted living complex closer to their daughter in Pasadena. They have reached that age where they need more assistance and their daughter thought it best they not go to the Seaview assisted living building but move closer to her."

Beverly was filling us in as she sped through the large parking lot that is in front of the two towers, all of which is roofed over in white aluminum, carport style. Seems like a very retro concept to me, covering an enormous parking lot with an aluminum roof but I'm sure it keeps the cars cool when it is hot and sunny. Today the developers would be too cheap to spend the money to cover the large flat top parking lot. Once we cleared the enormous carport we were on the entry drive and there were a couple of large Cadillacs, assorted Town Cars and taxi cabs queuing up for the *porte cochere* entry. Beverly shot through it all, honking the cart's surprisingly loud horn as she weaved past the cars right up to the automatic front doors. She parked in a prime "Management Only" spot just to the left of the front doors. The two, five-story white brick tower buildings are named "North" and "South" and so identified in large black, italic, metal lettering applied at the third story level of each building's front façade. Such original names and the large wording on each building must prevent a world of confusion I am sure. Each building is sited at an angle to take advantage of the water views. The Towers are joined together in the middle by a large, all glass, rectangular lobby building. Two uniformed doormen, dressed in green coats complete with tails and gold thread epaulets (probably from the same tailor who outfits the latest third world dictators *de jour*; not to be confused with the tailor who outfits the black suits for our first world corporate dictators) were busy ferrying old people with walkers and in wheelchairs out of the entry to waiting cars. Inside, a floor to ceiling Jetson-esque, steel water fountain was providing a nice white noise ambiance. Directly in front of the fountain was a massive white marbled front desk with three staff members at the ready behind it.

Beverly led the way, her clipboard in hand, briskly guiding us to the front desk. She stopped briefly by some flower planters, stooping to pick up a small flower petal that was lying on the immaculate light blue carpeting. A 20-something staffer with her hair pulled up in a bun and wearing the green Seaview blazer stood up straighter as Beverly approached. Beverly stepped up to the marble counter, "Smiles, you need to review your five S's Pamela." Beverly said while tapping her perfectly manicured short, pale pink nails on the counter's top. Hers were actually real fingernails. No glued on, 10 inch, acrylic nails for Beverly. "Now, Pamela we are here with Mrs. Ethel Kluntz to view the Ford's unit first. I am assuming their listing agent, a Miss Tiger Conley has arrived and is waiting for us?"

Pamela looked a bit panicked; perhaps she was trying to recall her five S's? She quickly plastered a huge smile on her face, "Ahh, yes good afternoon Mrs. LeFaye. A Ms. Conley signed in about 20 minutes ago and should be at the unit waiting for your showing.

Would you like for me to give her a call and let her know you are on your way now?"

Beverly wrinkled her nose a bit, reaching over the counter and straightening the gold name badge affixed to Pamela's green blazer's lapel, "Why, no Pamela that won't be necessary as we are going to be right on time for our scheduled appointment." She signed the visitor booklet Pamela put in front of her, snapping it shut and handing it back. "Oh Pamela, do be a dear and let's get out our counter top cleaning kit and give this counter a nice thorough polish. I do hate to see finger prints, it just mars the marble, don't you agree? I am surprised Pamela, you are now short two of the five S's and that is not the Seaview way! Remember, *smiles* and *shiny*? I'd hate to think we need to send you back for a core training recap Pamela, that wouldn't be any fun whatsoever, now would it?" Pamela quickly shook her head, no, in agreement. As Beverly was turning to lead us to the South Tower, she stopped at the far end of the front desk, "Oh Ricardo! Just look what I found on my way in, now can you believe it?" She said while dropping the wilted, yellow flower petal in his hand. "Let's get right on this Ricardo! Be a dear and get that manual floor sweeper out and let's just give the whole lobby a thorough run-through and spritz. I'm going to need to see the lobby maintenance log on my way out. It does not appear we are keeping to it, now does it?" He gave her a tight smile and a, "Yes, right away Mrs. LeFaye."

Beverly led us to the glass doors leading to the South Tower, "I find it is so important to keep staff on their toes, don't you agree Mrs. Kluntz? You can see, here at Seaview we *do* have our standards. In

26

fact, we have a zero tolerance policy for employees that do not give 110 percent. All employees go through a rigorous Seaview Training Core Program. I teach the manners, hygiene and decorum portion of their training. If you are interested Ethel, you can apply to serve on the committee that regularly does secret and mystery spot checks on the staff throughout Seaview. Sort of like a mystery shopper. We have our own trained volunteer citizens who regularly patrol and report on employees' behavior, housekeeping and grounds maintenance issues. I find it is so important to have a hands-on approach when maintaining our community's image and standards. I always say, cleanliness and good manners start with you and me!" She said, giving us a wide frosted pink lipstick smile. "Now we'll just scoot down to the end of this hall and the Fords' unit is on the right."

# 5

Down the long "Alice in Wonderland" hall we went. The walls are papered in pale vertical gold and yellow stripes and if you were remotely drunk or tripping on your old folk pharmaceuticals, this striped hallway could be a real challenge to navigate. Sure enough, the last door on the right was ajar and Beverly led us in, "Knock, knock! I have Mrs. Kluntz and her agent Alex Campbell here to show." Beverly called out in her crisp sing-song tone as she walked into the unit's large living room. There standing next to the opened patio door was a woman somewhere in her 50s, of average height. She was plump, with yellow blonde, over-dyed hair in sort of a retro Farah Fawcett style. She wore tight fitting black slacks and her blouse was a tan, leopard skin print, number with black sequins. It was literally bursting at the seams, the buttons straining to keep her D cup friends in place. Her eye lids were slathered with gobs of smoky eye shadow, and her chipmunk checks were swabbed with a pinkish tan blush. Her plumped-up lips were painted a glossy, candy apple red. She immediately lit up, her whitened teeth gleaming, "Why howdy there folks, thank ya'll for coming out today to see my new Seaview listing! I'm Tiger Conley and you know what Alex, I think we are office mates. I just moved here to Clinton and barely got my shingle out before my phone started to jingle and I took me some listings. And here I was thinking I was moving to Clinton to cut back on work and get me some more fun and play in!" This she said while walking over to us, her leopard skin spiky mule shoes making sharp snapping sounds against the bottom of her heels. She held her hand out to shake and I noted her stick-on finger nails matched her candy apple lipstick. This must be *the* Tiger that Stinky was all in a knot about. (see Volume Two)

Beverly looked Tiger up and down and gave her a closed mouth frosty, Nancy Reagan smile, "Well, Tiger you sure are *festive* in your animal print blouse. My goodness, you just don't waste any time procuring a listing now do you? Why the Fords told me they met you at bingo night in Clinton at the allied senior communities mixer. You apparently just swept them away Tiger. We were not even aware the Fords were considering leaving us."

Tiger didn't miss a beat, "Oh Bev you are so right, a good Tiger never rests, I suppose! Why I just seem to meet new clients wherever I go. Just yesterday at the salon when they were fixing up my hair, the rinser let me know about a client there who needs help selling her home. I met the Fords and learned their daughter was not local, well you know the tug of family and all. It's hard to blame them for wanting to move and be close to their loved ones now is it Bev? I am personally all in favor of family values and I told them anything I could do to help facilitate their move closer to their loved ones was alright by me and the big man up above."

Beverly looked straight at me, "Alex why don't you show Mrs. Kluntz this lovely unit. I see Tiger has her listing flyers set up here on the kitchen bar counter top. It looks as if we are going to have to review this printed collateral together Tiger. I'm afraid you have made some mistakes in terms of our rules and regulations for real estate printed matter here at Seaview." This she said as she removed all of the color flyers from the Lucite stand, clipping them on her clip board with a loud snap. "Oh and fiddle Tiger, I have to remove your business cards as well! We don't allow service people to leave business cards on the premises at any time." She handed the four-color glossy cards over to Tiger.

Tiger smiled, "Well not a problem Bev and thank you for letting me know! I'm just getting myself a crash course in all things Seaview today, boy howdy! Here Alex, why don't you and your client take a card in case ya'll have any questions? I pocketed a card, but not before I noticed her glamour mug shot on the front and her tag line, *Tiger Leads the Pack!* Gee, I suppose she didn't get the memo from Mother Nature as to the solitary, non-pack, orientation of tigers and all felines or that felines run in prides not packs. Obviously, Winterfrost had once again bent the rules for a "player" agent. Winterfrost business cards are only supposed to be printed by the Winterfrost approved printing company (at a substantial mark-up that the agent pays for) on matte finish card stock, not glossy stock. No personal taglines or sale phrases are supposedly allowed. Nothing like a blatant double standard to let you know you are working at Winterfrost.

I led Ethel down the short hallway and we took a gander at the master bedroom and bath. For a one bedroom unit, this was not a bad space. The Ford's décor was 1970s Ethan Allen, early American Colonial which is dull but perfect for a listing. Ethel let me know the unit was not spacious enough and she was not fond of the ground floor. I signaled to Beverly that we were done and thanked Tiger for coming out to meet us for the showing, "Oh the pleasure is all mine ya'll, really. Now Mrs. Kluntz you have yourself a fun little tour here with Bev and Alex and if you have any questions feel free to let me know. Bev it has been wonderful to meet you and thank you so much for filling me in on all the Seaview rule farts and whatnots! Alex I'm sure I'll see you in the office real soon." With that Tiger was closing the entry door but not before Beverly said, "Now Tiger, remember to lock the patio door and both locks on this door when you leave. I sure don't want you violating anymore house rules before the Fords get back home!"

Beverly led the way to the South Tower elevators, "My, that *is* a new listing agent we have there in terms of following our posted rules. You know, I find it such a shame just how vulgar certain elements can be these days and in a professional setting to boot, don't you agree Mrs. Kluntz? Why in our day a lady would never use bodily function oriented language and certainly not in public! And we will not discuss the clothing choices of this younger generation now will we Ethel?"

"*Oy*, don't you even get me started Beverly! You would not believe what my own son Norman is going around with! It is absolutely sinful and disrespectful Beverly. So sad, the disrespect these young people have, not like we raised them!"

Beverly hit the elevator up button, "My you are speaking to like minded company Ethel. I think you are going to fit right in here at Seaview. The rest of the world may be lewd and crude these days but we at Seaview do have our decorum and standards. And I find it is all so much more pleasant when common rules are adhered to, don't you?

Why here's the elevator, after you two." With that she promptly herded us in and pushed the button for the fourth floor.

# 6

We followed Beverly down the long fourth floor hallway until we reached Stinky's listing. Stinky is my secret nickname for Share (pronounced Sharee) Shelton who is the *grande* dame of Winterfrost Real Estate and a major cut throat agent. (see previous volumes) Beverly knocked on the door but there was no answer. Big surprise, it appeared Stinky was not there for the showing. Beverly appeared annoyed, "Well, this is certainly not to my liking! Share Shelton should have been here at least 10 minutes ago. I know we notified her there was to be a showing today, didn't we Alex. This is not the first time we have had this problem with her." With that she whipped out her cell phone and called the front desk, "Yes, Pamela has Share Shelton of Winterfrost signed in? She is supposed to be here for a showing of the Roland unit." Beverly gave us a vexed smile, "Ohh, I see. Well this is not good. I'm afraid we'll have to note this in the file, this is her second infraction. One more and she loses the listing per Seaview regulations! Pamela when Mrs. Shelton does arrive please let her know she needs to contact me immediately." Beverly hung up, shaking her head in disgust. "Well, I am terribly sorry Mrs. Kluntz but the listing agent for this unit is not doing her job. I'm afraid we'll have to wait and see if she is going to bother showing up or not. However, if you like, there is a unit on the fifth floor that I might be able to show you? A little bird tells me this top floor unit is going to be listing soon. Would you care to go up and see if we can take a quick peek at it while we are waiting?"

"That sounds good Beverly. You know the top floor might be nice." Ethel replied as I followed them back to the elevator. This was a bit out of bounds for Beverly to do as the multiple listing service prefers agents list a property first before showing it to anyone. But this kind of "pocket listing preview" does happen. Up we went and Beverly knocked on the door. She was smiling at us when we heard a grumpy old man call out, "Who the hell is there?"

Beverly smiled wider, "Oh, hello Harvey it's me Beverly LeFaye! Say, I have a client and her agent here who would just love to take a quick peek at your unit. I think your place might be the perfect match. Can we come in and take a gander? I promise we'll be out of your way in two shakes of a lamb's tail!"

The lock turned and the door opened with a jerk, "Lamb's tail my ass you old bag! You all just come on in. The place ain't for sale yet but it's true I'm getting the hell out of here and the sooner the better. Too bad you didn't interrupt me earlier today Beverly. I took my fiber and it was kicking in but good, a real stinker my bathroom was." Beverly wrinkled her nose but kept her pink frosted smile pasted on her face. Ethel didn't appear to be phased. As for me, well this old man was already Mr. Too Much Information in my book. He looked like an ancient billy goat, his chinos pulled up well above his navel, a wrinkled blue golf shirt and Seadogs baseball cap on top. He led us down the hall to his living room. I noted the ubiquitous old man smell that permeated the less than clean apartment. Beverly attempted small talk and tried to introduce us, "Mrs. Kluntz, Alex, this is Harvey Malloy and he has decided he'd rather live in a more independent venue that…"

"Yeah, cut the crap Beverly you old sunshiny whore! I'm Harvey and that there is my parrot Ralph. We've been here about a year and that's too long! My damn son conned me into buying this here place. Hell, Beverly is such a whore she probably gave my son a hand job to help trick me into buying into this prison. Don't let her goodie two shoes routine fool you folks, ain't that right Bev? Anyhow, your name is Kluntz you say? Well, you move here and you better like Beverly's rules and all the other Sea-shit they got going on around here. Practically have to fill out a permission slip if you want to take a piss! God damn communist country full of medicated zombies is what they got going on here!"

Beverly gave Harvey a very frosty look, "Yes, well Harvey you mind your potty mouth! Ladies ARE present. I have a good mind to put a bar of soap in your dirty mouth." I wouldn't be surprised if she really did have a bar of soap tucked away in her pocket book just for this purpose. To that Harvey flipped the bird at Beverly. "Ugh! That is just so common and unnecessary. You do realize Harvey that is one finger pointed at me and four fingers pointing back at you?" She shook her helmeted head and sighed with displeasure. "Why don't you go out on your balcony and I'll have Ethel and Alex out of your hair in a jiffy!"

"Hair? You stupid old windbag, I ain't got no hair! I ain't had any since 1975, that's what the ball cap is for you old whore! Don't you two let little Miss Prissy here fool ya'. She probably told you all

35

about her old days on the TV didn't she? Beverly was a fake little bitch back then and she still is, ain't that true Bev? Okay, don't get yer twat in a knot, I'm moving out to the balcony! Say, yer a real estate fella aren't ya? Lemme have one of your cards. Old Beverly here thinks she's gonna be listing and selling my place but that ain't quite decided yet, now is it Bev? See, I read them rules you bastards got and this here unit is one where I can choose the listing agent. You can't make me list with you and Sea-shit, you lying bitch!"

Oh god, a smelly old billy goat listing? Well the man asked me for my card, so I pulled one out of my pocket and put it in his rough paw. Beverly gave us a significant wink as Harvey exited onto the balcony, "Oh please do excuse him and his foul mouth. I think he has early onset Alzheimer's and we all know that can make one's mouth and actions become quite unpleasant."

"I heard that you lying sea hag! I don't have any Alzheimer's, I speak my mind. I always have and always will! You and Sea-shit can stuff it, you old biddy! Them face lifts ain't fooling me none, ya lying sea hag."

Beverly shook her head, "Mr. Malloy has not quite fit in. So the Seaview Board and he have decided it would be best for everyone concerned if he moved on and found another independent living venue that is more to his liking."

"Lying sea hag. Lying sea hag!" That shrieked missive came from Harvey's parrot, Ralph. The green, medium sized, red headed parrot was perched in his large cage on a wooden dowel, holding what appeared to be a green bean in one of his talons. He bit off a sizeable chunk of the bean, the rest promptly fell to the bottom of his messy cage.

Harvey started laughing, "You tell 'em Ralph!" he shouted from his balcony. Beverly rolled her eyes and proceeded to show us around the unit. It was a nice sunny condo and had full views of Warner Sound and a bird's eye view of the two swimming pools, gardens and gaming areas on the grounds below located between the two towers. The décor was almost nonexistent and what few pieces of furniture Harvey had appeared to be 40 year old Salvation Army rejects. There was a grey vinyl recliner, a mid-size TV set, a small round table with two white chairs in the dining nook. A queen size bed with no spread or headboard, a generic nightstand with a beige ceramic lamp was all the one bedroom had to offer. The nicest item in the whole condo was Ralph's cage. It was a deluxe blue metal cage that almost cleared six feet. That green bird had it all going on inside his abode. From the hanging wood mobiles and metal bells, to the dangling mirror, toys were everywhere. There were six different food dishes filled to overflowing with assorted fruits, vegetables and dried kibble, this bird lacked for nothing. He cocked his red head to the side while I looked over his living quarters and then he squawked, "Bitch. Bitch! My show's on damn it. My show's on damn it! Shut up Ralph. Shut up Ralph!" Obviously, Ralph was quite the listener and enjoyed parroting back the one-liners he picked up. Beverly was leading us out the door when Harvey called out goodbye, "I'll be in touch young feller to list this place and Beverly you eat shit and die you old bag!"

Ethel let out a sigh, "*Oy vay,* does that man have a mouth and so rude! His mother should die I'm sure if she heard such language! That place is not for me and it's not just that old man. The space is too small. I'm thinking I'm going to need a two bedroom at least. Isn't this fourth floor listing we are going to see a two bedroom?" I let Ethel know it was and Beverly herded us back down to the fourth floor.

# 7

Once again Beverly knocked on the door and no response. "Well this is just too inconsiderate!" Beverly exclaimed. "I'm going to have to resort to my master pass key and let us in." She started to look in her purse when her cell phone began to ring. As she picked up, I smelled Stinky. Share wears the strongest, sicky sweet perfume of anyone I've encountered and her vapor trail always precedes her and remains in her wake for at least 30 minutes. Sure enough my sniffer detected the scent of freesia, rose, musk and some other noxious spice wafting in strong waves down the hall way. Share's voice began to cackle from Beverly's cell phone, as it also echoed down the hall way. And there she was jangling down the hall as fast has her pointy bitch boots could carry her. "I'm here!" she called out waving at us while shouting into her rhinestone encrusted cell phone. Yes indeed, Stinky had arrived.

Today's ensemble consisted of camel toe tight, burnt orange slacks with flares at the bottom which covered her matching pointy, stiletto boots. Up top was a shiny violet colored blouse, unbuttoned almost to her navel and cinched at the waist by a wide copper metallic fabric belt. Piled in the freckled tit valley between her inflated friends was a chunky gold cross hanging from a thick gold chain. Stinky must have been meeting up with some kind of church people today, as her lapel pins and other symbolic jewelry always changes according to her clients. She wore thick jangling gold bracelets, a huge citrine ring and as always, her stick-on talons matched her blouse's color to a tee. Her orange/red hair was as spiky and crunchy as ever and had what appeared to be fresh yellow streaks in it. Her lips were lip lined and slathered in two shades of burnt orange. She tried to do a closed mouth smile, but forgot the corners of her lips are supposed to go up when smiling. With her lip corners turned down, she came off as majorly crampy and constipated. Her eyes were hidden behind shiny gold rectangular sunglasses with rhinestone logos on the sides.

"Oh looks like the gang's already here. Alex and his little client and of course, Beverly the queen of Seaview, all waiting for little old me! You know Beverly, the people at that gate really have to get with who I am and speed up the whole entry process. As you know, I am a very busy, premier agent and that crew out front is just too slow! They know who I am for god's sake! Of course if Seaview did not have this silly requirement that listing agents be present at all showings we could avoid all of this and get on with the business of serving our clients! Anyhow, here I am so let's get this show on the road." With that she stuck out her hand to Ethel, "Share Shelton, Winterfrost Real Estate's premier agent, happy to be here and assist you today. Prepare to be dazzled by my client's gorgeous two bedroom unit. It's the only two bedroom unit currently for sale in Seaview and I know you are going to love it!" With that she shook Ethel's hand, while swinging her hips, butting Beverly out from in front of the door and inserting her key in the lock. She had us herded inside in a blur of motion. Even Beverly was momentarily caught off guard.

Share was flipping on the lights while trying to mesmerize Ethel, "You will note the custom granite kitchen counter tops, the sunken double sink, all the appliance upgrades and custom cabinetry.

My client spared no expense and had a professional kitchen designer do this."

Ethel was nodding her head, "Nice, very nice and you know that appliance ratio appears to be correct. I can tell your seller had a designer who knew her appliance ratios. So important the ratios, if you want your kitchen work to flow smoothly. Ohh, and I love the living room curtains. Now Alex these are quality curtains, just look at this lining."

I was about to ask Share if the curtains conveyed or if the seller intended to keep them when Beverly interjected, "Oh yes they are lovely draperies aren't they, such a soothing rose color. Now why don't you and Alex just nose about and I'm going to review some things with Share while you two look things over. Share, we need to discuss your tardiness. This is the second infraction on your listing's record. As you know, one more strike and I'm afraid we have to say goodbye to you as the listing agent." This stopped Stinky dead in her tracks; she plopped her copper metallic pocket book down on the dining table and removed her gold sun glasses. Her talons began to tap on the table top.

"Sure, Alex you show your client around. I am going to speak with Beverly about real estate basics. Clearly she's never been to a Winterfrost core training class. Why you and I both know how this business really works. We are both professionals and work in the real world of real estate, not some spoon fed seniors playground, where we are handed in-house listings on a silver platter. Some people need to be schooled as to how this business really works, eh Alex?"

Beverly smiled bigger and coo-ed, "Oh that's right Alex, you and Ethel just look around and see if this size unit is more suitable, now that we can *finally* tour it. I'm going to write up Share's second strike in the listing file. Please do let me know if you have any questions Ethel!" Beverly sat down at the dining table and pulled a file off of her clip board. "Now Share, how *do* you spell your last name again? Fiddlesticks, I just can't remember the correct spelling from the last time I wrote you up for a listing infraction." Beverly looked up at Share with a demonic smile on her face, "Oh and mercy me! Why it appears you have a stain on your blouse Share. You know the best thing I have found for sloppy people who spill stuff on themselves, is to always carry a little spritzer of fresh lemon water with them. Why, I think I may have some in my purse, let me check. Ohh, but come to think of it, the lemon water only works on more traditional, daytime fabrics like cotton, not on shiny satin nighttime fabrics like you are wearing. No, for those bedroom appropriate fabrics, I find a solution of water with a bit of tartar mixed in works best. And of course I don't have a spritzer of that on hand as I am not home near the bedroom, now am I? Oh well, you make a note of that dear and when you get home perhaps it will help remove that spot for you." Share looked as if she was going to pounce on Beverly and scratch her eye balls out. I for one did not see a stain on Stinky's shiny blouse. Meanwhile, Ethel had moved down the hall to the master bedroom. I wanted to stay and see if the fur was going to fly in the dining area but decided I better do my job and follow my client.

# NO REST

The master bedroom was very light and had pale yellow walls with custom yellow curtains covering the windows. I was again pondering if the curtains would be staying with the unit when Ethel let out a loud gasp. I looked over and in the queen size bed lay what appeared to be an elderly woman with grey hair and pale blue eyes that were opened very wide and not blinking. That could only mean...

"OHHH my GAWD! Call 9-1-1, call 9-1-1!" Ethel shrieked as she grabbed my arm and pulled us into the hallway. "Agghh, there's a body in the bed! I think there's a dead woman in that bed!" She yelled as she ran out to the table where Stinky and Beverly were hissing at each other. Stinky jumped back and started to dial her rhinestone encrusted cell phone. Meanwhile Beverly sprang up and flew down the hall to the master bedroom. I guided Ethel over to the kitchen and got her a glass of water. She was already murmuring about the salts in her purse and I had her sit down at one of the kitchen counter bar stools.

# 8

The dead body sure put an end to Ethel's tour. Once the Seaview medics arrived and confirmed that Tina Roland was indeed deceased, then Seaview Security showed up and Beverly ferreted through their standard questions. The coroner would need to confirm but it was assumed Tina had some kind of coronary and passed away while in her bed. Beverly didn't miss the opportunity to tell us all about the Seaview Eternal Slumber Mortuary with a pet addition opening soon. She asked if we wanted to see the Seaview grief counselor, an on-call service they provide but we declined. She apologized for such an ending to our tour, winked at me and said I should call her with any questions and to reschedule a "fresh tour." I drove Ethel back to Wanda's house and as we pulled to the curb Wanda was standing out front on the sidewalk, hands on her hips, glaring back at her house.

"Well, 'bout time you got back here. So what did you buy today Mrs. Kluntz, got the offer paperwork all written up yet? Say, you two don't know nothing 'bout my front door now do you?" She said giving us both a significant up and down look.

"*Oy*, oh it was horrible Wanda, just horrible! I need to get right inside and have a nice lay down. Do you have any chicken stock on hand? I really think after my lay down, we should make some fresh chicken soup to help soothe this whole thing." With that Ethel bustled up the walk to the front door and let herself in.

Wanda called out after Ethel, "Well you know I'm asking about this here front door because when I left for work this morning it was a

44

nice bright orange. Seem like someone done decided to paint it brown and anyone who knows me knows, I ain't got no truck for no brown ass front door! Humpf!" Ethel waved her hand over her shoulder in response to Wanda and shut the front door. Wanda's eyes bugged out and she looked over to me, "Did you? You just saw what that old lady did? I don't need no Psychic Friends Network to tell me that lady painted my front door Alex! She got herself some nasty-ass, plain brown paint and that lady just up and went to work. My orange door! I'm telling you, this is it honey, ain't gonna be no more helping that lady out while she looking to buy. I don't care what her son done shacked up with or if he was a client of mine. I ain't got no more time for this here, no sir! Now you best be telling me Alex the old lady done bought herself a condo today at that old white folk's prison and she gonna be moving in within the next 30 days."

"Ahh, well, I'd like to ahh…"

"Oh hell no! Not any ahh nothing from you, you best be fixin' to tell me all about the great deal she getting over there at the Seaview."

"The thing is Wanda, Ethel did not buy anything today. In fact, we actually stumbled upon a dead body in the last listing we toured today. It is Stinky's listing, your favorite agent no less! We found the owner dead in her bed. That put a real damper on Ethel's enthusiasm. I think she's going to have to rest and regroup and we can…"

Wanda's eyes grew big, "You two done run into a damn dead body, say what? What is it with you and all these dead bodies, what you got some kind of hex on you? Can't show and sell without another stiff dropping in on you and your business every few months or so? I swear this just about the limit! Only good part of this here story is the fact that stiff be in Stinky's listing, I hope to hell it causes her a whole world of grief! Serious, a dead body stopped Ethel's tour? Damn! Okay, you know we gotta go out and get us some food and discuss this here. That's exactly what we gotta do." With that Wanda opened my passenger side door and got in. Once she shut the door, she glanced back up at me, "What you waiting for fool? I told you what we doing, now hurry your bony ass up and get this beater on over to Mama Honey's."

Mama Honey's sits at the bottom of the Highmont on the edge of downtown. It is an open kitchen, Cajun restaurant located in a yellow bricked, 1920s building that used to be a hardware store. It is most popular at lunch time but tonight there were two other tables seated. Mama Honey is in fact the proprietor and a kindly Jamaican woman somewhere in her 60s. "Nice to be havin' the both of you back and you both be lookin' as lovely as ever. Now let me seat you over here near de window and I'll bring out da beer and getcha the jambalaya all ready." We thanked her and sat down. We always have the same standing order, seafood jambalaya, bottled beer and for dessert her famous coconut cream pie. I suppose sometime we should actually request a menu and see what else may have been added over the years but this meal thus far has always been the winning race horse, so why change?

The food arrived and Wanda tucked in with a vengeance, stopping every now and then to look at new calls on her muted cell phone. "Damn, I tell you this market is just going straight down Alex. No doubt, the banker crooks have cooked this deal but good! You and me gonna have to ride it out and clean it up. You know how thorough I am with my clients and now even the squeaky clean, straight forward ones, ain't so anymore. I got appraisers, processors, calling me left and right all day long now. Even the high credit score, high income client is being called to the mat by the underwriters now. Seems like if the client flosses their teeth or uses a new shampoo that makes the underwriters nervous. And this, from just a while ago! Back then, if a person could make fog on a mirror, that's all it took to get them a home loan! Humph. So anyway, listen you gotta get Ethel out of my house honey 'cause I can't be dealing with her no more. You saw how she just up and painted my front door! I know that stripper her son is living with might not be no write home material. But still, every story has at least two sides and I'm sure Ethel just about drove Norman insane when he was growing up."

I filled Wanda in on Ethel's tour and described Beverly LeFaye to her as best I could. Buying in Seaview was definitely going to be a unique experience to put it politely. I let Wanda know I'd regroup with Ethel and we'd revisit Seaview and see if it would work out. While driving Wanda back home and trying to soothe talk her into not killing Ethel, she turned on my car stereo to drown me out. Jefferson Airplane's *She Has Funny Cars* started to blast and Wanda turned it down, "Damn, what decade is this car here driving in? You still listening to that hippie, white kid music and I still don't get it honey.

You are too young, you were barely a baby when this here song first played on the radio."

I nodded, "That's right Wanda but as we've gone over this before, my generation was a throw back. This music was popular again when I was a teenager and who could blame us? Who didn't find electric drum beats a bore and I was less than thrilled with "Thriller." There's only so much Dead Milkmen and Smiths you can listen too, hence the more authentic late 1960s music was popular."

Wanda shook her head, "Yeah, okay Mr. Sociology I've heard that there theory of yours before. I not so sure yo' mama didn't drop you on your head. Now just push down that damn pedal and get me home, I gotta see what Ethel is doing to my house now. I'm telling you, you best get that woman sold and settled and fast Alex!"

I dropped Wanda off, went home and took Clyde out for an evening walk. I noticed the decades vacant, three story brick, Conner Hasps factory building now sported a sold sign on its mostly faded, seemingly permanent for sale placard. Interesting, who would buy this abandoned factory and in my no-name neighborhood?

# 9

The next day I checked in with Ethel and she agreed to come and take another look at the "non-dead body" units at Seaview with me tomorrow. She said she was busy with a project and could not make it today. What "project" that might be, I am sure I'd soon being hearing about loud and clear from Wanda. I had a new client to meet at the Winterfrost office, so I quickly showered and put on my real estate drag. My hair was no doubt sticking up in the back but what the hell, people probably assume I purposely style it that way. I pulled into the Winterfrost parking lot, taking care not to side swipe any of the hulking SUVs that spilled over the narrow space lines. I noted Stinky's black, Mercedes SUV with its SOLD vanity plate was not there. I was happy my nose would not be assaulted by her fumes so early in the day. I saw a new, cherry red, two door Mercedes coupe which undoubtedly cost close to or over 100 grand. It had custom leopard skin seat covers and a leopard skin steering wheel cover as well. Just in case I was having a mental freeze, the vanity plate let me know this must be Tiger Conley's realtor mobile, as the license plate read, "GROWL3." I wondered if there were growl one and two vehicles for our animal print agent to roll around in? Inquiring minds never rest.

I took a breath and into the Viper Pit (a.k.a. the Winterfrost office) I went. Not too bad, only a few lost soul coffee klatch agents milling around the mail room, complaining about who knows what. It was only 10:00 a.m. so of course Todd Blund the designated broker/manager would not be in yet; too busy sleeping off last night's fun in a bottle I'm sure. As I made my way to the front conference room to meet with my new clients I saw what appeared to be a new agent training class going on in the back conference room. Through the conference room window I noticed a new agent Kenny Vance was passing out Snickers candy bars to everyone. Kenny is always passing out candy around the office. He is so wholesomely insincere and fake friendly, he makes my skin crawl. He is always pressed, dressed and shellacked like the perfect little Ken doll, even his blonde hair is brush cut and pomaded just so. However, this Ken doll is openly gay and doesn't want to live with Malibu Barbie. He's definitely a new viper to watch out for. In my viper world experience, anyone who is that squeaky clean and perky is bound to be a rotten apple.

I said hello to Nayina the receptionist who let me know my clients were waiting for me in the reception room. This client was a referral from a previous client of mine, Marc Hilson, a businessman with city council aspirations. (see Volume One) And there they were, mother and daughter, Vicky and Courtney Amanzo. I introduced myself and suggested we move to the front conference room. I noted Vicky was somewhere in her 50s and Courtney somewhere over 20 was my guess. Courtney barely looked up to shake hands, as she was busy texting on her magenta phone, her fingers clicking away. How she managed to type a message on that tiny phone is beyond me. I suppose if texting continues to take over, humans will morph and have appropriate sized mouse paws so they can easily text all day. Courtney was dressed in a pale pink sweat suit. The word "Joocey" spread across her plump ass let me know it wasn't just any pink sweat suit either. And Mommy? Vicky sported a powder blue matching sweat suit, except on her rear it should have read "Mushy" not "Joocey." Vicky and Courtney's hairstyles were almost identical reddish brown spiral perms, and they had matching white French manicured nails, glossy pink lips and both had enormous Gucci handbags hanging from their shoulders. Mommy Amanzo had her track top unzipped quite a bit to show off her enhanced cleavage. I guess Courtney's sweet 16 gift hadn't been new boobs like mommy's as her top was zipped up. Vicky wore spiky red stilettos, while Courtney had on black flip flops which didn't flip or flop as she just dragged her feet across the floor when walking. Vicky smiled big and wide, her whitened teeth shining brightly while Courtney scowled at her phone's screen and popped a wad of chewing gum.

Once we all sat down at the conference room table, I offered them coffee, which they thankfully declined or rather Vicky declined, Courtney couldn't be bothered to respond as she was still busy texting. Vicky let me know that Marc Hilson and his infamous wife Mary Beth used to live next door her in the Beaumont. She ran into Marc recently and he suggested they contact me to help Courtney find the perfect condo. Vicky said she and her husband wanted to support their daughter's move to college and living independently and they thought investing in a condo for Courtney would be a good step in that direction. I smiled and said that sounded nice and asked Courtney if she knew where she'd like to look, what kind of condo, etc.... Courtney popped her gum and continued texting and mumbled, "I dunna know. Whatev Moms picks is chill with me. Why I can't just live at home like now, but hey dads and moms wants to crib by themselves now, so you know, whatev!" there was a loud gum pop.

Vicky squirmed a bit and smiling wider, "Oh you see Alex, her father and I thought now would be the time to help get Courtney set up in her own little place. She's going to be starting school at Clinton Community College. Go C-3! She's just so excited to be starting college and her own life!" I wanted to add to that (as my high school French teacher used to say to me when I attempted to speak *en francaise*), are you asking me or telling me? But I kept my big mouth shut. "Yes, Courtney just turned 22 and she has decided a degree in cosmetology retail management is the right career move for her." You've got to be kidding me, they offer a specialized degree to run a fucking hair salon? Who makes this shit up? Obviously, Joocey is not the brightest candle in town nor the most congenial or motivated. But hey, why should she be when Mom and Dad are there to bank roll her chewing gum and texting habits?

I tried to feign enthusiasm, "Wow that is exciting for you Courtney! Are you psyched to find your own place, any idea what kind of condo you might like?" This elicited a pert gum snap and a shrug, as she continued texting. Maybe their private nick names should be Mushy and Pouty? Vicky quickly filled the dead air, "Oh, Alex her father and I were thinking at least a two bedroom unit, you know so she could get a roommate down the road if she wants. And I think something close to the school would be best. Courtney hasn't gotten her driver's license yet, so walking distance is probably good for now." I nodded in agreement meanwhile wondering how anyone could reach the age of 22 and not have their driver's license. I get those who grow up in New York City and have no need for a car but Clinton and most other cities really require that you have a driver's license if you are going to function in grown up world. Why Courtney was not chomping at the bit to get her driver's license at 16 and escape her gated life in the Beaumont is beyond me. Of course this is from someone who was regularly stealing the car and illegally driving at 13. Maybe I'm not the best to judge. Still, 22 and mommy drives you everywhere and you are not a former member of the short bus brigade or without arms and legs? Must be a new generation gap.

I went over my buyer packet with Vicky while Courtney chomped her gum and tapped away on her phone. Turns out Vicky and her husband would be paying all cash for this investment, so that makes things a lot easier when it is time to write up an offer. I reminded Vicky that I would need a funds availability letter from her bank or investment advisor and I'd have that on file to present with her offer once we found the right place. I could not get any more information from Courtney as to what kind of condo she might prefer, so I went on Vicky's two bedrooms and close to the community college criteria. I let Vicky know I would set up her search and email the applicable, active listings by tonight. I asked Courtney if she wanted me to email her the listings as well and she popped her gum and mumbled, "Sis-alright, my mom can do it." That wrapped it up and I shook Vicky's hand and let her know I'd be in touch and to call me if she had any questions. With that Mushy and Joocey left Winterfrost.

## CHARLES CHAPLIN

I was hoping to dash out of the office as fast as possible when my nose was bombarded with Stinky's odor. And there she was in the center of the office, standing in the open work room area. Share was decked out in a camel toe tight pants suit of deep violet with a shiny chartreuse green top, loads of costume bling, talons in matching deep violet with dual tone matching lips and of course, her spiked orange-ish hair. She appeared to be reading a promotional post card when who should also enter the work area but Tiger Conley. Tiger had on black stretchy pants, zebra skinned shoes which had wedge heels and tied around her ankles. Her top was also in a zebra fabric and fell almost to her knees, to cover her wide ass I guess. Her yellow blonde hair was feathered back and she wore huge zebra print feather earrings. She smiled big and wide, her glossy, cherry red lips glistening like fresh paint waiting to dry, "Well howdy there folks! Ohhh, look at Miss Share today! That is such a hot blouse you are wearin', where did you find that at girlfriend? 'Course you know I can't fit in that hot blouse, not with my big girl friends here." she said patting her boobs, "Boy howdy, my natural girls are just too big for that hot number you have on Share." To that she chortled and gave a wide smile. "You know Share, I can't wait for us gals to go out shopping together, 'cause I know me a classy lady friend for Tiger when I see one!" This she gushed as she moved over and patted Share's shoulder. Share tensed up thrusting her chest out, so her inflated friends and freckle spotted tit valley almost completely spilled out of her mostly unbuttoned blouse. Her dual colored violet lips turned down more as she grimaced and then she quickly caught herself, "Ohhh yes it's our new little

Winterfrost family member, Tiger! Out on the prowl so early in the morning?"

Tiger smiled wider, "You betcha Share! Why you are the pro Winterfrost agent. You know firsthand, ya gotta get up extra early and get out there and stalk your prey if you wanna keep eatin' them rib eye steaks!" With that she let out a deep belly laugh.

Share looked around for her audience and noted Nayina was refilling the paper in the copy machine and me. She stood up straighter and smiled, "Ohhh yes Tiger you are correct, you have to get out there early. And good thing you have your little animal costume on, I bet it helps you to blend right in and distracts your prey, huh? So cute, don't you think Alex? Her whole Tiger name and animal costume thing! Why when I pulled in the parking lot and saw that new, cherry red Mercedes with animal skin seat cushions, I knew right away who was in the office today. But you know, looking at your hair style I'd say a late 1970s Camaro might be more suitable for you. I guess you didn't hear *Charlie's Angels* was cancelled? So clever to market yourself in that animal way, it must help you attract the really stupid people out there or those who have some kind of kinky hots for animals, huh Tiger?"

Tiger just smiled bigger and purred, "Oh you! Share you get it, that's why Tiger always leads the pack! You know I used to have a Camaro back in high school, course that would have been when you were what, 30 Share? Guess we all have our eras, and you know your hair just says Annie Lennox to me, so 1980s retro and cute on you! Nothing like a boy's haircut to keep things easy, right Alex? They always say as you age that you should cut your hair shorter so the face doesn't appear to sag as much. Say, I heard from Beverly LeFaye that you lost your listing at Seaview Share? Alex, is it true there was a dead body in there when you toured with your client?" Tiger got all wide eyed and put on her concerned expression, "Why I can't imagine having a dead body in my listing! Share what did you do? You didn't scare your client to death did you? Or was it that Beverly? Ya'll know that lady is a real piece of work! She took all of my flyers and cards, says the Seafart rules don't allow for them. But hey, I am thankful I still have my listing there, no dead clients for me. Alex, what did your client think is she interested in my listing?"

Share pursed her lips and her eyes were staring daggers at Tiger who pretended not to notice as she smiled and stared straight at me. Oh god, a Winterfrost diva cat fight and me caught right in the middle of it. Too bad there isn't some kind of bug spray like, Tacky Divas Be Gone that I could just whip out and spray them with. "Ahh, well my client really wants a larger sized condo Tiger but we certainly appreciate the time you spent showing us your listing. Seaview sure has some uptight rules. My client was really shocked by the dead body, but I'm hoping to get her back out to Seaview tomorrow and have her look again."

Stinky snarled her lips, "Yes good for you Alex, take her out there again. What is it with you and dead bodies Alex? You know Tiger, Alex here has quite the history of running into dead bodies when he's listing places and now it seems his curse is carrying over and affecting his buyers as well. Ohh, I see Todd is here, I have to meet with him right away! He has to sign off on my new listing in the

Beaumont, some of us have to work. You enjoy your little day Alex doing whatever it is you do and Tiger you have fun leading your pack of wild kitties." And with that she stomped off in her spiky bitch boots, calling out to Todd, while waving listing forms.

"Boy this sure is a busy office, huh Alex? So what is your angle guy?" Tiger asked me.

"My angle, I don't understand what you mean?"

"Ohh, honey you can't be that new. Why all successful agents figure out their angle, their hook, and work it!"

Before I could provide her with an answer, the new agent class let out and there was Kenny Vance making his usual look-at-me scene. He spied us and called out, "Wait there Tiger, Alex! I have Snickers bars for you both!"

Is that what Tiger means by a hook, animal prints and candy bars? Oh, how cute, maybe my hook should be a good slap in the face to those that annoy me? With that thought, I quickly turned around and slipped out of the Viper Pit as fast as I could.

# 10

There must be something to the Law of Attraction that everyone is talking about, because no sooner had I escaped the Viper Pit thinking my gleeful, mean thoughts about how much fun it would be to slap all those who annoy me, when my cell phone began to ring. I picked up and immediately Harvey Malloy was barking in my ear, "Okay there son, I need you to get yer ass out here to Seaview this afternoon and list my place. I don't want no dilly-dallying, just bring your paper forms and let's get me out of here! Can you be here at 1:00 p.m? I would say earlier but Ralph likes to watch and sing to his favorite TV show, *Wheel of Fortune* and that comes on at noon. I'll let them mother fuckers at the front gate know yer comin' and to let you in."

Well this sure was short notice. A listing appointment and less than an hour and half to prepare, nothing like another day in real estate. Not my preference but what the hell. I told Harvey I'd be there and then I quickly went home to my computer to look up active and sold comps and slap together my listing presentation booklet. Clyde was excited to see me as I rushed in but he quickly caught on that I was in one of my work frenzies and so he gave me a few nasty looks, sighed and plopped down on the sofa. When I ran the comps, I noticed that Share's listing had already been changed to "temporarily off the market" as should happen when the owner is deceased. Have to give credit to her for taking care of that so fast. Now it would be interesting to see if she was able to keep the listing or if the listing would revert to Seaview or rather Beverly, per the Seaview rules. I gave Clyde a few strokes on the head, which he pretended to ignore and out the door I went, back to Seaview.

About 30 minutes later I pulled up to the Seaview front gate and the ever-so-friendly Dave was there to lead me through the entry fire drill again. Seriously, this guy must get a major hard-on playing wanna-be cop. Reminds me of the kind of kids who hung out in the back of shop class and pulled the wings off of flies for kicks. Since I was meeting a resident this time, I was told I could drive directly to the Towers and park in one of their visitor spots, number 17 to be precise. Off I went, driving at the obnoxious speed of 10 miles an hour while rolling over endless speed bumps. I went through the town square, noting they had a variety of small shops, a diner, a clothing store, even their own two screen movie house. I followed the signs and pulled into the drive for the Towers. Once again there were a couple of taxies and large Town Cars queuing up by the front door. I went toward the left to the Tower Visitor's Parking which is adjacent to the enormous resident carport parking lot. I found space 17 and made sure my two door beater was well between the freshly painted lines. I grabbed my listing packet and headed for the lobby.

The uniformed doormen were busy helping residents, but the automatic front doors whooshed open for me without pause. I walked over to the white marble reception desk and this time a woman named Nancy was there to help me. I wondered if Pamela had in fact been banished to retrain due to her five S's infractions. Nancy's hair was pulled back in a very tight knot, she showed me where to sign the register, and then called Harvey. I could hear Harvey yelling before she

could even get a word in, "Yes, you fucking moron, just send him up!"
Nancy tried to speak but evidently Harvey hung up on her. She looked
peeved, "Well, it appears Mr. Malloy is expecting you. Please go to
your left and take the South Tower elevator up to the fifth floor, his
unit number is 504." As I walked to the South Tower I noted one of
Ricardo's cohorts was busy with the manual floor sweeper, Beverly
sure kept them all on their toes. No doubt there would be no more
filthy, flower petals soiling the squeaky clean carpeting any time soon.
I passed an elderly woman with a blue rinse, in the South Tower
elevator area. She squinted her eyes, scowling while looking me up and
down and did not reply when I said hello. I didn't have on a visitor's
badge so it must be she has a sixth sense and can detect a non-resident.
She probably didn't want to waste energy being polite to a non-
Seaviewer, that or else her stool softener was causing her to cramp up
big time.

As I knocked on Harvey's door I could hear the game show on
the TV and Ralph squawking up a storm. The door burst open, "You
got here early! But come on in, his show is just about over." I
followed Harvey down the hall and into the living room. Ralph was
sitting on top of his cage, his red capped head cocked to one side
facing the TV set which was blasting out the end of a *Wheel of Fortune*
episode. Ralph glanced at me, his yellow eyes and pupils pin-wheeling
rapidly. A true sign the bird was excited and not in an attacking mode I
hoped. When the bell went ding to turn the letters on the show Ralph
went wild, going up and down the length of his cage, bobbing his head
up and down and chirping loudly. "Okay, that's enough strutting all

60

about now feller. Here Ralph, let's get back in the cage. I gotta get to work and spring us from this hell birdie." Harvey held his arm out and Ralph hopped on and then Harvey put him back on his perch inside the cage. He then shut off the TV set.

That move caused Ralph to go ballistic and he began walking up and down his wooden dowel, eyes pin wheeling all the while screeching. This caused Harvey to yell at him to shut up and that made Ralph all the louder, so Harvey led me out on the balcony.

"Let's get this paperwork done out here while he settles down. Damn bird can be loud. He gets all fussy if he don't get to finish his program clear to the end credits." We sat down in metal fold out chairs at a small, dented card table on the balcony and I proceeded to walk Harvey through my seller/listing packet. I went over the required state forms and other informational items, but Harvey really had zero interest. "Look, feller I just want to sign on the dotted line and get out of this hell hole as soon as I can."

I explained that I understood his desire to move out quickly but I like for all of my sellers to thoroughly review the listing information and read over the sample purchase and sale agreement first and then I usually come back and get the signatures. He did not look too pleased with this so I elaborated, "Look Mr. Malloy, I know you are eager to get out of Seaview and I can tell you do not like Beverly Ann LeFaye. I am sure you are happy that it turns out you are not legally required to use her as your listing agent. There are plenty of agents you could contact and use, so I am happy you decided to contact me first. However, it is in your best interest and mine too, if you spend at least a few hours reviewing this listing paperwork and other information I have here. I like all of my clients to be fully informed ahead of time as to exactly what they are getting into and be comfortable with the paperwork and my style of doing things. This is not how most agents work. If you are really eager to just sign and list without reviewing then I am sure you can find someone to come out here within the hour and do that for you. But that won't be me. Also, if you review things and we decide to work together, it takes some time before I actually list a property. Your condo needs to be in its best shape before we go live and especially in our market now. As you may know, nationally the real estate market is nose diving and now it is starting to hit here in Clinton. The days of instant sales are passing I'm afraid, so we are going to need to strategize and make your condo look the best it can before I list it. That is assuming you want to get top dollar for your condo? Otherwise I am sure there are plenty of insti-list agents you can contact who could have your place on the market by late this afternoon." I stood up to go back inside.

Harvey looked a bit taken aback but got up and led us inside. He turned around and said, "Okay, I think I get your angle here. Yer a real straight shooter I can tell and that's alright by me after living in this here bullshit village for a year now! I'll look over your pile of dead trees here and you plan on coming back over here tomorrow at the same time, maybe a bit later so Ralph's show will be completely over." Harvey looked over at Ralph who tilted his red capped head and appeared to give Harvey the go-ahead, "You bet I want top dollar, who doesn't? Okay so Ralph and I will give a gander to all your paper here."

I smiled and while I wasn't exactly chomping at the bit to take this listing and in Seaview no less, I too needed top dollar. "If it is okay with you, I think in order to get top dollar Mr. Malloy, we are going to need to spruce up your place a bit, maybe do a light staging. Something to lure as many potential buyers in as possible." That was code for your unit is ugly and filled with second hand crappy furniture. "Maybe I can bring someone by for some staging ideas? I always hire a professional photographer to shoot my listings. The photos are what get people's attention online, so I'll be hiring my friend Lexi to photograph this place once we have spruced it up a bit."

Harvey shook his head, "Yeah, okay then you do your stuff there and bring over your people to get this place taken care of. All I care about is getting the hell out this place before these old fogies drive me over the edge. Especially that Beverly bitch. You gotta watch out for that one I'm telling you, rotten apple to the core, that one is." I decided to be all grown up and professional and I managed to keep my mouth shut and my face blank.

I agreed to be there at 1:00 p.m. tomorrow and told Harvey to call me if he had any questions. And that was it. I made it out of the South Tower without encountering any more scowling prunes. But as I was heading for the huge automatic lobby doors, whose syrupy voice should I hear? "Ohh, Mr. Campbell, just a minute!" Beverly shot over from the white marble reception desk to where I was, all a flutter in her green Seaview blazer and a pale blue dress, her helmet hair not moving a follicle as she rushed over. "Why, I see you are visiting us again today, anyone in particular?" She asked while picking, what, imaginary lint or dust off the front of my shirt. "Ahh, yes hello Mrs. LeFaye, nice to see you again." I can be an awesome liar when I set my mind to it. "I was just visiting with Mr. Malloy. He called and asked me to come see about listing his condo but I've got to get it spruced up a bit first."

Beverly wrinkled her nose just a bit, "Well, you sure do have your work cut out for you with that man. I hope you'll be able to handle him and that foul mouth of his! Now I don't think you have ever listed a Seaview property before? I'll make sure you get one of our listing rule packets from Dave on your way out. I'm sure we won't have any compliance issues with you Alex. You are so respectful, not like those other two from your office. Anyhow, do keep me posted on all things Mr. Malloy! I think it is going to be much better for everyone if he transitions out of our wonderful town, and sooner rather than later. Oh now tell me, what is going on with your lovely Mrs. Kluntz? Wasn't that just too dreadful, finding Mrs. Roland in her bedroom and not breathing? I do hope that didn't scare Mrs. Kluntz too much. You know, I think she is just perfect Seaview material.

Unfortunately, the Roland unit is now off the market until her estate can be settled. She didn't sign one of our automatic listing forms when she purchased, which was before my time! I always make sure all of the new residents sign the automatic listing form, which gives Seaview the legal authority to list a former resident's property before they are even cremated. It's so important in this type of community, to keep things moving along and upbeat. We don't want our residents

64

dwelling on the negative or death, that's just not the Seaview way! Anyhow, I'm afraid that listing is off the market for now. I called over to your office and spoke with your Mr. Blund yesterday, just to make sure that Share Shelton removed the listing from active status in the multiple listing database." Well, that explains why Stinky actually did her job and changed the listing to temporarily off the market status so quickly. "Of course, Share will need to change the status to cancelled once she receives the letter from the Seaview attorney which explains that condo now reverts to an in-house Seaview listing. That is probably for the best, considering how inconsiderate some agents can be, don't you agree? I just know I am not going to have these issues with you as a listing agent here Alex, now am I?" She said with a perky frosted pink lipstick smile and a somewhat vicious gleam in her eyes.

"Ahh, no ma'am I'll pick up the Seaview listing rule packet and we'll make sure this all goes smoothly and Mr. Malloy can move on as quickly as possible. We are going to need to stage his unit a bit, given our current declining market but I still think it should sell reasonably fast."

"Oh, that's just grand. Now, what are we going to do with our little Mrs. Kluntz? It sounded like she preferred a two bedroom unit. You know a little bird tells me there may be another two bedroom unit coming on the market shortly in the North Tower! That's where I live. I will keep you posted about this Alex, hopefully it will be much sooner than later. Okay, well I am so delighted we have things all taken care of. Now you enjoy the rest of your day. Oh and Alex dear, tuck your shirt in a bit more, it looks a little loose and baggy. I find a shirt tucked in tight on men, especially when they are not wearing a sport coat, looks so much more comely. You know, I recommend you have your dry cleaners do a heavy starch on your shirts Alex. It keeps them fresher throughout your busy day. And when the late afternoon comes you can wear a sport coat to hide any wrinkles your shirt may have picked up during the day! And another little tip I used to give my viewers, I find if you tuck your shirt into your undergarment's waist band, that helps keep the shirt's front nice and flat, not all baggy like yours has become. Just a friendly tip, do give it a try, I'm sure you'll be just amazed with the results!" Beverly then gave me one of her winks and said she had to get back to reviewing things at the reception desk, "Such a mess they have Alex, why without me to oversee things I just couldn't imagine the disarray that would result!" Disarray? Tuck my shirt into my underwear? I know, perhaps I could just staple my shirt to my underwear every day, and then there would be no fear of it becoming slightly un-tucked.

I was turning toward the lobby doors when I heard Beverly let out an angry screech, "How awful! Oh, that dog! Stop right there, can't you see what your horrible little creature has done! Oh, curse word! Aggghhh, Carlos, Ricardo come here quickly! Pamela get the emergency clean up kit, NOW!" Sure as shit, literally, an old lady's small white dog had planted a turd right in the middle of the entry lobby.

The dog owner appeared a bit miffed, "Oh no, Mr. Jiggles why you really did have to go potty, didn't you baby? Oh bumpkins did a doody on the floor. Poor little dear, why these nice men will clean up your little boo-boo." With that she picked up Mr. Jiggles and began smooching him. Beverly was beside herself, motioning for the clean up to commence right away. She grabbed the dog owner's arm and began lecturing her about the pet rules at Seaview and saying she would have to cite her and there would be a fine as well. The old woman didn't appear to care, she just kissed Mr. Jiggles more which made Beverly's pink frosted lips turn down in a scowl. For a minute I thought she might throw up or I guess as Beverly would refer to it, up-chuck. "Oh quickly Ricardo, yes spray the disinfectant. Oh, I think we are going to have to have these carpets professionally cleaned now and Mrs. Runyard that is something *you* are going to have to pay for! We can't have this here at Seaview. No not at all, why your little dog is just not behaving properly. Not at all. This is most unsatisfactory dog behavior and we can't have this happening here Eileen. Why just the other day this ill behaved creature did this out by the pool!" As Beverly continued to fuss and rant, I made my exit.

The rest of the day was a blur of assorted errands and I called Mushy (Vicky) to make sure she received the condo listings I sent over. I called Wanda's house and Ethel picked up. I let her know the Roland unit was now temporarily off the market and what Beverly had told me about another two bedroom unit possibly listing soon.

"Not to worry Alex, I am not so sure about moving into a unit where we found a dead body. I'm concerned about Wanda. She seems so tense. I'm thinking she is not relaxing enough and you know that is not healthy. Say, do you know where Wanda keeps her tools? I need a good jig saw and some nice quarter inch nails." I told her I didn't know and she quickly replied, "Not a problem, no worries! I'm going to the Highmont Hardware store with Miss Lyla and then we are gonna hit that fabric remainder store on the way home. *Oy*, gotta run, I'm already late meeting her."

# 11

The next couple of days were the usual blur of what I call non-activity, meaning I showed a fair number of properties, especially to Mushy and Joocey but no cigar. Nothing any of my current buyers looked at hit the spot. I was beginning to hear murmurs from some that perhaps it might be best to wait and see if the market was going to go down like the rest of the country. That is a valid concern, but one that means much more wasted gas fumes for my two door beater. Of course if they stay in the their new place five to seven years as I advise all my clients, then the local statistics show that is the typical real estate cycle in Clinton. So worst case, they could remain there seven years, sell and break even or hopefully sell and make a profit. There are no guarantees as I tell everyone. There could be a down turn that defies the last 40 odd years of stats. In Vicky and Courtney's case, I'm sure Courtney would not be living in whatever they purchased for five to seven years. I had already advised Vicky that we should make sure the condominium complex where she purchases allows for rentals. This way she could rent the unit out if Courtney lives there for six months and suddenly has an epiphany that perhaps she needs to attend an international nail salon school in Asia to get her BA in Nailology. Vicky would not have a mortgage to cover if she rented out the condo and so she could ride out any hiccup in the real estate up and down cycle and hold until she could sell and break even or make some money. This was assuming I could find a place that would remotely excite Courtney. Thus far, not much made her stop popping her gum and look up from her phone.

# CHARLES CHAPLIN

I had spent a whole day with Harvey Malloy and gotten him through the listing paperwork, made sure he understood all the terms and legal notices. We arrived at what I thought was a viable list price and then I had to submit that price to the Seaview Review Board, headed by the lovely Beverly. She said they would meet tonight and review Harvey's list price and make sure it met with their approval. Harvey was good and pissed and I can't say I blame him but the review and approval is required at Seaview and he did sign and agree to those terms when he purchased.

In the mean time, Harvey actually asked me about having someone fix up his place, he wanted top dollar. I called one staging company I knew of but they only did top to bottom staging, meaning they are best suited for new construction model units or for a house that is completely vacant. The next company I called was out of business and the third sounded ridiculous. This woman runs Homestyle Vignettes By Tammi a company that supposedly specializes in creating a *homey atmosphere for less*. What that actually means is the company owner, Tammi, comes out to a property, places some candles, a small end table or two, some smell-good perfume sticks, colored glass chips in a vase, a few jars of colorful olives, an old cookbook opened on the kitchen counter, a couple of plush hand towels and wha-la, instant move-in feeling! And all for extremely high prices; creativity is costly after all. I tried explaining to her what I thought Harvey's unit needed, some painted walls, rearranging, a few nice *chotchkes* (not of the glass chips in a vase variety) and that should do it. Miss Homestyle Vignettes was not having any of it. She reminded me where her staging

70

degree was from (an esteemed mail-order/online institution) and who some of the agents are that she has worked with (Stinky naturally) and that she has been the sole reason many homes in the Beaumont sold so quickly. I thanked her for her time and crossed her off the list.

I knew what I had to do. I did not want to but it would definitely be in my client's best interest. So I dialed Percy Emerson's number and he picked up after half a ring. "Ohh, my best friend where have you been hiding? It's been just too long Alex! I had a feeling this morning when little Hadley and I were taking our walk that I'd be hearing from you and sure enough here's your jingle. So just tell me everything, catch me up and how's Miss Wanda doing? You know I really need to have you two over for a lovely dinner. You all would just be dazzled with my candlelight dinner, I'm known for them you know? You know the dining room is just ethereal when I light up all the candles. I light 100 candles to be precise and then let their warm glow mingle with the mirrored glass, the soft reflections are just stunning! I think I'll do one of my pork tenderloins, yes that's a good one for us I think. Why little Hadley and I are going right out to the butcher when we hang up and I will whip up the marinade, you know it takes at least two days to get the meat perfectly tenderized and..."

"Ahh, yes well Percy that sounds great. I am sure your dining room with all the lit candles is really something. In fact, that is why I am calling you Percy." I then explained to him about Harvey Malloy's condo and asked if he might be able to stage it for us. I made sure he knew it would be a special favor, as I knew he was indeed a professional decorator. The houses he has done have appeared in national magazines and his house is nothing to sneeze at. It's just Percy is a major pain. I ran into him at a dog park while walking Clyde (see Volume Two) and got my last listing that ended up not working out through him. Percy is an overweight, over middle aged, raging queen who is as pretentious as they come and lucky me, Wanda swears he has the hots for me. I'd rather live in denial but he *is* always trying to insert sexual innuendo into our conversations. I may cross the street but Percy lives in a permanent "do not cross" zone as far as I'm concerned. In Wanda's terms, his man pond is not the man pond for me. No thanks, I'll just stay on shore and look for rocks. Regardless of my opinion, Percy is a very talented decorator and I know he would do an awesome job fixing up Harvey's place and thus help me sell the old billy goat's unit as fast as possible.

"Ohh, Alex this sounds like something new and fun for me! You know I had a client at Seaview years ago, what was her name? Oh, well I recall she wanted pale blue chintz everywhere and insisted on swag draperies. Swag, I mean really, have you ever? Anyway, I do remember I finally overruled the old biddy and got that place looking as good as I possibly could, I mean given her budget. It was a laugh what she expected, I'm not a miracle worker! So I finished her unit and we did everything top to bottom and then she promptly died a month later. Such a shame really, of course those Seaview vultures were thrilled with my design work. It helped them sell that place in one day. If I recall it was a two bedroom in that newer tower complex they have, not the old towers, you know the ones with the great sound views? Anyhow I just thought..."

"Yes, Percy I am sure you did an awesome job with that woman's condo. Now what I need you to do for my client is just simple things, prior to listing. He's a grumpy bachelor but he does agree if we fluff the place up a bit he'll get more money. So, would you be able to come out to Seaview with me and take a look? I have to warn you, this geezer is very cheap so this would be a very budgeted job."

"Well, I know what you are describing Alex and these kinds of clients are always such a pain. You know I don't do staging and there are companies that specialize in that kind of work. But as you must know, most of those companies are wanna-be designers who think a vase full of silk roses and a Pottery Barn poster are just the height of sophistication. Now I know that *you* know the difference and can appreciate what I do. So only for you Alex would I even consider such a project this trite. But we are friends and friends are supposed to help friends out and best of all, you will owe me a big favor after this one!"

Oh god. We talked a bit more and Percy agreed to take a look and he could actually come out this afternoon with me. I called Harvey and he was fine with us stopping by as long as we made sure we arrived after 1:00 p.m., nothing interrupts Ralph's *Wheel of Fortune* hour. I tried to suggest that Harvey needed to be on his best behavior and respect the decorator I was bringing over, that he was doing this as a special favor and is nationally known, etc....

"Yeah, yeah, I getcha there son! I didn't just fall off the turnip truck. So yer bringing one of them butt stuffers to my place here? Well it won't be the first time Ralph and me ever met a fairy. No need to get yer pants in a knot, I ain't stupid. If it's a man and a decorator then it's gotta be a queer, right? So yeah, Ralph and me will make nice. I don't really give no monkey fuck what the butt stuffer does in his own time, makes no never mind to me. I just want top dollar for this here hell hole and Ralph and me are outta here! You hear that birdie? You and me are springing this here fucking coop!" With that, Ralph began to squawk and chirp extra loud so I shouted out the time we'd be there and hung up.

I left a quick message for Wanda letting her know that Ethel said she and Miss Lyla were visiting the hardware store. That was kind of mean on my part, as I knew hearing that would cause Wanda's blood to curdle. No doubt, I was going to have to get Ethel out looking and hopefully buying and soon because Wanda was just about to her limit. I made a note to see if the two bedroom unit Beverly had mentioned would be listing soon. I then made sure my clothes were Seaview presentable. They were reasonably pressed, no obvious food stains. I tucked in my *Leave it to Beaver* plaid shirt but much to Beverly's dismay I did not tuck it into my underwear and my stapler was empty so no chance I could employ my genius shirt tucking-in idea. I gave Clyde a bit more kibble, hugged him and out the door I went.

I drove over to Capitol Heights and pulled up to the curb outside of Percy's two story contemporary house. Capitol Heights sits just south of the old money neighborhood The Bluffs and just north of the Lee District which is where newly minted lawyers and doctors and yuppies just starting out typically live. Capitol Heights is comprised of houses built between 1915 and 1935. The houses are upscale, while the lots are mostly narrow as it was designed to be a more urban neighborhood. It has some really nice arts and crafts style houses that have views of Warner Sound and generally Capitol Heights is where the rebellious trust fund babies settle, usually the sons and daughters of The Bluffs estates. The neighborhood professes to be nothing but accepting and down with the people but the vaults of inherited and corporate money that back these enlightened opinions make it the perfect armchair liberal haven in my humble opinion. Most Capitol Heights residents have nothing but scorn for the toney estates in The Bluffs and view themselves as "everyday people." Any agent who works with these types of folks in the Heights knows, they may be "down with the people" but these Neiman Marcus hippies can get mighty testy if you dare suggest their humble abodes are not the million dollar plus babies they think they are. Funny how money can be dressed up and expressed in so many ways but underneath it all lies the same cord of fear and lack.

I glanced at the mustard yellow stucco house next to Percy's, my former listing. Sure enough it appeared my former client's relatives were still in residence (see Volume Two). The lawn patch was now completely brown and dusty, there were cardboard boxes and what looked like old tire rims piled up by the front door steps. Her once shiny, new white Range Rover was now best described as a shade of dusty beige with two hub caps missing and the rear window was cracked. Yep, Darla and Ronnie were still living large in Serenity's house.

# CHARLES CHAPLIN

Percy was bustling down his front walk as I pulled to the curb. He was wearing a lavender button down shirt, starched within an inch of its life with equally stiff chinos. His ample gut was spilling over his leather, monogrammed fanny pack and he appeared to be carrying a blue blazer on one arm while flapping one of his monogrammed handkerchiefs at me in some sort of waive or salute. No doubt, Percy stuffed his shirts in his underwear as they stayed as flat as they could given his girth or perhaps he employed my shirt stapling idea which knowing Percy, I would not be surprised.

"Oh my, can you believe the state of Serenity's house? Did you see how filthy her car is now?" Percy said while getting in my car. "It's just too trailer park and in Capitol Heights, can you imagine? I just pray that estate is settled soon and you can relist that house and get them out! I mean, you would think they would be missing life in Indiana by now wouldn't you? Who are those smoking fiends going to associate with here in Clinton? Well you are just right on time Alex! I am thinking you and Wanda should come for dinner this Friday, around eight-ish. I am going to pick up the pork tenderloin later today." With that he continued to prattle on non-stop for 40 minutes until I was pulling up to the Seaview front gate, where Dave once again put led us through the entry fire drill. I was instructed to park in the Towers' visitor parking lot, this time in space number 13, I hope that wasn't some kind of omen.

# 12

The front desk routine was quick and painless. Pamela was back and apparently her five S's were in order as she smiled right off the bat and kept smiling as Harvey barked at her when she called his unit. I led us to the elevators, Percy bustling in tow as he made comments, "Oh, this lobby really needs an updated look Alex! This white marble and powder blue carpeting, it's all so dated. I know these old people probably like familiar things but really we could do better! Aghh, and look at this wall paper Alex! These halls are enough to make you dizzy with the vertical stripes, oh my!" This continued as we made our way up to Harvey's condo. I barely managed to knock on the door before Harvey yanked it open.

I introduced Harvey to Percy, "Oh it is just wonderful to meet you Mr. Malloy." He said offering his pudgy hand to shake his a palm facing down, in a kiss my hand manner. Harvey looked at Percy's limp hand a bit confused but managed to paw Percy's fingers a bit as a way of shaking hands. "I am Percival Emerson, Percy to all my friends. Alas, I do not hale from *the* Emerson clan I am afraid, but my mother's side does descend from President Woodrow Wilson. Now let me have a look here at your water view home and see what magic I can perform to help you transform and sell this place." Harvey looked a bit suspicious but simply nodded his head in agreement and we proceeded to look around. Percy actually has a very good game face and did not reveal what were most likely his appalled thoughts at such an undecorated and drab cave. Ralph took note of us and immediately his eyes began to pinwheel as he darted back and forth on the main dowel in his cage. He gave a few loud chirps but no words or loud song routines this time, his TV show must have worn him out. Percy looked in each room and then stood in the living room, nodding his head while thinking. "Well now, you certainly have a fine condominium here Mr. Malloy. Why your view is simply stunning! As you know, I am here as a favor to Alex. I do not normally do staging work as I am a professional and a well known interior designer. You may have seen some of my work in the upper end national publications?"

Harvey looked irritated, "No I don't read them lady magazines, only subscriptions I have is *Popular Mechanics* and *Bird World*. I'll take yer word for it that you know how to fix up a place. Just so long as you don't paint this place all pink like your shirt there."

Percy didn't skip a beat, "Actually my shirt is lavender and no, we won't be painting anything this color. Well as I said, I agreed to help Alex as a very special favor. What I have in mind is to repaint your whole condo with fresh white paint and then paint one wall in each room an accent color, not pink but something cheerful. You know Mr. Malloy, your Red Lored Amazon parrot there will really appreciate some color on the walls. Parrots see a much wider spectrum of color than we humans do and I am sure these dull white walls are simply not stimulating for your bird." This appeared to pique Harvey's curiosity and he tilted his head to the side almost exactly like Ralph's head was tilted. "Next, we'll need to remove some of the few pieces of furniture you have in here and they can easily be replaced with simple, more up-to-date items. This way, potential clients do not focus on your furniture but can imagine themselves living here." I suppose that was Percy code for get rid of your Salvation Army shit and make the place not appear to be someone's basement filled with cast-offs from four decades ago. "We can put a simple bedspread on your bed and maybe find an inexpensive headboard for it. There are some pieces of furniture that I think would really compliment this space and I can get them on loan for us to use so you don't have to purchase them. I am sure Alex has explained how these simple staging touches will get you more money when you sell."

Harvey nodded but then his eyes became a bit squinty, "Okay now I hear what yer sayin' feller. Give this place a woman's touch and all and I'm sure yer real good at that. So what's it gonna cost me? 'Cause I ain't paying no king's ransom to make this here place a show pony for Liberace!"

Percy calmly replied, "The bottom line is this project is going to cost you $5,000 and that includes labor, materials and anything I can manage to get on loan. Keep in mind this is a low bid considering what the staging companies charge and I am only agreeing to do this as a special favor to Alex."

Harvey looked aghast, "What did you say, $5,000? Have you plum lost yer mind there fella? That much money for a bucket of paint and some lady do-dahs set all around, that's crazy! Who do you think I am, some senile rich fool who will just throw money at ya?"

Percy became dead serious and his tone was cold, "That's a non negotiable price Mr. Malloy and as I mentioned that price is well below rate and a special favor. Most people would simply die to have me agree to help them stage their home for sale. You can think this over and let Alex know your decision by this evening. Now Alex, I have to get back. It's been a pleasure meeting you Mr. Malloy and your parrot." With that Percy turned and went straight out the front door. I turned to Harvey and told him I would call him later today but to take a moment and think things through, the price to stage was not so bad if it increased the buyer appeal and led to a sale. I reminded him the market was slowing and it was in his best interest to do everything he could to help sell his place. I headed to the door and then turned and offered my own zinger, "Besides Mr. Malloy, I know you and Ralph do not want to have to stay here for months on end while your unit sits on the market. I am sure you would enjoy getting on with your life and leaving Beverly LeFaye and Seaview behind."

Percy and I made our way back to the lobby and Beverly was there making her rounds. The minute she caught sight of me she flew across the lobby. For a woman of whatever age she is past 70, Beverly is quite spry. "Alex, I am so glad I caught you. I want to let you know that we will be meeting tonight to review Mr. Malloy's list price and make sure you have all of your listing ducks in a row." She then reached out and grasped my arm, "With you, I am almost certain all of your forms and paperwork are going to be in order, not like the others. You know Share Shelton has lost her listing since Tina Roland passed away, those are the rules. So I will have that on the market very soon. Share just listed one of our bungalows for sale, the Menendez cottage. Seems they are going to leave Seaview and move closer to their children, of course that's probably in Mexico or somewhere down there." She said with a sly smile, giving us a slow wink. "Anyhow, that

Share had them listing with her in no time, she's good at that you know. We'll be reviewing her suggested list price for that place when we meet tonight as well. Alex, maybe you can help her out with her paperwork, as she doesn't seem to be able to grasp our requirements. I'm afraid one more infraction and well, we are just going to have to call a special meeting with your office's designated broker, that's Todd Blund isn't it?

Oh my, always something. And just the worst news! Sonya Chalmers passed this morning and she has a two bedroom unit in the North Tower. I'm afraid that is another listing I am going to have to tend to. I don't think this one will disturb Mrs. Kluntz because Sonya passed away in the elevator, one of those heart things I imagine, so much of that in a senior community. Such a blessing we have the crematorium and the Seaview Eternal Slumber Mortuary and Mausoleum here onsite, keeps it all so easy. And that is such a dear comfort to all our residents; the whole family just stays right here. Did I tell you Alex that we are adding services for our residents' pets afterlife care as well? That should be ready to go shortly. Anyhow, I'll certainly give you a ring as soon as I have the Chalmers unit all set and you can have Mrs. Kluntz come out and take a look. It's just getting so busy!

Oh, and who have we here with us today?" She said putting her hand out to Percy and coyly turning her helmet hair head to the side, her frosted pink lips going up in a wide, almost manic smile. I quickly introduced Beverly to Percy and he went through his usual family lineage routine. Beverly just gave her best closed mouth smile while Percy prattled on, "You should call me Percy, all my best friends do and I can just tell we are going to be friends Beverly!  And my, you know I don't think I've been in Seaview in almost 10 years now, god I'm dating myself now aren't I?  Anyhow, we'll see if Mr. Malloy comes to his senses and realizes what an opportunity and good fortune it is to have someone of my caliber help him with the staging of his unit.  As I mentioned, I don't usually do such a thing but I always help out my best friends!  Speaking of interior design projects Beverly, it appears the lobby and tower hallways here could use some updating.  That wall paper in the halls is enough to make you dizzy!  Here's my card, perhaps you and Board would like to meet with me to discuss some interior design options?"

Beverly smiled wider as her eyes got a certain glint, "Why thank you, Mr. Emerson is it?  I don't think it is quite appropriate to call you by your first name, seeing as we really aren't friends yet, now are we?  I find it is best to keep things formal, especially in business life and I'm sure a man of your age would agree, now wouldn't you Mr. Emerson?  Why I bet in just a year or so you are going to be old enough to consider living in Seaview.  I'll put your business card on file.  But you should know, I myself have quite the eye for decorating and I've had my mind on doing some redecorating here since I moved in.  I think the Board would be more comfortable working with me on a redecorating project since I am a resident and since I run the real estate office, serve on the Board, manage some of the committees, host the weekly TV show, gosh it just goes on and on!  But I will keep you in mind Mr. Emerson."

Beverly then smiled at me and reached out and patted my shirt front, "Oh Alex that is so much better. It's nice when people find value in my advice. Doesn't his shirt front look much better Mr. Emerson? No bulging fabric, all smooth and flat like it should be, gives such a better impression." God the old bag was right, my shirt wasn't bunching out. Must be a miracle because it sure as shit wasn't tucked into my boxers. I pondered telling Beverly about my stapler idea but she breezed on before I could open my mouth. "Now Alex, you should find out the name of the dry cleaner that presses Mr. Emerson's shirts. See how nice and crisp his shirt is? Oh, I'll get you all fixed up Alex, just one step at a time! Notice how Mr. Emerson's shirt *does* bulge but that's not the fabric bunching up now is it Mr. Emerson? You know, when you consider moving to Seaview Mr. Emerson, we have quite the exercise facility for our residents. Why I bet a couple of months on our machines with one of our specially trained senior workout coaches and you won't have that belly bulge anymore! It's so important not to let one's self go in one's golden years. No one said you have to become senile *and* fat when you age, now did they? I lead a weekly motivational class for some of our residents here, all about the wonderful power of positive thinking. I believe everyone can benefit from that, why just look at me! It's important for me to set a good example in my figure and disposition each and every day. It gives our Seaviewers such hope and inspiration.

Now I do hate to be a spoil sport and dash off but I have to get over to the crematorium to help them with the paperwork and the processing of Miss Chalmers. Of course I have to be the bearer of bad news and pull up her file and call her loved ones. I just hate making those phone calls but we do have to keep moving forward now don't we?" With that Beverly patted both our arms, "I'm just so happy we got a chance to see each other Alex. Mr. Emerson it has been such a pleasure to make your acquaintance." And with that, off she shot out the front doors, into her electric cart and sped off, cutting off a taxi and Town Car in the process.

Percy appeared a bit taken aback, "Well, hells bells Alex, that woman is something else! The only good thing out of her mouth was the fact she does not care for Share Shelton. God she's like the witch of Seaview and telling me she's a decorator? Why that's a complete laugh, she doesn't even use the proper industry terminology, interior designer. Decorator, ohh that *is* a laugh! Given her pastel dress and unmovable hair, I'd say she still thinks Ronald Reagan or maybe even Jimmy Carter is in office. Oh, I can *just* imagine her decorating skills, god! Now, we need to go have a nice long lunch and recover from this. So where are you taking me? I think this new charming French bistro is just the place. It just opened up on the edge of the Lee District and the owner is this dreamy Frenchman with large brown eyes and an ass that is to die for! Of course he can't hold a flame to you Alex and I am assuming you are still saying you are bisexual? Well I'm still banking on my 50 percent chance!"

T.M.I! And lunch? Who said anything about lunch with pervy? Thankfully before I could respond, my cell rang and it was Wanda. She immediately started barking in my ear about Ethel but I quickly cut her off and told her she was coming to lunch with Percy and me. Before she could respond I passed my phone to Percy and told him to give her directions.

# 13

The French bistro is called *Le Godet*. How or why anyone would name their restaurant "the bucket" is beyond me. I suppose bucket is not as unappetizing as the seafood place Wanda and I sometimes frequent called Barnacles. Crusty crap on the bottom of boats and piers, gee I'm starving. Percy did not shut his mouth from the time we left Seaview until we pulled up to the curb outside of *Le Godet*. I played more of my hippie music, as Wanda refers to it, at a low volume and pictured Grace Slick and spinning mandalas as I maneuvered up the streets. It worked wonders in tuning out the babbling brook called Percy. I suppose that's what people mean when they refer to their "happy place." Wanda's emerald green boat of a car was parked at the curb by the restaurant's entry and I let Percy out. I said I'd circle around the block and find parking. As I scouted for parking I thought about just driving home and going for a nice walk with Clyde in the greenbelt south of my house. But I suppose that would entail more trouble explaining than it was worth. Besides, Wanda was already semi homicidal from Ethel living in her house. So I parked my car, took a deep breath and went in to see what the bucket's lunch time specials were.

Wanda and Percy were seated at a round table in the corner, complete with a fresh blue and white checkerboard table cloth, flowers and wine glasses. The restaurant was half full and clearly *Le Godet* was trying to be the next trendy eatery in the Lee District. Expensive with checkerboard table cloths at lunch and probably really expensive and snooty at dinner with white table linens and at least two wine glasses with each place setting. Wanda was decked out in a magenta dress, a large turquoise necklace and matching chandelier earrings. Her hair was puffed up really high today. I've noticed whenever her hair gets closer to god, Wanda's mood tends to be in the angry range. Sort of akin to a bird fluffing up it feathers when it is trying to ward off a predator I suppose. "Humph, well look what finally made its bony ass way to lunch Percy." She said while taking a pull on her glass of red wine. "We all having this here bottle of *merlot* something another, so just give in and for once have a sip of Satan's kool-aide at lunch Alex. They don't make no slushies here, so Frenchy wine gonna have to hit it. I'm telling you both, between the crazy shit going down in my mortgage world and the crap Miss Liz is pulling over at Salon Wanda, telling me she done went ahead and ordered two more dryer stations without even getting my permission." Wanda owns her own hair salon, a business she started prior to becoming a top mortgage broker. The salon is infamous for its pornographic statue in the courtyard out back. (see Volume One) "Then this here Ethel all up in my crib playing on my very last nerve, well hell it ain't no wonder I'm starting to drink!" Starting? "Yeah, you go ahead and sit your bony butt down Alex but you best be telling me that you got that Ethel all set and she gonna be moving out like yesterday. I just told Percy here how that woman went and painted my front door brown and she is now best pals with Miz Lyla! Them two old birds is truckin' all over the damn Highmont and all of it on some new mission to fix up my house." I thought it best to keep my mouth shut about their foray to the hardware store today, as clearly Wanda had not checked her messages yet. Miss Lyla is a high spirited, ancient woman who lives up the street from Wanda. "So when is Ethel moving Alex?"

"Ahh, I just ran into Beverly LeFaye at Seaview when Percy and I were there and she says there is a new two bedroom unit that will be on the market very soon in the North Tower. Sounds like it might be a good fit for Ethel as the owner of this unit did not die in the unit but on the elevator."

"Yeah, well old lady gonna be dying in my house if she don't get her ass moving and buy soon! I tell you, them old birds sure drop like flies out at that Seaview; must be a gold mine for old Beverly and company. Percy was filling me in on Beverly, and honey she sound like a real bitch. Sort of like one of them old school housewife bitches. Humpf, makes no never mind to me, you just get Ethel out of my house Alex. Ohh, these garlic bread thangs is just nasty! Here Alex pass me the butter, I'm gonna slab some more on these here."

I gave Wanda a curious look, "What you lookin at bony, you forget your name? Oh, the bread. Well see once again you actin' way too old for your age Alex. Everyone knows that nasty is the new bomb. Here let me translate that for you white boy. Nasty means it's really good. I'm sure Percy here is up on the new nasty, huh Perce?"

That was just plain annoying, Ethel or no Ethel living in her house, "Oh yes Wanda I'm sure Percy is all up on the new nasty! Why aren't we all just nasty? I wish I too could speak 16 year old all day or talk in text. Aim high, that's my motto." I reached over and grabbed the bread basket and took out a mini garlic bread loaf, taking a loud and crunchy bite right in Wanda's face. Ewwee, these bread things were truly nasty and not in the new nasty way either. I managed to swallow the bite and started chugging water.

Wanda let out a chuckle, "See there Percy, he doesn't like them, which ain't no big surprise to me, 'cause he's got the food pickiness of a finicky four year old. Here Percy, have yourself one-a these here, take a bite of nasty!"

I tried to glare at Wanda as I chugged more water. Percy took out mini bread loaf and proceeded to slather enough butter on top to make Paula Deen proud. "My, my ladies looks like you two are just a wee testy today. Now settle down. We all have our time of the month but you two are well past your once a month quotas. You two are going to have to play nice because you'll be coming to my house this Saturday night for a fabulous candlelight dinner. I'm going to marinate the pork tenderloin tonight. We can celebrate Alex' new listing and my gig to help that poor cranky man make his place sale ready. Have either of you ever seen Beverly LeFaye's weekly show on the cable access station?" I nodded no, as I don't have a television and Wanda no doubt hadn't seen it as she usually has something better to do with herself on a Saturday night than watch a local cable access station. "Well, we'll all watch her show at my house. You have got to check out this time warp bitch in action. So I'll see you two Saturday night at around 7:30. Ohhh, we are going to have so much fun! Why we could even make it a slumber party, sleep over and---"

"Ah, Percy I can't do the sleep over thing." Over my dead body was I gonna end up at some sleep over at this perv-on-the-make's house, not to mention who could possibly sleep in his dollhouse, museum? It is so clean and shiny you'd be afraid to unmake the bed much less sleep in it.

"Humpf, well old no-sex, bony there might not do no sleep over but hell yeah, I'm bringing my overnight bag! You got any of them bath salts and facial mud mask stuff at yo' crib Percy? You know I'll just stop by the salon and pick us up some beauty treatment aids. I'll call Miz Liz and get her to put us up some stuff. We can fix ourselves up, have us a rejuvenation spa moment right there at your house. Get me a nice break from the Ethel. I am telling you Alex, you best get that woman sold and soon or we gonna be attending her wake."

I calmly suggested, "Well you could always ask Ethel to leave, it's not like she's *your* mother after all. We could have driven her to a nice hotel when she had her falling out with Norman, no one said you were required to house your mortgage client's mother. I mean it really is all about boundaries Wanda. It's not our fault Ethel Kluntz came here all the way from Philadelphia unannounced to surprise her son only discover he has a live-in girlfriend she doesn't approve of." If looks could kill, I'd be dust.

Wanda sat up straighter, "Oh no! You did not just start that psycho babble boundary bullshit with me again did you? Who drove this woman to my house? Who suggested to her that I had comfortable mattresses? For that matter bony ass, you could've used your boundary crap and taken old lady to a hotel, made some boundaries for me. But ohhhh no, you didn't go there now did ya? I'm telling you I just----"

Percy put his wine glass down, "Now girls please! This is supposed to a nice little lunch with friends at this gorgeous French restaurant. Let's not start all this bickering. Really it is so unnecessary. Now Miss Wanda, I am sure our friend Alex here is going to have Ethel Kluntz moved into a great new condo in Seaview as soon as possible. Really, play nice you two. I do hate when my friends squabble, it just makes me eat more. Oh look, speaking of French and gorgeous, here's our waiter with our entrees."

From there, lunch was served and Percy distracted Wanda by asking her about beauty treatments they could do together at the sleep over. They babbled back and forth, squealing like two perky teenage girls. All of this prattle, while Percy managed to literally drool over the French waiter. There I sat, counting the minutes and thinking about how I could rearrange the shoes in my closet.

Lunch finally ended without any more squabbles or a homicide and Wanda told Percy she'd give him a lift home. As I was walking to my car, my cell rang and it was Beverly. "Ohh, I'm just so happy I reached you Alex! Why I just got all of Miss Chalmers' papers processed and notified the family that I'm so sorry for their loss and they have 10 calendar days to clear out her condo, and we start the countdown tomorrow. So, why don't you bring Ethel over and I'll let her have a pre-listing preview of this terrific unit. I know this is the one for her Alex and between you and me, Ethel is Seaview material and we need to get her moved in and living here in a jiffy. Don't you agree? Why don't you all come by around 5:00 today? I will meet you at the building and notify the gate you all are coming. Oh, this is just grand when things work out like this. I'll see you soon!" And with that she hung up. I never even said hello. She didn't ask if my client was interested or if we were available today to tour and she did not let me know what the list price of this unit would be. No qualms on Beverly's part about violating the local multiple listing service rules and showing a property before it listed and was input in the MLS system. Nope, just see you at 5:00. I was tweaked but on the other hand, getting Ethel moved out of Wanda's as quickly as possible seemed to be the order of the day. I got in my car and called Ethel. I filled her in and she shouted back that she would be at Wanda's house at 4:15. Apparently she and Miss Lyla were out and about in the Highmont and were coming back from some kind of errand. I could not hear her clearly but it sounded like she said they had visited some kind of shelter.

# 14

I checked in on my little ranch and took Clyde for a long walk along the rotting piers, stopped by to say hello to Daynia at Sasser's Bakery and had a cup of their extra-strong coffee. We were passing by the Conner Hasps Factory and I was again noticing the sold sign on the front of the old brick three story building. I also noted a city land use/development board had been installed. I was stepping up to read it when a shiny black Hummer with tinted windows and out of state license plates pulled up in front, parking next to the curb. Out of the car came a glitzy looking couple. They set off my real estate agent radar but I'd never seen these two before. They were all bright smiles and shimmering sunglasses as they walked up to Clyde and me. "What a cute little puppy dog you have there. I take it you live around here?" asked the woman. She was about 40 with a pricey bottle blonde, page boy hair cut and wearing expensive blue jeans (the kind well-to-do people wear when they want to dress down to blend in with the everyday people). She had on a crisply starched, coral blouse and matching sandals. Her lips were glossed in peach and she wore a thick gold bracelet and sported an enormous diamond wedding ring. She removed her black sunglasses and smiled wider. "Hi, I'm Kackie Bendle and this my husband Rick. We are the new owners of this building and if you live in the area, we have great news for you! You are finally going to get a real neighborhood. Rick and I are professional developers and neighborhood rehabilitation specialists. We have done projects all over the country and we discovered this gem of an unknown neighborhood while we were here in Clinton last spring. We just knew this had to be our next baby, isn't that right honey?"

Honey smiled wider and removed his gold sunglasses. He was around 40 as well, six feet tall with brownish hair that had expensive blonde highlights. He wore a light blue polo shirt and a huge gold watch was strapped to his left wrist. He also wore 'I'm down with the people' overpriced blue jeans which appeared to be starched and black loafers, the kind with the long toes that curl up like elf shoes. He held out his hand to shake, "Yes, this is our next baby for sure. We are going to put 50 luxury loft style condos in this old building and we also just purchased the old Stynum Tile Factory building right over there on Baylor Avenue. That will be our phase two. We hope to add shopping amenities and max out at 100 units. We've got options on several other buildings along the water front and the vision is to make that rotting waterfront the happening nightlife scene of Clinton. Kackie is hard at work with her people creating a new neighborhood name for this area. The right grease to the city wheels and within a year you current home owners should be rolling in instant equity! I hope to be able to put in an upscale grocery store once the two buildings are in development. Say, how long have you lived in this area? Do you know anyone that is interested in joining our new community development committee? We want everyone involved in improving this undiscovered gem of a neighborhood."

Oh shit, did this shark just say they are here to develop my 'hood? Just what we need, another tromping ground for upper middle class people who want to live their sanitized funky version of inner city.

Suburb living with a hip and urban flavor, I'm sure. Goodbye Sasser's and hello generic coffee chain. "Hi, I'm Alex Campbell. I live down that dead end street up there. Ahh, you know most people here like things pretty quiet and prefer things as they are. This really is not a real neighborhood. I sell residential real estate and there are not many folks in Clinton who are interested in living in this area, much less really know it exists."

Kackie perked up, "Oh exactly Alex! Great, you are a local real estate man. Why you are probably just the local real estate liaison Rick and I have been looking for and you already live here to boot! Oh, it doesn't get better than this, huh honey? Yes, Rick and I move around the country finding great undiscovered/underdeveloped urban areas like this one and then we turn them into gold mines. Rehabbing inner city venues and making our venture backers a whole lot of money in the process and for ourselves as well! Now that's what we call a win-win for everybody. The real estate boom has just been too wild, seriously. It's slowed in parts but we think there is life enough here in Clinton to turn this project around. So awesome that we met you. You know, like how random is that? Here's our card and let me have yours Alex. We definitely need to all have a sit down, don't we honey?"

I took the card from her. I contemplated telling her I didn't have a business card on me but before I could lie, Rick whipped out his phone. "Hey Alex, just give me your vites and I'll key them in here on my phone. Kackie is still all old school with business cards and all but I'll just plug you in here and we'll be in touch guy. Honey, it looks like that might be the city land use blob. You wanna go run the meet and greet interface on that one and I'll finish up here with our new local real estate liaison friend." Kackie smiled, "Roger that. Say it was great meeting you Alex and we look forward to our sit down and exploring mutually beneficial working options." She walked down the street to meet the city drone who had pulled up in one of the white Clinton municipal sedans. Oh fuck, this was real! I reluctantly gave Rick my phone number and email address and barely managed a nice to meet you before he took off to 'interface' with the city drone. This was my worst nightmare coming true right in front of me. The jackals had discovered my undiscovered 'hood and were ready to feast.

Clyde too was ready to feast and he woofed down a bowl of kibble when I got us back home. I locked up the house, put Clyde in the fenced in back yard so he could do his squirrel patrol and drove off in my two door beater to fetch Ethel.

As I pulled up to Wanda's house, Ethel was already waiting for me at the curb. I noted the front door was still brown. Wanda's house has a brown front door. I need to take a photo because this won't last for long. "*Oy*, you are running a bit late Alex." It was two minutes before our appointed pick up time. "Such a day I've had, let me tell you! Miss Lyla and I have been so busy. It's hard work trying to get Wanda's house and life in shape, you just wouldn't believe it Alex. So we are going to see a two bedroom unit in the North Tower you say, a new listing? You are sure this one the owner did not pass in Alex? I can't see myself resting comfortably in a home where someone has passed. You know who called me today Alex? Just guess. Yes, my son

Norman calls me. Normie is still insisting he has done nothing wrong. Oh no, my Norman has done nothing wrong. *Feh*! You raise a child, you sweat and break your back for years, years I tell you, and what do you get Alex? What you get is an ungrateful son who is committing all sorts of untold sins with a *goyishe* hussy, that's what you get. You should never treat your mother in such a way Alex. Take it from me, it would just kill her. Take the years right off her very own life I tell you.

You know these freeways here in Clinton are smaller than the ones in Philly but I tell you, you still have to drive for everyone else wherever you go. You can't rely on other drivers to be alert. Especially these days what with all their phones and computers! I always used to tell my late husband, Herman, gawd rest his soul, Herman you need to drive for yourself and all the other cars around you. That's what I would say, but did he ever listen, did he? And that's why he wrecked our brand new 1969 AMC Rambler Alex. Brand new I tell you! Why the paper liners were still on the floor mats, that's how new we are talking Alex. I can remember it as if it were yesterday. We were just getting on the Schuylkill Expressway, which you know everyone in Philly refers to as the Surekill and for good reason I tell you. Anyway, our little Norman, he was just a little child back then. Well Normie was in the back seat and just scared to death when his father rear ended that gold Cadillac Fleetwood. I tell you I thought I'd never be able to take that poor child with in a car again! And why I ask you, why Alex, because his father was not driving for everyone else. I warned him that Cadillac was gonna slow up; I did as sure as I'm sitting here now in your front seat. So he turns to snap at me, calling me a big nag he was when he drove right into the back of the very car I told him was gonna slow up. Not that I wanted to be right mind you! But Herman Moishe Kluntz got his but good that day! That man didn't call me a nag again, ever, well at least not in a loud voice. Alex, watch that red convertible up over there, that woman is not paying attention. Oh and just look at that revealing halter top that harlot is wearing! She must be good friends with my son's hussy."

This continual monologue went on for the entire 40 minute drive, until I pulled into the visitor parking space (this time assigned space 16 out of the 80 or so vacant spaces). The only thing that shut Ethel up was the syrupy witch Beverly who was eagerly awaiting our arrival by the automatic entry doors. Well not exactly waiting, she was instructing the doorman in dictator drag on how best to spit-polish the already shining, silver door handles which incidentally are never touched as the doors are automatic. "Oh, hello friends! Why Carlos this is Mrs. Ethel Kluntz and she is going to be our latest Seaviewer family member. I just know it will be the case, once she sees this gorgeous unit! And here is Alex, right on time again. My that's another plus mark in my book, no tardies in your column Alex! But who's keeping attendance?" she said while winking at us. Apparently you are bitch. "Anyway, Alex is just too young to live here with us Carlos, otherwise I think we'd just move him in right away, well once he got his cowlicked hair under control. But we welcome him here none-the-less. And my, your shirt is still properly tucked in and it is late in the afternoon Alex. Oh, I am just thrilled my helpful dressing tips are working for you! Now remind me dear and I'll give you some hair grooming tips. You know that cowlick could use a good dousing. Why if I were your mommy, I'd just lick my little hand right now and give it a good rub down, ha, ha, ha…." Touch my hair and die.

"Ahh, yes it's nice to see you again Beverly. Ethel is interested in seeing what this unit looks like, so why don't you lead the way."

Beverly looked slightly peeved that I indicated we should move along but she quickly snapped to attention and led us through the lobby doors. The lobby was as spotless as ever and Beverly led us through the doors to the North Tower elevator, all the while babbling on about how sad for Sonya Chalmers to have passed but what a great opportunity for Ethel. Up to the fifth floor we went. Beverly winked at us again as she unlocked the door, "Now you all know this unit won't be listed until tomorrow but I like to give my favorite people exclusive previews when I can." With that she opened the door and hit the hall lights.

The condo was really nice with water views and an enormous balcony. The kitchen had been updated sometime in the early 2000s and Ethel was all excited because the appliance ratio was correct. The entire unit was covered in thick, sage colored carpeting with black marble tile flooring installed in the kitchen, baths and entry. "Oh Alex look, the curtains are quality. See here, now that's a liner!" Ethel exclaimed while inspecting the green floral print draperies in the living room. On to the bedrooms we went. Both were spacious and had full baths and the master bedroom had a smaller balcony. Again the draperies in the bedroom were quality or so I was told. Beverly led us back to the living room and opened the slider door, leading us out on to the large balcony. Below were the swimming pools, and straight out was the sparkling water of Warner Sound with a few sail boats bobbing around. Beverly smiled, "Now if you look to your right, my penthouse unit is right down there on the end. I just can't wait to show you all my lovely home and get you moved in here Ethel. It would be so nice to replace Sonya with someone who is quality, such as yourself Ethel. I love knowing my immediate neighbors are just, well simpatico. Sonya could be a bit difficult at times. We have a tight little group up here on the fifth floor and I think you'll just love it. Why our floor started the Seaview Secret Santa Cookie club! Each floor rotates the Santa and every week the Secret Cookie Santa is supposed to make a batch of cookies and surprise a fellow floor member with them! Isn't that just too cute and it is such fun and so neighborly!"

Ethel nodded in agreement, "Oh I hear you Beverly and I too agree, good neighbors are important. I do like what I see here, you can't go wrong with quality curtains and a correct appliance ratio. When did you say this place is going to list and what is the list price going to be?"

Yes, nothing like doing a showing before you've listed the property Beverly or before the former owner has even cooled in the morgue for 24 hours. "Oh, well the list price has to be approved by our Board first, but you know I am the president. Since you are someone we would really prefer to have living here, I am quite certain we can come up with an agreeable list price Ethel. I'll let Alex know what that approved price is as soon as I can and the minute this listing goes live, you can have Alex put in an offer for you." Again with her conspicuous wink and sly grin. "There is the unpleasant business of Sonya Chalmers' relatives and clearing out this unit. Fortunately, the Seaview rules are very direct about clearing out a former resident's living space and they will need to have this all taken care of and the unit all neat and tidy in 10 days time. Why, I bet we might even have you in here with us within a few weeks Ethel! Oh it will just be so exciting, a new addition to our fifth floor gang.

Ethel was now smiling, "This I like; yes I do. Yes, you get the list price to Alex as soon as you can. I have my son's mortgage person to help, she's the woman I am currently living with Beverly. I am not sure if I will do a mortgage or pay cash for this unit, we'll see how the numbers add up. *Oy*, and now I need to contact my cousin Letti in Philly and get my town house back there on the market. I am just going to have her supervise having my house packed up and ship everything right out here. I see no need to waste time on that. I need to be here to get Norman's life back on track and you know, I think a change of living will do me wonders. Now Beverly, what did you say about these curtains, they come with right?"

Beverly's frosted pink lips pulled up more, well as much as the plastic surgery would allow, "Oh that is just grand Ethel. And you know, a little bird tells me that these lovely draperies will be staying in this unit."

Beverly bid us *adieu* and assured me she would be in touch with the list price and expected time/date the listing would go live. Yes, a rigged deal but it wasn't me breaking the rules and besides, Wanda needs Ethel to move out and fast. I half listened while Ethel did a 40 minute drive back monologue. As I was pulling up to Wanda's, I noticed something strange poking out of Wanda's front hedge. I rubbed my eyes but it was still there. Ethel looked up and saw the horse's ass, "OY! I thought Lyla and I tied Sammy up really good out back. Now how do you suppose he got around here to the front?" With that she took off around the hedge. I stepped onto Wanda's front walk and sure as shit, there was an elderly looking brown horse camped out in Wanda's tiny front yard. Thankfully, he had not ventured out onto the sidewalk or street. I looked at Ethel, "What is a horse doing here? How did you---"

"Enough! This poor horse needs a short term home, so Miss Lyla and I rescued old Sammy. Miss Lyla's yard is really not the best place for Sammy and so we decided to put him up here short term. Wanda's back yard is plenty big and he is hardly going to be noticed out back there. Why I bet Wanda won't even know he's here. I'm gonna take this lead rope and guide old Sammy out back where we had him. He's hard of seeing you know, poor little lamb. I thought Miss Lyla tied him to the dogwood tree back there nice and tight but it looks like our Sammy here is a regular Houdini. Okay, Alex you call me as soon as you hear from Beverly, I don't wanna miss this one." With that she started leading Sammy around the side of Wanda's house. I then heard the tell-tale rumble of Miss Emerald's V-8 engine. Oh shit.

Yep, Wanda was home and parking her late 1980s emerald green Lincoln Town Car out front. "Hey baby. What you doing coming out of my yard? You just drop Ethel off here? I hope you are gonna tell me that old lady done bought herself a new place to live today. That's what your are fixing to say, ain't it?"

I sputtered a bit and quickly walked towards my car. "Yep, that's right Wanda. Ethel found a great Seaview condo and Beverly says she can place an offer in a day or two. Ethel could be out of your hair and living in Seaview within a few weeks. Isn't that great? Sorry, I've gotta run, just got a call. I'll fill you in later, bye!" I shut my car door and had my Volvo fired up and moving out before Wanda could respond. Whew! I did not want to be within a 20 block radius of her when she discovered old Sammy in her back yard.

# 15

I had a message that night from Harvey and he said he wanted to have "that doughboy fairy" decorate his place but he would only pay $4,000 for the work. I called Harvey back and let him know that I knew Percy would not go any lower in his price but I could check with him and see if he would not do certain staging things in order to reduce the price. I again reminded Harvey it would be in his best interest to just pay the money, have it done right as we needed his place to look its best in a slower market. He was grumbling when I hung up. Around 10:30 p.m. there was a loud knock on my front door. I looked out the spy hole and there was Wanda. I opened the door and she practically knocked Clyde and me over as she burst in.

"I don't know what in the hell you know about that old lady and a horse in my back yard, I'm not sure I want to know. Get that blender down that I bought you for your birthday because we are fixing to have us some serious slushy time. I bought my own bottle of rum here. Ethel tells me she and Miz Lyla were out looking around today when they stopped by the Highmont Animal Shelter. Said she was looking for a cat for me. A cat?! Woman says I need a pet in my home. Here put more rum in that pitcher and cut up some limes. Turns out, while they was looking for a cat for me, a man stopped by with a horse in the back of his trailer. Fool wanted to leave the old horse there at the damn shelter. Shelter lady told him no way, no how, no pay day. So that's where old Ethel and Miz Lyla step in and decide to help out. Help out my ass! Told that man they'd take the old horse and save it for him, didn't want old Sammy turning into glue. Put more ice in there and turn that thing on high honey. Hit that switch for your garage door opener wall or whatever the hell it is, we gonna sit out on your patio there. So them old birds ride with the man and the horse over to my house and they put that horse in my back yard! Say it's just a temporary fix until they can find it a nice home, a field to live in. Grab the big green glasses up there and pour. Tell me it's good practice for me to be having Sammy the horse in my backyard because it will get me used to caring for a pet. They still think they are going to get me a cat! I don't even like cats that much and whose damn house and life is this anyway? I had to get out of that house and have me a good break before I just let that old lady have it. No wonder her son be dating a skanky, pole dancer woman. Damn, she lucky he even speaks to her. You oughta let that old lady have your stupid boundary book, 'cause I can tell you she wouldn't know a boundary if it up and bit her on the ass. Ohh, this tastes good! And that Miz Lyla in on all this too! I tell you Ethel Kluntz is just a bad influence, yep nothing more than a bad influence. So now that we are sitting out here and I'm hearing your nice waterfall, you are gonna tell me that you for real, found that old lady a new home today right?"

Fortunately that is exactly what I told Wanda and I assured her we would get Ethel out of her house as quickly as possible. I was going to mention she could kick Ethel out but given Wanda's mood I didn't want to suggest a thing. I had an idea for the horse, "Wanda why don't we call Lexi up and see if she might be able to take Sammy? She's got all that open land around her art farm out there and—"

105

Wanda's eyes grew wide, "Oh praise it all, Alex you solved the puzzle! Damn let me ring that girl up right now. Yep, Lexi is the answer, she got the room, her place is a total artist dump and she would probably like the company or she could somehow use Sammy in one of her interactive art thangs she's doing these days." With that Wanda was dialing. Lexi is an installation artist somewhere in her 60s who has a house/land on the outskirts of Clinton. She does all kinds of art installations for the city, mostly rusted out crap in my opinion but hey, she's the artist. We have been friends with Lexi for years and she is a great person, eccentric but interesting and helpful. She's the whole reason Wanda and I are now on a first name basis with Tony the mob boss (see previous volumes). Wanda got Lexi's voice mail but left her a message, "Girl I got you a great pet/gift. It's a horse, and his name is Sammy and honey I'm gonna let him come live with you! He needs himself a good home and your art farm is just the place. You are gonna love him, I know it. Call me."

With that done, I proceeded to fill Wanda in as to the condo that Ethel would hopefully be purchasing and after a pitcher or so of slushies she was calm and decided she could go back to her house and not kill Wanda or her new temporary pet horse, Sammy.

The next day was off with a bang, Beverly called and let me know the list price and that it would be going live at noon. I raced to get the paperwork filled out, zipped over to Wanda's and had Ethel sign the forms. I had them faxed and emailed to Beverly by 12:05. I didn't want to but I called Percy and he did agree to Harvey's $4,000 price but said he wouldn't add as much fluff. He reminded me again this was only as a special favor to me and he expected me for his dinner/sleep over. I reminded him it would be dinner only for me, thank you very much. I zipped down to Seaview, went through their whole entry song and dance which was faster this time as Dave was not on duty. I met up with Harvey to collect the funds for Percy. We had two weeks to get things all set. With the market starting to decline, every day was becoming crucial. Percy said his people would be painting Harvey's unit and moving crap in and out in two days, so this barely gave us time for the paint to dry before his listing went live. I was hoping to notify the witch of Seaview about all of this via email when naturally who should I run into in the lobby of the towers but old sweetness and sunshine herself.

"Well I see you are out and about doing business here today Alex. You must be a bit rushed today dear; your belt does not match your shoes! Why we need to find you a good little wife don't we? Mercy and I just want to spray that rebellious cowlick of yours down with some good old hair spray. Hair spray is just so underutilized these days. You know on my show Alex, I once did an entire segment on the many non hair styling uses for hair spray. Why did you know a spritz of hair spray will act as a wonderful fixative for many kinds of craft projects and…."

"Ah, no Beverly I don't believe I did know that but I'll take your word for it." Matching belt, hell I was doing good to even have a belt on, I hate them almost as much as I hate wearing socks and shoes. "Anyway, I got Ethel Kluntz's offer in and hopefully we'll hear back from you all very soon, as I know she is anxious to move in."

Beverly's frosted pink lip smile pulled up to the limits of her plastic surgery, "I see that she is offering all cash, which of course you and I just adore! Nothing like an all-cash deal to just move that closing date right along. I know you asked for two weeks for closing but I think we could even move that up to a week or 10 days if everyone is game! I love quick and easy deals, don't you Alex? And we can get Mrs. Kluntz in here and settled in no time. I know she is going to be the perfect Seaviewer. I do love when we find just the right people to live here. It makes it so much more fun and homey, now don't you agree? Oh and Alex, I just met with Mr. Malloy and I hear that Mr. Emerson is going to get to work on staging his unit the day after tomorrow. They'll be painting and cleaning and moving a few pieces of furniture in and out and it should go live in the multiple listing service in a week or so I'm told. We can't get him out of here fast enough. My word, the potty mouth that man has and that bird too!"

Beverly's frosted pink lips pursed a tad as she tilted her helmet hair head to the side, "Alex, you are the busy bee today, no wonder your belt does not match your shoes. You know, I've found laying out your outfit for the next day the night before, including your accessories such as your belt and shoes, helps when we have these busy little days. Once you have polished your shoes, you just lay that matching belt right out there. It's so important for a man especially, to make sure his footwear is polished and shiny each day. Makes for such a better presentation, now don't you agree?" She said as she looked down at my dusty, never once polished, scuffed up, brown shoes. "I did many shows on helpful wardrobe preparation tips in my day. Why you know, I can have myself put together and be front-door ready in a jiffy when I get pressed for time. I used to joke with my sister when we were younger, that I could be front-door ready in under five minutes. We raced each other many times and well, I always won!

I will have to look up the handy weekly wardrobe chart that I used to use on my show. It helps you plan and prepare your weekly outfits a week in advance, the same way you plan your weekly meals I'm sure. It's really just a matter of personal discipline and consideration for how one presents oneself to the world Alex. Anyhow, I do have Ethel's offer and I'm just sure we are going to get to mutual agreement on this by tonight. You tell Mrs. Kluntz I said to start packing!

Now Mr. Malloy, well better you than me to work with that potty mouthed, nasty man. But you will need to have him complete our worker release/unit maintenance forms Alex before I can allow Mr. Emerson to commence any work in his unit. I'll have Carlos drop those forms off with him shortly. I would just *hate* to have to write him up for any more violations. You know he is just not a team player and we here at Seaview do have our rules and regulations. I don't think Mr. Emerson is on our approved vendor/unit maintenance list but since I met him personally with you, I don't see why I can't just speed that whole approval process along. After all, it's in everyone's best interest to have Mr. Malloy out of here as soon as possible. Oh, I'd love to talk more with you Alex but I see that Pamela is back at the front desk and we do need to have a little chat. I just have to stay on top of everything around here, but I'm not complaining, some of us are just natural do-ers and more caring and concerned than others I suppose." With that she gave me a long wink and scurried off to attack Pamela, who when she caught sight of the incoming Beverly looked like a rabbit watching a hawk swoop in.

As I was about to leave when there was a loud uproar in the lobby near the South Tower doors. "The flasher! He's back! Aggh, the flasher, get him!" Sure as shit, there was a man wearing an open green raincoat, black army boots, a black ski mask and nothing else. He shook his wang around and then took off down the South Tower hallway. Beverly was frantically searching for the doormen and motioning for them to pursue. Ah, senior living.

The next two weeks went by in a flash (pun intended). I came down with a 24 hour bug and had to miss out on Percy's dinner and sleep over. It was a really tough bug. I had to watch three movies at home, clean out my waterfall system and order in pizza for Clyde and me. Naturally Wanda didn't believe a word but Percy took it at face value and is already planning the next *soirée*. With her all cash offer, Ethel did in fact close on her new Seaview condo in record time, 10 days, and so within 11 days she was moving out of Wanda's and into Seaview.

None too soon either, as Wanda was beginning to frighten me a bit with her threats to evict Ethel from her home and worse. Wanda has been busy getting her home and life back in order, the way she thinks it should be. Norman tried to help Ethel on her move-in day but she told him she could not tolerate seeing him until he gave up his wayward life and began to behave the way she and Herman raised him.

He looked anguished. I however thought he should be thrilled and just go with mommy's cold shoulder routine but that's easy for me to say because Ethel ain't mine! We got Harvey's condo just about ready for listing ahead of schedule and I was currently inputting his listing into the multiple listing service. I was pondering what to do next when my cell rang. It was Mushy. She wanted to know if I could show her and little Joocey a new condo listing I had sent them the night before. Without anything else really going on, I said sure how about we meet there in an hour.

# 16

Clinton Community College is located out near the interstate to the east of Rosedale and southeast of the Beaumont where Courtney and family currently live. By going to school here she'd have her new found "independence" but be about 15 to 20 minutes away from the parental units. The college was started in the mid 1970s and sits on a fairly large suburban style campus. Over the decades it has expanded in size and scope and now offers dorms, and a fairly large sports complex. Developers have pretty much built a mini city on the outskirts of the campus, so there are plenty of apartment complexes, strip malls and condos as well. Lexi occasionally teaches an art course at "C cubed" as the school is sometimes called. However of late, with all of her city art commissions, Lexi has not been teaching.

The condo that caught Vicky's interest is a newer complex to the north of the college. It sits on wooded acres and consists of townhouse style condos and some multi unit condo buildings with carport style parking and a huge community swimming pool and gym complex for residents. This meandering complex is called Cedar Lakes and it was originally started in 1999 and is now up to phase four. Why it is called Cedar Lakes is beyond my comprehension as there are absolutely no cedar trees anywhere on the compound's property (in fact all of the trees are deciduous). What they call the "lakes" is actually a single blue cement bottomed "lake" at the complex's entry that has a huge water spray feature in its center and is lit up at night with multi colored lights embedded in the shallow "lake's" cement bottom. There were tons of colorful promotional flags and for sale banners on the street lamp posts guiding me to the newly completed "Phase Four" which the banners assured me is "Cedar Lakes Living at its Best!" I was also encouraged to ask about their no money down purchase option and reminded that phase four was already over 40 percent sold.

Per the listing report, the sales office was only open on weekends and I was instructed to use one of the main key boxes, each of which contains a pass key that opens all of the available unit doors. I logged in on one of the boxes, picked up a key and then drove farther down the winding road to building D of phase four. I spied a new white Ranger Rover with white interior and gleaming silver hub caps and I noted the Beaumont pass, Clinton Community College stickers on the rear window. So I knew Vicky and Courtney were there and waiting. Vicky hopped out all perky and smiles. She had a huge gold colored shoulder bag and was wearing a green Clinton Community College athletic shirt which was about two sizes too small and ripped at the collar to make it a v-neck to accommodate her inflatable friends. She was wearing sky blue skin tight gym shorts, almost of the bikini bottom variety and had gold colored high heeled shoes which looked like some kind of kinky bondage wraps around her ankles—all sorts of gold leather straps interweaving around her ankles. Up top, her bushed out hair was all contained under a yellow canvas baseball cap with rhinestones that read, "Bad Hair Day" across the front. She had a huge iced coffee drink in one hand, which she held out to the side of her body as she walked up to me and air kissed while removing her oversized white framed sunglasses, "Alex so good to see you! We are

113

so excited to have a look at this condo! Oh my god! I told Courtney as we drove in this complex, I can just *feel* this is the place. Her very own bachelorette crib! Damn, my little dawg is gonna be all down, huh baby? And look Alex, Courtney can just walk down that paved trail over there and she's like right there at the C-3 campus! So exciting! Courtney aren't you just dying!?"

Courtney semi snorted as she shuffled over. She had on her black flip flops and today wore brown velour sweat pants which had "Joocey" spelled out in red rhinestones across her ass. She too had an enormous shoulder bag, hers in silver metallic, and she wore a loose orange t-shirt with some designer something across the chest. Her spiraled hair was all bunched up on top and held together with what appeared to be a red plastic chip bag holder. She was holding her magenta phone in one hand and an enormous iced coffee drink in her other paw, which she was slurping on through a black straw.

Vicky squealed really loud, jostling Courtney as she approached, causing her enormous drink to almost spill. "Jesus Christ bitch! Settle the fuck down mom! God, you almost caused me to spill my iced green tea, caramel, triple shot, low fat, macchiato, jesus!"

Vicky ignored her and turned to me, "See Alex, we are all ready and psyched here! School starts really soon and I'm just feeling this is it! Look, I even already got my mommy team spirit college t-shirt on!" Yeah, and mommy apparently forget what size shirt she currently wears, as her shirt would have probably have fit Joocey when she was seven. The shirt barley covered her inflated friends and worse, her bare fake baked belly was exposed and sported a ruby/diamond combo thing where her belly button should be.

I smiled big and wide and turned toward the complex, "Oh terrific, well ladies let's go check out the condo and see how you feel once you see it. That is a great feature Vicky, the path that goes right to the campus, especially since Courtney doesn't drive."

Vicky beamed, following along as we walked up to the complex, "You got it Alex! Courtney can just hop down that trail to class after a hard night of partying and you know there is even a campus shuttle bus that does regular loops through this complex, so Courtney won't have to walk if she doesn't feel up to it."

Yes, we must not let our lazy and apathetic spawn exercise too much and by the way she drags her feet she'd probably wear her flip flops down to little rubber nubs in four blocks flat. "Okay, here we are unit D-8. As you already know, from the listing report, it is two bedrooms and two and half baths. I unlocked the door and Vicky flew in with Joocey dragging behind her.

"Oh my God! I'm feeling it Courtney, you are home honey! Oh baby look, there's even a gas fireplace and check out that balcony! Courtney think of the fun parties you can throw; a keg-ger on the balcony and you know they have hot tubs down there by the pool, think of all the frat boys you'll have over here! Oh, Court this is da bomb, chicka! Ohh, do you likes your new crib?" Is there anything more nauseous than a 50 plus year old white woman trying to talk ghetto with her spoiled brat who is 22 going on 13? From here, Mushy went ape shit and was all over the condo, opening drawers, bouncing all around oohh-ing and ahh-ing over every little thing while Joocey just stood in the middle of the living room texting, slurping up her coffee drink, and chomping away on her gum which she occasionally popped.

Once Vicky was finished doing her cartwheels all over the condo's interior, I led them back outside and locked up. I was about to ask if they would like to go look at the pool and clubhouse when Vicky asked if they could write up an offer right now. Break my finger, "Certainly Vicky. We can meet at my office or I am happy to prepare the paperwork and bring it over to your house?" She opted for the office. Back to Winterfrost we caravanned. I phoned ahead and Nayina had the front conference room reserved for us when we arrived. The Viper Pit was practically dead, only two coffee pot whiners and one other stray agent in the computer work room. I noticed a Snicker's bar in my in-box. What kind of agent leaves candy bars for other agents? A naïve and major butt kissing one named Kenny that's who. Seriously, save your candy bar allowance and work on schmoozing with the public who will hopefully be buying something with you, dumb ass.

I got the paperwork ready and met Vicky and Courtney in the front conference room. Vicky was literally buzzing and when I asked her what she wanted the offer price to be and she replied before I could even put a question mark to my question, "We love it and it's worth the list price so just fill in the list price and we are good! Right honey? Ohhh, Courtney I am so psyched. Oh my god, it'll be like your very own *MTV Real World Clinton* crib!" To that Vicky shot her a withering look and snorted, "Yeah right old lady, like it would be all MTV Clinton if it were still 1995. God you are so lame!" Vicky chose not to hear that retort and continued making her way through the various forms, signing her name and initialing where necessary. Next up it was Courtney's turn to sign. Mommy and daddy had apparently decided to make it a mother/daughter co-owned unit. My question was who was actually going to attend college and use it, Mushy or Joocey? Courtney snarled, sighed, slurped, and gum popped her way through the purchase and sale forms, deigning to scribble her signatures and initials on pages like an overworked soap opera star signing autographs after a hard day's taping. When done, she promptly tossed the pen on the table and announced that her hand hurt to which Vicky chimed in, "Oh, okay baby, not to worry we'll stop by the nail spa on our way back. I'll get Haunchin to give you one of her special hand massages. Ohhh, my baby is all grown up and gonna have her own crib now!" To which she let out a loud screeching whoop which startled me. I'd give anything to see Beverly's face and reaction to such a public display of excitement from a grown "lady." I assured them I'd be in touch as soon as I had word from the seller, Cedar Lakes Phase Four, LLC.

On the way out of the office I was cornered by a wild tiger near the in-boxes. I quickly tried to ward her off, "Hi Tiger, gee I'm in a big hurry but nice to see you. Would you like this Snickers bar?"

Tiger's smoky smudged eyes lit up as and she snatched the candy bar Kenny had left from my hand, her cherry red talons scratching me in the process, "Damn, does a fat girl want a Snickers bar, are you shitting me? Course I do and I'll just put her away here for safe keeping." She said with a sly grin as she placed the candy bar in between her exploding cleavage. She then adjusted her silky red and brown leopard skin print blouse so the Snickers bar disappeared. God only knows what else she may have down there with her girls for safe keeping. Did I really want to know? "Say, did ya'll hear the shout out from Miss Beverly today? Seems she is fixing to have a big ole' sale party out there on her TV show this coming Saturday. She wants all us listing agents to be there for the show and hawk our listings. Now ain't that just something? And she said its formal aay-tire only. Wants us ladies to wear evening gowns. Don't that just beat all? I gotta get my fancy clothes outta my storage space. That's gonna be something huh? Us up there with Share and what not, telling all them old folks to bring their friends on along and buy our listings. Now what do you think Share is gonna wear? I want to make sure we all are looking our best, ya' know? Say, you hear about that new stiff they found down the hall from my listing out there? Got another old lady who kicked and you can guess who is gonna be listing that one in a red hot, New York minute, now can't ya?" Before I could respond, her cell phone began to ring or rather it let out recorded growling sounds, which I suppose was a tape of a tiger growling; so clever. With that she gave me a half handed wave and started waddling down the hall, her red mules making sharp snapping sounds with each step, "Well howdy there stranger! Why of course I can get my butt out there and take a gander at y'alls home! I think I'll pick us up a bucket on the way. Mama always said, nothing like some fried chicken to make things more fun...."

118

# 17

The next day was the brokers' open for Harvey's condo. Each listing area has its standard brokers' open day and time and Wednesdays from 11:00 to 1:00 is the Seaview area's time slot. Brokers' opens are where the listing agent holds the newly listed property open so that other agents can tour it and hopefully sell it. These were very important back in the day before all the listings were online. In those days, new listings were published in a book that was printed by the local multiple listing service and delivered once week to the subscribing real estate offices. Thus, brokers' opens were a way to get a lot of exposure for your new listing. Now, it's all live instantly and available for agents and the public to see right away. Brokers' opens do however linger on, although the number of agents that actually tour them is rapidly declining.

I stopped and picked up Wanda at her office, as she likes to do brokers' opens with me. She had on a billowing turquoise dress, big white earrings and a matching necklace; a sedate outfit for Wanda. She was carrying a stack of mortgage flyers outlining different purchasing strategies for Harvey's condo and she had ordered some doughnuts and coffee for us to pick up in Seaview. Per the law, we would be splitting the cost 50/50. "It's about time you got your bony butt over here, you know we still got to pick up the food and this thing starts at 11:00 right?"

Yes, hello to you too and I'm actually five minutes early but whose counting, "Hi Wanda. I'll get us there in plenty of time assuming all is right with Dave at the security gate. It seems odd to have a brokers' open at Seaview, by the time any visiting agents get through security, the open house will be over. Anyway, thanks again for coming and wait until you meet Harvey and company. I still haven't seen the final touches Percy did to his place. I couldn't be there when Lexi took the photos, so I've only seen pictures. Ethel called to remind me that we are to stop by her new place around 2:30 but she warned us her place isn't completely unpacked yet. I guess we can kill the hour and half tooling around Seaview."

Wanda nodded her head while I pulled onto the interstate highway, "Ahhum, I guess we should see that old lady. Still, I'm telling you that woman just about broke my very last nerve, all up in my home and business, repainting my damn door, redoing my closets, making drapes and you know that Sammy is still in my back yard! Miz Lyla be coming over every day now to feed him, asking if I don't think he's cute, saying he'll grow on me. I called Lexi again but I think she is purposely ignoring my phone calls. I don't know why she don't want some old horse out there on her art farm. Humph, I put a call into the shelter too but they say we can't return him, he wasn't supposed to be going there in the first place. It's an aggravation and we got to find us a real home for him and soon, otherwise we both gonna have a nice supply of glue on our hands and I ain't lying.

It's gonna be nice to see what Percy has done with this old man's crib. Old man sounds awful mouthy to me. You know I find mouthy people to be an aggravation, all that talking and mouthing off about every little thing. It reminds of me Ethel, just nonstop opinions on this and opinions on that." Really, this from Wanda? If the pot wasn't calling the kettle black then I don't know shit.

"Yes Wanda, Harvey is a talker. You should see him and Berverly LeFaye go at it. I'm sure she will be stopping by and you can finally meet her for yourself and see what all the talk is about. Speaking of, I have to go to Seaview this Saturday evening to be on Beverly's damn TV show. It's a Seaview listing show and I have to wear the penguin suit. She requires everyone appearing on the show to dress in formal wear, seriously. I can get you an audience guest pass if you want to attend."

Wanda chuckled, "Honey, I ain't missing that show for nothing. You get a pass for Percy too, I want him to be there and see it live as well. You know Percy and I already saw her TV show on that local cable access channel and baby you are really in for it. Course you would've seen a preview of the show too if you had attended Percy's dinner and sleep over." She said giving me a knowing look. I fiddled with the air conditioning knob while trying to appear very intent on driving carefully on the long, straight interstate, scouting ahead for the Seaview exit. "Don't get all I'm so into my driving with me! You know you weren't having no stomach flu that night. I know you and Clyde just hung out at that little house of yours and ate yourselves some pizza. Don't even! Anyway, you don't have to worry none, 'cause Percy is already planning the next one and I'm gonna be picking you up myself for this one. It was fun, really. And you all up there in your tree like some cat, too good or too scared to come on down out of that tree and have some fun with us."

Fortunately, our exit appeared and I had us rolling up to the gate. Mr. Hardass, Dave, was there yet again, putting us through the whole fire drill. This time our designated parking space number outside of the towers was 22. I inched the car slowly through the Seaview streets until we finally hit the town center. I pulled into the national chain grocery store's parking lot and followed Wanda inside. It looked like a normal chain grocery store; harsh lighting, dead processed food on most of the aisles, an anemic fresh vegetable and fruit section, miles of frozen foods and the stench of cooking sugar and white flour piped in throughout. This branch had colorful photograph banners of Seaview lining its walls and hanging from the ceiling. All grey haired models appearing to be having the time of their lives while posed at various Seaview venues. There's no way those healthy looking elderly models ate the junk food this store sold. The only thing that was missing was a photo of a couple hanging out in claw footed bathtubs while perched on a cliff and staring out at the horizon. Oh wait, that's the icon for the old dude who now has to take a pill to make his wrinkled dick hard, go figure. The stench of white flour and cooking sugar became more intense at the bakery counter. Wanda picked up her box of preservatives and artificial ingredients posing as pastries and out we went.

Next stop, Clinton's very own, national chain coffee shop. The only thing different about this one was everyone inside was over 70 except for the help. The various people sitting around with their caffeine fixes did not appear very lively, in fact they all seemed to have permanent scowls etched on their faces. Wanda commented, "Must be problems with the Metamucil around here, they all look crabby and constipated." I nodded and noted that it sounded like they were playing Muzak in the background. We got our to-go box of drip coffee and headed off to the Towers. Along the way I spotted one of Share's A-board signs pointing in the direction of the cottages. Got to a hand it to Stinky, she didn't waste time after she lost the last listing picking up another one in Seaview.

I found parking space 22 and in we went, past the doormen in dictator drag, across the spotless pale blue carpeting and to the front desk where we signed in with Pamela. Her smile was almost scary it was so big and wide. Clearly Beverly had set her back on track with her five S's regime. The fountain's whooshing sound in the lobby was soothing but once we got in the South Tower hallway, I immediately noticed music. As we walked to the elevators I heard fairly loud, old school Muzak playing. I looked up at the walls, trying not to get too dizzy from the vertical stripes and noted there were speakers built in the hallway walls at evenly spaced intervals. And these speakers were now live and playing what sounded like a Rolling Stones instrumental hit. It was even louder in the elevator. Wanda looked at me as we rode up, "Who let the lambs out? Damn all them white men and women singing them bah-bah's, it sound like a bunch of lambs got out of their pen and are trying to find their way home. This is some serious old school white folks shit they got going on in this place Alex. Mmph!" She wasn't wrong; there were syrupy sounding men and women making bah-bah sounds to an instrumental version of *As Tears Go By*. No actual lyrics, just bah-bah-bah. What the fuck? At the song's end a very mellow and drugged sounding DJ announced that song was by the New Classic Singers. Next up was an instrumental version of Barbara Streisand's *Prisoner*. Prisoner, resident what's the difference at Seaview?

As we walked up to Unit 504, out popped Harvey. "Bout time you got up here. Damn if this tour thing you are doing ain't going to cut into Ralph's *Wheel of Fortune* time." He said while leading us into his condo. "But don't you worry birdy," he called out to Ralph who was looking at us with pin wheel eyes from inside his enormous cage, "I got yer *Wheel* all set up there on the recorder and we'll play it later on today once all these assholes get outta here and leave us be! See what yer fairy did to my place? Can't hardly sleep in this place now! Not comfortable at all and look at these here colors that lady man painted my walls!

Who the hell are you?" he said noticing Wanda next to me. "You two ain't some kind of couple or nothing is you? Not that I got me any problem with the races but I don't want no necking going on in my place here while I'm away. Nope, no makin' none of them Coffee-Mate looking babies on my ship mister! Speaking of necking, you'd really hear any action going on in here now, 'cause that fairy went and put up a damn headboard thing in the bedroom and painted the wall behind the bed orange! Looks like a god damn fruity orange juice can is what it looks like. Now you two mind Ralph here and watch out for that old bitch Beverly. I'm sure she'll be stopping by to see that you two ain't breaking none of her damn rules. Old bitch, I oughta bang her against that headboard and orange wall in there shouldn't I Ralph? Biddy could stand for a man-stuffin' to put her back in her place.

124

That's why the whole world has gone ta shit in a bucket, goddamn women libbers. Okay, well you do yer sellin' there feller and don't let Ralph get bothered by no one and I'll be right back here at one o'clock to kick your asses out. Get the sellin' done, 'cause the sooner I'm out of this here shit hole the better, ain't that right Ralphy?"

Ralph perked up and promptly started screeching, "Old bitch, old bitch! Old bitch!" Harvey smiled and yelled out over his shoulder as he left, "That's right Ralph, you tell 'em!"

Wanda set the pastry box down on the kitchen bar top counter. "Mm--mph, you got yourself one live old white motherfucker there Alex! Damn, he's all fiery that one is. Him and his Coffee-Mate babies. Hell Alex, only thang you be making anytime soon will be your bed! And look at this here green, red topped bird. Say your name is Ralph? You sure got yourself a mouth on you Ralph, now don't cha?" Wanda said as she walked over to his cage. Ralph became very excited and started strutting up and down his main dowel, his yellow eyes pin wheeling faster as he tilted his head and chirped at Wanda. Wanda put her finger up to his cage and Ralph momentarily squawked and snapped his beak at her but then he quickly became enamored again and started up again with his happy chirp sounds and strutting while squawking out an occasional "old bitch" and "motherfucker."

"You got yourself a new friend there Wanda, he is really trying to show off for you. Wow, look what Percy has done to this place and that old hemorrhoid has the nerve to complain? You should have seen this dump two weeks ago Wanda." I set down the coffee box and walked around taking it all in while I turned on the lights, pulled up the blinds and made the place broker open ready. Percy had painted the entire condo stark white, the carpets were all recently cleaned and now white and not dish water grey. Each room had one accent color wall. In the living room, the main wall was now a vibrant kiwi green; there was a real sofa and chair which were covered in cerulean blue leather. A chrome and glass coffee table sat between them and beneath was a matching blue and green area rug. Ralph's cage was still the main event but now at least things were facing out toward the great sound view. Over the large water facing windows, Percy had installed window cornices on top of the window frames which were covered in fabric that matched the area rug. Ethel would be proud although she would want matching curtains with the headers. I'm guessing Harvey's budget did not allow for it. The TV was now hidden away in a honey colored, faux antique armoire. Percy had put two modern chrome and Lucite bar stools alongside the kitchen countertop bar. The back wall in the kitchen was painted a lighter shade of cerulean blue and copper molds and a rack of copper pots had been put up on the wall. The kitchen cabinetry was painted white to match the appliances with new, chrome cabinet doorknobs. The main bath was now a cerulean blue with accent towels and a shower curtain in matching fabric. In the master bedroom, what Harvey called orange was in reality a deep soothing apricot color and the bed was covered in a patterned apricot bedspread. The bed had a simple cherry wood headboard, and matching wooden side tables, each with a sizable glass crystal ball style lamp with matching apricot shades. A cherry wood dresser was in the corner with a mirror and a small Chinese red ceramic lamp on top. A couple of potted, leafy green plants filled the odd corners. Here too, Percy had put a window cornice above the bedroom window in the same bedspread fabric.

When I went back in the living room, I noticed there were three large silver framed mirrors hanging on the green wall which Ralph apparently loved to stare at. He was currently admiring his reflection while Wanda was busy setting up the coffee and pastries on the kitchen bar's counter top. I opened the balcony's sliding glass door and out there were potted white geraniums in large blue and green ceramic pots. A small stone water fountain on a plain black pedestal had been added at the south end and it was making a nice gurgling sound. On the north end was a white, circular, metal garden table with a pot of Gerber daises and four matching chairs with green and blue cushions. Gone was the dingy beige card table and broken down metal folding chairs that had previously filled this space. There were wind chimes hanging in the corner giving off a feint tinkling sound. Percy sure knows how to fix up on a budget.

# 18

Back inside, Wanda and I were set up and awaiting the hordes of brokers who would be touring. We were armed with caffeine and sugar; great motivators for type-A nuts and fatties. "Damn Alex, even I think these maple bar thangs look nasty and not the new nasty either. Humph, I'm gonna pass on these. I should have known the bakery in the geezerville grocery would sell this kind of old-style crap. I'm telling you, old people live for this here sugar shit." Wanda said while turning the pastry box just so on the counter and filling up a cup of coffee for herself. "And honey, what is up with that music in the hallways? I feel like I'm 10 years old and out shopping with my grandma or something, all time warp like I don't---"

"Knock, knock! Are we all set up for our broker's open Alex?" Beverly's sing-song voice called out from the front door. "Ohh, and who do we have here with you today? A little bird at the front desk tells me you brought company with you today Alex. You all heard our wonderful new music in the hallways? Isn't it just grand. I was finally able to get the old Muzak system repaired and now we are awash with pleasant upbeat tunes day and night! Just the way Seaview used to be before Muzak went bankrupt the first time. I find it so relaxing and uplifting and it's already a sure fire hit with our residents. We now download from the cable network's Yesteryear's Instrumentals station. My next project is to get the golf course wired so this pleasant music can be enjoyed while out on the links. Now wouldn't that improve anyone's game? Think how much the birds will appreciate it! I find myself just humming right along. Why there are so many old tunes and favorites playing, it puts an extra spring my step.

What a lovely dress you are wearing. You know I think it is just so much nicer when ladies wear dresses, now don't you agree? I am Beverly LeFaye and I bet Alex has already told you all about me, why my middle name is practically Seaview!" this Beverly said while walking towards Wanda to shake her hand. Beverly was decked out in a pastel lavender dress complete with her name badge, pearls and sensible matching pumps.

Wanda perked up and shook Beverly's hand, "Hey lady, how you doing? I'm Wanda Billings from Safety Mortgage. I'm here doing the open house with Alex today."

Beverly's pink lips pulled up higher, "Oh my, why it is just so nice to make your acquaintance Wanda. I'm sure if you are here with Alex then you are quality. And so nice to meet another mortgage person. You know we have a person named RG Boysun who does a lot of the mortgages here at Seaview and even runs a little reverse mortgage investment club that is quite popular with our residents. RG is a bit different, but the residents sure do like her and her returns! We must talk some more because I think it would be just lovely to have some more mortgage people circulating out here at Seaview. And any lady who wears a dress and matching shoes and accessories is already earning a plus mark in my book! Those earrings of yours are lovely but I bet they do get a bit heavy on your ears, what with them being so big. We just need to get you in some pantyhose and then you really are getting a star in my ledger. You know, I feel practically naked if I don't have on a good pair of pantyhose whenever I go out in public. Oh my Wanda, look at Alex's shirt! Why it's all tucked in and flat and properly starched. You know he's my special project these days." She said while giving Wanda one of her conspicuous winks. "My next step is to put some hair spray on that cowlick of his and make it stay down and behave properly! I can see you too are a woman who knows and appreciates the many wonders of hairspray." She said while eyeing Wanda's hair which was piled up extra high in a quasi beehive style.

"And you two did bring refreshments I see. Now that is just lovely. Although, I do find the proper presentation of refreshments really is important or otherwise what is the point? But I don't suppose old Mr. Malloy has an attractive serving tray or a ceramic platter handy? I guess you are forced to use that unattractive bakery box. You know Alex, I think you should invest in a nice silver party platter that you can easily store in the trunk of your car. And you can keep a roll of wax paper or really what would be better would be a box of those handy white paper tray liners. You can purchase those from any catering supply company. That way, when you run into these kinds of presentation dilemmas, why your solution is right there in the trunk of your car! But he's learning now isn't he Wanda?" Beverly said while giving Wanda another slow wink.

Presentation my ass bitch. "So Beverly, help yourself there to a maple bar. They are fresh from your very own Seaview bakery and there's Seaview coffee as well." I said while giving Wanda one of my sideways looks.

# NO REST

"My, aren't you just too sweet. They do look delicious but a lady must always watch her figure and especially me. You know I run the weekly ladies dieting group here at Seaview and I do have to set a good example. Some of our weight challenged ladies here just need to see me for inspiration and to realize that they too can improve. It's just so tragic how fat and slovenly so many of our seniors are becoming these days. Why I have a special guest dietician coming to our next meeting all the way from merry old England! Yes, the Seaview Thin to Win group is alive and flourishing. Not to brag but you know I am the one who started the group. I just can't seem to help myself, being such a giver and all. I see a need and before you know it, there I am leading the troops. Busy as bee, that's me!

So Wanda, I do hope Alex has put you on our little guest list for this Saturday night's show. Did you know he's going be a TV star on Saturday?" Again with the fucking wink. "We are going to have all our listing agents present for my show to let everyone know about their listings."

"Oh yes Beverly, Alex has got me and Percy Emerson already on the guest list and you can bet we won't be missing your live show this Saturday. That's some serious appointment TV and in person too. Percy and I caught your show on TV a couple of weeks ago, on the Clinton local access cable channel and honey, you sure do put on a show!"

Beverly was glowing, "Why you! That's just wonderful of you enjoying my show. And you are bringing Mr. Emerson with you? Now he does have nicely starched shirts even if he does need to lose

131

that pot belly. Well, at least he managed to fix this place up. I had to review the redecoration of this unit with Mr. Emerson and Mr. Malloy. You know we do have to sign off on final interior renovations and decorations; page 167 item 351 clearly states that is the rule. I only had to suggest they redo a couple of things. It's so nice when it all works out that way.

Anyway, Wanda, I don't like to brag but you know I am *the* Beverly LeFaye from back in the day. I hosted the award winning *The Ladies Hour with Beverly Ann LeFaye* on Channel Four which ran weekdays from 1964 until 1979. You probably recall the show if you grew up here. It was the number one rated show in Clinton for many years. So my Saturday evening show harkens back a bit to the golden days of television. I do try to fill that hour up with lively, informative and entertaining guests. It is geared towards our Seaview audience but I find there are quite a few fans in Clinton who greatly enjoy my efforts too. Of course this show is not just geared to ladies and while I do still try to give out some helpful homemaking and home economic tips, it's a wider entertainment format. Such fun we do have!

Oh, I just can't wait to see you both on Saturday. But you know this busy bee has just got to fly. I'm afraid we've had another little passing in our Seaview family this morning and I have to get that cottage all ready to list, along with the Masons' unit here on the first floor. Oh my, I do need to check in on that Tiger Conley and her broker's open and make sure she's following the rules. Why Alex, it is just such a shame but Share Shelton has broken yet another one of our Seaview rules. She did show up today for the required broker's open of her new cottage listing but gosh darn if she didn't put out her own A-board signs. And we all know that is simply not allowed. No, I'm afraid Carlos is out there right now with the cart confiscating her A-boards. I'm going to have to give your office's managing broker Todd a call about this. I mean really, too many more infractions and Share is going to be banned from listing properties here in Seaview. And we wouldn't want that to happen, now would we?" she said as she winked yet again.

Ralph perked up when she winked and let loose a long string of "old bitch, motherfucker" and other assorted expletives while his yellow eyes pin wheeled with excitement. "Oh how awful! Such a potty mouth bird! If I could, I would put my bar of soap right there in your pointy beak you nasty little excuse for company. I just wonder where you learned all those naughty words." She said while shaking her helmet haired head and rolling her eyes at us. "Well on that fine note, I've got to skedaddle, get back on task and keep things running around here. I'll sure look forward to seeing you two this Saturday. Now Alex, don't forget to arrive an hour early and read over our show rules again, it's in the show packet I emailed you." With that she sprinted out the door to corner a tiger on the first floor I suppose.

The broker's open was a complete dud. Not one agent came to visit. The only visitors were a group of three old ladies who lived in the building. They nosed all around Harvey's place for almost an hour, commenting on Percy's makeover while consuming six of the maple bars and as many cups of coffee. We gave them three more maple bars as a parting prize. That left us with three maple bars to unload and we still had an hour or so to kill in geezerville before we were supposed to meet Ethel and check out her new digs. Wanda and I decided to head down to the pool and recreation area, check it out and give away the remaining sugar bombs. Ralph coo-ed over Wanda again and this time she actually pet his head a bit through his cage. He seemed quite taken and he squawked a few "mother fuckers" in appreciation of Wanda's attention. We locked up and ran into Harvey at the elevator. He was bitching nonstop about Beverly, as he apparently ran into her in the lobby.

"You let me know when we got us an offer there feller and the sooner the better. That old woman is the limit, telling me it's a good thing I'm selling because she finds Ralph offensive! Says she would put a vote to the board to have him removed from Seaview if it weren't for me selling. Damn bitch that woman is. I'd like to let old Ralphy loose on her; just let him peck her eyes out, I would! I'm telling you that woman is one sneaky skank. Don'cha let her sweet apple pie routine fool ya' none. I used to know them TV people back in the day and they all said she was hell on wheels to be around. Just watch yer' selves with that one is all I'm sayin'. Can't wait for me and Ralph to get out of this hell house. Damn communist country that they got going on 'round here."

O n the ride down in the elevator, Wanda and I were serenaded in
full stereo by the instrumental version of *Tie a Yellow Ribbon
'Round the Old Oak Tree*, to which Wanda muttered, "Makes me wanna
cut down that damn tree." By the time we reached the pool and rec
area, *Cabaret* by Herb Alpert and the Tijuana Band was blaring. Wanda
and I stopped and stood there taking it all in. "Mumph, those are
some big ass swimming pools they got here Alex. Check out them old
honky women out there with the matching flower swim hats, doing
some swim dance routine. And look at them geezers by the *bocce* ball
courts. I'm telling you, this is one time warped place they got going on!
Let's see if those old birds at that table over there want the maple
bars." Wanda led us over to a white round poolside table complete
with a green Seaview logo umbrella. Four elderly women were sipping
iced tea and a huge pile of catalogues was spread out on the table with
a sizeable box of more catalogues sitting next to the table. "Hey ladies,
looks like you all are enjoying the sun today and checking out the
catalogues? Say, we just had us an open house up there and have these
maple bars left over. Would you all like them?" Wanda said placing
the bakery box in front of them. The fattest old lady snapped the box
open and they all gawked at the three maple bars like crows around
some fresh road kill. "Well, this is very kind of you honey. But there
are only three doughnuts in here and there are four of us. Oh but wait,
Sara you are on that restricted diet, so I guess three is just perfect. I've
always been partial to maple bars! Ohh my, these *are* tasty. Mmmuph,

so what unit were you all holding open today? There hasn't been another death has there?" this the fat lady in the pink sweat suit said with her mouth full of maple bar.

I explained we were holding open Harvey's unit and he was still alive but Beverly had mentioned another death that she had to attend to. "Oh, yes I heard about the new one, just this morning." A frail woman with grey hair dressed in a pale blue sweat suit piped in while the other three nodded. "Yes, there certainly have been a lot of deaths lately. Word is they want to keep that crematorium in full use." They all giggled but then the fat woman replied with her mouth still full, "More like keep Beverly LeFaye in some prime listings! You know her sister Ellen just passed through here a short while ago with her emergency kit; you don't suppose there's been another death? Just too creepy if you ask me, but not nearly as creepy as this new music they have playing everywhere now." The others agreed.

I cleared my throat, "Well ladies, I hope you all enjoy the maple bars. It sure is a nice, sunny—"

There was a loud shriek from one of the ground floor, pool side units, "Ooohhhhh no, MR. JIGGLES, No! Oh my Lord, Mr. Jiggles is DEAD! Help, OH HELP!" We quickly rushed over to the patio where the screaming was coming from. An elderly woman with dyed black hair was on the floor inside her living room sobbing hysterically. We went in through the open patio door and I let out a gasp when I saw what appeared to be a dead white dog on the floor, foam coming from its mouth, its brown eyes wide open and not blinking. Wanda started soothing the woman and the old people were now crowding around the unit's patio and murmuring. I heard someone say to call the front desk.

There was a swirl of activity, with front desk staff, Beverly and what appeared to be a nurse of some sort coming in and out. The nurse was around 60, heavy set or big boned. She wore hospital staff clothing, blue scrub pants, white crock style rubber shoes, a purple and blue matching work top with a green name badge which read, "Ellen Hansen, Nurse's Aide." She had long dishwater colored hair which went all the way down to her wide ass and it was wrapped up in a braided pony tail with a pink squeegee twist. She wore no make-up and her demeanor was efficient but cold and detached. The old lady was now sobbing hysterically, "Oh but Ellen, you just looked at Mr. Jiggles and you said he was fine." She looked up at Ellen and then over at Beverly who had just arrived, "Beverly you said your sister used to be vet and she would make Mr. Jiggles behave. No more doodies in the lobby or by the pool. Oh now look, he is gone!" Ellen rolled her eyes as she stood up and shrugged as if to say, that's that. Beverly quickly went into action. She walked over to the woman, helping her stand up.

"Now Eileen dear, I know this is just too awful. Here, let's go have a seat by the pool and let Ellen and Carlos here take care of things. You know Mr. Jiggles is now in a better place and we are going to take perfect care of him and he'll always be here in our Seaview world dear. You know we now have the pet mortuary. Mr. Jiggles is going to be looked after, don't you fret. Why I bet he's already happier, he can't have any more accidents that embarrass him and his owner. No more soiled carpets to pay for or fines. Why dear, you just come right along outside and let's get some fresh air. My, isn't the sunshine just lovely? Come along let's go sit. Pamela bring us some iced tea right away and I think Father Boyland is on call today. Why don't I go get him, I think he's in the elder care building. Alex, Wanda could you two do me a favor, could you all sit with Eileen while I get Father Boyland? He doesn't always answer his on-call phone, so I need to just go grab him." We nodded yes. "Fine, now Eileen you come right over here and sit with my good friends Alex and Wanda. I will be back before your next tear drop falls. Oh listen Eileen, the angels are already speaking to you! Why isn't that an appropriate song to be playing now? God is letting you know that Mr. Jiggles is safe and flying away to doggy heaven right now!" With that Beverly gave Wanda me one of her winks and took off, her lavender dress billowing behind her like a motor boat's wake. The instrumental number now blaring by the pool was, *Wind Beneath My Wings*. Wanda and I exchanged looks and sat down with the whimpering Eileen.

Per orders, Pamela arrived with a silver serving tray complete with the proper white tray liner Beverly is so fond of. She set a huge glass pitcher of iced tea down on the table, a silver bowl of lemon wedges with tongs and a silver sugar bowl with tongs. She then placed three green, iced tea glasses on white paper napkins which had the green Seaview logo printed on them. While Pamela filled the glasses, Eileen continued to cry. "But Mr. Jiggles was completely fine, he was only six years old. I don't understand. And Beverly said Ellen would help him get over his doody problem. I just don't understand!"

Wanda raised her eyes at me, "Honey, what exactly did this Ellen lady do with Mr. Jiggles when she looked at him? Did you say she had come by earlier today to take a look at him?"

Eileen, stopped sobbing a bit and appeared to think, "Yes, Ellen came by about a half hour before Mr. Jiggles," sob "before he starting to spasm and then Beverly stopped by just after Ellen left to check on him and ohhh---" with that she burst into a fresh round of tears. Wanda's eye brows raised higher, "It's okay baby. Now you tell me, what did this Ellen do with your Mr. Jiggles when she was there?"

Eileen kept sobbing, "Well, she gave him a vitamin shot. Said it would make him feel better and should help his bowels. She used to be a vet you know. I thought she would help him and now—" with that came another round of wailing and tears.

Before Wanda could ask more questions, Beverly was marching over to our table with what appeared to be a man of the cloth in tow. This man was about five foot four, a bit chubby like a cherub. He had clean cut brown hair, which appeared to be dyed and was decked out in black preacher garb, a black dress (robe) that reached his ankles and a tight white clerical collar up top. He carried a small maroon prayer book. He gave us a standard sympathy greeting smile and shook our hands. I thought his chubby hand lingered a bit too long in mine but who am I to tell? I'd prefer if we all just bowed like the Japanese and did away with all this hand shaking. With his boyish face, he could be anywhere from 15 to 60. He placed his small hands on Eileen's shoulders and commenced to console her with a whole litany of prayer book platitudes.

Beverly eyed Wanda and me, her eyes commanding we get up and follow her. "Now Eileen you are in good hands. Father Boyland is here to comfort you in your hour of need dear. Have some of that fresh iced tea, it will help boost your spirits. Well, we are going to scoot and let you get to your grieving. I am going to personally ensure that Mr. Jiggles is taken care of this afternoon at the mortuary. We can plan a ceremony for him tomorrow dear. You are all safe here and taken care of. Your Seaview family is here in your darkest hour. Why, when you are ready Eileen, there is our weekly Turning Grief Into Smiles support group. Now Father, you see to it that this girl drinks her glass of tea. I just know it will help her."

"Oh, yes indeed Beverly!" he replied in a crisp lispy voice. "I am right here to console and help Eileen. We are going to pray together and let go and let Heavenly Father whisk Mr. Jiggles home to pet heaven." With that Wanda and I followed Beverly to the lobby.

Beverly paused at the front desk, inquiring about Mr. Jiggles remains. "Well that is just too dreadful now isn't it? Thank you both for helping us out there. Mrs. Runyard is one of the overly emotional ones around here. Good thing Father Boyland is on call to help sort these things out. Now are you two on your way out?"

"Ahh, we are just killing some time here Beverly before we meet up with Ethel. She wants to show us her place, now that her furniture and everything is all just about put away. Looks like we have about 40 minutes left before we are to meet her and---"

Beverly perked up, "Oh, that's grand! I am sure you two are going to enjoy visiting Mrs. Kluntz, our new little fifth floorer! Say, why don't you and Wanda tag along with me and I can show you two our Seaview Mortuary and Crematorium. We are quite proud of our after care facilities here and you know Mr. Jiggles there is going to be our first animal loved one to go through our new pet after care program. Here, you take the box and you two follow me. Pamela, call me if there is anything urgent." With that she picked up a sturdy gray cardboard box with "Remains" printed on its lid and thrust it into my arms. Sure as shit, she had me carrying the dog's body. Eeewww!

# 20

Out the automatic glass doors past doormen in dictator drag we went. Beverly's cart was parked right out front in its special spot. She took the dead doggy box from me, cavalierly tossing it on the third bench seat in the back of the cart. "Okay, well all aboard my friends!" Beverly exclaimed with her pink frosted lipstick smile. You two just make yourselves comfortable in the row behind me and I'll get us over to the Mortuary in a jiffy. Notice the new orange flashing light up top on my little cart? I had that and a power booster installed just last week. The Board thought it best if my cart had emergency features so I can readily get to where I am needed. And as you two can tell, it appears I am needed just nonstop these days. Oh well, hop in and enjoy the scenery and the music! Isn't it just grand how this wireless thing they installed in my cart allows me to enjoy the pleasant music while scooting all about! I am going to have to see about getting these wireless gadgets for our resident's golf carts and personal mobility carts as well."

With that she picked up the corded microphone and cleared her destination with the mortuary, apparently giving them a code to let them know she had the cart in emergency mode. I suppose getting the remains of Mr. Jiggles to the undertaker qualifies as a full tilt emergency in Seaview. She clicked on the orange flashing light switch, popped the cart into drive and we literally burned rubber out of the entry's drive. Beverly wasn't kidding, this cart had a huge power boost. She was going at least 40 miles an hour, cutting off cars, doing *Streets of San Francisco* style jumps over the speed bumps, and nearly running over people and other carts on the paths as she sped over to the mortuary building. Along the way she turned up the music, while she looked back at us and smiled, nearly side swiping another golf cart in the process. Wanda's and my ears were assaulted with a plucky instrumental version of The Beach Boys' *I Get Around*—how appropriate. Wanda placed her hand on the back of the front seat to steady herself, and used her other hand to keep her hair in place. I clutched the seat's side arm and prayed we'd reach the mortuary as visitors and not customers. In no time she sped through the "downtown" part of Seaview and had us in the rear docking station of the Seaview After Care building. An attendant in a white lab coat came rushing out to meet the cart as Beverly nearly crashed into the building. Beverly hopped out, "Oh Don, the dead dog's in the back. Just let me know when you are all set to process him. It's the first time we've used the pet cremator. Why I feel like I should have ordered us champagne for the inaugural run. I'm going to show my friends around Don, just buzz me when it's time."

Don scurried to the back of the cart to get the box which incidentally had popped open during the rough ride. Wanda and I followed Beverly inside. The back part of this rather large building was all gleaming white tiles, and stainless steel. Beverly pointed out the morgue and the human crematorium room and then she showed us the new pet crematorium room. "It's large enough to accommodate pets up to the size of a pony, can you imagine? Well since we have a pet weight limit restriction of 25 pounds and under, I think this model has got our needs covered! Now follow me and let me show you the public rooms. We went through some doors and then we were in the entry/reception room. The room was paneled in a honey oak wood, the floor carpeted in deep burgundy, there were brass urns with ferns in them scattered about, along with various upholstered chairs and benches and an American, state and Seaview flag all hung limply on gold poles as a centerpiece. Beverly showed us a viewing room which had a casket and chairs all set up for a service that afternoon. A reception room was set up next to it, "This is our after-service room and as you can see we can make it larger or smaller with these attractive fabric paneled wall dividers. This way when a member of our Seaview family passes on, who is less than popular, those attending can be placed in a smaller setting so the deceased's unpopularity isn't so painfully obvious with a large empty room."

She then showed us the adjoining viewing room which was currently being "staged" as she called it. On the other side of the entry reception hall was one room full of display caskets and then the next room was filled with hundreds of urns all displayed on lighted shelving with brass plaques in front of them. Like the caskets for sale, the urns all had comforting names, "Eternal Beauty, Serenity, Gentle Dawn, Restful Sleep" just to name a few. Beverly then led us to a smaller shelving section, "And these are the pet remain urns. Aren't they just too cute? Why now a Seaviewer can have his little friend with him at all times. They come in such attractive designs, you can display them on your coffee table or maybe place the urn on your dining room sideboard. Eileen is going to be the first one to get to purchase one of these!"

144

Wanda was taking it all in, "You got it all covered here Beverly, no doubt about that. Damn, Alex would you look at all this!" Beverly perked right up like a cat being stroked. "And lady, you got the caskets going on in that other room. I thought everyone at Seaview had to be cremated per your rules?"

"Absolutely Wanda. But some people still prefer a traditional service with a casket. So we provide that and then the body and casket are taken care of in the crematorium. After that, the ashes are placed in one of these gorgeous urns that we provide, well actually sell, to our members."

"Girl, go on! You sell them the casket AND the urn? Now don't that just beat all. You are one sharp businesswoman Beverly LeFaye! You know, I own a hair salon in Clinton, called Salon Wanda. That's how I first started out before I moved over to mortgages. I can appreciate me a woman with some business sense. Humph, this here is something else." Wanda was nodding her head and taking in all the urns while Beverly appeared to be a second grade school girl getting an A plus from her teacher. "Oh golly Wanda, I sure do try my best. Why, I see Don is here. Looks like we can go over to the pet crematorium and watch our first little friend be processed! Shall we?"

I would prefer to go home and hammer my thumb but Wanda pulled my arm and we tagged along behind Beverly back into the clinical side of the building. Along the way we passed Ellen who was carrying a clipboard and reviewing some kind of chart while slurping away on a can of root beer. Beverly looked straight ahead and passed by her but Ellen called out without looking up from her clip board,

"Bev the dog's getting fired up next and according to this chart we got the stiff from the bungalows about to be processed too. Word from the family is to just cremate, no need to do the casket drill. Looks like you are out the casket commission on that one."

Beverly stopped dead in her tracks, her shoulders stiffened, "Ellen, I have told you how many times we are NOT to refer to our Seaview family members as *stiffs* when they have passed away. Now please, we really must---"

Ellen interrupted her with a loud root beer belch, flipping her long braided pony tail over her shoulder and calling out, "Whatever" as she slowly walked down the hall. That being the polite one word version of, "Fuck you."

"Ugh. You two must please excuse Ellen's lack of decorum. I am afraid she is younger than me, though you'd never know it from the way she keeps herself. She was part of that whole grubby little hippie generation and well, you two can see where that got her! Mother just so spoiled Ellen. Here, I always wanted us to have fun together and maybe have a wonderful little singing group like the Lennon Sisters. Oh how I adored them and their must-see appearances on the fabulous *Lawrence Welk Show*! Why my cousins Patsy and Louise were all keen on forming a singing group but not Ellen. And when I was in the Miss America pageant do you think she was proud of her sister? Absolutely not! Did Ellen bother to watch my highly successful television show in all the 15 plus years it ran? No sir! She could have cared less and trust you me, she could really have benefited from my ladies show. See how unkempt and sloppy she is? Sigh, I just don't know what to do sometimes. I can't help it if I am so successful, more attractive and keep myself up, now can I? And I had to give her a job here. I mean after her problem, what is a sister to do? But her nasty attitude is just so bothersome and I had to draw the line with letting her live here at Seaview. I mean she doesn't remotely qualify financially and why should I pull strings for someone as uncouth as she? Oh well, never mind me and my cross to bear. Let's go see our new Seaview pet crematorium at work!"

After Beverly's "Mr. Toad's Wild Ride," and the sickening pet crematorium live show, Wanda and I elected to walk back to the North Tower for our appointment with Ethel. There was a nice walking path which led us through parts of the golf course and we noticed what appeared to be utility men installing speakers on the course. "Damn if that woman ain't kidding Alex. Look those men are putting in that horrible music out there on the course! I'm gonna tell you, that lady is crazy. Seriously, did you see how happy she was when they fired up that poor dead dog?"

"She is completely bat shit but I'm not so sure the gleam in her eye and the smile on her face when they burned the dog's corpse wasn't from her happiness with her new crematorium toy and how efficient things are running. This place is definitely its own world. I wonder how Ethel likes it here, thus far?" This I asked hoping Wanda wasn't going to go where I thought she might. She did.

"Oh, we'll be finding out all about Miss Ethel in a few minutes. But what I want to find out is what the deal is between that sister Ellen and Beverly? I can't even believe those two are sisters. You saw how Ellen acted. Did you see how she was when she checked up on the dog at Eileen's? And what is up with all these old people dying around here? I know you are gonna say they are old and that's true but it sure seems like they have a lot of deaths happening here. You heard them old ladies talking about how those deaths mean more listings for Beverly. Something ain't right around here. I guess we already know this place is old time honky crazy. But these deaths and that Beverly and her sister, I'm telling you Alex that there is something way more crazy than the average old white folks crazy going on here."

I let out a sigh, "Wanda just don't go there, leave it be. I can sell Harvey's place and be out of here. Hopefully Ethel likes it here and she can visit us whenever she wants out of the old folk's asylum. And what's with all of this 'honky' and 'old white folks' talk? What if I said the 'n' word or referred to something as 'old black folks crazy' wouldn't that get your panties in a knot?"

"Humph, you got a point but you know damn well what I'm talking about and don't pretend not to. Honey we both know this place is wall-to-wall white folks. Well okay, maybe they have one or two Huxtables living here but they might as well be white. I'm just calling it like I see it and the main skin color here, happens to be white. If the main skin color here was black, I'd be calling it crazy black folks shit and you know, I might even use that 'n' word too, although I have to say I'm not a real fan of that word personally.

I think we need to come up with new bad word to describe the lowlifes of all colors and nationalities. Call it the new 'n' word except it applies to everyone, rednecks, gang bangers, all the scum out there in all their assorted flavors and colors. Then nobody could get their self-righteous ass in a knot and go on CNN to spout off about how awful such-and-such a word is and how it hurts their specific people. Yep, we need us a generic nasty word to use. This is America, we should'a had us a bad word like this a long time ago. A melting pot bad word that covers everyone equally; equal opportunity potty mouth as Beverly would call it, that's what I'm talking about. I think we should spend some time working on this new bad word Alex, it could be our way of giving back to the community—you know that whole give back spin they all do? Anyhow, the main thing here is that people are kicking the bucket, a lot! Hell most of them probably ain't even half way through their bucket list. Speaking of which, what is all this bucket list crap? They got some seminar going on at Safety Mortgage that we are supposed to attend and it's all about the damn bucket list. Bunch of crap, if you ask me! Only bucket I need to spend my time thinking about is the one from KFC, and keeping my bucket full of money. Well, we both know something is up here and not in no good way. I think you and me need to pay attention and start looking into things. Maybe we can---"

I put my hands over my ears for a second, "Not hearing this Wanda, do not go there. We are not private detectives. I am here to sell this stupid listing, avoid getting mauled or preened to death by Beverly, and move on. If you want to become the Nancy Drew of Seaview, have at it but leave me out. I don't need any more listings with dead bodies or fucked up families listing with me, thank you very much. I've got one fucked up family, I don't need another one."

Wanda ignored me and was pondering out loud the number of recent deaths in Seaview as we approached the rear lobby entry door to the towers complex. We checked in with Pamela who rang up Ethel. As we walked down the North Tower hallway and rode the elevator, we were serenaded by a snappy musical tune called, *No Matter What Shape Your Stomach's In* by the New Classic Singers.

"There you two are! You are late, here come, you have to see. Take your shoes off and follow me." This Ethel shouted out as we approached her unit's door. And late? Yes, I suppose it was three minutes past the appointed meeting time. We followed Ethel inside. There were a few unpacked boxes stacked in the living room but everything else was unpacked and set up. A large, low slung, 1960s vintage sofa upholstered in nubby aqua marine fabric and tightly wrapped in clear vinyl upholstery covers dominated the living room. On each side of the sofa were matching end tables, each with a large mustard colored ceramic lamp with white and gold lamp shades, which were also sealed in clear vinyl. A large kidney shaped coffee table held an array of coasters, a small artificial fern in a turquoise pot, and a white dish with individually wrapped butterscotch candies. The new issue of *TV Guide* was carefully laid out on the coffee table, as were the latest issues of *Ladies Home Journal* and *The Economist* and *The Harvard Business Review*. A dog eared crossword puzzle book with a blue pen inserted in it was lying face down on one end of the sofa. Behind the sofa was a large rectangular mirror, encased in an ornate gold frame. On either side of the sofa were two identical 1950s Danish modern chairs in a rose and aqua marine nubby fabric and sealed tight in clear vinyl as well. When I looked at the floor, I noticed there were thick clear vinyl floor runners laid out everywhere on top of the plush carpeting. They were like railroad tracks, indicating where you should walk. In the corner was a large curio cabinet which was lit up. On each large shelf were assorted knick-knacks and silver framed family photos. On the top shelf was a large color photo of Norman and judging from the cap and gown it must have been his high school graduation day. Next to the curio cabinet was an enormous television, stereo entertainment consol unit, circa 1980. On top, an avocado green ceramic lamp with a vinyl covered black lamp shade sat next to a bronze bowl filled with plastic fruit. The water views from the large living room windows were great.

Ethel was scurrying around, "Sit! I've got water for coffee already made. You see my view? Isn't that great? I didn't have that view back in Philly. I hope to have that balcony fixed up by next week. *Oy*, so much work to do, I tell you I never rest. No, there is no rest for me here at Seaview." Wanda and I had barely sat down on the squeaky vinyl covered sofa before Ethel was setting a large silver tray down on the coffee table. The tray had three white mugs each with a spoon tucked inside, a sugar bowl, cream, a white tea pot and a large jar of instant coffee crystals. Ethel put the mugs in our hands, and handed Wanda the instant coffee bottle. "Scoop and pass, here let me pour your water. I've got some terrific day-old pastries from that bakery near Alex's house. I'll get them once we've poured. I tell you that Seaview bakery, who can eat such *chozzerai*? I have half a mind to start up my own bakery and deli here; I tell you these people don't know food from *opfal*." This she said while simultaneously filling our mugs with hot water and scooping endless spoonfuls of instant coffee into her mug. "These people here, I don't know. But I have to give myself some time, join the groups. I am going to Beverly's TV show this Saturday and she tells me that you are going to be a guest Alex! That's exciting, have your told your mother? I don't know why my Norman can't get rid of that *kurva* he lives with and get himself on a respectable television show. Oh, your mother will be so proud Alex; you should tape it and send it to her as a memento."

I grimaced, because of the nasty instant coffee taste, not because of her comment and replied, "Considering I haven't spoken with the vessel that spawned me in almost 20 years, I doubt I'm going to send her a tape of my illustrious appearance on Beverly's show. So how's life at Seaview? You are right Ethel; you've only been here what a couple of weeks? It takes time to adjust. Your place is looking great and you have everything all set up. It must be a relief to be settling in your own place now."

Ethel took a sip of her coffee and then promptly added another teaspoon of coffee crystals, "*Oy*, that you should talk like that about your mother! At least you aren't living with a *kurva* in sin. Yes, this place is coming along nicely for me. Wanda, I put in that good shelf liner in my kitchen, just like I put in yours. You know there's a bingo event I am going to tonight, it's a big deal around here. These people take their bingo very seriously. They have special card stampers, visor hats, lucky charms and most run 20 cards or more at a time. This I don't know but I'll see what it's all about. I used to tell my husband, Herman, gawd rest his soul, Herman you have to try new things and keep moving or else you are going to stop living. Did he listen? Well we all know who has passed, now don't we? And speaking of passing on, I tell you this place is like a non-stop death factory. Someone here is passing away every other day or getting moved into their assisted living building which is just a euphemism for god's waiting room. This

153

I don't know, but I gotta try the new things and that Beverly is after me to give this line dancing class they have a whirl. Who knows, maybe I'm going to be Ethel Kluntz the queen of seniors line dancing; get me a purple cow girl hat and call it good. Oh here, have some day-old, they taste great dipped in the coffee. So Wanda how's that Sammy coming along? I bet he keeps your grass out back nice and trim. You know I'm going to come over to your neighborhood next week. I'm going out tomorrow to go car shopping. I figure a new life in a new town, time for a new car. I gave my cousin, Letti, in Philly my Chrysler LeBaron. It is a good car, one owner, only 53,000 miles on it, she should be so lucky to have. This lady down the hall here, Mrs. Myers, she is going to take me to look at cars tomorrow. She's about the only person I know here who actually ever leaves this place and thank gawd for her or else I'd have no day-old to share; they all seem to stay within the gates here. Very strange and boring, if you ask me. So Miss Lyla and I are going to have a day out together, once I have my new car. You know she never leaves the Highmont? She's at least 80-something or more and the woman has never left that neighborhood, once! But we have lots of fun together. I tell you it's not like these people here with all their clubs and social agendas. *Oy!* Got to keep a positive attitude and give it all a try, just like I used to tell my Herman. More hot water, Alex? Scoop some more crystals in while I pour, that makes it taste better if you add while I pour. So what's new with you two and life in Clinton?"

From there we filled Ethel in on our less than glamorous lives and Wanda managed to bite her tongue and not go off on Ethel's

154

comments about the shelf liners and Sammy the horse. She did however, quiz Ethel extensively about the deaths at Seaview but Nancy Drew wanna-be didn't uncover any thrilling clues or twists. On our way out of the building, I got a call from Harvey. "I had a call from some agent who said she was gonna show my place tonight. Then she calls me back and says they ain't gonna make it. You need to tell them whores to make up their darn minds! I can't be having Ralph and my schedule interrupted and changed like this."

"Ah, I am sorry to hear the agent cancelled on showing your unit Mr. Malloy. Unfortunately, I have no control over whether or not a buyer's agent follows through with a showing or not. In fact, many agents do not even have the courtesy to call the home owner and cancel, they just don't show up. Did you get this agent's name? I'll be happy to call her and follow up if you like?"

Ralph let out some loud chirps and there were some rattling sounds, "No, I didn't get the damn fool's name, some woman supposed to show tonight at 7 p.m. and then she calls an hour later and cancels. That ain't no way to run a business! Well, at least we won't be bothered none, you know the new *Wheel of Fortune* shows run at that time. And Ralph really likes the new shows the best, he can tell when it's a rerun. Well, I guess we'll just be happy that agent won't be bothering us but you people really need to learn how to do business! Oh and that plate of cookies you all left, I'm assuming you don't plan on coming back for them? Just as well, I'm gonna eat them while Ralph and me watch the *Wheel* tonight." And with that he hung up.

"Wanda we didn't leave any cookies at Mr. Malloy's place did we?" Wanda shook her head no. "He must be getting senile. He said there is a plate of cookies there that we left and he plans on eating them tonight while he watches TV with Ralph. He was all grouchy because a buyer's agent cancelled her showing tonight, as if I have any control over that."

Just then there were shouts and screams from the entry's *port cochere*. "The Flasher, agghhh help it's the flasher! Get him!" Sure enough there he was again in his army boots, rain coat and ski mask letting all hang out for all of the world to see. He quickly took off, weaving between the taxis and limos and ran off to the side of the North Tower. The doormen were giving chase but were far behind. Pamela came up and was giving the flasher's where abouts over her walkie talkie. "Oh that dirty old man again! Mrs. LeFaye is going to be fit to be tied."

Wanda shook her head, "Oh baby that weren't no old man there. His little dingle ain't no old man dingle. That guy's got a middle age dingle and he sure can run. Damn, this is most definitely one fucked up honky town scene going on here for sure."

## 22

Unfortunately, Saturday rolled around all too soon and there I was dragging out my penguin suit from the back of my closet and cursing like a sailor as I put it on. Luckily the damn bow tie was a pre-tied thing and I was able to easily slip it on, otherwise much to Beverly's horror, I would have been showing up without a tie to go with my tux. I drew the line at polishing the black shoes, the ones reserved for crap like this event and the rare funeral. I don't do weddings period, so no need for the black shoes for those horrific events. Although perhaps I should reconsider and go into the wedding industry, talk about a cash cow. Especially when you consider the average American wedding now costs $15,000 and 41 percent of all first marriages in the U.S. end in divorce. What sort of brainwashed, overly sentimental, dumb asses go into hock for these pseudo princess/prince-for-a-day events, only to have the marriage not work out? A lot of dumb asses, that's who! The black shoes weren't dirty but you sure as shit couldn't see your face reflected in them. I certainly wasn't going to find some polish and make them shine. I was betting old Beverly would be the first to notice and comment.

I poured Clyde some scrumptious kibble, which he sniffed and promptly ignored. He hopped on my bed, did his walk in a circle routine and plopped down to sleep while I struggled to put on the cuff links. How did I ever allow myself to agree to do this---oh never mind! I gave Clyde a pat on his shaggy head, told him to watch the ranch and headed out the front door to fire up my two door beater. Down to Seaview I headed.

Again, with the entry gate fire drill with Dave, such an asshole. Then I sped along at two miles per hour, over a million speed bumps, through the town center, finally arriving at the community building and auditorium to which the Seaview TV station is attached. I pulled into one of the designated guest show parking spots, put the laminated parking pass on my dash and went in.

Inside was a cluster fuck of official geriatrics with Seaview TV lanyard name badges. They were busy scurrying all about in preparation for tonight's live broadcast. I signed in and was directed to the make up/guest reception area. It was quite nice, my frame of reference being my experience with the local Clinton Channel Four station. I have to say, the Seaview TV station is no sloppy outfit. Beverly was not kidding, the people running this station must be retired television industry workers. A producer's assistant signed me in again, and told me they'd page me for make-up in a few minutes. I killed the time by checking out the guest refreshment table, helping myself to a slice of pepperoni pizza which wasn't too bad considering it came from the Seaview Pizzeria. I walked to the soundstage and took a peek. They were busy setting up the lighting, doing camera tests, dusting the set furniture. The audience risers were pale blue upholstered, movie theater style chairs, nice compared with most TV studio audience accommodations. It looked like it seated about 150 people. The stage was almost as big as Channel Four's sound stage. It had a huge living room area, with room for a full orchestra band, which was busy setting up their musical equipment. There were two smaller segment sets to the right, one prepared for some kind of kitchen demo and the other appeared to be a craft room of some sort. I was walking back to the reception area when I heard a very deep, baritone woman's voice bellowing, "EEEEE!! Over here right now and give that woman my special make-up kit, NOW!" That could only be one person, the always charming RG Boysun and her lapdog husband Eddie.

When I rounded the corner, there was RG decked out in an all white, man's suit. She was busy bossing everyone around while wolfing down pizza. This was odd considering the last time I crossed her path she was all into her Power-Up Serenity protein drinks and diet. (see Volume Two) I stopped to take it all in. RG is about six feet tall, built like a linebacker, only dresses in white, men's suits, has a crew cut that is dyed an alarming yellow hue, sports a small slab of pale lipstick on her thin lips which are accented by her small beady eyes and pig's nose. Her husband Eddie barely clears five feet, weighs no more than 98 pounds, is completely shiny bald up top and spots a long ZZ Top style beard. He is constantly chasing after RG and doing her bidding, basically being treated like total shit. Such a fun couple. RG is a mortgage broker with Coopers Hawk Mortgage and she is all about self promotion. She was still stuffing her mouth when she spied me and immediately began bellowing at me while spewing pizza as she roared, "OOHHH! It's Al Campbell, we meet again. Say Al, haven't you been receiving my important weekly loan updates? I'm surprised I have not seen you at some of my monthly sphere networking events. You know when you are a VIP like me, it's important to remember to invite people such as yourself to attend events. I'm sure you must have had an email glitch as no one would be so foolish as to miss out on one of my special invitation-only events. This show is different from our last TV appearance together, this time I need my make-up bag. You can probably tell how jet lagged I am.

I just got in from Vegas. I was at one of the power circle, VIP events there that JC Zander puts on. Most important event, only the top players are invited to participate in Zander's gold circle events. I learned so much about powering up my business cycle and infusing it with synchronicity while letting the momentum actually power the ride. Most important information, awesome contacts there and of course, I could gamble all night as well. Nothing like letting off some steam in Vegas! But seriously, the event changed my life, my whole business philosophy. I am signing up for some of JC Zander's personal monthly call-in circles. Very few are selected and able to join those circles. Naturally, I'll be sharing some of what I learn in my email updates to my sphere. I might even start my own JC subsidiary circle here in Clinton; it's by invitation only. But I have to see how it all plays out, JC doesn't just grant anyone an exclusive circle territory you know! I have to first complete the subsidiary training course and then go to JC's Guru Camp that he holds once a year in Atlantic City for those who are applying to be the subsidiary trainer in a local market."

She stuffed more pizza in her thin lipped, smug, little mouth, her pig nostrils flaring out as she inhaled the food and continued talking with her mouth full, "Beverly told me you have a listing here and I am sure Beverly has informed you that I am the official mortgage professional here at Seaview. I run a very exclusive, VIP only investment club here for the Seaview members. Players only, that's my style! Such a pity about Serenity (see Volume Two) but I've processed, found closure and my life is moving on. You're not still doing business with that Wanda woman are you? Really Al, you need to get Eddie here to hook you up with an appointment with me real soon and upgrade. I'm sure we can do some real power networking together." With that she scooped up two more slices of pizza, and barked at Eddie to follow her, "Great seeing you Al, but I've got to get to my dressing room. I need solitude before going on live, must-see, TV. Beverly has made sure I have a private, VIP dressing room. I'm frequently on her show, what with all the business I do here at Seaview. Eddie, give him my card and hurry up, I don't have all night to prepare for my appearance!" With that she lurched off down the hallway; for a second I swear I saw a bull dressed in white moving down that hall. Eddie sheepishly smiled at me, quickly handed me her business card and scampered off down the hall behind her, his arms overflowing with boxes, a make-up kit, garment bag, and the paper plate of pizza, which RG had flung at him, was precariously perched on top.

I was then told it was time to have glop put on my face. Into the make-up room I went. I sat down in a barber's chair, and they put a green vinyl smock over me. The woman proceeded to make me look orange, sort of like that agent who is well known in Clinton, Kevin Carver of Johnny Lane Realtors. He lives for his spray tans and three piece business suits with matching bow tie and handkerchief and a white carnation always pinned to his lapel. He looks a former football player, grandfather advertisement model type and has a voice that sounds like a high pitched, squeaky dog. And not so incidentally,

161

Kevin is one of the biggest gossips around. He constantly lies to the public about other agents in order to land listings, all the while playing Mr. Congenial. Mr. Passive Aggressive, such a charm. I was pondering this when my nose noted the distinct sickening odor of freesia, musk, rose and some other noxious spice. Bingo, there was Stinky live and in person. She was ready for prime time, decked out in a tight fitting pant suit in bright red and covered in shiny sequins. Just red and shiny from head to toe, all she needed was horns and a pitch fork. Her girls up top were barely secured and sporting a huge ruby and gold necklace. She was clacking around in matching pointy boots which added at least a foot to her height. Her hair was recently re-flamed with red and orange streaks and spikier than ever.

She sneered at me in the mirror as she walked in the make-up room, her two toned red lips snarling downward, "Ohhh, looky who we have here and getting all pretty for TV? My Alex, you sure are letting them put war paint on you, what are you trying to become a mini version of Kevin Carver? Now there's an angle you can work, become Winterfrost's very own younger version of Kevin. Might help your sales improve, just a thought. You know word is Kevin's had another face lift. Ohhh, and you are here early to boot, getting brownie points with the old B are you? Well, I'm here early and she can duly note that in her tight-ass notebook. It's not like I don't have more important business to attend to, but hey it's required and I have to do all I can for my seller/listing, now don't I?" She said while hoisting herself up in the barber's chair to my right. She grimaced at the make-up lady, "Obviously I'm all ready for the camera, so just a little touch up on me and we'll use my own make-up, you are not turning me into some orange, ass clown like him. But you can get out your nail kit and repair this chip for me. The damn door out there chipped my nail and do you know how expensive my manicure is? I've got the custom polish here in my bag for you to touch it up with. I'm assuming you are qualified to address my nail repair needs?" The make-up woman didn't bat an eye and continued glopping crap on my face while telling Stinky, she'd let her know when they were ready for her. "Ohh it's like that around here, huh? Well no worries busy lady, because I clearly don't need much help with my make-up. I'll just cool it here a bit before old sweetness shows up." With that her cell phone lit up with its *Yellow Rose in Texas* ringtone and she picked up and began yakking away.

I was trying to think non Stinky perfume thoughts when the tiger arrived. "Howdy-ho folks, Tiger is in the house!" she shouted while chuckling and plopping down in the barber chair on my left. Tiger's plump body was squeezed (like a sausage in a too small casing) into a floor length, tan and brown leopard print evening dress. Her cleavage was spilling out and putting Elvira to shame. Two thin and strained spaghetti straps were barely holding her girls in place. "Damn, if that ain't the show house they got out there, huh? Not every day you get to be on the TV. I've got a friend who's gonna tape me tonight. I figure I can somehow use this here clip on the YouTube, great way to recruit new victims, I mean clients!" With that Tiger winked at me in the mirror and let out a loud belly laugh which caused her to rip a loud fart and that sent her reeling into spasms of hysterical laughter and

163

snorts. Stinky promptly turned in Tiger's direction and scowled at her. She asked her caller to hold on. Out of her ruby red sequined hand bag Stinky pulled out her dreaded atomizer and proceeded to spray a cloud of her killer vapor right at me. She then fanned her hands to push the stink cloud over towards Tiger. "My god, are you three years old and playing trick or treat? If you don't mind, I'm on the phone with an important client trying to do business and be a professional Tiger." With that she started to pick up her phone and then hesitated, aiming her atomizer right at me she squeezed out another whoosh, "There Alex, you poor thing, stuck right next to that smelly animal agent. Really, someone here needs to go to a Winterfrost professional guidelines class, don't you think Alex?" With that Share picked up her rhinestone cell phone and began to ooze and apologize to her client on the other end. I began to cough, as her last whoosh of stink went right in my lungs. I wiped my mouth with my arm, which now reeked of Stinky's perfume and I got some orange glop on my tux's sleeve. Make-up lady sprang into action with a damp cloth and began rubbing my sleeve.

Meanwhile Tiger was finishing up her hysterical laughter spell and noting that her eyes had gone more raccoon due to her laughter's tears. Make-up lady assured her that would get fixed. Tiger calmed down a bit and looked over at me, "Well, I guess Miss Im-port-tant over there can't be bothered to have no fun now can she? Oh well, get yer' sequins all in a knot but boy howdy when the party's on we all know who in this room's gonna be rockin' it with the listings y'all! Tiger always leads the pack!"

# NO REST

The rest of this festive make-up session continued without incident and soon Beverly's three little pig agents were all cake-faced up and ready for prime time. A producer of some sort came in and said it was time for roll call, Beverly would be there shortly. So, it was off with the vinyl capes and out the door to the reception area. There were assistants and assorted musicians all scurrying about as the countdown to show time was quickly approaching. The producer person had us line up to the side and I could hear Beverly's loud and syrupy voice coming down the hallway. Stinky put her cell phone away and then said she needed to find the ladies room. Tiger quickly chimed in, "Oh you need the can, Share? Yeah, I had to tinx like a race horse when I first got here. Nothing like one of them Big Gulps to bring on the pee! You just go right down that hall over there, the ladies can is on the left." Stinky didn't bother to acknowledge Tiger but took off down the hall, from which Beverly's voice was coming. I could hear the murmurs as they met in the hallway and some kind of loud discussion ensued, a door slammed. And then, there she was the star of her own show, Beverly LeFaye!

Beverly was wearing a full flowing sequined gown of pale blue and midnight blue and up top, a pale blue boa trim went around her neck and along her balloon sleeve cuffs. She looked like a cross between Endora from *Bewitched* and one of the Muppets. Her hair was extra bouffant-ed and shellacked into an unmovable gray helmet. She held blue note cards in one hand and a small pale blue hanky with her initials embroidered on it in the other. "Oh I am just sooo delighted to have everyone here this evening to share this special live television

165

moment with me. It's always such fun! A little bird tells me that RG is in her own dressing room and coming out shortly. Now I'll have the producer, Gill, run you all through the show's format. You are going to be seated on my living room set's sofa for the show's duration. Now there is no need to worry or get those crazy little on-camera butterflies, I'll be right there on stage with you all and guiding everything along nicely. Gill will explain it all to you, won't you Gill? Anyway, I'm just so thrilled we are all here tonight and ready to make television magic together! I've got to go speak with our band master Tommy and make sure the bubble machine is filled up. We are live in 15 folks, so break a leg!" With that she sprang off to the sound stage.

Gill proceeded to fill us in. He took us out to the set and arranged us on the enormous blue sofa. To the left of the sofa was a large chair in white for Beverly and a side table. To the far right was the band area and what appeared to be a small dance floor. To the left of Beverly's chair were the other mini stage set ups, the kitchen and then the craft room. The make-up lady came out, fussed over us and the lighting and boom mike people did likewise. The band was warming up and the audience seats were quickly filling up to capacity, though it was hard to see anyone in the audience as the lights just got brighter as show time approached. Gill pointed out the large "Live" sign and "Off Air" sign, told us to watch those and warned us about cursing on air and allowing Beverly to ask all questions and run the dialogue. RG made an entrance with Eddie in tow. An assistant helped her get situated on the sofa as she needed to be on the far end to do some special investment club monologue. The first spot on the sofa was reserved for Beverly's special guest and then that person would leave and we'd all move down during the commercial break and she'd be back to collectively interview us, talk about our listings. Then Beverly would do some segue way segments on the mini stages and back to us and then fade out with Beverly walking across the set to the dance floor area. Not real difficult but some sunglasses would be nice with all the bright lights, not to mention more air conditioning. I felt like a pumpkin baking in the hot sun and I'm sure my orange face matched that image. The sofa was very uncomfortable, there was zero back support and they wanted you to sit up very straight, not cross your legs and always look at Beverly not the cameras.

Beverly smiled at us all as she sat down in her chair the band started to play softly as the producer did the countdown. When he hit "one" and pointed to Beverly, the audience burst into loud applause and the plucky theme music cued up in full. Beverly promptly switched into action, "Oh hello everyone in Seaview, it's time once again for our little weekly get together and Saturday night fun time! I'm, of course, Beverly LeFaye, your hostess here to guide our party along tonight and I am just delighted to be with you again. I have with me my special guests and of course yours and my favorite, the Seatones, our house band is starting tonight's show off with an old favorite of mine, Mel Torme's *Games People Play*. Our very own Mr. Marvin Tuttle, is tonight's singer. Let's listen to this neglected classic and enjoy the bubbles as we go to break. You freshen up your tea or tini" which she said while conspicuously winking directly at the camera, "and I'll be back with you in two shakes of a lamb's tail. So stay tuned and enjoy!" The music then got louder and an old geezer in black tie and wearing a maroon velvet tux jacket with his enormous baby-on-board belly hanging over his black cummerbund was out on the dance floor belting out Mel's neglected masterpiece. Sure as shit, there were two bubble machines spewing out a swarm of bubbles as the camera panned over to the music area and we went to break.

We went to commercial and the music continued along with Marvin's howling and the bubbles spewing. Beverly shuffled her blue cue cards and smiled out at the audience while the make-up lady quickly powder puffed her nose and a producer prompted Tiger to sit up straighter. As the song was ending, the commercial break ended and we were live again. "Oh, I wish you all out there could have heard Marvin's wonderful rendition of that classic while we were on our break. Thank you so much Marvin, let's give him a hand. Now don't forget, you can hear Marvin and our fabulous Seatones live at our famous Halloween shindig that is coming up in just a short while. My how time flies around here when you are having fun! I'm sure you already have your tickets but for those of you out there who like to dilly dally, just a gentle reminder that you can purchase your tickets at any of our fine Seaview stores. You are allowed to bring a maximum of two off-site guests as long as you follow the pre-registration rules and regulations. It's an event I know you won't want to miss and I'll be there, of course, to keep the party going! We are going to have a song contest and best costume contest and of course there will be dancing to till midnight with the Seatones. I'll plan on seeing each of you there. It will be such fun!"

Again, another wink at the camera. She then went down the line and introduced each of us and said we'd all chat soon but first she was just thrilled to introduce tonight's special guest, "Yes, we are just thrilled and honored tonight to have in our Seaview studio a very special guest who has come here all the way from Cleveland to visit with us! Please help me welcome Miss Patricia Weaver!" Again the applause and out came this elderly woman who was also sporting a helmet hairdo (hers in red) and wearing a floor length gown of black sequins. She shook all of our hands and Beverly gave her a light lady hug. Once seated, Beverly took off.

"Oh, I am just so delighted you could be with us tonight Patricia. I feel like we are just old school chums already! Now I'm sure everyone in our audience already knows you from your past book, Swinging and Saging Past Seventy and I know one our many book clubs here at Seaview just had the best time reading that gem a few years back. Such an important message there, the whole aspect of being a wise sage while aging, it is *just* profound. But now you are back at it and here, let's get the camera to zoom in on the cover. This is your new book, Eighty is the New Sixty. This is going to be in bookstores next week I believe and why don't you just share with us the important message this book has in store for us. I can already feel another great Seaview book reading club forming around this new title Patricia!"

Patricia smiled at the camera, "Oh thank you for having me visit Beverly. It's not often I get to enjoy the company of a real lady and in a proper seniors-only town like Seaview. Why you know, I might move here myself someday. But this book, well it just comes straight from my heart and it really is true Beverly, I do think 80 really is the new 60!" Huge applause from the audience geezers. "It's not just the medical break-throughs we have now and our fine medical care system it's more a mind set. We just aren't going to be old! And why should we?  I want everyone who reads this book to walk away with a new attitude; life is just starting at 80.  Why Beverly, you are a woman of 80 or so and you can certainly testify that you don't feel old.  I've seen you out and about, and you certainly have the energy of a 60 year old."  Beverly's face instantly became blank and I noticed that gleam in her pale blue eyes flaring up.  Oh Patricia was treading on thin ice, as Beverly is only in her early 70s.

"Well, Patricia you certainly have a youthful philosophy in your new book!  And I am sure you can inspire us all to take up that youthful outlook of yours.  You know, I am surprised you didn't name your book something more inspirational and closer to your own situation, something like <u>Ninety is the New Seventy</u>.  Now don't you think that would be more inspirational and age appropriate?"  Before Patricia could react, much less reply, Beverly added, "Oh fiddlesticks!  My producer Gill is letting me know that we are just plum out of time Patricia!  But thank you so much for coming all this way to promote your special little book.  I am just certain the Seaview family will enjoy reading it and take great inspiration from your wise *nine* decades of earned wisdom on this fabulous planet.  Oh dear, do I hear the break music starting?"  Beverly said while staring directly at Tommy the band leader who quickly snapped to attention, waived his baton and started the band playing a musical version of The Ronettes, *My Boyfriend's Back*.

Once the "Off Air" sign lit up, Beverly tossed the book at an assistant who had come out to help lead Patricia off the stage. Patricia was looking very puzzled and asking the assistant why the segment was cut so short, wasn't she scheduled to talk in depth about her book and its wellness program for 10 minutes? Beverly reshuffled her cards, took a sip from a bottle of water with a straw in it that another aide held out for her. Gill was by her side and they were muttering about reformatting the time for each segment. Once done, Beverly snapped back into her frosted pink lipstick lady self and smiled at us, "All ready to talk about our listings now? Oh, and where is our Share Shelton? My, is she not participating? Such a shame. I saw her in the hallway back stage just before we started. Oh well, I hope she's not ill. And Tiger dear, please do sit up straight; we want the camera to catch you in the best light possible. And Alex, my, your shirt is behaving beautifully this evening all flat and they even got your little cowlick tamed as well! It's really too bad dear that you don't have your shoes properly polished, now that's going to look just awful on camera but you just keep your feet down there on the floor and the coffee table might hide your dusty, scuffed shoes. RG are you ready to inspire us with some great reverse mortgage tips and give us the latest on the Seaview investment club? Before RG could answer, they were counting Beverly down back to live air.

"Well here we are again friends, I trust everyone is enjoying their tea and evening in Seaview? Such a fun book to learn about but now I have my main guests here tonight to tell you all about the new listings here at Seaview. So take out your pad of paper and pen and take notes as I'm sure you have friends who will want to visit and possibly buy!" Just as she started in with me and Harvey's listing, there was a loud banging coming from back stage and then a huge crash. Beverly attempted to talk over it but out onto the set burst Stinky and

172

she was as fiery mad as her pant suit is red. "Started the show I see!" she said as she shoved RG over and sat down on the sofa's end. "I'll just introduce myself, I'm Share Shelton with Winterfrost Real Estate, Clinton's premier agent. I was here on time but *someone* locked me in the ladies room back stage and apparently everyone around here is deaf, as I have been banging on that door for a good 15 minutes now. Finally, I broke open the door using a hammer I found in the bathroom's maintenance closet. Anyway, I have a spectacular new bungalow listing here at Seaview and it has two bedrooms, a---"

Beverly cut her off, "Yes, well so nice of you to finally join us Share! I don't know why you had a problem with our rest room's door; we've never had that issue come up. Although it is funny, when I was a contestant in the Miss America pageant the same darn thing happened to that willful Miss New Jersey. By accident, she too, got locked in the ladies room. But Share, I guess you wouldn't know too much about beauty pageants now would you dear?" she said while looking her up and down. "Well, we all make do the best we can with what we have and move gaily forward with confidence and enthusiasm! Now don't we folks?" the audience burst into applause. "The show started some time ago but I'm not surprised you are tardy. Share you don't seem to ever be on time; certainly not when it comes to showing units for your clients here at Seaview. You know, I used to do a wonderful time management segment on my old TV show and folks, I think we might just revive that segment on this show so people such as Share can learn the importance of managing one's time and obligations properly. It is just common courtesy after all, not to keep others

173

waiting. Anyway, yes Share does have a new listing, the Menendez's bungalow I think it is?

Unfortunately, Share lost her other listing in the towers to me but now that's all water under the bridge, isn't it Share? Oh my!" Beverly exclaimed with wide eyes while looking Share up and down. "I guess you didn't read my memo that each guest receives on proper show attire. I specifically ask all of the ladies on my show to wear full length evening gowns and gentlemen to dress in a tux. It makes things so much more festive and fun and we all greatly enjoying dressing up here at Seaview. It's a pity you had to show up wearing a pant suit. Now personally, I find pants on women just so unbecoming. Well, at any rate you did make the effort to wear something more suitable for the evening, what with the red and sequins. Red seems so appropriate for you and your personality Share. But don't you think you ought to put away those bright hues now? You know once we get past a certain age, it is time to trend towards a more subtle and refined color palette. Why you might find my segment next week on coordinating one's fall wardrobe palette helpful Share. Anyway, you've interrupted us here on live television but don't let us stop you Share, go ahead and give us the details of your yummy new listing, we are all ears!"

If looks could kill, but Share quickly turned toward the camera and spouted off her listing's details concluding, "I know you all are going to just love it as much as the Menendezs do! Please make an appointment to visit and as always, if you or any of your family and friends needs premier real estate service here in Seaview or in Clinton, just know I am merely a phone call away to helping you achieve all of your housing and lifestyle dreams."

Beverly smiled and tilted her head slightly, "Oh, Share thank you for that introduction to your listing. Share will be on site tomorrow, with the rest of our agents here from noon until five for anyone who wants to tour and see firsthand the new offerings."

Share looked confused, "What? No, I have a premier open house tomorrow in the Beaumont for my new $1.6 million dollar listing on Divot Drive. That's just off the golf course and I'll be there from two thirty until three tomorrow, please stop by."

Beverly shook her head while smiling, "No, I'm afraid someone failed to read the required open house memo that she was sent last week. Oh my Share! What *are* we going to do? I'm afraid that is another infraction on your lengthy chart but we'll talk about that off-camera. Folks, Share will be here onsite tomorrow from noon until five as required. Okay, so Tiger Conley why don't you tell us about your cute listing?" Share was completely flustered and fuming as Tiger began to yammer.

# 24

Tiger was wrapping up her pitch, "So ya'll can see this is a real deal condo there in the Towers! So get y'alls butts on over there tomorrow. I'm gonna be cookin' up some of my mama's famous deep fried chicken chili with refried beans in it. Ya'll know I'm gonna be keeping that patio door open, 'cause what with all them beans being eaten it's gonna be a pooter factory!" She then burst into a loud chuckle and leaned over so the camera got a full-on shot of her huge tit valley. "Boy howdy are we gonna have us some kick ass fartin' fun out there tomorrow, I'll see ya'll there!"

Beverly's eyes bugged out, "Oh my, oh no! We do NOT curse on television much less in public. Oh Tiger that is just not acceptable. And that chili comment on live television, really! I mean, really. Oh well, you *are* festive and I'm sure our Seaview family can appreciate that. At least you wore a floor length evening gown of some sort. Well, I'm not sure, is it a dress or is that some kind of negligee you are wearing, Tiger? First Share insists on wearing pants in a street walker's shade of red and now you Tiger, apparently you do not know your nightgowns from your evening gowns. Oh my! See folks, what a crazy world it is out there, outside of Seaview! This just reminds us of why we are here, now doesn't it? And you know it is awfully kind of these people to come and share details with us about their listings here at Seaview and take the time tomorrow to be here with us. Let's give them a round of applause for that. We can help them with grooming tips on another show." With that she winked while the audience burst into applause on cue. Before anyone could speak, Beverly suggested

RG fill everyone in on her reverse mortgage tips and investment club. The camera man tried to zoom in on RG but since Share had bumped her down the sofa and was perched on the end it was difficult to get a full frame close up of RG.

RG's deep baritone was droning away, "And after you've checked out doing a reverse mortgage with me, your exclusive Seaview mortgage provider, you can find out more about my Seaview members-only investment club. It's a very special and exclusive club just for Seaview residents with a one time member pool contribution and awesome potential investment returns. Just last month, the average club member's returns were over 30 percent and with our special financial planning, most members can bank their returns without paying taxes. So contact me today to find out more, you don't want to miss out! My next VIPs-only informational meeting will be Tuesday at 4 p.m. at the general meeting room in the activities building. Contact my personal assistant Eddie for more details." This she ended with a smug, thin lipped smile.

Share quickly cut in before Beverly could take control, "Oh, so you have an investment club here at Seaview? My, how Bernie Madoff of you, I'm sure. And I just want to point out to everyone here, that *MISS* RG here is wearing a man's suit. So apparently Beverly, you have some kind of amnesia in your old age, as your frequent guest here comes on your show in full drag at least once a month. You know, I think you need to read that other old bag's book about 80 making you young or something Beverly, because you appear to be slipping."

Beverly began to sputter but RG cut in, "Excuse me, Share is it? I happen to be a regular VIP guest on this very important show and as such I am not required to follow regular guest dress protocol. In fact, this white suit is my signature look, my brand. If you knew anything about marketing and how influential VIPs get to their level of greatness, then you would know that they all have signature looks, such as mine. It's a pity you are so uninformed about that or my exclusive investment opportunity club. I really pity you as surely you do not know when you are in the presence of greatness in the making. Now perhaps you can shut your pie hole and let our host here lead her show. It is HER show after all." With that RG gave another smug thin lipped smile this time while looking towards Beverly.

Beverly recovered her placid smile, "Oh yes, well thank you RG. It's always so pleasant to have an old pro on the show with me who knows how things work here. Okay, I think we are going to break now and when we come back you all get your pen and paper ready again as I'm going to be demonstrating a simply scrumptious salad recipe in our kitchen for you!" Applause cued and fade to commercial. It was then that RG pushed Stinky off the sofa's end and she landed flat on her ass. "Oh me, you fell. I'm sorry I didn't see you there but then again, you weren't supposed to sit on the sofa's end, as this is my permanent spot when I'm on the show for my special segment." An aide quickly stepped over to help a shocked Share get up. They sat Stinky right next to me on the sofa. Aaaahhhh, the scent of Stinky up close and personal. Meanwhile, Beverly ignored everything and was off to the kitchen set with the producer and make-up lady in tow.

# NO REST

Live on air again and this time was Beverly's cooking segment which she did wearing her feather boa gown along with a green "Seaview is Cooking" apron. Today's yummy special was a "Ginger Ale Fruit Salad." This involved a pound of marshmallows, two cups of ginger ale, a half cup of maraschino cherries, a cup of mayonnaise, a can of peaches with syrup and a cup of Cool Whip; optional was a half cup of crushed canned pineapple. Beverly proceeded to melt the marshmallows with the peach syrup. Then once cooled, she showed the audience how to mix in the Cool Whip, mayonnaise, cherries, peaches and ginger ale. "Feel free to substitute some Fresca if you don't happen to care for ginger ale. I find that Fresca gives it a nice tangy taste." Into a shallow metal tray the glop went, "You just spread this out evenly, and pop it in the freezer. Why the next morning, it will look just like this!" She said removing a tray from the set's freezer. "Isn't that just lovely? Such a tasty treat, straight from your freezer! Now we simply cut it into squares like so, place one square on an attractive salad or dessert plate such as the one I am using. You can garnish with a teaspoon of mayonnaise and a single pecan like so, or get really wild and put a dab of Cool Whip on it with a cherry. Yummy! And you know these are simply delicious, ready-made refreshments for whenever company stops by, or for a side dish with your dinner or for dessert. I just know you'll love them as much as I do!" Wink at camera. "Now be sure and be here next week with me when I'll be making my famous recipe from 1965, my candied ham and banana surprise *entre*! You'll want to check and make sure your pantry has a nice canned ham at the ready. And now while we go to break, please take a moment to read on your screen this little gem I used to use quite frequently back in the day when I hosted *The Ladies Hour with Beverly Ann LeFaye*."

As the camera pulled back I saw on a monitor, "Beverly's Recipe for Friendship" which was: *1 cup of friendship, 1 cup of thoughtfulness, creamed together with a pinch of powdered tenderness, very lightly beaten in a bowl of loyalty. Add: 1 cup of faith, 1 cup of hope, 1 cup of charity and a dash of good manners. Be sure to add a spoonful of gayety that sings and the ability to laugh at little things! Moisten with sudden tears of heartfelt joy and serve repeatedly. Serves: All!*

There was a quick commercial break and then back to Beverly who was now on her craft segment set. "Friends, don't you find it so unpleasant to visit the gas station these days? Remember back when, they would fill up your car for you, check the tire pressure and oil, wash the windows and all with a smile? Oh my how things have changed. Why even here at Seaview, our service station is forbidden by state law from offering you full service." Sigh. "So we must make do and this led me to create this week's useful and attractive craft project. When you pull into the gas station, you have to unscrew the gas cap and hold that icky gas pump handle. It is certainly unsanitary and often leaves a residual gasoline odor on your hands, which is most unattractive.

Well folks, I've solved our little problem. Gas mitts! You can start making these now and have them ready for all of your friends and family for Christmas! First, you purchase an attractive oven mitt, like I have here. You want the kind that your whole hand slides into. You will also need to buy Velcro strips. Now these can be sewn on like I have done here or you can use your glue gun to attach the Velcro strips to the mitt like so. Oh and speaking of glue guns, don't forget to tune in next week when I will have fellow Seaviewers Dottie and Elsie back with me again for more Glue Gun Madness! You won't want to miss out on that one; it's always a fun time with those two around. Anyhow, you are going to prepare an appropriate sized square of needlepoint canvas and then create a personalized design. Now you can see I've made one here for someone whose initials are AC and one for someone with the initials WB. These two do not know it but the other day I spotted them at our Seaview service station filling up their car and doing so without a gas mitt or even using the paper towels! And all before attending a public event! Well my friends won't have to suffer through that ordeal ever again. Aren't these mitts just lovely? I find the simple pleasure of needle pointing is just so overlooked these days, now don't you? Anyway, you are going to attach your personalized needlepoint square to the back side of your oven mitt via the Velcro. This way the personalized needlepoint monogram can be easily removed and you pop your gas mitt in the washer for a thorough cleaning. Just keep this attractive gas mitt in your car's trunk and there you are, no more mess when filling up your car!

Now for a quick break and I'll be back with tonight's Lovely Lady Moment. So the gentlemen out there can go mix up a nice new pitcher of tini's for the Mrs. while we are having our moment!" Close up on her sicky smile and wink and fade to commercial.

Beverly moved back to her chair in the living room set and they counted her down, "I'm back and here with my friends again! As I promised, here is this week's Lovely Lady Moment. When you get frazzled in your busy day with all of your duties and obligations, just take a moment to stop and refresh. Hum a happy tune, gaze at a lovely blue bird, think of how nice it feels once all of your silver has been thoroughly polished, or recall your mother's delicious apple pie. It's guaranteed to put a smile on your face! No need for all those silly yoga classes the young women are now going to. All that deep breathing, skin tight clothing, lewd positions and perspiring in public! No, we Seaview ladies know better, now don't we? All you need is a quiet lady moment of inner reflection.

You know tonight's show is an excellent example of this. When Share burst out on our set tonight and interrupted everyone, she needed to have a lovely lady moment, now didn't she? I could have reacted just as immaturely as Share but I chose not to. Why is that you may ask? Well, I've trained myself to simply stop and have a quiet lovely lady moment! Tonight while Share was disrupting things, I simply sat here calmly in my chair and I recalled an absolutely delicious turkey dinner I made, oh it must have been 20 or so Thanksgivings ago. I'm sure you too have a favorite holiday dinner moment yourself, where it all turned out so perfect and smelled so yummy! Well that's where I briefly went while Share chose to make such a scene.

Now of course this example is not meant to embarrass Share, we wouldn't do that now would we? It's just meant to help illustrate my point. I thank Share for such poor decorum and behavior on her part as it is wonderful unexpected inspiration and a chance for all of us to grow and learn, together. This is the magic of live television, these unexpected moments of inspiration. Next week's Lovely Lady Moment segment is going to be longer and I am going to have my special guest, Bunny Hueser here. She has a simply wonderful charm bracelet collection that she is going to share with us. So I know you all will want to dig around in your jewelry boxes and have yours out too. It's sure to start a new Seaview dressing fad! And Share, I know you are obviously a big jewelry fan and I think, yes, right there on your arm aren't you wearing a charm bracelet? Bill, see if you can get a close up on her bracelet for the viewers to see. Yes, that is a sort of charm bracelet. A big gold dollar symbol is it and oh, a religious cross, both together on….hummm, a bit gaudy and crass for my taste but still a charm bracelet! Now see, we do have our fingers on the pulse for new fashion trends here at Seaview! Okay, so don't miss next week's show.

Well I see we are just about out of time tonight, so I want to thank all of our guests for appearing on tonight's show and let's get our special audience dance winners up here on our little dance stage now. Okay, now we have bubbles and music and let's all enjoy this old song and a dance and I'll see you all next week! Beverly, grabbed my hand and dragged me over to the dance floor. The band was playing *Sentimental Journey* and Beverly insisted on waltzing around with me. There were selected audience members also on the stage waltzing around. Then I noticed Tiger had jumped on the floor and cut in on some old couple. She had hiked her dress/nightgown whatever, up to her waist and was twerking with some old gray haired man who was beaming with joy while his ancient wife looked on scowling. Beverly caught a glimpse of Tiger's dance moves, dropped my hands and took off across the dance floor while shouting at the camera man, "Bill pull back and focus on the band and the other dancers! Bill move that camera now! Tiger you need to leave the dance floor, immediately! Tiger do you hear me? I simply cannot believe, I mean this is completely...."

# 25

After the show wrapped, Beverly was busy lecturing Tiger and Stinky was trying to butt in so she could argue with Beverly. Stinky claimed Beverly locked her in the bathroom and was threatening legal action. RG held an impromptu meeting with some of her investment club members who had been in the audience. I was looking for a path through the crowd for the nearest exit when Wanda and Percy found me. That's how I got dragged out to the Seaview Bar & Grill. It was around 9:30 when we arrived at the place and the only thing hopping was the bar. I noted the early bird dinner started at 3 p.m. and ended daily at 6 p.m., my guess would be that was their rush time. The bar was filled with elderly people soaking up the suds by the gallon. We found a table and the waitress informed us that dinner was no longer being served but we could order from the bar's appetizer menu. I didn't really care, I wanted to go home, scour off the nasty scent of Stinky's perfume, scrub the remaining orange goo off my face and hang out with Clyde but that was not to be. Wanda immediately ordered a pitcher of slushies, with extra rum and Percy ordered enough appetizers to fill the table from end to end.

"Didn't I tell you that show was too unreal to believe? And did you see Beverly's time warp dress and then she did that cooking demo in that dress with the apron? I'm telling you that woman is living in another decade. Wanda and I could not even look at each other and still we were laughing nonstop Alex! I did find out from my other seatmate that Beverly's sister Ellen is known around Seaview for her anti Beverly attitude and she used to be a veterinarian in Clinton. Too strange, an ex-animal doctor is now a nurse's aide in Seaview." Percy said as he immediately snatched up the first plate of appetizers to arrive and started stuffing his mouth with some kind of potato cheese things which were floating in a plate of some kind of oil. Gross.

"Don't sneer," Wanda said with her mouth full, "they got the mini pizza thangs coming and you can eat them. Here have a long sip of your slushy and let the cool crushed ice relax your mind baby. Damn if them bitches just weren't all up in each other's business tonight! I'm telling you just a bit more and we could'a called it the Seaview White Women World of Rasslin!" Wanda took a huge pull on her slushy drink and popped a potato slime thing in her mouth. "Honey, when that Patty lady started up with calling Beverly 80 something, I thought I was gonna bust a rib. Old Beverly's face, did you see it?" With that Wanda and Percy collapsed into a peel of laughter.

I took another sip of my slushy and quietly commented, "A better book idea would be something like <u>Twenty is the New Ten</u>, now there's a concept Mushy and Joocey could get behind."

Wanda noticed I wasn't laughing, "What, you didn't see any of these things going on while you were on the set? Don't worry, cause Percy taped it and you can watch it. Now that is some entertainment TV they got happening here. And baby, when old red Stinky bitch came storming out, I just about up and died right there. I had to laugh into my arm to keep quiet, I thought they was gonna throw me out. But the very best part was when old man Boss Hog knocked red bitch

186

off that sofa, just pushed her flat out on her bony ass. You probably heard us howling then, 'cause honey there wasn't any holding back from then on!" The plate of pizza things arrived and Wanda scooped up two, tossed a couple on a small plate for me and commenced draining her slushy glass.

I took a bite; the pizza thing wasn't so bad. "I am glad to know you two were so entertained. I however, could have done quite well not being a part of that show or whatever it is. You should have seen backstage, Stinky actually sprayed her perfume thing right on me, in my mouth!"

Wanda's eyes wrinkled up while she popped a pizza thing in her mouth, "Ahhum, I thought I smelled me something nasty and not the new nasty either. I'm telling you that is cat fight central over there. But seriously, what is the deal with this Ellen being a vet and now working as Beverly's step and fetch? Makes no sense. A good veterinarian can earn themselves some serious bank and she looks all animal and earthy, unlike her sister Beverly. I'm telling you, this whole place just doesn't add up. And you heard old Stinky calling out RG as a Bernie Madoff, and you know that's gotta be true! I don't know no investments that bring in no 30 percent monthly returns, that's just crazy. No, I'm telling you there is all kinds of crazy going on right here in this seniors-only, honky town."

I took another sip of slushy, a bit heavy on the rum but not bad, "Yes it's all bat shit here in honky town Wanda, no doubt about it. But, we are going to do our open house, sell Harvey's place, and be on our way."

Wanda ignored me and began speaking directly to Percy who was busy working on an appetizer plate full of stuffed mushrooms, "Ah ha Percy, we got us a five hour open house out here tomorrow and you can best bet I'm gonna be spending a good portion of that time collecting me some clues. Cause you know I got a sixth sense about these here things and something is all catty ca-ca out here in Seaview." Percy nodded while chewing.

"Oh god," I exhaled, "you are correct we have five long hours here tomorrow. Who in the hell does open houses for five hours and in a limited access, gated community like this? It's insane. So with that happy event in mind, I am going to say good night to you both, here's a 20 for my portion and Wanda I'll pick you up tomorrow around 11:15." I got up to leave, they protested a bit but realized I was not yielding and so I escaped. But not before Wanda tossed me my monogrammed gas mitt which caused all of us to burst out laughing. I was back at my little ranch as fast as my two door beater would carry me, petting Clyde and using every kind of soap I had in the house to try and remove Stinky's stench.

Tomorrow rolled around far too fast and I dragged Clyde out for a long walk through the neighborhood. I noted Kackie and Rick Bendle's new development sign was now implanted in the skinny lawn next to the rotting Conner Hasps Factory. Oh shit, the jackals were coming, the jackals were coming! Their enormous, colorful sign informed me it was to be the premier building of the "New and Improved Southtown District or So-Town!" I guess they chose an official name and a corporate cutesy nickname as well for us, how kind.

Once I had Clyde walked, peed, kibbled, and back in his spot on the bed, I locked up the ranch, made sure my open house crap was in the trunk and headed off to the Highmont to pick up Wanda.

She was waiting out front of her bungalow dressed in a just-from-church, billowing pumpkin orange dress. "Damn this is a first, me waiting on you!" She said as she got in and dropped her box of mortgage bunk in the back seat. We got us an appointment later, gonna go visit this vet out near Lexi's who might know someone who can take Sammy. That poor horse can't see Alex and he sure as shit can't be staying in my yard, he's chewed up everything back there! Lexi finally called me back this morning. Bitch is out of town and didn't even tell us. She couldn't talk long, cause she's in Europe and her calling plan costs a fortune there. Said she's got some commission there for some kind of sister city installation art project. I don't know, some new art thang she's going to be doing. She has to kiss some European butt and get them to hire her as their Clinton art ambassador or some kind of shit like that. Damn that girl gets around. But she could've told us she was leaving, much less going out of the country. Anyway, she can't take Sammy but she gave me the vet's name, he's some old time friend of hers. He asked me to take some pictures of Sammy and said we can stop by after this open house today and he'll let us know what he can do. Now I'm telling you, that horse has got to go! And you can best bet that Miz Lyla and Ethel sure as shit ain't helping me find Sammy no home. Nope, Miz Lyla was at church this morning, ducking around me at the after service buffet, acting all busy like she couldn't see me. Humph. She best be ducking, old lady put some fool blind horse in my yard for temporary keeping and then don't have another word to say about nothing."

Wanda continued her diatribe and soon enough we had gone through the Seaview gate and I was pulling into assigned space number seven. "The good news is I don't have put out any A-boards Wanda, they don't allow them. The bad news is I have no idea how we are going to stay awake for five hours." This I said as we passed through the automatic doors and headed over to the front desk to sign in. Pamela was on duty and all smiles. She called Harvey's unit but there was no answer. "Well, I guess Mr. Malloy stepped out early today. He knows today is the open house, so I'm sure it is okay for you all to go on up, just sign in here please." Pamela said while she hung up the phone and wiped off the marble counter top with a white cloth. Beverly must be on patrol but good these days.

Off to the South Tower elevators we went, this time serenaded by a musical version of Wham's *Wake Me Up*. The only thing big about that lame 1980s hit was their boy bouffant hairdos. "Least they got the lambs all back home now. I don't hear any bah-bah-ing in this pom-pom song." Wanda said as she rolled her eyes and pushed the button for Harvey's floor. We reached Harvey's door and I knocked but there was no answer, just the sound of Ralph squawking.

Great, five hours in an open house with a squawking parrot. I had not thought of this. Agggh! I used my key copy and unlocked Harvey's door. The TV was blaring away with a *Family Feud* rerun. Ralph was really wild, his eyes pin wheeling, lots of squawking and flapping going on in his cage. We put our stuff down on the kitchen bar's counter and Wanda went over to talk to Ralph while I started turning on the lights. "How's Mr. Green, the potty mouth parrot of Seaview doing today? You look tuckered out honey, too much game show action going on here for you Mr. Ralph? What you and Harvey do, stay up all night?" I was turning on the living room lights and walking toward the TV to look for the remote to turn off the damn game show. Out of the corner of my eye I spied Harvey in his recliner. His eyes were closed and his skin was very grey. I let out a gasp and yep, once I touched Harvey's arm I knew it, he was dead. Oh fuck, not again!

Once Wanda clued into what I'd found, she called the front desk and asked for the police, a medic, whatever, letting them know we had a stiff in Unit 504. While waiting for chaos to ensue, Wanda took a closer look at Harvey. "Ah ha, you are correct, this man is stone dead, no doubt about it. I wonder how long he's been hanging here like this and poor Ralph over there all concerned. Look Alex, Harvey's mouth is open and he's got food crumbs on his lips and all over his lap. What do you think that is all about? There's a plate on the floor. How long do you think he's been here like this?"

"I don't know Wanda but he's dead. This open house is off and the listing goes back to Beverly and company, so we are really out of here. Say our goodbyes and leave this bizarre honky town as you refer to it, behind us."

"Mmmm, I don't know about this Alex. It's too strange, old Harvey just up and kicking, crumbs all over himself, it doesn't make sense. And who is gonna take care of Ralph here? How long has this bird been here by himself?" Ralph gave Wanda a little chirp and she moved over to his cage and stroked his beak through the cage. "Humm, from the looks of his water and food dishes, Ralphy here has been alone for some time, unless his bowls were not kept full but knowing how much Harvey loved old Ralph, I'm guessing his dishes were always full. Oh, Ralph it's too sad, your daddy has flown the coop green bird."

Ralph tilted his head to the side and then let out a loud stream, "Bitch, bitch, Beverly the bitch!" Wanda's eyes bugged a bit, "Why do you think potty mouth Ralph is talking about Beverly Alex?"

I held up my hand, "Don't go there, leave it be. Like I said, we are done here. They can all enjoy themselves here in Seaview and you and me are back to Clinton and doing our thing. Which happens to be, selling real estate and securing loans for people Wanda, NOT playing junior detective."

"Ah, humm." She mumbled as she took a closer look at Harvey's body. "Get me my handbag baby and hurry." I shook my head but went to the kitchen counter and brought her back her 50 pound orange pocket book (handbag my ass). Wanda dug through her bag and pulled out an unused plastic sandwich bag. She opened it and took a pen and scrapped off some of the food crumbs on Harvey's lips into the sandwich bag, sealed it up and put it in the vortex better known as her pocket book. She then looked up and smiled at me as we heard the rush of people coming down the hall and opening the door.

# 26

First to arrive were the Seaview paramedics, who immediately set about making sure Harvey was indeed dead. Wanda quizzed them about how long he'd been dead, what did they make of the food crumbs, etc.... They mostly bustled about and did not respond to her questions. Then sunshine and sweetness arrived with Pamela in tow, "Oh this is just too dreadful, another passing this week! How awful for you and Wanda to have to find this! And here you were all ready for your big open house. Such a shame. You boys are going to get him over to the mortuary right now. Pamela, call the office and get them to pull Mr. Malloy's emergency contact file. I'll have to call his son right away. You know I can't say I'm too surprised he has passed away. What with his hateful heart and foul mouth, why it's just a wonder he hung around this long.

Oh this is a real pity Alex, you finally had his place looking somewhat presentable. You know, I'm going to see if I can pull some strings here and let you stay on as the co-listing agent on this place Alex. I'll be a sport and pay you a five percent referral fee when it closes. After all the work you've put into to this listing, it just doesn't seem fair to have it all turn over to me. You are such a conscientious agent and do try to observe all of our rules here. Yes, that's exactly what I'm going to do for you Alex, don't you fret. Why once they have this dirty old man's body cleared out, I'll get Carlos up here with some nice Lysol spray for a quick cleaning. We'll still have the open house! You and Wanda just go ahead and get set up and stay here. I'm going to follow the body and get things all squared away at the mortuary. I'll come back before five to have you sign the co-listing agreement and we'll just be all fine and dandy!" She then smiled and gave a little sigh as the paramedics loaded Harvey's body onto the gurney cart.

Ralph began to franticly move around his cage while squawking up a storm. He was clearly upset they were taking Harvey away. Wanda went over to his cage to try and soothe him. Beverly shook her head, "Oh, that noisy potty mouth bird! Why it won't be too soon to have you out of here as well. You know, I wonder if we should just let him loose on the balcony, get him to fly away?" She said giving first me and then Wanda a questioning look to which Wanda gave her a stony stare right back. "Well, I guess I should just call the animal shelter and see if someone can come take him away." To that Ralph let out a loud retort, "Big bitch! Big bitch!" Beverly's eyes flared, "Or we do have our after care for pets now available, you dirty little creature! Perhaps it might be best for you and your disgusting human to share in the eternal here-after together! It's such a shame that Mr. Malloy's remains can be interred here at Seaview. Perhaps his son will see that it is best to take his ashes elsewhere. I mean really, I don't think Mr. Malloy is quite cut out for eternity here in our Seaview community. It's just not proper if you ask me. I sure hope Mr. Malloy likes it hot because I'm sure where he is heading now is just broiling." Beverly then shook her head again and followed the paramedics and Harvey's body out the door.

Wanda's eyes were narrowing, "Did you hear what that old bitch was saying Alex?"

I groaned, "Oh, I know! We still have to do the open house. Some nerve she has, she'll *give* me the listing for a fucking five percent referral fee when the going referral rate is a minimum 25 percent! Like I'm goin--"

"No fool! What that old bat said about Ralph here! Bitch gonna try and kill him too. I am not letting that old lady nowhere near this here bird. No way, no sir! Ralph, you are coming home with me today. Temporarily, you understand? No way am I leaving this poor green bird with that old witch lurking around. I think old lady killed your Harvey, Ralph. I really do think that old syrupy lady is a killer. Alex, Seaview has got itself a serial killer named Beverly on the loose!"

"Please not this Wanda. I hear you about Ralph and all but Beverly killing people? Let's just not go there. And you are seriously going to take Ralph home with you today, for real?"

Wanda nodded her head, "Hell yes I am! You can come watch your *Wheel* at Wanda's honey and then we'll find you a new home. Damn, I already got a blind horse that I gotta find a home for, what's a small bird like Ralph gonna do? He's a piece of cake compared with Sammy and all the food that Sammy is eating."

Ralph perked up a bit and began to move up and down along his main dowel.

Like clockwork Carlos appeared with a whole cart of cleaning supplies. He almost asphyxiated us with Lysol spray, then he ran the vacuum over all the carpets. I kept telling him it was all good but he wouldn't hear of it, "Oh no, Mrs. LeFaye will be back up here checking and there's no way I can afford no minus marks from her today."

Carlos finished up and our open house was now an hour and some into its scheduled time. Slowly the old geezers started trickling in. They were all agog over Harvey's death, news travels fast in Seaview. They nosed around while wondering out loud if the son would be taking the TV set with him or did I think he might want to sell it? Seems a Mrs. Sylvia Farkle had taken it upon herself to test out Harvey's bed and deemed his mattress just right for her back. "It would be such a shame, to have that perfectly good mattress just go to waste. And you know that's just what happens when people pass here. The Goodwill truck hauls most of it away before we can even get a look at the things. Now some folks are superstitious and all about a dead person's mattress but not me. So could you please pass my name and number along to his son, along with my condolences of course. I'd really like to take this mattress off his hands, it would make emptying out this place so much easier for him in his time of grief and all, don't you think?"

Think? Sounds to me like the Seaview vultures don't waste time swooping in. "Certainly Mrs. Farkle, I'll pass your note along to Mr. Malloy's son. Thank you for coming to our open house today and do enjoy your afternoon." I was guiding her toward the front door. She slowed up next to some other old biddies at the kitchen counter. They were looking over the mortgage flyers Wanda had set out and one very sour old lady in a dusty rose, velour track suit loudly commented, "You know it's a real pity the way they sell real estate these days, don't you agree Sylvia? I mean really, these two don't even have any candies set out, much less doughnuts and coffee. I hear that Tiger agent down on the first floor has some chili cooking.  Come on girls, let's take our business down there."  Yes, why don't you move your "business" along downstairs and hopefully Tiger's chili won't soil your Depends too much.

"You ladies enjoy your tour and don't forget to visit Share Shelton's bungalow listing that's also open today.  Rumor has it she hired caterers and is serving all kinds of appetizers."  I smiled as they shuffled out.

Wanda gave me the once over, "Stinky hired a caterer?"  I nodded.  "Humph, I'd say that Tiger has got old smelly by the tail!  Anyhow, I need to find us a portable cage for Ralph.  You think old man Malloy had one?  We'll have to come back later for his big cage here I suppose.  But there's got to be a portable cage, that's what would be used to take Ralph to the vet."

"Wanda are you seriously taking Ralph with us when we leave?  I mean, I suppose you are right and we have to find someone to look after him but we could find someone here, maybe Ethel?"

"Ethel my ass.  She'd be polishing his feathers and probably wouldn't let the bird chill.  Let me tell you honey, I know all about living with *the Ethel* and I don't wish that on this here bird for nothing.  Okay, now help me hunt up his portable cage.  I know there's one in here somewhere" she said as she opened the hall linen closet.  Wanda was looking in the back of the closet on the floor when she pulled out a small cardboard box, on top was written "Seaview Case."  She opened up the top and inside was a spiral notebook filled with dates and comments that appeared to track all of the Seaview deaths and admittances into Seaview Critical Care for the past year. It had notations as to Beverly's whereabouts for each date. It was clearly a log attempting to show a pattern linking Beverly to all the residents who either passed away or became sick and had to be transferred to the critical care unit and thus give up their condo. Sale prices of each unit were also noted in Harvey's surprisingly neat scrawl. Also in the box was a manila folder of *Clinton Observer* articles (some photocopied from the library), all about Beverly. The articles tracked Beverly from her young Miss America pageant days, to her being named hostess of her own TV show, mentions about her and her show in the media over the years, the cancellation of her show, her husband's obituary, and her growing role at Seaview. All there in chronological order.

Then like a ghost, there was Beverly, "Oh, there you two are! I've got my referral forms all ready for you Alex. What are you looking for down there? Almost time to wrap up our open house. You know I've found over the years Alex, that serving refreshments at an open house always brings in more traffic. I will say that Tiger Conley did indeed cook chili today. I'm afraid it's going to take days to air out that unit what with all of those spices she used but at least she did serve food. And I almost fainted when I popped in on Share's open and she had a caterer there serving formal appetizers and hot apple cider. Can you imagine? Must be the competition from Tiger got her goat. Anyway, what are you looking for down there in Mr. Malloy's closet?"

Wanda and I both were very startled but fortunately I was able to place the items back inside the box and shove it to the back of the closet all the while pretending to be searching for the bird cage. Wanda distracted Beverly by purposely knocking some towels on the floor.

"Oh my, fresh towels on the floor! Now there's a dilemma. Do they need to be re-laundered or just put back on the shelf? Why silly me, Mr. Malloy won't be using them again and anyway even if he were still among us, I'm sure that dirty old man wouldn't know the difference between freshly laundered towels and those that have picked up ickies on the floor. What exactly are you two doing?"

I stammered and Wanda cut in, "Well, we are taking Ralph home today so you all won't be bothered anymore by his offensive mouth. I'm going to find him a new home, unless Mr. Malloy's son wants him when he gets here. We are trying to find a portable bird cage for him. I'm sure Mr. Malloy has one, you know to carry the bird to the vet and all?"

Beverly nodded, "Why that is so wonderful of you to take that creature out of here Wanda. Really, I hope his potty mouth won't offend you too much while you find him a new home. I'm sure his son probably won't want that dirty bird but we'll find out. He's going to arrive the day after tomorrow to finish things up here. Such a relief, we won't have to deal with that old man anymore. You say you need a smaller, portable cage for the bird? You are right, one would think Harvey would have one of those but with him who knows. Why don't I help you. I'll look in his bedroom closet; you check the hall coat closet and Alex dear, you check the storage closet out on the balcony."

And that's just what we did. I found the prize, a smaller steel cage on rollers that we could wheel Ralph out to my car in. The cage part could lift off and easily fit in the back seat and the roller stand could go in my trunk. Beverly was pleased, "I just so love when things work out, as they always do! Alex here's our little referral form. You just sign and date. I'll get it all turned into the Seaview Board and to the multiple listing service tonight. You'll be the new co-listing agent with me. Normally, I wouldn't dare agree to give you a five percent referral fee but as we've discussed, you deserve it with all the work you've done with that miserable old man. This will be our little agreement and it will be such fun working together! I've never had a co-listing before but something tells me this is going to be a start of some great team work, now don't you agree? Anyhow, you go ahead and take that potty mouth bird and lock up and I am sure we'll all see each other soon. Make sure you both scrub your hands after handling that dirty bird, you know they carry diseases don't you? I'd love to stay and chat but duty calls and there are only so many hours in each day, now isn't that true?" She snapped up the paper I had signed and zipped out the door.

"Damn bitch ripping me off with the listing, five percent referral fee my ass. It should be me as the sole listing agent and if there were a referral fee it should be five percent going to her not the other way around. What could be worse, my co-listing with Share (see Volume One) or a co-listing with the Queen of Seaview? I guess I'll find out."

Wanda perked up, "Okay, look let's get Ralph in this portable cage and beat it. And we have to take that box with us. Did you see that stuff Alex? I told you I was right about things going on around here. It seems like our man Harvey was already on to it. I tell you, I have a sixth sense about this kind of shit. We gotta make sure we get this box out of here without anyone catching on—I can put some of Ralph's toys there on top so it looks like its all bird stuff we are taking."

I pondered telling Wanda that I thought we should leave the box and forget it all but in truth, now I was curious.

# 27

Ralph was excited to be in the car and leaving Seaview behind. The minute we pulled out of the gates, he let out a long stream of very loud squawks from the back seat where his cage was secured by a seat belt. This must be what parents with small children deal with every day. Sure reinforces my bright idea not to produce any rug rats. Eventually Ralph cooled down and I was soon turning off the interstate and following Wanda's directions to the South Clinton Farm Animal Clinic. The nondescript, white aluminum siding building is situated right next to a farm and has a gravel parking lot which was empty except for a dusty brown, Ford Bronco. "They finished up clinic hours at 4 p.m. today but the vet said he'd be here doing some work and for us to stop by." Wanda said as she got out of the car. "Crack the windows a bit for Ralph, I think he will be okay waiting here, won't you Ralph?" Ralph replied to her by pin wheeling his yellow eyes and lightly chirping. We knocked on the glass entry door.

A tall man somewhere around 60 or so came to the door, "Hi, I'm Dr. Boyd Baxter, and you must be Wanda?"

Inside we went and Wanda filled Dr. Baxter in on Sammy the horse and showed him the pictures of Sammy that were stored on her phone. "Yes, that's definitely an elderly horse and you say he's blind? That's probably some natural aging degeneration to his corneas, not uncommon in old horses. You say he's currently in your back yard, in Clinton? If the city gets wind of that, you are going to face some pretty steep fines. It'd be best to place him in a nice field for his final days. I know you are a friend of Lexi and you see I've got my farm right out behind the clinic here. If you can arrange to get Sammy here, I'll just take him for you and let him live out his final days here. It's a great thing you did, saving him. Otherwise, I'm sure he would have ended up at a kill lot and in a bottle of glue. Do you know anyone that can help you transport him here?"

Wanda appeared relieved, "Not off hand I don't but don't you worry, the old birds that had him delivered to me will be helping me figure out how to get him out here. Thank you so much, this is nice of you and I know Sammy will appreciate it and so will my back yard! You do mostly farm animals and all but I just got me a temporary parrot this afternoon. His owner passed away and I'm going to be looking after him until I can find him a good home. Would you be able to take a quick look at him, and sell me some bird food or whatever it is I should be feeding him?" Dr. Baxter agreed and Wanda went out to the car to get Ralph. While waiting, I told Dr. Baxter about the open house and where we were coming from.

He shook his head, "Oh, Seaview. God isn't that place just hell on earth? I'm dying right here on my farm and not in some prison like Seaview or else I'm not dying at all. I bet you know that Beverly LeFaye lady. She runs that place like it's her own North Korea. Have you come across her sister Ellen? Last I heard, Ellen was working out there as a nurse's aide. It's a real pity about her. For years, Ellen was a well known vet in Clinton and then there was the scandal and she lost her license. Such a shame, I never did quite figure that woman out. I wonder how she could even be remotely related to Beverly LeFaye. I'm not sure what pushed Ellen to do what she did but hey, we all have our own paths to walk." With that said, Wanda came back in. The bell hanging on the door knob jangled loudly setting Ralph off into a fresh round of squawks and, "Big bitch, big bitch. Damn fool!" This rant continued until Dr. Baxter calmed him down and started to look him over. "He seems in good health to me. You don't know who his regular vet is do you?" We shook our heads. "I'll bet you it's Robin States. She has the largest aviary vet practice in the area. Her clinic is located up near the interstate, east of Rosedale. I'd give her office a call tomorrow and see if Ralph here is one of their patients. I don't have any bird food here, as I don't actually include birds as part of my practice. You can feed him some sugar free dried fruits, veggies, raw pasta, a few pumpkin seeds but watch giving him too many seeds. You can pick those items up at the Clinton Co-op and that should tide you over until you can get in to see Robin. You'll want to make sure he doesn't have a chance to get out of the house, as his wings are not clipped. You can test and see if he's okay being out of the cage in your house. Maybe keep him loose in your bathroom, they like using the shower rod as a perch. Of course, whoever adopts him will want to get a larger cage for him to hang out in. I'm sure Robin can fill you in on all things bird world but from my cursory look, you have a healthy and very mouthy Red Lored Amazon parrot.

We were done and Wanda was relieved. "Okay, turn this car on the airport connector road over there. You and me are going by the Tiki Bar and have us a post open house, getting Sammy placed, saving Ralph, celebratory rum slushies and appetizers.

I wasn't so keen, "But we need to go by the Clinton Co-op and get food for Ralph and we can't leave Ralph in the car Wanda."

She held her hand up to me and pointed up the road, "Drive! Clinton Co-op stays open until 11 p.m. Ralph is coming in with us, sitting with us in his cage in the booth and we are gonna take a load off and relax our minds for a spell. Now move it." That said, she promptly started listening to voice mail messages and returning mortgage related phone calls as I drove toward the airport. The Tiki Bar is an aging drinkery that was opened probably around 1962 and time has stood still. It was one of the first airport floozy bars to sprout up around the then new Clinton Airport. It is sited right on the airport connector road which runs parallel to the interstate about one block away from the airport's entrance. The Tiki is the last stop for alcohol until you are actually inside the airport and through the entire search you over, under, sideways, down, security related drills.

I pulled in the gravel parking lot and there were about five or so cars parked, not too bad for an early Sunday evening I suppose. Wanda pointed at the box we took from Harvey's, indicating I should bring it inside. She promptly picked up Ralph's cage, hoisted her huge, orange pocket book over her shoulder and kept gabbing away on her cell. Inside the Tiki Bar, it is very dark with thousands of colored string lights shining and rattan and bamboo for miles. On the left side is a long polished wooden bar with vinyl turquoise bar stools which were filled to about a third of capacity; mostly air travelers, some with their luggage next to their bar stools. On the right side is a long wall of very large booths also upholstered in turquoise vinyl. Each booth has a mini palm leaf, thatched roof over it. Wanda knows the owners, so she just waived at them and picked out a booth. She put Ralph's cage on our booth's table and rummaged through her pocket book for a pen and paper. About five minutes later, the waiter brought over two big turquoise mugs in the shape of a smiling, pot bellied, Buddha. In each mug was a colorful straw, a bright umbrella, and a skewer stick with pineapple and maraschino cherries. Wanda smiled, mouthed thank you and pointed to her mouth. The waiter completely knew what she wanted and off he went. He didn't even bat an eye at Ralph sitting in his cage on top of the table. Ralph was completely entranced, his head cocked to the side looking all around. He was intrigued by the colored string lights and colored lanterns that were hanging off every available surface in this narrow, retro bar.

The waiter returned with a large platter of assorted Polynesian style appetizers. Wanda finally got off her phone, popped a coconut prawn in her mouth and tore open the box we stole from Harvey's. "Damn you are not kidding. While Harvey lived there, he kept long detailed records of all the deaths in Seaview, the dates and times. Look at these notes Alex, he's wondering what could make all these people have heart attacks. He's written it out plain as day. He thought Beverly was offing these old folks so she could get herself some new listings."

"I see his notes here and yes, Harvey appears to be establishing a pattern Wanda but there is zero evidence of anything. Nothing. There are dead bodies. Old people die every day and in a place like Seaview the death rates are even higher due to the demographics."

# NO REST

Wanda took a pull on her slushy and rolled her eyes, "There you go, taking all of the dick, out of Dick Tracy! Ralph, we are here sharing us some Buddha-love slushies with Mr. Wet Blanket himself. Alex, you gotta use your imagination. Didn't you watch yourself some *Romper Room* with that Miss Linda when you were little? You know, when she'd tell everyone to put on their imagination hats? Humph, must have been before your time. Look at it this way, you think Columbo ever solved a case accepting everything as fact like you are doing? I mean really, you gotta spread your wings and apply a little *Murder She Wrote* to this here information. Not the original old lady version but that new one they got with my woman Octavia starring in it. Now that is some serious mystery solving, you know that's true! Here, let's look at this file Harvey has of newspaper copies of Beverly LeFaye through the decades."

I passed her the newspaper file and tried out one of the fried clam strips. They weren't too bad, once I scraped off the sweet fried dough gunk. Ralph was making very content chortling/chirp murmurs and appeared to be hypnotized by the colored lights. "See this one," Wanda said holding up a photocopied page, "this is when Beverly took over that ladies show. It's all about how the other lady who was the host got too ill and tells how Beverly who was just subbing for the summer, will become the new full time host. It's talking about how the new show's name will be *The Ladies Hour with Beverly Ann LeFaye*. Humm, she looks younger then but you know her hair hasn't changed too much since 1964. Damn, she puts my mama's 1960s wigs to shame but good. That girl had some serious helmeted height going on, still does! The article talks about how Beverly was a finalist in the Miss America pageant in 1962 and she'll be bringing a fresher and younger approach to the noon time weekly show. You gotta hand it to her, bitch could work it. Work it but good honey. Look, these articles are all talking about how the show is taking off. Here's 1966, she's now the number one ranked show in the regional market, not just Clinton. Damn, back in the day, Miss Beverly was a mini-Oprah in the making! Here, she's Clinton's television personality of the year 1970. In 1973 she is presenting some award to the Clinton homemaker of the year. Homemaker of the year, you sure don't hear 'bout that shit anymore. What did they do, have a contest to see who could bake the best cookies while waxing their kitchen linoleum? Aup, here in 1976 is an article questioning if Beverly's show is still relevant to women today. Here's a 1978 one mentioning her show's rating are tanking. And here's the end in 1979, the show is cancelled.

This article is about her new show *Women Are Talking* and here is another article about its cancellation in 1981. And look Alex, an article about her husband, Leon LeFaye, passing away and a copy of his obituary. Says he was a long time Clinton TV Producer and Executive and responsible for her popular show. Says he passed peacefully in his sleep. He was only 57 years old. She's his only surviving relative, no kids, no siblings, no family. So 1984 and Beverly is a single lady. These pages appear to be quick mentions of Beverly at charity functions in the late 1980s and 90s. But here we go! This is January 2002 and it's all about Ellen Hansen, owner of Simple Animal Care, and how they are temporarily suspending her veterinary license in order to investigate complaints about animal neglect at her clinic. Here's some more articles after that about Ellen, showing she has lost her license and is facing charges for animal cruelty and neglect. Looks like she was sentenced to eight months in the big house, but that got waived in favor of a stay at the Clinton Psychiatric Hospital and Asylum. So Ellen was in the loony bin. I wonder what that woman did? You think she was beating the animals?"

I sighed, "Well Nancy Drew, I don't think we'll find out from those articles. Dr. Baxter alluded to Ellen being involved in a scandal but he didn't reveal much more. I think Harvey was just an old and lonely man who spent his time trying to dig up some dirt on his nemesis Beverly."

Wanda took a long pull on her straw, "Ahh, hum, yeah well you think that then. Look here, a big article from 2005 announcing old Beverly will be the new Seaview Community Recruitment Director and help revamp their real estate practices model. See there, she's making her power grab and turning Seaview into her own cash cow."

Wanda's phone rang and in no time she was figuring out loan payments for a buyer who was making an offer on a property.

# 28

The investigative pow-wow at the Tiki Bar ended shortly after Wanda's call. She had to go to her office to pull up a client file and re-run the numbers. Seems another buyer had been duped by their real estate agent and agreed to look at listings above their pre-approval cap. Naturally they liked the more expensive property and now wanted to see if Wanda could work some kind of miracle so they could be pre-approved at a higher price point in order to purchase it. Their agent had led them to believe that this should be something Wanda could easily work out for them. Always the sign of a stellar agent when they profess to know the numbers better than the loan person. Stellar, as in major time waster. Not the way I do business and certainly not how Wanda prefers to run hers but they are her clients so Wanda was off to see if something could be done to increase their buying power.

After dropping Wanda and Ralph off at her office, I was rolling back home when I got a call from the shill at Cedar Lakes Phase Four, LLC. He let me know they had reviewed Mushy and Joocey's offer and accepted it. Just one fine point, they wanted to shorten the inspection contingency by one day. One day less, talk about pissing in the litter box. I told him I'd contact the buyers, check my email for the counter offer and be back in touch. Jesus. I swung by Winterfrost, happily noting the parking lot was empty, no one there on an early Sunday evening. Once I'd printed out the counter offer and made sure there were not any other changes included that the developers had thrown in and not mentioned to me, I called Mushy. Her scream of excitement when I told her the news just about blasted my ear off.

Once I had her calmed down and let her know that I needed to get their initials on the inspection contingency change, she was a bit more focused. Like me, she didn't quite understand the shortening by one day but she said I could come over anytime and she and Joocey would be standing by to initial. Then we'd be off to mutual agreement land.

Before heading out to the Beaumont, I stopped by my ranch and picked up Clyde. He had been home alone almost all day and I figured he'd enjoy the car ride and airing out. He jumped up on me and did his usual greeting dance. Once he'd watered a small patch of front lawn, he was thrilled to be buckled in the front seat and co-piloting the two door beater. We were heading across town and up to the Beaumont when Wanda called. "Pick me up and we are going to go visit our old friend Norman, he's gonna use his chemistry lab at work and test the cookie crumbs I took off of Harvey." I could hear Ralph squawking in the background. I tried unsuccessfully to tell her I was on my way to a client's house, deaf ears. Wanda did not care, just pick her and the bird up, they'd wait while I got my papers signed. Norman's house in the Rosedale was the next neighborhood over from the Beaumont so it all worked out nicely, at least in Wanda's mind.

I picked up Wanda and Ralph at Safety Mortgage and listened as I drove us to the Beaumont. Her clients had gone completely AWOL and put in an offer that morning which the seller accepted, only problem was the buyers did not have the money, pre-approval, to purchase it. I don't know who was more incompetent the buyer's agent for submitting an offer that had zero financial backing or the seller's agent for not urging her seller to require a pre-approval letter from the buyer's loan person before reviewing, much less accepting, the offer. Stupid never sleeps. So the buyers were extremely dismayed and angry, after all someone has to be blamed for them not being able to afford what they want and who was a more convenient target right now than Wanda? I'll hand it to Wanda, she doesn't let unfounded anger from clients get under her skin and was quite confident they would soon figure out it was their agent who was the true imbecile at work. "Who knows, once the fool agent gets them out of this deal, assuming she had them submit a financing contingency, then maybe they'll wake up and come work with you Alex." This she said from the back seat, where she and Ralph were buckled in. I was a bit leery as to how the bird and Clyde were going to react to one another but Clyde seemed oblivious that there was a Red Lored Amazon parrot in a cage in the back seat, steadily squawking a stream of expletives. And Ralph seemed very intrigued by the shaggy, tan, creature buckled in the front passenger seat, his eyes showing his excitement by endlessly pin wheeling. It was clear to me that Ralph didn't get out a lot and apparently getting out was fine by him.

We got through the gated entry at the Beaumont in record time; especially when you compare it with the Seaview shake down. Winding all around we found our way to Turn Key Drive and up on the right was a magnificent fiber glass columned mac-mansion spilling over the confines of its shoe box size lot. This one was just as charming as the rest of Beaumont. A four car garage took up most of the house's frontage, and enormous white columns stood out like sore thumbs against the pale rose and yellowish brick façade. There was an oversized Italian looking fountain with cupids of all description spewing in the middle of the small front brick walk, and rose colored lights illuminating it. The house was early 2000s and eclectic as we politely say in the industry. Meaning: the oversized garage doors look like Heidi just dropped in, the rose and yellow brick façade is actually just thin slivers of brick masonry attached to sheathing, the white fiberglass columns remind one of Mississippi and the cobble stoned entry porch rivals the worst country cottage in England. Meanwhile the steep pitch of the two story house's roof resembles a New England barn. There is even an oversized brass rooster weathervane at the center of the roof's peak. Large vinyl framed windows with stick-on plastic panes and undersized black aluminum shutters flank each side of the enormous front door which was the *piece de resistance*. It is a faux bronze, multi paneled monstrosity capable of allowing baby elephants to easily pass through, with one huge dinner plate sized knob in its center. It's the type of heavy door which requires a system of built-in weights and levers to actually allow the home owner to open the damn thing. Perhaps they purchased it from an old department store or bank demolition? Illuminating the narrow cobblestone entry porch was a large black urn shaped chandelier held in place by sturdy swag chains. *Feng shui* aside, it is very creepy having that heavy light fixture hanging over your head while standing beneath it at the front door. Naturally the door bell played some pseudo mini symphony and I could hear the yelling and squealing of Mushy approaching.

"Oh my God! Here you are! Baby, Alex is here honey. Come down we need to sign right away! Come in Alex and let's seal the deal.

Courtney! Down here now, we gotta sign!" Vicky screeched as we walked through the checkerboard tiled foyer with matching oversized curving stairway and landing. Into the great room we went. Meaning an enormous kitchen complete with den/media room, bar, dining area, fireplace, everything but an indoor swimming pool. My small house would easily fit inside Vicky's kitchen/great room with plenty of space left over for part of my yard as well. She indicated I should park it on an oversized bar stool at one of the kitchen's three hulking islands. These bar stools were wooden French country style swivel stools painted a washed out baby blue with foot rests. They were upholstered in a bright red and black cheetah skin print fabric. Tiger would be envious. Across the cavern, I noticed perched on a ship sized sectional sofa (upholstered in mustard velvet fabric), was a huge puffy yellowy fur ball; an elderly cat. His beady blue eyes were shooting daggers at me as if daring me to come over and try and pet him.

"We've got *Pinot* open, Alex, you want?" Vicky said holding up her partially filled, fish bowl sized wine glass with her fuchsia lipstick smudge on it. "Oh, no thank you Vicky, it sounds nice but I never drink while on the job." Although, at the rate my business was progressing lately, that rule might have to be revisited. Vicky nodded while taking a swig, screeching for Courtney again while picking up the remote to mute the home shopping channel that was currently blaring away on the plasma TV set. A TV set that was easily the size of a ping pong table and hanging over the great room's fireplace, the central focal point of the entire space. "COURTNEY GABRIELA

ROSEMARIE AMANZO down here NOW!" Vicky thundered and then gave me a demure lady like smile while swigging her *vino*.

"What-the-FUCK-ev, bitch! Don't lose your tampon! I'm like right here already." This Courtney announced as she gum popped, flip flop shuffled, and texted her way across the enormous great room. "Oh wait, I forget you don't have tampons anymore 'cause you're like all old-lady menopausal bitch now, right moms?" She snickered as she parked her ass on one of the swivel stools at the rose granite countertop. "Now, what the fuck do I sign? I got like stuff goin' on Mom."

Vicky nodded at me and I pulled the paperwork out of my briefcase and proceeded to line it up for initials while Vicky coo-ed to Courtney, "Now honey I know this is tense for you. Baby is getting her first condo. So exciting! But just please put down your phone baby, and let's sign where Alex tells us to. It won't take very long, I promise. When we are done here, I'll make us up a batch of vanilla watermelon *Mohitos*, the ones you really like and me and you can go chill-ax in the hot tub girl, and discuss fun stuff like furniture! You know Courtney, I already found this really bitchin' fabric for your sofa and I was thinking some of that fun new shag carpeting they have out now in a rad color of course and we—"

Courtney looked up and snorted, "WE? Really bitch, we? There is no 'we' in MY condo mom. It's mine! You can go all faggy decorator with some other retard daughter but I'm tricking out my place the way I want to, so just back off the pedal bitch. Why don't you and dad go on another old fart couples learning-how-to-fuck-again

215

retreat thing or something and just leave me alone, huh?" With that she put her phone down and tapped her acrylic nails on the counter, ready to sign.

Such a charm, and so deserving. I passed the pages back between Joocey and Mushy and soon enough we were good. The counter-offer was signed around. Once I had it back to the listing agent, we would have mutual agreement. One step closer to closing, thank the lord! As I was getting up, I accidentally knocked over a metal organizer container that was on the counter top. Out spilled pens, post-it pads, a couple sets of keys, lipsticks and other assorted catch-all crap. A few pens and a prescription medicine bottle fell on the floor which I quickly set about retrieving. I apologized and Vicky sprung into action picking up the items on the counter while telling me "No worries Alex, no worry at all! That stupid thing really shouldn't sit up on this counter anyway but as you can see we put all sorts of stuff in it." Courtney just slouched on her stool and gave me a disgusted look. I handed Vicky the prescription bottle and put the pens back in the metal thing. "Oh! Alex, you da' bomb! This is great! Look honey, its Butterpuff's medicine. Alex we've been looking all over for this. Why he hasn't had his medicine for a couple of days now, I don't know how this got put in here." Butterpuff? That glowering poof of fur is named Butterpuff? No wonder he shoots daggers with his beady blue eyes. I noted the name on the bottle and it was from the Seaview Pharmacy. Huh? "Ah, Vicky if I may ask, why do you get Butterpuff's meds at Seaview? Isn't that a bit out of your way? I'm currently working on a listing down there."

Vicky smiled, "That's awesome! Did you hear that honey? Alex has a listing at Grammie and Grandpa's place. You should have told me Alex, we'll all have to meet up down there sometime. We are overdue for a parent check-in visit, isn't that right Courtney? I know they are gonna be so excited to hear all about your new condo! Anyway Alex, it's the strangest place that Seaview, right? I mean, thank god you and me have got miles to go before we are there, am I right?" she said as she attempted to fist bump my hand. Joocey now gave us both disgusted and withering looks. "Yeah, we got my mom and dad living down there and they love it. Mr. Butterpuff over there is getting up in years and he wasn't acting right. Unfortunately, his vet over in the Lee, Dr. Crantz, was out of town and I didn't like the lady covering for him. So Courtney and I were visiting mom and pop down at Seaview and that nice woman there heard me talking about Butterpuff. Turns out one of the nurses there was like a vet or something before she started working at Seaview. So that nice lady Beverly who runs everything at Seaview went and got the nurse who used to be a vet. She could tell what it was that was wrong with Butterpuff just by listening to me. Beverly offered up an Rx right there on the spot for Butterpuff. She wouldn't take any money for it either. See, that's just how they are at Seaview, always so helpful and all. It was a real relief I tell you. The pills did seem to pep old Butterpuff up."

"Oh, you probably got the pills from Ellen, she's the nurse's aide there who used to be a vet here in Clinton but there was some scandal and her sister Beverly got her a job there. Beverly LeFaye is the woman who is in charge of everything at Seaview."

217

"Yep, that's the one Alex. Beverly and the long haired nurse who was the vet. Wow, I would have never guessed those two were related. Anyway, Beverly is so kind to mom and dad and their friends, keeps them happy with their meds and at that point in life, hey why not, right? She makes sure they all have fun activities every day and is so cheerful and the old folks really like that kind of peppy attitude. Mom later told me that the nurse who used to be a vet, that the police like trumped up some kind of charges against her. I don't know about that but I do know that Beverly is just an angel and old Butterpuff there is all perky again thanks to her help.

I smiled and we chit-chatted a bit more as I walked out. Vicky demanded I meet her and her parents at Seaview, so I told her I'd let her know when the next open house would be.

# 29

Back in the car, Wanda was busy with her new past time, texting. Ralph was making low chortling sounds and Clyde was sitting up straight, his doggie seat belt still clicked in place. "Go on ahead up to Norman's house, he knows we are on our way and I know you are going to be all stressed to get that counter-offer you just got acknowledged sent in. I asked Norman if you could use his scanner and computer when I drop off the crumbs and he said no problem. And watch how you are swerving, it's affecting my texting."

Affecting her texting? How Wanda manages to text with her long stick-on nails is beyond me. For that matter, how most humans manage to text is beyond me, unless they have mouse sized hands. Must be why text messages are mostly incomprehensible, have no proper punctuation and are creating a generation that most likely will not know what a capital letter is used for. But that's my old fart rant. Seems to me, I'm too young for such rants but such is life. Personally, my cell phone is blocked from receiving text messages and I warn all clients I don't go there. Naturally my phone service provider does not have a customer service option for clients such as me. Anyone who does text me does not receive a bounce back message letting them know the number does not receive text messages. So helpful, the wireless carriers are but why be helpful when your industry has purchased the law makers and regulators? So much for free enterprise and consumer choice.

# CHARLES CHAPLIN

The drive to Norman's house in the Rosedale went by quickly and only the sound of the chortling bird and the clacking of Wanda's texting filled the car. Norman greeted us at the door. "I've got the computer turned on in the office Alex, and Wanda you have a bag of food crumbs you want me to analyze? You said it came off of a dead man at mother's complex?" Wanda nodded as we followed Norman down his split level stairs to his basement office. "You know I get the feeling mother is not very happy out there at Seaview. Of course she is very short with me when we talk, what with Amy living with me. Here Alex, you can feed the paper in there and it should make a PDF for you. Anyway, when I do speak with mother I can tell she is not a match for that place. She is too active. I could have told her that before she purchased but you know she was not speaking to me at that point. Mother doesn't know it but Amy and I have plans to get married this coming spring. Her career is really taking off. She's entering the regional pole dancing tournament and we all think she is going to nail it. She could end up in the nationals. Amy is now headlining three nights a week at Scandals and her performances are now their top draw. I'm so proud of her. I just can't seem to get mother to come around on this."

Ah, good luck on that one, "Thanks Norman this should do it. Now I'll send it from your email here and auto fax it as well." One task down. "Yeah, your mom never struck me as the Seaview type but that's where she wanted to look, so that is where I took her. She might settle in though, we saw her place and it looks nice."

"I bet she has the plastic vinyl on everything and her vinyl floor runners right? I think that might be why I originally became interested in chemistry, all that vinyl and plastic on everything. I was always in awe of how it kept anything from being ruined when I spilled or tracked in mud. Started me wondering how plastic could do that. Anyway, maybe someday mother will like Amy." Hope springs eternal. "Mother did mention to me this past week that she thinks too many people die at Seaview. I tried to tell her that statistically that is indeed within the norm but she's not having it. She seems to think something nefarious is up. Guess that's why you are having me analyze these cookie crumbs Wanda?"

"You got that right Spanky. And honey don't you miss a beat when you do all that analyzing, you make sure you find out what kind of poison they put in them cookies, 'cause I can tell you they are what off-ed our Harvey and that ain't no lie. 'Course bony butt here don't agree but we'll prove him wrong now won't we Norman?" Wanda said giving Norman a significant look.

On the way out, Norman showed us the converted basement rec room which was now Amy's pole dancing studio. It had turned out quite well; huge shiny pole, stage platform, disco ball, lights, mirrors, sound system—what more could a stay-at-home stripper want?

Possible poisoned cookie crumbs dropped off, paperwork sent in, Wanda next insisted I take her home and we eat dinner there. So back to *Chateau* Wanda we all went. As I was pulling up to the curb outside her house I noticed Miss Lyla farther up the street. She took a long look at my car and started to high tail it back up the walk to her house. Wanda got out of the car and was unbuckling Ralph's cage as she watched Miss Lyla retreating. She yelled out, "That's right lady, you just go right on back and hide in your house baby! I know you been down here in my yard tending to Sammy. Ain't found him no home yet, now did ya? Hey lady, no need to worry none, we just found Mr. Sammy a home this afternoon. You be off my voodoo list before ya know it girl." This caused Miss Lyla to pause a bit at her doorstep and then she and Wanda both burst out into loud, guffawing laughter. So much for bearing a grudge. I let Clyde sniff the camellia bush hedge and then we headed up Wanda's front stoop.

As I walked in the front door, I noted a can of hot pink paint sitting next to the front door. "Yep, you see my paint there huh? Gonna get this brown crap off my door tomorrow. Ain't that right Ralphy? You birds like bright colors too, so we gonna fix my door back to right." Wanda plunked Ralph's cage down on the kitchen island. She immediately headed back into the living room calling out to me, "There's a bag of limes in the refrigerator, start juicing them for some slushies. I'm gonna run back and put on some at-home clothes." Wanda said while turning and looking at Ralph. "Here, let him out of his cage and let's see what he thinks of the place. He could probably use some flapping time." This she said while she opened the cage door and within seconds, Ralph shot out of the cage and promptly took off. He was flapping all around. Circling around the kitchen and into the open dining room with its box beam ceilings and bay window seating nook and out into the living room. I don't know who was more excited, Wanda or Ralph. I held tightly onto Clyde's leash but he was completely uninterested in Ralph or anything, besides sniffing Wanda's floor for food crumbs.

Soon enough, Wanda had fired up her stereo and from her living room a Funkadelic song was thumping. She grabbed Clyde by his two front paws and was dancing with him all over the living room, which seemed to rev Ralph up even more, as his flapping from room to room increased. Wanda turned the music down a bit, Clyde plopped down on her chocolate leather sofa and Ralph settled atop the dining room's vintage brass and milk globe chandelier. He seemed to smile at Wanda and me as he cocked his red capped head to one side and promptly dropped an enormous white and green bird splat on top of Wanda's heirloom dining room table. The very table she religiously polishes once a week. The table most humans do not dine on when visiting *Chateau* Wanda, much less touch. I looked at Wanda and she looked back at me, her face was expressionless. Just as I was about to try and step in and save Ralph, Wanda let out an enormous belly laugh, "Ohh, birdy just letting us know he's getting comfortable, aren't you, you little green devil? Alex hand me the paper towels. Oh, little Ralphy is making a mess of my grand mama's table." To which Ralph squawked loudly and then replied, "Damn, bitch, damn bitch." This started another round of Wanda's endearments as I handed her the paper towels. I knew then the die was cast and potty mouth Ralph had found his new home and human. Wanda with a parrot. Seems kind of natural but who would've guessed?

The evening progressed with a batch of lime/rum slushies and Wanda fried up some of her famous spicy chicken. Naturally she prepared a special plate for Clyde. Ralph seemed content to watch everything from his central location atop the dining room chandelier. Dinner over, I had the bright idea to call up Arnie and see if she knew of anyone who might be able to transport Sammy to his new home. Arnie is a terrific handyman, well technically woman, who is reliable and does an all around great job. I'd discovered Arnie via Percy during my last listing. (see Volume Two) "Yep, this is Arn, what can I do ya for? Hummm, off hand I know of this horse chick who might be able to lend us her transport trolley, we could load up the horse and git 'em where he belongs. Let me try and reach her tomorrow and I'll get back at you Alex. Gotta run now, it's my turn to bowl—it's league night. My team, the Lane Ladies, is kicking some major man butt out here at Clinton South Bowling. Just gotta get me a strike and sure enough our undefeated streak will continue with the butt whoppin' of the Baptist Men's Bowling League. Praise god! Gotta run." Click.

I had the call on speaker and Wanda paused to give me a look and then went back to scrubbing the frying pan, "Humph, well you go Arnie! Damn you know that woman can sure 'nuff kick their asses flat Alex. Okay, well I hope she can get us that horse trolley thang and get Mr. Sammy out of my yard." Just then the first chords of "Respect" started up and Wanda turned off the water. "My phone; it's there on the counter Alex, push speaker. I did. It was Ethel. She had heard about Harvey Malloy's death. She'd also spoken with Norman and knew we'd dropped off cookie crumbs for him to analyze. Ethel was all worked up, "Listen you two, I know there is something *bupkes* with this Seaview place. Since you dropped off the crumbs from Mr. Malloy with my boy Norman, you two are clearly starting to see it too. I'm telling you there are some weird things taking place out here. I just went to this investment club meeting earlier tonight and that RG mortgage person was there. 30 percent returns she's offering these people! 30 percent! Who does that? Who I ask you? Bernie Madoff, that's who! No, I'm telling you it's all strange here. Can you two come visit with me soon? I've got some things I want to share with you and it sounds like you two are already on the case, so that's good. Don't you have to be back out here soon Alex, to meet Mr. Malloy's relatives, settle the listing or what not?" I explained his son would be there the day after tomorrow and Wanda and I told Ethel we'd set up a time and come see her then. Ethel agreed but said we should watch our backs because she thought Beverly was on to us. On to us? "*Oy*, I spoke to Norman late this afternoon and he told me you two were bringing over some cookie crumbs for him to analyze. I let it slip to Beverly tonight that you two had found some cookie crumbs and my son the chemist was going to check them out. Now I know I probably should not have done that but you know that Beverly just has a way about her, she's so pleasant and it's like she can just get you to talk. Anyway I'll see you two soon, be safe."

I clicked off while Wanda was drying her hands, "Be safe? That Ethel is telling us to be safe after she went and spilled the beans to the old syrupy spider lady? Seriously! Humph, I'm telling you this is all 'bout to get as messy as what Mr. Ralph did on my grandma's table. I think this here calls for a fresh round of slushy, don't it Clyde?"

From there the night progressed and it was close to midnight before Clyde and I made it home.

# 30

The next day whizzed by without a word from Norman and I enjoyed hanging out with Clyde at Sasser's Bakery most of the morning. In the afternoon, I did some yard cleanup work and I was out front attempting to edge the small patch of grass posing as my front lawn, when who should pull up to the curb in their shiny black Hummer but the Bendles. It was too late for me to hide or go inside as Kackie was out of the passenger door before their civilian tank even came to a complete stop. "Just the man we are looking for, Alex Campbell! Funny, how the tax records always lead you to the person you are looking for. Cute place you have here! I can see the rehab effort you have made. I think you've got some developer blood in you Alex." Perish the thought. "Anyhow, Rick and I wanted to drop by for a little face-to-face time, see if we can synch up and mobilize a cohesive plan of action. Right, honey?" Honey hopped out of his militarized civilian vehicle, his teeth so white they blinded in the sun, "Roger that baby. Yes, you have quite a fixer-upper here Alex. Why not dream big and grow with us? Kackie and I have decided to expand our little neighborhood reinvention plan and since you are literally the local liaison, we want you involved. It's such a win-win for everyone. We get to grow our project and put it on a fast track and you get the dream neighborhood I am sure you have been waiting for!" The dream neighborhood I have been waiting for? It sounds more like *A Nightmare on Elm Street* and these two must be the new Freddy Kruegers.

"Ah yeah, well Rick, Kackie, I really enjoy my neighborhood just as it is and you know I don't think I'm really the best match for your project."

They smiled wider and Kackie chimed in, "Oh go on Alex! Of course you are perfect for our project. Is this your hold-out strategy, to get more? Honey, we've got quite a negotiator on our hands." Hold-out strategy? How scheming and calculating are these two? Oh wait, they are jackals, they don't deal in or know how to be honest and direct. "Seriously Alex, hold-out negotiation tactics aside, let us help you maximize and monetize your full potential and in doing so, help to create a new wealth niche for Clinton in this awesome undiscovered oasis. We now want to buy out your block and a few others, expand our window of development opportunity. We know as a local real estate agent and a neighborhood resident, you will be awesome collateral as our community ambassador of good will. You can help us turn the locals so they sell low and we can help you to move up to the good life. We were thinking part of your compensation might be, oh I don't know, a PENTHOUSE in the new So-Town Lofts!"

Fucking so-what lofts, huh? Kackie and Rick started to get back in their Hummer. Rick took a call on his cell and Kackie smiled, as her tinted window rolled down and she called out, "You ponder the good life Alex, it's going to be yours! Rick and I will be in touch soon so we can formalize. We just wanted to touch base quickly today so you can start to strategize, get your mind up to speed on the new you and your new lux lifestyle. Talk soon!" With that, the poor excuse for a penis extender lurched off down the street. What the fuck?

# NO REST

What the fuck indeed. I didn't have long to ponder because my cell rang and it was Mushy all in a knot. She told me that Joocey wants to have the whole condo tricked out in hardwood flooring before she moves in. I had to explain to her that first, it would not be possible to start any remodeling work until the deal actually closed and they were the new owners. Also, it was highly doubtful the condominium board was going to permit hardwood flooring be installed. Most condos do not allow it, due to the noise carry-over issues.

You would have thought I'd taken a shit right in her double latte, whatchamacallit. No hardwoods for precious? How could I deprive her? Why wouldn't the bad old condo board allow it and why couldn't they start doing the upgrade work before the deal closed? Why stupid? Well because if you did start doing remodeling work and the deal does not close, guess who gets all of your then free, home improvements? Not to mention the liability and insurance issues involved. Who wants to start rehabbing a place before they own it? Local Einsteins-in-the-making, Mushy and Joocey, that's who. Not on my watch.

She then tried to start taking it out on me, the old kill the messenger routine, but I was not going there. She should thank her mushy ass that she has an agent like me to keep her from completely doing something bat shit insane. I politely told her that I had to go and reminded her if she wanted to verify what I told her, she was free to check it out with any of the local real estate attorneys that are on my list in her buyer intake packet.

To quote Ethel, *Oy!* Soon after that call, Beverly rang to let me know Harvey Malloy's son Steve would be there tomorrow afternoon to pack up the place. She thought it would be good if I could stop by and say hello, seeing how I am the co-listing agent. Co-lister indeed you greedy bitch. But I remained pleasant and said, yes Wanda and I would both stop by. "Oh that's just grand Alex! Why it will be my pleasure to see you two tomorrow and say let's make sure we all look sharp. We don't want our new client to think we are all wrinkled and not on top of our game, now do we?" Oh, I don't know perhaps my cut off shorts, the ripped tank top I mow the lawn in, barefoot or Jesus sandals? I guess it just depends how my feet feel.

The next day came soon enough and Wanda and I headed off to Seaview in her car. She was hoping Harvey's son would let her have Ralph's big cage and if so, she planned to somehow fit the thing in her car's enormous trunk. While rolling down the highway, Wanda was talking up a storm, "And that's when I told Miz Liz that there weren't no way in hell I was gonna let him add no more dryer stations to MY salon until I approved the budget. You know she took attitude with me? Seriously, bitch took some 'tude with ME, talking 'bout how can't no proper salon be run without enough dryer stations and the only good ones is the ones from Sweden. Sweden, Alex? As in in long, blonde Barbie doll, Swiss-Miss hair? Like that dryer shit is gonna dry my client's hair and extensions. No, I don't think so! Oh, here's the exit!" She said swerving her lurching Town Car off of the highway. "So you know, we up for a lunch visit with Ethel here today. I spoke with the lady and she says she has some information for us. Said

230

Norman ain't done with the cookie crumbs yet but it should be soon. Humph, we gotta have us a planning meeting Alex, get this case all sorted. I bought my note pad so we can take down what Ethel has got for us. You know at some point we gotta give that Pete Davies a call, let him know we are on a new case. It don't hurt none to keep the fuzz posted as to our in the field activities and---"

"And?! And nothing, Wanda. First, we are not on a case, we are not even investigators. And it doesn't matter what your mind thinks, we are not P.I.'s so just get over it. Focus on your loans, your hair place, whatever, but please no more of this 'case' crap. Second, I highly doubt Pete Davies wants to ever hear from you or me again. Third, right now I really don't give a rat's ass what is going on at Seaview. Just be happy Ethel is out of your house. I can help the happy witch sell Harvey's place and hopefully we are done and out of there for good."

Wanda shook her head as she pulled up to the Seaview gate and the ever charming Dave appeared. "Ahh, hum. You just keep on telling yourself that Alex. It don't take no federal i.d. badge to make us P.I.'s. Ain't that right my little P.I? Oh howdy, you must be the rent-a-cop, my friend here and everyone else seems to always be bitchin' about. Dave is your name? Well honey, let's get this entry do-dah dance done with, we got an appointment with a bird cage." That went over well.

Our entry time was doubled but eventually we cleared Seaview Customs and proceeded to the Tower's parking lot, space number 27 this time. As we walked up to the entry doors, *The Days of Wine and*

231

*Roses* musical version was blasting away for all to hear, indoors and out.
To the front desk we went where Pamela greeted us. Her hair was in
an even tighter knot/bun and her smile a bit more frantic/manic than
the last time. Beverly must be out and about today, busting asses left
and right, keeping those five S's all tick-tock. As we were signing in the
music changed over to a plucky strings musical version of the Dave
Clark Five's *Glad All Over* and who came bouncing over as chirpy and
syrupy as ever? "Why I see the gang's all here again! Oh what fun we
are having today. Mr. Malloy's son Steve is already up in that dingy
unit, packing up and I have just been notified the movers are at the
front gate. Oh, what a relief to have this going so well." Sugar-puff
was dressed in a flowing, soft peach, dress with sensible low healed
taupe pumps, a string of white pearls and a "lovely" white rose was
pinned near her dress's neckline. Her hair was as shellacked and
immobile as ever and her frosty pink lips all smiley.

 "My, it's been how many days since I last saw you both? And
how many days has it been since my television show? You know, I was
thinking this morning when I was outlining the spots for this week's
show, that the mail must be especially slow right now. I don't seem to
recall getting any thank you notes for the lovely personalized,
needlepoint gas mitts which I am sure you both are thoroughly
enjoying. Now don't either of you feel bad, I know it's the postal
service. You know, I have heard that they just sit on letters and then
postmark them when they feel like delivering them. Can you imagine?
So when I do receive your gracious thank you notes, don't you even
give it a second thought that the postmark date on the envelope will

probably be today's date. My, and Wanda, I see we are in slacks today? It must not be a work day. Purple slacks. My…, they sure do say, here I am! And that multi color blouse, why it picks up the purple tones beautifully Wanda. Dear, I still don't see how your poor little ear lobes can handle those big earrings, all that weight just pulling them down all day long. Why you don't want to have old lady ear lobes before you move in here, do you? You are just too young for that Wanda. Oh, and Wanda would you look at Alex. I see we are having a dress down theme today! Alex, your shirt is bulging out in front again dear. Were you rushed this morning, is that the problem? I'm telling you, it just takes a few seconds to secure your shirt in your undergarments and off you go, all professional, tucked in and crisp. Good thing our new Malloy client, Steve, well he's all dressed down in dungarees and sneakers! Of course he is packing up everything I suppose. Say, why don't we just go on up there and pop in. I'll introduce you." The only thing I'd like to pop is you old lady.

We then went with Beverly and were serenaded by a plucky musical version of *Quinn the Eskimo* while waiting for and riding the elevator. Beverly was as pleasant as ever, "A little bird tells me that you two, or somebody, took some cookie crumbs that were apparently found with Mr. Malloy?"

I gave Wanda a big eyed look and Wanda cut in, "Oh that's right. I thought it was wise to collect a few crumbs. See, I'm a curious one and I've got a friend who is a chemist and I thought I'd just get them crumbs analyzed. That's sort of my hobby, stuff like that. Just make sure everything all checks out."

Beverly smiled, "I see somebody who reads too many mystery novels! Well, I think that is just grand that you are making sure all the I's are dotted Wanda. However, you do know dear that Seaview has a renowned police department and I am sure if they suspected any kind of foul play, why they would bend over backwards to upturn every little stone. The police report to me and the Board and you know, I am known for my attention to detail. But in this case, those cookies Mr. Malloy ate were from his hall's Secret Cookie Santa of that I am quite sure. But it is just great that you have such an interest and concern for our citizen's welfare Wanda. See, I knew you were someone of quality and I do know a bright and shiny penny when I see one! I want to discuss your helping out with our mortgage needs here at Seaview. Aup, here's our floor, after you." She said holding the door and smiling at us with her frosty pink lips and that certain gleam in her pale blue eyes.

Steve appeared to be around 50 and he looked a bit like Harvey but he was more slick. Once he introduced himself and said he was a pharmaceutical sales rep that explained it. Harvey Malloy's son, a pharmaceutical sales rep. Guess we all know how he chose to rebel. Harvey must have never let him hear the end of it. Beverly piped in, "Now Steve just so you know, the front gate tells me the moving van is arriving. And as you know, we do have our strict move out time limit, so it is probably best if we just get all these things here packed away as quickly as possible. No pressure dear, just a statement of fact." Wanda then proceeded to ask Steve if he wanted Ralph, to which Steve immediately said no. Then she asked for the big cage and she got it.

"Well alright then. Alex and me will get that big cage out of here. I can keep Ralph temporarily until I find him a good home. Say, Beverly do you have a luggage cart or something that we can set the cage on? Looks like Harvey removed the rollers that were on it. If we can get us a cart, we can just roll the cage out to the car and I think it's gonna fit in my trunk."

Beverly looked a bit peeved as she smiled, "Oh Wanda, I am afraid that is just a no-can-do. You see, we have our rules for moving in and out and only Steve's movers are the approved moving company. Only the approved moving company is allowed to load their truck in the docking bay. They are not permitted to load items into more than one approved transport vehicle. It keeps things running so much more smoothly this way; no loading up cars and trucks and who knows what! It's part of our Seaview decorum and standards, I'm sure you understand. We can't have you pull your car around, and have that unsightly cage put in your trunk. Then have you drive through all of Seaview looking like *The Beverly Hillbillies* on parade with that cage poking out the back of your car's unclosed trunk, now can we? Besides, for you and Alex to try and lug that big cage out of the building would require prior Board approval, an application fee, and submission of your request at least two weeks in advance."

Wanda smiled back, "Humph. Is that so? Well Beverly I don't understand how Steve here can be moving out today since it's not been two weeks between his father's passing."

Beverly smiled wider, "Ohh, Wanda. You are correct but in the case of a death and re-listing a property, the Board has given me special authority to over-ride that move out stipulation. You see it is in everyone's best interest to hurry along the clearing out process once a Seaviewer has passed. It keeps things so much more life focused and upbeat around here. It also allows us to give the opportunity for a deserving person to move in to Seaview and enjoy life here with us much more quickly. I believe this is what the negotiators call a win-win."

Wanda's eyes started to open wider, "Now let me get this straight, Alex and I have helped you and Steve here by taking Mr. Malloy's bird. A bird you have flat out said you can't stand. Now we are back here and I am offering to take that big bird cage off of your hands, help Mr. Malloy's son out and you are going all Seaview bureaucrat on me Beverly? See to get us to a win-win, you gonna have to help us get this here cage out of here today."

Beverly was a bit flustered, "Oh my, I see those purple slacks just bring out the persistent side of you. I really---"

Steve slammed a box down on the kitchen counter, "Enough! Look here Beverly, I know my father was a hard pill to swallow and probably not the best fit for Seaview, and I know you two did not get along. So you should be thrilled he is gone and I am here so quickly emptying out his place. That bird cage is leaving today and my movers are going to load it in this kind lady's car. If you don't like it, to quote my dad, you can go fuck yourself! Now get the hell out of here so I can get this move taken care of." I guess the apple doesn't fall too far from the tree after all.

Beverly's eyes bugged out, "Ugh, well I never, I mean really! I can now see the resemblance of your father in you Steven Malloy! It must just be your nasty Irish genes flaring up because I cannot understand the need you people have to be so uncooperative and vulgar. Good day Mr. Malloy and *you* just remember, I have to sign the final form before your moving truck is allowed to leave these premises. I sure hope I don't become delayed this afternoon and have to keep you waiting, those movers do charge by the hour." With that she turned around and headed for the door.

Steve glared at Beverly's back and shouted, "Lady you delay me one fucking minute this afternoon and you'll really find out first hand just what my fiery Irish genes can do!"

# 31

S teve told Wanda he would have the movers take the bird cage to the loading dock and when we left, we could pull her car around and they would load it up for us. We offered to help out but Steve said he had it covered. We were on our way down to meet Ethel and waiting for the elevator while rocking out to a mystical musical version of *Highway to Hell.* Who picks these songs and then bastardizes them via the perky, musical strings machine? Do these geezers even know who AC/DC is? Is that musical demographic now part of geezerdom?

On the ride down, a scowling prune was already occupying the elevator; she glared at Wanda and me like we were dipped in dog shit. As we were exiting the elevator Wanda piped up, "Looks like somebody needs their diapers changed and a nap. Hmpf, oh, look Alex, Ethel just texted me. She wants us to meet up at the dining room in the Tower's pool clubhouse. Here let me just hit her back and tell her we are heading over there now. I sure hope they got some good eats in this damn place, cause I am powerful hungry this afternoon. Talking with that old TV witch made me hungry. And did you catch that old bat saying how we need to send her a thank you note for that gas mitt shit? Ain't that rich, Miz Proper there basically asking for a thank you. My mama always taught me you don't ask for a thank you, it's not polite. I wonder if they offer slushies at the pool house? I think they have to, seeing how they just cater to old farts and we all know them farts drink their way to the bottom of the ocean most every day."

I could only wonder and what was this whole Ethel texting crap? Has the whole world grown miniature mouse fingers except for me? Who the hell has the patience to type out all that crap, why not just call or better yet just set a fucking date and time and show up?

On our way out to the pool house dining room, we passed by the *bocce* ball courts and right next to the pool seated at the same table as before, were the group of old ladies in sweats that we gave the doughnuts to the day Jiggles died. They were again busy at work looking through mail order catalogues but the larger one looked up, must be her sixth sense for potential free food kicking in, "Oh, you two are back here again, huh? No doughnuts today I see. What brings you all back to Seaview, any sales we should know about or a new listing perhaps?" This, the grandma in pink velour asked while the rest of her old crow cohorts, looked up from their must-read mail order catalogues.

"Ah, no. No doughnuts today ladies and no new listings or sales that I know of. We are here to pick up the bird cage from Harvey Malloy's unit and we are going to have lunch with Ethel Kluntz." I said, hoping to keep moving along.

Pink velour wasn't having it, "Oh, that's nice of you to help out Mr. Malloy's son. I heard Mary Willis got that great TV set of Mr. Malloy's and Sylvia Farkle was going to try and take the mattress off his hands. You are here for lunch you say, with Mrs. Kluntz? You know she's really adding some fire and interest to this place, right girls?" The other crows bobbed their heads in unison. "Yes, Ethel is attending meetings and classes. You know she won at bingo twice just two

239

nights ago. She is setting up some new interest groups and you can better believe that sure is getting under Beverly LeFaye's skin. Am I right girls?" Again they all nodded and coo-ed in agreement. "So have you two heard the latest Seaview *de jour*? That's French, for today. Anyhow, we had yet another resident pass away just this morning, not less than an hour or so ago. I just saw Ellen leading the morgue people over there to the South Tower. To that end unit way down there. Marvin Holton lives there, seems he had a cardiac arrest. You better believe Beverly is going to be down here and all over this. I think it's another one of those guaranteed in-house listings. Never a dull moment around here, seems like the grim reaper is always on call, right girls?" Again with the synchronized nodding heads. "Anyhow, you two enjoy your lunch and you tell Ethel we'll look forward to seeing her tonight at the Towers association meeting. I can bet you she is going to have some more suggestions and it should be fun watching her and Beverly go back and forth."

We left the velour, pastel colored track suited crows to their catalogues and made our way to the pool house dining room. "Alex, Wanda over here! I'm so glad we could have lunch, it's my treat. Order what you like. Me, I'm getting the daily special which is bologna with your choice of cheese and bread and half a salad. It's a good size portion and three dollars off. But you, you just take it all in and don't let my wallet or the discounted specials interfere with your choosing." We ordered lunch specials and Wanda and Ethel both got some kind of rum slushy, I opted for iced tea much to Wanda's eye rolling derision. We filled Ethel in on the morning's events, she already knew about the recent heart attack, death—news like that travels almost instantaneously at Seaview. Wanda asked Ethel what exactly was going down with Beverly, as the old ladies by the pool implied they were now adversaries.

"*Oy*, that one! I tell you I thought she was a *goodnik*. A stick up her *tochas* maybe, but still a good person, you know sort of like a younger Pat Nixon? Well, I tell you that one is something. She runs this whole place with an iron fist, everything has to be Beverly's way, or approved by Beverly. I suggested we start a Towers walking club. She was concerned it might be too strenuous for the residents and she didn't want the trails clogged with walkers. What is that I ask you? Walkers, isn't that what the walking trails are for? So then we ask that they change the free weekly movie night so they show some better movies, right? They have the free movie night at the Seaview Auditorium once a week and a lot of us want to see some more interesting and current movies. They only show these old Doris Day and surfing movies, fluff like that. I thought something like that movie, *Chinatown* or *The Boys From Brazil* might be more interesting, get people thinking and talking but that suggestion just about made Beverly *plotz* on the spot. Seems she is going to elect a committee to review movies that might be more up-to-date and suitable for Seaview, whatever that's supposed to mean.

Then Beverly got wind that there was a group of Seaviewers who were setting up some kind of gambling related bingo night and that almost made her cancel the official Seaview bingo night indefinitely. Yours truly had to talk her down on that one at the last meeting. Of course I don't know what the issue is with some gambling bingo, seeing how she's all behind that RG person's investor's club, which is nothing more than a ponzi scheme. I tell you, I attended one of those investor meetings and that RG is fleecing these people here. The returns she promises, make no sense! But that is all Beverly approved and sponsored. I can tell you when I raised that issue at the last meeting, Beverly just shot me daggers with her eyes, turned my microphone off, and moved on to another topic. This I don't like, who does she think she is Mrs. Chairman Mao or what? I thought she was a nice lady when we met her Alex but this I no longer know.

I got a notice from Beverly on my door yesterday, a warning. It seems the potted geraniums on my balcony are not an approved color. They don't allow the bright reds, just pale pink and white. What is that? And I tell you the last item that I brought up at the meeting, to explore possibly changing this music or just getting rid of it, at least at night time. I thought Beverly was going to burst a vein! I didn't realize the whole music thing was her baby. It plays in all the public areas 24-7 and now she's got it out on the golf course and walking trails. You can hear it now, as we eat! I ask you, who can properly masticate when there is this endless melody playing? Your mind tries to figure out the original song they are instrumentalizing and who sang it, and when. OY! It's too much, day and night I tell you. I like nice instrumentals as much as the next gal but all day long, all night long?

But enough of all that hub-bub, what I really want to discuss with you two is all the deaths in this place. You heard, just this morning another heart attack? This is not good. I'm glad my Norman is analyzing those cookie crumbs Wanda because I tell you there is something *shlekcht* going on here. They drop like flies and who is this all benefiting, I ask you?"

Wanda perked right up, "Ahh-hum, who is right. We all know who is making their bang from the buck with all these deaths, old Beverly LeFaye, that's who! I always say, you gotta follow the money, don't I Alex? Ethel you don't need to worry none 'cause me and Alex are on the case. Your Norman is checking out the crumbs and we are starting our investigation. Beverly told us she knows about the crumbs. She says those crumbs are part of the cookie Santa thing. We'll find out won't we? We could use you as our inside lookout, sort of like a satellite, on-site deputy."

A satellite what? Is she nuts?

Ethel purred, "Ohh, this I like Wanda. Yes, I will keep my ear to the ground. Oh, that cookie Santa thing! Someone left me the worst tasting batch of prune bars I have ever tasted. I never imagined someone could be poisoning us with cookies! This is not good. You really think someone like Beverly could be behind some of these deaths? I've seen the daggers shoot from her eyes, but murder, this I'm not so sure. But I do know something is not right here and we need to get to the bottom of all this and fast before there's another one, before it's me! I mean bad tasting cookies is one thing but death cookies?"

"Mmmum--hum, you got that right. We are with you Ethel, ain't we Alex? We have solved some other cases and you know this is just right up our alley. I'm thinking someone is doing some poisoning around here.  It will be interesting to see what is in those cookie crumbs."

Ethel nodded, "Yes, this is good.  I don't think it is all just poisoned cookies here though.  There has to be some other way they are causing all these old folks to have heart attacks, to die in their sleep.  Die in their sleep!  Do you know how many of those there are around here?  Alex and I ran into a die-in-their-sleep when we were touring here.  She was dead in her bed.  And just last week, there was another one of those, Betsy Shelland, she too passed in her sleep.  Well you might say, what's the big deal, it's an old folks community, people they pass in their sleep.  But I tell you, I know as sure as my own mother's mother would know, something is not right here, it's *meshuga*.  I don't know if it is Beverly or someone or some group or what, but something is not right here.  This I know."  And to add emphasis, Ethel looked at us wide eyed through her enormous blue glasses and took a final crunchy bite of her salad while vigorously nodding her head up and down.

Wanda nodded back, "Amen to that one sister.  I too know it ain't right what all is happening here and we are on the case baby!  Now I think we gotta come up with a plan and start tailing our suspect.  You gonna have to help get us in here more so we can start hanging out and watching."

"Ahh, I hate to spoil the party ladies but first of all, we are not investigators.  Second, we have no proof any crimes are being committed here, and third---"

Wanda cut me off, "Third nothing. Finish eating your sandwich and sit back and learn something fool. Don't you pay no mind to him Ethel, you just leave it to me. I'm wondering if we can maybe get ourselves in Beverly's office or her condo. Where ever it is, old sugar coated does all her work. See if we can prowl around undercover and find us some--"

I had to let out a huge sigh, "See if we can break and enter and illegally search and---"

"Damn, shut up! As if we ain't done no B and E before! We got Ethel here on the inside to help us out this time. I think we just need to check things out, see if there is anything we can find to lead us to the killer. You know come to think of it, we need us a name for all this here. Something like the Seaview Slayer or Slasher or well, I guess I'll have to work on that one. Anyway, Ethel, you think you could help us get into Beverly's place this Saturday night while she is live on the air doing her show? We could check out her crib and if she has an office visit it too. Old cynical-before-his-time here might be right. We might not find anything but at least we could sure take a look and see."

Ethel perked up, "This I like! Such a mind; the mortgages, the hair and now this, the investigating! That's a great idea Wanda. I'll have to see about getting the pass key that unlocks all the doors here. They have a pass key, this I know because we all have to sign a consent form before moving in. If you haven't shown up for a meal or an event in a couple of days, they use that pass key to enter your unit and make sure you are still breathing. Some of the antisocial ones here really resent that. I guess it makes sense, a rotting body can start to smell really bad. Maybe I can finagle that pass key from Pamela at the front desk. She's easily flustered you know. They have a pass key there at the desk. I could get a hold of it and then make a break from here and get it copied in Clinton. Did I tell you, I now have new wheels? I have a terrific like-new, Buick LeSabre and it is red! *Oy,* would my mother turn if she knew her daughter Ethel was driving around in a red car! I think it's time for a little mixing it up; my cars have always been white. Turns out I didn't even have to go into Clinton to go car shopping. The folks here sell their cars just about every day. They move in, don't want to leave or end up as one of Beverly's stiffs and there you have it, instant used car market! This car only has 5,000 miles on it. A lady in the other tower complex was letting it go for a song, said she always hated driving and now there was no need for it. Her loss, my wheels to freedom. This pass key copy job I will do, and let's plan on you two coming here this Saturday night. Deal?"

Before I could open my mouth to protest, Wanda agreed with Ethel by fist bumping her. As Ethel is so fond of saying, *oy!* And to that I add, what the fuck!

# 32

What the fuck indeed. We drove Wanda's boat of car around to the loading dock. The movers barely managed to fit Ralph's big cage in her trunk. The trunk was left open and secured with rope by the movers. I thought I glanced Beverly approaching as we pulled out but it could have been another Seaview golf cart. At any rate, we did manage to escape Witch Mountain, I mean Seaview, and I helped Wanda lug the big cage into her house.

Wanda popped her head into her bathroom to say a quick hello to Ralph, who appeared to be quite happy, perched on her shower curtain rod while admiring himself in her vanity's large mirror. I read somewhere parrots are intrigued by their reflections in mirrors and can spend hours admiring themselves. Hum, sounds like he and Wanda might have some grooming and admiration traits in common. Between Wanda's large bathroom vanity and her "make-up" table thing in her bedroom and her closet's full length mirrors, she has got all the angles covered, literally. Must be a girl "thang" as she would say.

Ralph cocked his head to stare in our direction and let out a string of expletives as his greeting, "Dumb bitch, bitch, son a of a bastard, commie bitch...."

"Ahh, there's my little greenie! All decked out in the shower, checking himself out. Ready for action with the lady birds, right Ralph?" His yellow eyes did their pin wheeling thing in response. "Okay Alex, let's set this cage up here in the dining room. That way Ralph can be in on the action in the kitchen, dining and living room. I am glad I opened up this house. I didn't realize at the time it would be

247

for no bird's benefit though. But, this is only temporary, until we find him the right home. I ain't no bird lady, that is for sure! Humm, let's move my grandma's sideboard thing out of here and put his cage up against that wall, it should fit. Then he can look out the window seat windows and see the city below and still see all the rooms and action out here. I guess we will have to set the sideboard out on the back porch. I think it will fit next to the washer and dryer. Come to think of it, that sideboard should make a nice folding counter out there for me. Just temporary but I can get something else to put out there for a folding counter once we get it moved back in the dining room."

Moved back? It's clear to me that Ralph the potty mouth bird is putting down roots at *Chateau* Wanda. Wanda never moves her furniture around, much less her grandmother's sideboard out onto her laundry porch to make room for a bird cage. "Ah yeah, that's a good idea Wanda. Let's lift it on three."

We got the bird cage all set up and Wanda put Ralph in and he went to town checking out his old/new digs. Wanda decided we needed some late afternoon slushies so she was busy cutting up limes and dumping ice in the blender. I was watching her, mesmerized at how fast and efficient she can whip up a batch of slushies. I suppose she could add bartender to that long list of professional accomplishments Ethel outlined earlier. I got a phone call from a number I did not recognize and for some reason I picked up. It was Kackie Bendle calling. I put it on speaker phone so Wanda could listen in on the fun. Kackie was all friendly wanting to know when we could meet to seal the deal and look at the plans for my soon to be penthouse at the So-Town Lofts. I told her I really was not interested but best of luck. Kackie said she would not take no for an answer, that was not an option. She said she and Rick would be in touch. Whatever.

I hung up and Wanda hit the blender "on" button. Once she had the slushies ready, she poured out two glasses and said, "Now explain to me what the hell a Kackie Bendle is? And what is she talking about you living in some ho-town loft penthouse? Is this one of those reality shows where you go live in one of them phoney ass, spoiled-brats-in-the-inner-city, tricked out pads with a bunch of asshole people? Then you fight over nothing on purpose, just so you can get your ugly up there on TV?"

I filled her in on Kackie and Rick while we took our drinks outside and sat on her rear deck. Sammy was down below, swishing his tail every so often while he slowly chewed one of Wanda's bushes. Wanda noticed me looking at the horse, "Oh, him. We got it all set now, me and that Arnie you put me in touch with. Sammy is on his way out to his greener pastures this coming Friday and none too soon as my bushes out there will tell you. I already told Miz Lyla that she and Ethel would be buying me some new plants once his shaggy butt is out of here. I gave up trying to make him stop chewing on my things out there, he don't listen." She took a long pull on her slushy. "Well, that neighborhood redevelopment thing sounds crazy. How do they think they are going to pull this off in this economy? Guess that's what makes them speculators. Still, you should string them along, see what they'll pay you, cause you know it's never gonna work out."

I disagreed and I let her know I wasn't too sure these people weren't going to gut my neighborhood, they were already moving along at a warp speed.

The next couple of days were mundane. Mushy had calmed down and was resolved to the fact that precious wouldn't be having hardwoods in her new condo. I had a call from some guy who lives in Nebraska. He said he found my agent profile online and was interested in relocating to Clinton. As the conversation continued, I learned that he had no job, but plenty of money—right. He also let me know that he was going to Singapore soon to "pick up his bride." And when he returned he thought they would buy a house in Clinton. Huh? He is picking up a bride in Singapore, what kind of crap is that? He made it sound like he's going to stop off at the market and pick up some cleaning supplies. As Ethel would say, "this one, I don't know." I didn't comment but then asked him his price range. It was hilarious. He thought he should be able to easily purchase a "nice" three bedroom house in Clinton for say $40,000. Maybe, if it was 1953. What? I then tried to politely fill him in on home prices in Clinton and said I am sure prices in Nebraska are lower. That might be true but I don't think there are many "nice" 3 bedroom houses available in Nebraska for $40,000. He wasn't having it. So I ended the call by letting him know I would email him the current 3 bedroom listings on the outskirts of Clinton and he could see firsthand what kind of money bought what. He'd be lucky to find something less than a half hour outside of Clinton that was habitable for less than $200,000 and certainly not anything with 3 bedrooms. I should have just hung up but I felt it was only right to at least send crazy the active listings. Maybe then he'd realize how unrealistic his plans for his Singapore bride and himself are. Some days.

On Friday, Wanda and I were just finishing up helping Arnie load Sammy in the horse transport truck for his new home when I got a call from Norman. Turns out the cookie crumbs had nothing suspicious in them. Wanda grabbed the phone and proceeded to quiz him but to no avail, the crumbs were clean. I was about to say, so much for our Beverly-the-Seaview-Slasher theory, when her phone rang. It was Ethel. She'd heard about the crumbs already but she was excited because she had a copy of the Seaview pass key. Of course it was a secure key that could not be legally copied. So unbeknownst to me, Wanda had put Ethel in touch with our "friend" Tony the mob boss who took care of copying the key for her. This I did not know, this I did not want to know! Ethel said she wanted us to be at her place tomorrow night at 7:30. Wanda told her we'd be there and hung up.

"Why are we still going out there tomorrow to break into Beverly's place? You just heard, Norman didn't find anything and---"

"Shut it. Ethel got us that pass key--"

"Yes, thanks to Tony. You never told me you were involving Tony in--"

"And we are still going to go do some investigating, check this sugary bitch out. You know something ain't right at that place and we are gonna figure it out, poisoned cookies or no poisoned cookies."

I sighed and resigned myself to the fact we'd be sneaking around Seaview on Saturday night, yee-haw.

At least this nighttime visit to Seaview did not involve a penguin suit and formal attire. I had taken Clyde for a very long walk and he was resting at home on my bed. I put on dark blue jeans and a navy button down shirt, my dark and blah, B and E attire I suppose. Alas my shirt was not tucked into my underwear so I'm sure that ever-so-annoying shirt bulge would appear in no time. I swung by Wanda's and she was actually out on the sidewalk waiting for me. Her B and E attire consisted of black slacks with black spiky shoes—the new weird kind that look like animal hooves on spiky heels and cost god only knows how many car payments. Women's shoes, what a racket! Up top, Wanda wore a black and orange swirly patterned top with billowing sleeves and black multi hooped earrings. Her hair was piled up high on her head and held up with a black fabric thing. Hanging off her left shoulder was an enormous black pocket book that easily weighed 50 pounds. This all to blend in for the B and E. Wanda was busy texting as I pulled up and she barely stopped typing while opening the door and plopping down in the passenger's seat. Her rapid clicking continued as I pulled away from the curb. "Well hello to you to Ms. Billings and I see you are all decked out for tonight's illegal venture."

She finally stopped clicking and looked up, "Oh yeah, hey. I was just giving Ethel an ETA and then my niece, Sherice, was filling me in on my sister, Syreeta. She says her hoarding is getting way out of hand. Nothing new to that story. My sister has been saving crap forever."

# NO REST

I had us at the Seaview gate right on time but there was a long line of cars waiting to get in, probably all the the visitors coming for a hot time on Saturday night at Seaview. We made it to the Towers parking lot and had set things up to make it look as if we were visiting Ethel. The front desk cleared us and up to Ethel's unit we went, to the charming instrumental version of The Association's *Cherish* which was even more syrupy than the original. Wanda tapped her orange stick-on talons against the elevator key pad as we rode up, "Only thing I'm gonna 'cherish' in this damn place is when Ethel gets the plug pulled on this here crap-fire music."

Ethel had her door open and was peeking out as we exited the elevator and she motioned us down the hall to her door. "I was beginning to think you two got held up at the gate or by security, quick come in. Just stand right there by the door and you can leave your shoes on. I'll go get the key. She was back in a flash and handed me the illegally copied Medco pass key. "Okay you know Beverly's unit is to the left and at the end of the hall. I don't think anyone who lives in the unit next to her is home this evening, I'm pretty sure Pete and Penny are attending her show, which should have started 20 minutes ago now. I figure you two can snoop in her place first and then if you think it's necessary, you can try her office which is in the visitor's center. This way, at least you are out of here before she might return home."

Wanda patted Ethel's shoulder, "No worry baby, we are on it. Now if anything strange comes up you can just text me and we'll do the same on our end but this should be a piece of cake, we have got it all covered now."

I headed off down the hall. Right, we have *it* covered. Whatever "it" is. We are going to break into the sunshine bitch's condo and snoop around hoping to find what, the Seaview Slasher mask and sword? Has my life really come to this? Well, yes.

Not a soul was in the hallway and the pass key easily unlatched the door. We were inside Beverly LeFaye's lair in no time. The first thing that struck me was that she had the music piped in her unit and it was louder than in the public places. Right now there was a string filled version of *Stranger in Paradise* playing. I noticed her rose colored marble entry complete with an antique mini chest of drawers with a *potpourri* bowl and two small antique figurines of ladies in period costume. Above it was a gilded antique mirror, probably there to check your face and make sure you are "front door ready" before opening the door. Then there were miles of dusty rose colored carpeting. It was extra plush carpeting and it felt as if you were sinking into a sandy beach with each step. Her overhead light fixtures in the long entry hall were mini crystal chandeliers with gold gilt and pink hued bulbs burning in them. Naturally her place smelled of freshly baked apple pie, go figure. We walked down the long hallway and at the end was a spacious, open living room with a white corkscrew spiral staircase leading up and an open kitchen. Everything was wall-to-wall dusty rose carpeting and the only other colors were powder blue and white. She had an enormous sectional sofa in powder blue ultra suede material with assorted sized white needlepoint pillows, all with homey sayings stitched on them. On either side of the sofa, there were two large white ceramic lamps shaped like Grecian urns with white ceramic roses winding around them and each was lit up, casting a soft, pinkish glow. A large, stark white, faux bear skin rug was in front of the sofa and on top of it was a long, gleaming glass and copper coffee table with the latest issues of all the ladies and craft magazines perfectly fanned out. Assorted copper coasters were strategically placed to accommodate any seated person's drink. On either side of the sofa were large matching colonial style wing back chairs covered in white material, each with its own pink and blue needlepoint pillow arranged just so. The centerpiece of this seating arrangement was the large white brick fireplace flanked by large, plate glass windows overlooking the balcony and water views. Centered over the white brick fireplace was a big portrait of Beverly in which she appeared ageless. She was seated (or perched like a proper lady is more like it) on a white Chippendale style chair, wearing a flowing full length pale blue evening dress, her immaculate bouffant and shellacked hair just so, and her left hand was holding a pale pink rose just up to the edge of her chin as she dreamily peered off into the distance with an eternal sparkle in her pale blue eyes. The frame was an off white, gold gilt affair with a brass light up top which lit up the portrait in a soft light. Wanda and I stopped and took this in. For some odd reason, the portrait reminded me of something Imelda Marcos would appreciate. In the far left corner of the living room was a white baby grand piano with tons of silver framed photographs of who else but Beverly on top. Beverly throughout the decades all smiley and pink lip-sticked prissy as ever, a bit tighter as the face lifts progressed.

Wanda pointed at the portrait, "Humph it's the ageless sugar witch all decked out for everyone to see! Damn, don't she look like one of those old-school, lady romance novelists or something? You know, just looking around this place Alex, you and me better make damn sure we aren't tracking in no dirt or dust! We should probably have done this B and E in the nude wrapped up in Saran Wrap or something, to keep everything spotless. Now this place is what my mama would call scary clean!"

"No shit. Okay, Nancy Drew you dragged us into this spotless hell, now let's get on with it and get out of here."

On the other side of the living room seating area was the open kitchen which had three white bar stools, perfectly lined up at the eat-in bar; each with a pink and white checked gingham cushion, which was secured to each stool top's corners with perky, heavily starched bows. In front of each stool was a soft blue place mat, matching cloth napkin with copper napkin ring and full dinner service, complete with wine glasses and a white ceramic vase with pink and blue silk flowers. Someone apparently got the real estate staging bug and lived it in their own home. Frightening!

Her kitchen overhead lights were turned on and the kitchen cabinetry was a faux country look, painted white with copper door hinges and knobs. There were top of the line matching white appliances, a white porcelain sink, and white marble counter tops which were so clean they reflected everything in the bright kitchen lighting. In the center of the kitchen was a spotless work island with a built-in wood chopping block, which was stained and polished and it appeared to be brand new. However, knowing Beverly I'm sure she sands and refinishes it every month. Above the island hung a large, oval shaped, copper, pot rack. Off of it dangled every sized copper pot imaginable, all shining so brightly they almost appeared white. Most likely Beverly polishes that rack and those pots every week if not more often.

We started to snoop about and I noticed the music was piped into every single room, including the bathrooms and even the master bedroom's walk-in closet. The master bedroom was a powder blue bomb. From the carpeting to the bedspread and the lush curtains, everything was baby soft blue and white. Beverly's king sized bed had a large elaborate French style headboard, with inlaid, tufted blue ultra suede fabric. There was a big skirted, make-up table with an old style tri-fold mirror on top, also in the same rococo French style as the bed, complete with its matching cushioned stool. The skirting was rigidly pleated blue and white fabric which just touched the floor and covered the table's legs. On top were assorted ornamental perfume bottles, atomizers, a silver brush and comb and other old lady dress up bunk. A wall of windows and a sliding glass door showed off the private master bedroom balcony. On it were potted white and pale pink geraniums, and a white, curlicue, wrought iron metal table. Two matching white metal chairs were perfectly positioned to take in the sound view. It reminded me of a *Pepe Le Pew* cartoon. Those silly chairs which no one can possibly sit in for more than five minutes without their ass breaking from the too small and very uncomfortable metal seats. Wanda took note at the same time and commented, "Sure as shit no one is parking their ass out there on those pretend chairs; looks like dollhouse furniture to me. Humph, no surprise. Okay, so let's get in that closet of hers and prowl around; seems like she'd hide shit there or maybe under the bed?"

258

We set to work and we found nothing, not even a hint of a dust bunny under her bed or in her closet's corners. All of her clothes were arranged by type and in color and then hue order. All the shoes perfectly lined up on the built-in custom shelving, and next to them her matching lady purses. Wanda did unearth an ancient looking small, pearl handled revolver behind some shoes. It looked like a dainty old lady gun but no doubt it could kill. She left it in its hiding place. There was a three-way mirror station with custom lighting in the closet's corner, complete with a mini block to stand on, the kind of thing you run into at a tailor's. Next to it was a dry erase board on which the month had been gridded and every day each outfit was pre-planned down to the accessories (as she called them) and some days as many as two or three outfits were mapped out. And of course, there were hundreds of pastel lady dresses and evening gowns in all kinds of shiny, feathery, wispy material. But there was absolutely nothing out of the ordinary or any "evidence" as Wanda would put it. Her master bath was located just off of the huge closet and it was covered floor to ceiling in rose marble. Three small dusty rose carpeted steps led up to its masterpiece, a large soaking tub with gold faucets and a marble dish of small pastel soaps, two candles on white pedestals along with a white vase with pale pink silk flowers in it. The Muzak echoed a bit in here and now they were entertaining Seaview with silky smooth version of *Some Enchanted Evening*.

Back out to the living room we went. From there we explored the two guest bedrooms and a full bath and half bath. Each bedroom staged to perfection but not a shred of anything remotely interesting and certainly no dust bunnies in site anywhere. We scoured the gleaming white laundry room. Nothing interesting there, just perfectly arranged bottles of bleach, assorted laundry detergent bottles, a case of starch, a huge ironing board with a professional style iron and built-in racks to hang her "delicates" on to drip dry. There were two pairs of nude colored panty hose hanging there and that was it. The last place to look was up the white spiral staircase that took up the north corner of her large living room. Up we went. On top was a good size rectangular room, this one covered in plush powder blue carpeting. It was completely ringed in windows, like a look out nest of sorts. This room is what gave the unit its coveted penthouse status. The realtor in me could not help taking in the amazing water views, automatically calculating the best lighting to snag listing photos and the "penthouse view" marketing verbiage began stirring in my brain. Aggh!

From up here, Beverly could survey all of Seaview, the town, roads, golf course, entry, all under her watchful eye. This was truly her lair. A small glass door led out to a metal fire escape style platform which made a great outdoors observation deck and it had metal stairs which led down to the large main balcony below. In the center of the room was a white desk and behind it a pale blue leather, executive chair. A white multi-line landline took up a corner of the desk along with a white lamp. The other side held a computer; its screen saver was on, showing an aerial view of Seaview. A wall of white, two-drawer style filing cabinets lined one wall just underneath the windows. A green potted plant on top and nothing else except for a table top, brass telescope which was pointed down at the Seaview after-care complex. Even up here, the music continued with a misty musical rendition of *Mandy*. Wanda took to the computer and motioned me to hit the filing cabinets. I was not finding much of anything, just Seaview records, listing files, board meeting minutes, endless activities files. The last drawer, did have her personal files. These include her will. "Okay we have her will and some other personal files here."

Wanda looked up, "Nothing on this computer that is worth a thing. Here let me come down there and I've got my iPad in my bag. We can use it to scan in any document that is worthwhile." We quickly scanned the pertinent parts of her will, and next was a file that Beverly made notes about various Seaview employees which we figured might be useful. There was a file entitled "Ellen" and it had money transfers, legal bill receipts all of which Wanda scanned. There were tons of files from her old TV show, every homemaking and craft tip known to woman. Finally one last file folder, which was red and had no name on it. In it appeared to be a list of Latin names, chemical related information, hand written notes in the margins noting liquid or powder. It was a lot to take in. We were just about to start scanning the red file, when we heard the front door opening below. Wanda's eyes bugged out at me. Whoever was down below was making tracks into the living room. Wanda motioned to the door and quietly opened it, we were both standing outside on the small observation deck when we heard the first steps on the metal spiral staircase. As whomever it was ascended, we descended outside down to the main balcony below. I briefly caught a glimpse of a tennis shoe on one of the upper steps inside but not enough to identify anyone. From outside the livingroom balcony windows, no one else appeared to be in Beverly's condo. Wanda pulled my shirt sleeve and we crouched up underneath the metal stairs at the far end of the balcony. Out here, the damn music continued to play so we couldn't hear whoever it was inside. But whoever it was, they opened the door and stepped out onto the platform above. They made a movement and seemed to pause at the top of the stairs. I thought I'd pass out because if anyone came down the stairs they would then see us. Fortunately, whoever it was turned back and went inside shutting the door behind them. This was going to be dicey. As they came downstairs, we had to go back up, so they would not see us on the balcony. We crouched at the bottom of the stairs and at the first glimmer of the metal spiral staircase inside moving, up Wanda and I went. I don't recall my feet touching a single step. We cowered on the platform. The main balcony door opened below but then quickly shut. Whoever it was, decided not to go outside. We waited for what seemed an eternity but after about 10 minutes I thought it was safe to venture back inside. Slowly we opened the door, and we stood perched just inside like two cats frozen with their ears perked up, trying to pick up any sounds or movements. Nothing, just the fucking theme to *Love Story*. I whispered to Wanda, "I think the coast is clear and whoever that was is gone."

Before she could respond I noticed a small glass vial with a red top partially filled with white powder, sitting in the middle of Beverly's desk. Wanda gave a quiet gasp and whispered, "You see that? What the hell is that? Did that person just leave a vial of blow on Beverly's desk? Say what? She can't be no blow queen. Now I can see the old

witch strung out on some valium or other happy pills but not on no
blow."

I was still freaked out and shushed her, "Let's just get the fuck
out of here right now."

Wanda nodded, and then she picked up the vial and put it in
her pocket book. I was shaking my head no, but she ignored me. She
was leaning down and pulling out the red file. I motioned for her to
come on and now! But then the front door opened again and this time
is was Mrs. Sing-Song. We could hear her cheery voice calling out to
other residents in the hallway, "Well you all enjoy your evening too!
Oh it was such a grand show, now wasn't it Penny? I'm just going to
go get all tucked in my jammies and have pleasant dreams about all of
our fun. I will see you and Pete bright and early at our sunrise
breakfast! It's going to be a melon ball special tomorrow, so make sure
you all get there bright and early! Good night." Oh fuck.

In came the witch. She was humming along to the theme to
*Love Story* as she walked into her kitchen. We heard the ice dispenser
fill up a glass. Then Beverly, let out a long sigh and said to herself, "It
is time for a soothing bath." And thankfully that is where she headed.
When we heard the water in the bath start to run, we were about to
high tail it down the stairs. But then Beverly came out of the bedroom
and back to the kitchen. This time, the sound of a cork. It sounded
like she poured herself some wine and she let out a little "Ahhh."
Then the bath water stopped and we waited. It seemed as if she'd now
be soaking, so I nodded at Wanda and we went down the spiral stairs
as quietly as possible. The coast was clear! We took off past her

bedroom door and down the entry hall. Unfortunately, Wanda's huge pocket book snagged the crap on top of the small entry chest of drawers. The ceramic bowl of *potpourri* and the two lady figurines, flew off the top and crashed onto the marble entry floor. We were completely startled and froze. Broken china shards were all over and Beverly called out, "Who's there?" We heard the bath water sloshing and it was clear she was coming out. "I SAID, who's there? I have a gun and I'm calling security as I speak." I pulled the front door open and grabbed Wanda's arm, pulling her out, the door slamming shut behind us. What to do? If we ran down the long hallway, she'd spot us the minute she made it to her front door. I spied the stairwell exit just to the left of her unit door and motioned for Wanda to follow.

But Wanda had other plans. She quickly dashed across the hallway and pulled down the fire alarm. With that, the music abruptly stopped and a very loud siren when off and emergency lights began to flash along the hallway. A male, mechanical voice started bellowing out through the speakers, "Alert! This is the fire alarm. Do not panic! Proceed to the nearest stairwell immediately. Do not take the elevators! If you cannot take the stairs, remain in your unit with the door closed. Help is on the way. Alert! This is the...." I didn't have time to ask Wanda what she was doing. She ran back to me and down the stairs we went. Two floors down, there were geezers joining us on the stairs, Wanda pulled my arm and we went inside the third floor. The alarm and voice were even louder and more old people in their nightclothes were peering out of their doorways and some were heading for the stairs. Wanda led us down the long hallway to the other end of the building. There was an emergency stairwell on this end as well and that's where we followed a group of old people.

# 34

We ended up outside the North Tower in a service vehicle area, near the loading dock. There was a growing pool of residents gathering under the harsh halogen lights. We kept walking as the fire engines were rolling up. Wanda led us to the trails and kept hoofing it. I glanced back and it was total chaos at the North Tower. Wanda finally slowed down as we approached the backside of Visitor's Center. I was about to start in but she held up her hand to stop me. "Don't! We can recap later. Now, let's get into Beverly's office here and see if there is anything interesting. I don't want to hear it, so don't even! We have the pass key, it is now total honkies a-go-go over there at Beverly's fort, so no one is gonna be checking out her office here in the next little while, except for you and me." And with that she walked through the manicured grass and up to the rear, service door for the Visitor Center. Inside it was eerily quiet. Apparently the music turns off system wide when there is a fire alarm emergency. Thankfully inside there was no alarm or mechanical voice, just dead silence, which made my ears ring and my skin crawl. The door led us into a kitchen. We made our way out to the reception desk area and then into Beverly's office where Ethel and I had first met the old witch. There was an old fashioned wood paneled desk and the first couple of drawers had the usual office supplies in them. The bottom drawer on the right side was locked. Wanda dug around in her pocket book. First she pulled out a mini flash light and told me to hold it over her purse so she could see. She then pulled out what looked like some kind of file. She slid it in the drawer's lock and jiggled it around. I was

266

about to warn her about damaging the lock when it popped open.
Inside were some Seaview financial files but behind them at the back
was a small cardboard box. Wanda open it and there were more glass
vials similar to what we found on her desk, along with some syringes,
and vials of liquid for use with the syringes.

Wanda put the box on the desk, "Well BIN-go! Damn, Alex
would you look at this shit here? Didn't I tell you that old lady was up
to no good? You see firsthand here, my sixth sense is right and here is
the evidence!" I was about to respond when outside the office
windows, through the sheer curtains, a golf cart's headlights appeared.
"Oh hell no!" Wanda exclaimed, stuffing the box in her bag, as I
pulled her out of the office. In the reception area we were totally
exposed. I was frantically looking around when I noticed an alarm pad
by the entry doors with a red flashing light. Apparently this building
was silently alarmed. Holy shit. A couple of men got out of the cart
and as we hightailed it back to the kitchen their flashlights began to
bounce all over the reception room. I heard a key in the door as we
made it to the kitchen. Right to the back door we went and as quietly
as possible I opened the door, almost out. But then once again
Wanda's damn bag struck! She knocked a metal mixing bowl off of the
counter and the noise of it clanging onto the linoleum floor made my
heart leap into my throat. We were running towards the walking path
but Wanda snagged my sleeve and steered us over to a clump of trees
that ran along the side of the building towards the front parking lot.
We could hear the back door opening and voices calling out when
Wanda pulled us across the lot to a Seaview golf cart. "Get in and hold

tight. Wanda hit the pedal and the cart lurched forward towards the front doors. She turned sharply to the right, the wheels bouncing off the curb almost toppling the cart but somehow it got back down on all four wheels and she jammed the pedal to the floor. We took off across the lot, the security guards running around the building yelling, their flash lights bouncing off the back of the cart. I spied a button that read "boost" and hit it and sure as shit, the cart kicked into heavy duty and we started to gain a lot of speed. Apparently Beverly's cart wasn't the only one with a power booster on board. Wanda steered us down the main road until she came upon access to the cart path and she quickly dropped us down on the path, taking us around the perimeter of "downtown" Seaview. I was looking back but I didn't see anyone following, yet. I yelled out to Wanda, "We gotta ditch this cart!" She looked over to answer me and that was it. The cart hit a rock or bump or something and right off the path we went, flying across the golf course and straight into a sand trap. When we hit the trap, the whole cart just slammed down and rolled into the deep embankment on the sand trap's far end. Half of the front of the cart was embedded in sand and I was flung out to the side and landed on my ass in the damp sand. I saw stars for a moment. Across the seat Wanda flew out right behind me landing within inches of me on her side. We were dazed. "You still here with me bony ass?" Wanda asked.

"Yep, I think so." I replied. "Let's see if we can stand up. And then we have to get out of here."

"Damn right, pork rib barbeque and all that's sacred, what the hell was that? Okay I'm up and I can move. My bag is still here on my shoulder and there is my missing shoe. Yeah, we gotta get out of here now."

We slowly climbed out of the sand trap and looked around. Fortunately we didn't see or hear anyone approaching. We decided it would be best to walk back to the North Tower. We chose to walk out on the golf course rather than take the walking or cart paths back. This way we could not be spotted as easily and we could duck into the woods for cover if necessary. Wanda had to take her spiky shoes off and walk barefoot, as her shoes immediately sunk into the damp greens. The walk towards the lit up Towers was in silence. We were both too stunned to speak. We finally made it to the path right behind the North Tower. It appeared people were now heading back inside. I didn't see any sign of Beverly. We hopped over a low wall onto the poolside terrace and both sat down at one of the dark, umbrella covered tables. Wanda plopped her bag down on the table and peered inside, "Thank the sweet baby Jesus himself, all our evidence is still here, we did good Alex! My phone is vibrating. I got texts here from Ethel. She's wondering where we are, what's up, the fire alarm, etc...."

I let out a huge sigh of relief, "Text her back and ask her if it is safe for you and me to leave? If so, tell her we are okay and we'll talk to her tomorrow, we will fill her in then."

Wanda nodded and started clicking. "Yep, she say it's okay and all clear. I told her if anyone asks, about us just say we left her place after getting caught up in the fire alarm evacuation."

We stood up and brushed ourselves off. I had sand in my hair, Wanda tried to put her hair back, finally she just pulled it into some kind of knot. "We don't wanna look like we've been running. Tuck your shirt back in Alex and my sleeve here is ripped but I think my bag will hide it okay."

With that we walked back to the Tower's poolside entry doors and in through the lobby, which seemed extra bright after being out in the dark for so long. The crew at the desk were busy helping stray geezers in their bathrobes, as were the doormen. We made it out the front doors, noting the two Seaview police cars parked right at the front door, most likely responding to Beverly's break-in. Finally, back to our parking space and my two door beater! As we slowly drove out of Seaview, we noted security carts and the Seaview police pulled up at the Visitor's Center. At the gate, the guard was completely pre-occupied with the in-field radio calls and he barely looked up at us when I handed him our parking pass back.

As I pulled onto the interstate I let out a huge sigh of relief and said, "This time, I'm the one who is telling us we are going to go have slushies and actually lots of slushy. I'd like to go somewhere besides our houses, so we don't have to make them, that's how completely fried I am Wanda. But, I'd like a clean, smoke free, and most of all quiet place and I don't know of any bars like that."

Wanda sighed as well, "Any bars? Humpf, when's the last time, if ever, you sat your bony ass down at no bar? Well I got us a place that is gonna become your favorite hangout Mr. Campbell. It's called Om, as in the whole Indian, yoga, meditation, bead thing. Percy and I went there the other night. It is exactly what you just described and I for one am in complete agreement with you on this one! Knock my fat ass into next Friday, what the hell was all that back there? Anyway, take the second Clinton exit and head toward the Lee District, I'll direct us to Om. Yes sir, Miss Wanda here could be using herself some serious Om and slushy!"

I rolled down Dalton Street into the Lee District and Wanda had me turn up a small side street off of the main strip. We scored a legal parking space on the block right before the street took on a steep hill. "Just push me." Wanda said in jest as we walked up the hill. This side street was not busy and at the top of the hill the residential section started. On this hill were two old brick apartment buildings, a shoe repair shop, legal offices and half way up the hill was a blue neon sign "Om" on the side of a 1910 or so two story brick building. Below the Om part it read, "the QUIET bar…" in green neon. The glass entry door was painted over in black and a large stenciled sign on the door let us know the following: *Om patrons agree to turn all electronic devices off prior to entering. Cell phone use of any kind is prohibited and you will be asked to leave. This is a quiet zone, no loud talking, music, etc… is permitted.* Hmm, I'm liking this already. In we went.

It was dark inside with soothing blue and green lighting and candles burning throughout. The theme was quasi Indian/Tibetan with a bit of high tech thrown in. There were 1970s style conversation pits, recessed areas in the flooring; i.e. you sat on a huge floor cushion pulled up to your low built-in table. Other tables you could sit at had large yoga balls to rock on while seated, and there were conventional tables with comfy chairs, a living room area set up around a fireplace, and a mid-size bar in dark wood with swivel bar stools. About six or so built-in booths lined the wall opposite the bar. All the liquor bottles were on glass shelves which were lit up by cobalt blue lights. From the top of the bar's back counter to the ceiling was a large continuous stream waterfall that stretched the entire length of the bar behind the liquor bottles. It was lit from above with more blue lighting. In the center of the waterfall, was a repeat of the outside neon sign, Om. The bar was about two thirds full with a wide assortment of people; there was no predominant age, color or freak/type demographic in this place, a true mixture. Definitely, my kind of bar. Everyone was speaking in hushed tones and piped in at a low volume was soothing Tibetan bells and monk chanting music.

Wanda briefly pondered one of the tables with the yoga balls for chairs but instead led us to the last empty booth. It had cushy turquoise and purple colored cushions and a soothing white pillar candle was burning on the table top. When the server arrived we could barely hear him speak, they take the quiet rule very seriously. Wanda ordered us the old-school stand by slushy drink, a pitcher of pina coladas, and two items from their appetizers-only menu. I watched the bar tender as he began to prepare our slushies and was fascinated to discover that the bar had the blenders built into some kind of sound proof box. When he turned the blender on to crush the ice and make our drinks, there was no sound. Now if they would allow Clyde to hang out here with me, I might easily become an Om bar room floozy and regular.

Soon enough our pitcher of pina coladas arrived along with a plate of mini seaweed wrap things and another plate of European cheese, *prosciutto* and vegetable kebobs. Wanda took a long swig of her slushy, "Now that was some serious B and E action tonight Alex! Damn, it even fried me. I can't figure out who that was in her place but we made out good." She said while she dug in her pocket book and pulled out the small cardboard box, the vial of white powder and the red file. All the fun items we stole from Beverly this evening. This caused me to take a long pull on my slushy.

"Holy crap, Wanda, just look at that. You should put that box and vial back in your pocket book, someone could see it! I cannot believe we have this shit, we stole this shit! What are we going to do when Beverly misses this stuff? What are we even going to do with it?"

Wanda finished swallowing a seaweed thing, "Zip it. You need more slushy, and less thinking. We had us a very successful run tonight. Now I will admit it was a bit more stressful than I bargained for but we are an awesome P.I. team. See how you found the stairwell so fast and I pulled the alarm to create us a much needed diversion? Now that is true team work."

"No Wanda, that is five to seven years in the federal penitentiary! I don't think you would take kindly to those accommodations, as you would not like wearing orange every day. Also, I don't think the available love life scene there is to your liking, unless you've changed your game plan since our last dip into the lady pond at the Hairy Beav?" (see Volume Two)

Wanda glared at me, "Hell to the no, on all that! You know, you are just getting worked up for nothing. All P.I.s do what we did tonight but most probably are not as quick on their feet as we are.

Now, we are gonna get all this here shit analyzed by Norman and find out what the fuck they got going on down there. Then we gonna bust that sugar psychopath and help save Seaview and that's no lie." She finished off her glass and poured herself another round. "You, me and Ethel have got to have us a meeting tomorrow and go over all of this stuff, revise our plan. I knew my sixth sense wasn't playing no game on me! I'm gonna text Ethel now, tell her to be at my house tomorrow at 2:00 p.m. You bring Clyde with you and pick up some cookies or something sweet at Sasser's. Me and Ralph will make us a big salad. They have one of the last Sunday farmer's markets of the year at the Highmont Community Center tomorrow morning. Sound good?"

I reluctantly nodded my head and Wanda proceeded to refill my glass and force one of the kebobs on me. We talked more about the night's drama and I had Wanda home by 1:00. I was home and thankfully chilling with Clyde by 1:30.

# 35

Clyde and I slept in and around 11:30 we managed to make it out the door. We went for a long walk, covering the rotting piers, then back up to peer at the Bendles' new billboard sized signage in front of the Conner Hasps factory. It was an attention getting bright orange sign with green accents, announcing So-Town, and the lofts. There were master plan drawings on it, their website, QR code, and of course smiling and generic, young models living in urban ecstasy. This along with every phony PC, corporate do-gooder phrase and pseudo organization, designation, logo one could imagine. A load of bullshit but the buying public sure seems to eat it up with a big shovel so *touché*. I guess that all falls into the old category of, "We wanna believe, we wanna believe." To which I add, "in nothing." Ugh.

My stomach duly churned. I then walked Clyde over to Sasser's Bakery and we holed up there for a good hour. Daynia was ecstatic to see Clyde and I needed a couple of her extra strong coffees to shake off last night's bullshit. Before leaving, I purchased a bunch of assorted cookies to take to Wanda's. As I approached my little house my neighbor, Mrs. Starns, motioned me over to her yard. Mrs. Starns has lived in the same little clapboard house since at least 1955 and her husband worked at one of the local factories his whole life until he passed away in 1980. She has to be somewhere over 85 but I'm not sure. She still gets about okay but I don't usually see her very often. "Oh, Mr. Campbell I see that you and your dog are out enjoying our fall sunshine. I think my marigolds here are going to hold out for another week or two and then it is goodbye. Been to the bakery I see, never was too fond of that place myself but my husband sure used to enjoy it. Have you been approached by those developer people yet? I got a letter in the mail and then that couple appeared here last week. Very pushy sorts, tried to invite themselves inside my home but I didn't allow for that. They seem to think that my house is worth a lot of money and say they will give me all cash and pay to move me out if I agree to do so in the next 90 days. They said you are in on this project and that everyone else is selling."

Me, in on this project? "Ah, Mrs. Starns I am very sorry to hear that the Bendles visited you. I don't know why they told you that I am involved in their redevelopment project but that is untrue. I have no intention of selling my house and moving and I hope no one else in the neighborhood does either. Those folks most likely are ripping you off, I would suggest you ignore them."

We chatted some more and she seemed reassured by my thoughts on the redevelopment subject. She said she'd pass what I said along to the other neighbors. I could tell I was going to have to make sure the Bendles were not actually telling people I was on board with their crappy project. This was definitely starting to kick into high gear, I might have to help organize or something. However, that would have to happen later, as Clyde and I needed to get over to Wanda's.

We pulled up to Wanda's house and I noticed a red Buick LeSabre out in front of her house, the front tire was actually up on the curb. Ethel must already be here. I unbuckled Clyde and let him out to sniff the walkway. I noted Wanda's front door was now hot pink, all signs of Ethel's residency had been erased. Well almost, as Ethel and

Wanda were coming around the side of her house. Wanda had apparently been pointing out the specific bushes, and plants that Ethel and Miss Lyla needed to replace, due to Sammy's stay. Ethel was dutifully agreeing and actually taking notes in a small memo pad. Clyde immediately pulled me over to Wanda and then jumped up on her and they started their usual meet and greet dance. Finally we all went inside and Ralph, who was hanging out in his large cage, began to serenade all of us but thankfully his extremely loud squawking and expletive chanting calmed down fairly soon. In fact, he stopped once Wanda popped in a CD in her stereo. "Ralph here likes Miles Davis, so if I play it softly he usually shuts up. Now if we need to rev him up, he really likes himself some old Motown, must be the drums or something cause this here bird starts bouncing all up and down on his dowel and moving his head. You'll have to check that out but not now, cause I've had enough of loudmouth greenie for one afternoon, ain't that right Ralph?" He cocked his head sideways and then started pecking at his food dish.

Wanda actually had her dining room table all formally decked out and Ethel coo-ed in appreciation. I put the cookie box on the kitchen counter and we all sat down for an enormous salad Wanda had fixed along with iced tea. Once we'd grazed, Wanda made coffee and we scarfed down some cookies and Wanda pulled out last night's spoils; the small cardboard box, the glass vial with powder and the red file. We filled Ethel in on how things went, where we found what, etc.... Ethel nodded in appreciation, "When I heard that alarm, I told myself that must be you two. I texted you but didn't hear back, so I knew something was up. This I did not expect, each minute was like an hour I tell you! I was so relieved when you responded and I knew you were not caught or something. Oh it was sheer chaos there last night. Beverly was beside herself, they had the police at her unit and everything was just madness. The only upside is they didn't turn that music back on last night, pure silence. But then first thing this morning it starts up again. *Oy--* it is so annoying! And look what you found and in her home office and her Seaview office no less. I think this woman is a killer! Look at this, syringes and powders! Okay, I have to call my Normie right now. We are going to have him run tests on this stuff." With that she whipped out her cell and called Norman. It sounded as if he and Amy were in the middle of something but Ethel wasn't having it, "NORMAN, you get right in your car and drive over here to Wanda's house right now! This is a matter of life and death I tell you. Here, Wanda will give you her address. Oh and Normie, make sure you wear your jacket, there's a chill outside today. I'm serious, you could catch your death Norman that's all it takes especially when the seasons are changing. Of course, you live with that person who hardly wears any clothes, so how would you know the difference anymore?"

Wanda took the phone and gave Norman her address. I looked at the stack of print outs that Wanda had made from the files she scanned to her iPad. There were various bank transfers from Beverly's account to Ellen's account. They appeared to be somewhat regular transfers. "All this shows is that Beverly routinely gives her sister, Ellen, money and paid for her legal bills when Ellen ran into trouble with the law a while back. This means nothing." I then picked up the red file we had swiped and I shook my head, "We shouldn't have this file. Beverly is bound to notice it is missing."

Wanda piped in, "Who cares if old sugar knows the red file is missing, she gonna be praying whoever has it doesn't tell nobody about her little box of potions and needles here that were swiped with it! What is she gonna do, tell the Seaview police that someone stole the shit she is using to kill people with and by the way they also swiped a red file too. No, we don't have to worry none about Beverly mouthing off nothing. Bitch is scared now, we got the goods on her and she don't know who has it. These names in this file are Latin and I looked them up this morning. Guess what they are?" Ethel and I both gave her go ahead looks. "These are Latin names for plants. Some are flowers, others shrubs. I thought why all this Latin gardening shit in her locked filing cabinet, right? Why? Because they are all plants that are toxic, they'll kill you! Then she's got some other shit on here that aren't from plants like some stuff called thallium. You know what that is? That's some serious shit they used to put in rat poison. It's odorless and tasteless. Seems there were some serial killers back in the day who used to favor this shit, put it in their victim's tea. Sounds all Agatha Christie I know but it's for real! Now why would old sugar have all this written out and researched? Cause she's a killer! Once Norman tests this stuff, we can call up Pete Davies and Seaview and bust her ass. Here, pass me that box of cookies, I need me another one of them sugar ones with the white icing, this P.I. work makes you work up an appetite for sure."

I passed her the box, "I don't know Wanda. I agree this is some bizarre stuff to have in your office desk drawer. But I still don't know if I can see Beverly as a killer, there's no real gain for her. Based on her bank account transfers, she's got plenty of money to spare."

Ethel jumped in, "No, you underestimate the power of greed Alex. She might be flush with cash but you know every time one of those people passes, there she is to snap up the listing. It could all be about her gaining market share, not really about the money. The money could just be a perk or bonus. Beverly is completely into controlling and running Seaview, this I know too well! We don't know what kind of inner demons might be making her commit these crimes."

"But as Wanda always says, follow the money and so this doesn't make sense, Beverly has money."

Wanda humpfed, "Yeah, Alex, I always say follow the money but in this case I have to agree with Ethel. I think old sugar there has got some serious demons that be all up in her perfectly fixed hair and are making her do some evil doing. That's what I think. No, I have to revise my saying, 'cause I think this here all shows us that it's not always about the money."

"Okay a revision to your theory but what about this vial?" I said picking up the red capped vial of white powder. "This was put on her desk while we were there! Who put it there? What's in this vial and why was it put on her desk while she was out last night?"

Wanda then filled Ethel in as to the lovely game of hide and seek we played last night, more like countdown to an early heart attack. Wanda held the vial up to the sunlight, "I'm guessing this here is some nose candy and that was her very own Seaview dealer delivering. It makes sense, how she always has energy and is all peppy and sweet. In addition to being a killer, old lady is a total coke head, that's where I'm placing my bets."

Ethel's eyes bugged behind her large blue framed glasses, "You mean Beverly is snorting cocaine? Oh this I don't know. That's the stuff all the hoodlums in my Norman's high school were doing. It was very popular back in the day. Not like my friend Rose Marie's son's high school where they all smoked that pot but her son was older, a different generation. Beverly and cocaine? Well, they always say those celebrity and TV types are on that stuff. They say that's why Johnny Carson always rubbed his nose. Now I always thought that was a nervous tick but that's not what my cousin Letti and others thought back when. *Oy*, this! Well, my Norman can run tests on that vial too and let us know if it is the cocaine. What a world."

I piped in, "Well if it is coke, why would her dealer deliver it to her condo while she is away and leave it on her desk? That makes no sense to me. And I'd like to know who that delivery man was because it just about scared me to death. Whoever it was sure spent time just hanging around her place. They checked out the view up top and they were not in any hurry to leave that's for sure. Also, they had to have a copy of Beverly's house key or a pass key copy."

Wanda put the vial in the box with the other assorted presumed poisons, "Well like Ethel says, soon Norman will let us know."

We stewed a bit more. Then Norman knocked on the door. Wanda asked him to come in but he said he couldn't. Ethel picked up the box and a copy of the red file's list of Latin names and walked over to the door. When she reached the door Norman tried to kiss her cheek but she pulled away and said, "As I have told you Norman, you need to straighten out your life and once she's gone we'll talk. You know, with all this here, there is a good chance I will be leaving Seaview. If you can see to get your own house in good standing, then I might just move in with you, as originally planned. You do good with testing this stuff Norman and then we'll talk." I peered out of the living room window and noticed Amy getting out of Norman's grey Honda Accord. Oh shit. Up the front walk she came, decked out in her stripper Sunday best. Sunday best consisted of: clear plastic spiky platform stripper heels, a yellow and red spandex tube-top mini dress, mini being the operative word, and her stick-on talons in red with matching inflated lips. "OH, Mother Ethel it's so nice for you to call us over to visit! Normie has been dying for us three to get together. You have to come over for Sunday dinner today! We are entertaining some friends from the club and there's plenty of food and I made these awesome vodka Jello shooters. You haven't even visited since we moved in. You should just see the gorgeous practice room my Normie has built for me in the basement." This she said as she walked up the steps and placed her arms around Norman's shoulders.

Ethel pounced out onto Wanda' front stoop, Norman quickly backing down the steps, one arm behind him shooing Amy back to the sidewalk and car and the arm other tightly clasping the box and papers to his chest. "Ah, mother, I'll ah, get this done as soon as I can. Amy ah, we need to leave, mother can't make it to dinner tonight baby."

282

Ethel was fuming, "BABY? You call this *kurva* a baby and on a public street no less! NORMAN ANTHONY KLUNTZ, this is not the son I raised! Just look at *this* and you! It's disgraceful. You are killing me Norman. *Oy*, what your father, Herman Moishe Kluntz gawd rest his soul, what he would say about all this? We worked our *tuchases* off for years! We put you through Temple and then graduate school and for what, this? I never asked you for much, just some grandchildren but not with this, *feh*! You, get that stuff tested. If I'm still alive when you have the results, let me know." And with that Ethel went back inside Wanda's house, calling back, "Wanda! Where are your salts, I need salts I just can't take this betrayal!"

Norman pulled Amy to the car and beat a hasty retreat. He said it might take a day or so to complete a full work up on the samples but he'd be in touch.

# 36

The next few days were more chopping wood and carrying the water bullshit. I spent some time doing chores around the house, took Clyde for a long walk and sent the Bendles an email, asking they not tell anyone I was associated with their redevelopment project and that I did not wish to be affiliated with it. Basically, I politely told them to kiss my ass. Wednesday rolled around and it was off to Referee Escrow where I was to meet Vicky and Courtney for their signing appointment. I thought since business was slow and I had the time, I might as well show up for their signing appointment. An agent is not required to attend their client's signing appointment and Clinton is not in a state that does simultaneous signing and closing; i.e. there are always a couple of days between signing and the actual closing, or the legal transfer of the property's title. Also, the signing appointment is where the buyer signs any lender related documents and if there are none of those (as was the case with the Amanzos' cash deal) just basic documents for title and recording are signed. There is usually no role or need for the real estate agent to be present at signing, except to smile and hand hold. Any questions that arise are most likely not something the agent can address or even help out with.

For some reason, many mistaken people in the industry seem to associate being a "good" agent with attending your buyers' signing appointments. A complete misperception as the agent has no power or active role in how a HUD form is filled out or the terms of the buyer's loan. Yes an agent can show up and schmooze and hand hold but beyond acting like a Vanna White, there isn't anything of substance for an agent to do at a signing appointment.

Referee Escrow is located just down the road from the Cedar Lakes complex. I went in and was directed to a conference room where Tiffany a perky, late 20-something, escrow officer was seated along with Vicky and Courtney. Today's mother/daughter fashion statement did not disappoint. Vicky was decked out in a Joocey electric blue, velour track suit, which was unzipped halfway down so the girls could get some fresh air. She was wearing one of those retro 1970s gold necklaces, the kind with her name in cursive letters and her face was completely slathered in war paint, ready to face the day! Her spiral perm was bunched up under a white, rhinestone encrusted baseball cap but alas, this one didn't let me know if it was a, "bad hair day." Down below she wore spiky hooker heels also in white with rhinestones to match her cap. Courtney was wearing an identical Joocey sweat suit in light yellow and hers was mostly zipped up. Her spiral perm was being held up by what appeared to be a purple potato chip bag clip on top of her head. Clearly 11:30 a.m. was early for her as she barely had on any make-up. She of course, was wearing her scraped down to a nub, black flip-flops.

Tiffany offered me coffee and filled me in, "We are just waiting for an updated report from the title company. I had all of the documents ready, the developer has already signed but title said they needed to run one last update report. Once I have that we should be ready to sign here. Not a real difficult signing since it is all cash! And Courtney you must be so excited, your first place, all cash and starting

285

school. Oh my god, that is like so many good things all in a bundle, I mean wow!"

Vicky beamed and nodded her head, while Courtney ignored everyone and continued texting while slouched over the conference room table, with one leg propped up on an empty chair. Tiffany gave me a split second look as if to say, who is this spoiled bitch? But then she hopped up, "I'm just gonna check my computer and see if the title company has sent over that final report and then we'll be ready. Everyone sure they are good on coffee?"

Vicky and I nodded yes and Courtney snorted and said in a low voice, "As if we'd want your cheap-ass *office* coffee!" and then she let out a loud gum snap. Vicky quickly replied, "Now honey, the lady is just trying to be nice. I know their coffee here is probably sucky but we've just got to sign the papers babe and then like I promised we will stop and get some real coffee afterwards." Courtney looked up and sneered, "Yeah well it better fucking be soon, 'cause the at-home espresso shit you made me this morning sure isn't any good either. Jesus, why did we have to come here so fucking early? I told you I needed my sleep. What the fuck do they need my signature for anyway; can't they just like give me the damn keys already? I mean I've got like shit to do mom." To that she sighed loudly and continued clicking away on her phone while chomping and popping her wad of chewing gum.

Before Vicky could respond, Tiffany appeared at the door way, papers in hand but she looked very surprised. She entered and quickly closed the door behind her. "Well, I'm afraid there is a real issue here that I am not sure you all are aware of. Ah, it seems the title company just did their final background sweep on Courtney here and ah, it appears there is a problem. Umm, it says here that there is an active and outstanding warrant for the arrest of a Ms. Courtney Gabriela Rosemarie Amanzo issued a year or so ago in Clark County."

Vicky let out a huge gasp, "Oh, this must be a mistake, there must be a mix up, I mean right Courtney?"

Courtney actually stopped texting and sat up a bit, "Ahh, like I don't know what you are talking about. Arrest? Why would I be arrested? What's this got to do with my fucking condo mom?" She said as she pulled some pink chewing gum out of her mouth and twisted it on her index finger.

Tiffany placed the report down in front of Vicky, "Well I would say perhaps there was a name mix up but the age appears to be the same as Courtney's age. Ah, Courtney did something maybe happen a year ago down in Clark County, and maybe you forgot about it?"

Courtney slammed her phone down, "This is total bullshit! They can't just like interrupt all this. I don't even know where the fuck Clark County is. Mom this is total crap!"

Mushy leaned in and put her arm around Joocey's shoulders, "Of course it's total crap Courtney." She said as she looked at the report. "But honey is does state that someone your age with your same name evaded arrest last April down in Clark County. I'm sure it's a mix up but let's think where you were last April baby. Didn't you and Sherry and Larry all go down there for that outdoors Rasta festival thing? You know the thing your dad and I didn't want you to go to and then we found out later from Sherry's mom that you went while we were away on our couples retreat thing?"

Joocey was growing red in the face, "Yeah you and dad on your geezer fuck weekend thing. NO, yes! We went and fuckhead Sherry's mom of course had to have a complete cow and like ground her and call you. Fucking bitch that woman, I mean grounding Sherry and calling you!"

Vicky was looking a bit perplexed, "Well then honey, that concert event was in Clark County and it says here that someone with your name evaded arrest and there is an outstanding warrant issued for your arrest. Courtney, this is serious! I have a feeling there is more to the story about that concert weekend than Sherry's mom or I know about. Are you not telling me something? Look, we gotta know baby, otherwise we can't clear this up and close on your condo honey."

Then Courtney started up the water works, which caused Tiffany to dash out for a box of Kleenex, "Fuck mom. It wasn't anything, just some asshole cops who said we were dealing shit or some crap like that. They arrested Larry and like Sherry and I took off into the crowd when they were cuffing him. I mean it's not like it is any big deal. We just had some extra, ah stuff and there were some kids who wanted to buy and like how the fuck were we to know one was an undercover narc! He was black and had dreadlocks, so like who would ever think that guy could be an asshole cop?"

Vicky was soothing Courtney, "Of course honey. And you've had to keep this all bottled up inside all this time, oh baby! You two probably should have stayed there with Larry but I totally understand honey, of course you and Sherry made a run for it. Why I bet it was Larry who gave you two up. Now do you see why I sometimes question the friends you choose to hang out with? I mean Courtney, a real friend would never have ratted you out to the cops, not like that. Oh honey, it's gonna be alright. Here let me call daddy and he can get the lawyer to handle all of this. Oh sweetheart, I'm so sorry this had to happen on your special condo signing day!"

With that, Joocey's water works turned off and she made some sniffle sounds. Tiffany and Vicky talked about the warrant and Vicky called daddy Amanzo. It was decided that she and Courtney were going to zip over to daddy's attorney's office right away and Tiffany gave her a copy of the title report with the warrant details on it to take with them. Vicky let me know she'd be in touch and Tiffany told us that signing and most likely closing would be delayed until this matter could be cleared up but she would be standing by. As Mushy led Joocey out, Courtney sniffled a bit more and then said, "Before we go to the fucking lawyer's office, you gotta stop for coffee mom, I mean it. I really need an extra large caramel, triple nonfat, macchiato, with light whip and extra butterscotch syrup, like right now! This has like fucked up my whole day."

"I understand baby, oh this is so traumatic for you. Don't worry, we'll get you your coffee and get this all fixed. Alex, I'll call you later."

And with that, Tiffany and I watched as their low-rider, velour covered asses with *Joocey* spelled out in red sequin things jiggled out the door. Vicky's ass with a yellow thong peeking out and Courtney apparently going commando as her butt crack was showing (gee I know a plumber I can set her up with).

I smiled and looked up at Tiffany, "Well that sure was a fun surprise, huh? I can assure you mommy and daddy Amanzo are going to make all of this work, they want Courtney in her own living space. So I'll call you as soon as their attorney figures it out. I imagine we might need to have title put in the parents' names so we can close this and then later they can quit claim it to their stellar off-spring." Tiffany let out a loud laugh and thanked me.

I was just about to pull out of the parking lot when I got a call from Wanda. She wanted me to meet her at Barnacles for lunch and said that Norman had gotten the test work done and I'd definitely want to see the results. Well, curiosity is one way to entice me to come to lunch even when it is at a seafood restaurant named after crusty crap on the bottom of ship hulls. I made it across town without any delays and went inside to find Wanda. Barnacles is a wharf restaurant that actually is sited on pilings out in Warmer Sound. It's been there forever and the interior is varnished, honey colored pine wood, with ancient stuffed fish hanging on the walls and a million assorted black and white framed photos of Barnacles customers going back to at least the 1940s. Their regular fare is mostly artery clogging, deep fried, crap and sweetened iced tea that really should be called sugar with tea. Fortunately, they do have a couple of fresh fish entrees that are not deep fried and if you know who to ask, you can get unsweetened iced tea, although you will most likely get a strange look from your server.

And those items are exactly what I ordered while Wanda got deep fried dead fish, with hush puppy things and sugar with tea in it. We had a great booth right at the end of the long, open restaurant with a huge picture window allowing us to look straight out in the sound. It was a gorgeous sunny day, and assorted boats were bobbing all around, even a few water skiers were out enjoying the early October, last gasp of Indian summer. The views make Barnacles a worthwhile place in my book.

Wanda pulled some papers out of her enormous orange pocket book, "Wait until you see here what Norman found! I'm telling you the sea witch is busted but good Alex." She said as she popped a deep fried thing in her mouth.

I put my fork down and picked up the sheets of papers. These were toxicology lab reports with some graphs and base line for each of the analyzed substances. The results showed positive for: thallium, ketamine and rocuronium and another one that could not be properly identified.

Wanda piped in, "See that shit? All those there are some serious mother fucking poisons Alex. We got her! Nailed and busted. I told you we would bag this case."

"Just a minute there Lacey, and no that does not make me Cagney, this case as you call it is far from bagged. Okay, so these are some poisons and they were in vials in a little box in Beverly's desk. That proves absolutely nothing Wanda, except Beverly keeps some strange shit in her desk drawers."

# CHARLES CHAPLIN

"Now you just don't get it, do you? It must be those lighter shades of blonde in your hair impairing your reasoning capacity. Honey, these poisons killed them people. But don't take it from me, let me read you what Norman says about these poison samples." With that she pulled out her reading glasses, gave me a look as if to dare me to say a word about her needing glasses to read and then she proceeded, "Thallium is an odorless and tasteless powder that used to be a common ingredient in rat poison. It has been linked to many murders and was commonly placed in a beverage served to an unsuspecting victim. Ketamine used to be used in the veterinarian field, gee who could have supplied old syrup with that I wonder? It is a heavy duty tranquilizer that can knock a subject out instantly and can cause a heart attack. Our last poison is rocuronium, a liquid that when injected, paralyses all of a victim's muscles from head to toe and they remain fully conscious but completely unable to move or communicate for about 10 minutes until they suffocate due to their immobile body parts. My, my said the spider to fly and all that shit, huh? Damn if these here poisons don't match right up with what them old people die of out at Seaview. Heart attacks, they stop breathing, only nobody knows old syrup there is causing it all with her evil lady ways." Wanda pulled her reading glasses, off, looked at me triumphantly and took a long pull on her sugar with tea.

I sighed, "Okay, so we have some identifiable poisons and yes they do seem to pair up nicely with the types of deaths that are occurring at Seaview. It still proves nothing. First, we have no idea if those vials and syringes are in fact Beverly's or maybe someone planted them in her desk? And what was the deal with the red capped glass vial that someone put on her desk while we were there?"

Wanda rolled her eyes a bit, "That vial, well that vial it says here had the thallium powder in it. So Beverly wasn't getting no personal snow delivery, she was getting her personal let-me-kill-you-with-rat-poison-in-your-tea delivery. Guess, this means old sugar ain't no coke head and she really is just naturally energetic after all. Humpf."

"Okay, someone placed a vial of poison on her desk while we were there and we know it was not her as she was live on the air. So who put that shit on her desk and why? Next, the crap in the box still could have been planted."

Wanda sat up a bit straighter, "Ahhum. That is true but what do you have to say about that red file and these substance names and Latin words written down in it? What the fuck did old lady have that all written out and researched for? Seems to me that old lady is good at doing her homework. She might be annoying but can't nobody say Beverly is stupid. She did her research Alex and she has been offing them geezers as it suits her and her pocketbook, snapping up all them in-house listings."

I peered out at a sailboat with an emerald green sail far off in the distance, "Well she is a thorough person. But I'm sorry, I still cannot see Beverly as a killer. Greedy, manipulative, spiteful, mean, insane, etc…, they all apply but for me I don't see killer added to that list. I don't know what it is but I think there is something far more complex happening."

"Damn, you always gotta go and over think and complicate things now don't cha? I'm still betting my money on Beverly as the Seaview Slayer. But okay, you got your points, so what are we gonna do, this case is unsolved and open."

Unsolved and open? "Can we just remember Wanda that we are NOT private investigators. We do not earn money or brownie points for ending up in all these half assed situations? I had no idea I was signing up for a Lucy and Ethel rerun style of life. Jesus, I'd like to just make some simple real estate sales and live in my bubble."

"Humpf, well too bad Sinbad, cause I'm here to pop that damn bubble of yours and if you got problems with that, you can just take that one up with your spiritual attorney once you pass over. Right now we need to get this sorted and we gotta remember there are people dying at Seaview. Old lady could be fixing some of that thal-whatever tea right as I'm here talking."

"Great, so what is our plan? We have all of this information. We obtained the samples illegally by breaking and entering. We have no concrete proof anyone is a killer or that anyone is really being killed at Seaview. True, there are an unusual number of deaths happening but again someone could say that's just pure statistics at work. Also, they cremate everyone at Seaview, remember? So unless someone has been running complete toxicology screens, doing thorough autopsies, we again have no evidence of murder."

Wanda pondered this a bit, while pushing remainders of fried bits around on her plate. "Okay, that's all true. I know who we gotta talk to and so do you. It's time to call the hot cop, Pete Davies. See if he has anything to advise."

"Please tell me you are joking? Pete Davies works in Clinton, not in Seaview Wanda. He has no interest in or authority with Seaview. Plus, we are the very last people he would like to hear from, of that I can assure you."

"Of course you say that. But you know as well as I do that we have unofficially helped him and the Clinton PD solve some cases, whether they like it or acknowledge it. I know he thinks we are crazy but that's his problem not mine honey! I know what I see here and I need a badge to review it and give me their opinion." With that she promptly picked up her cell phone and called up Detective Davies.

Wanda actually reached Detective Davies, must be a slow day for him to take our call. He said he was out on in the field and he could meet us at Salon Wanda in 40 minutes. I took that to mean, he didn't want to be caught dead talking to the likes of us, the notorious unofficial PI's of Clinton, at his office. I tailed Wanda over to the salon. Salon Wanda is located at the bottom of the Highmont District and is in a converted 1930s clapboard style house that is now painted lime green with a vivid fuchsia front door. It does a booming hair styling business and was Wanda's original brainchild and stomping ground. We parked in the gravel lot, which several businesses ago, was most likely the house's front yard. Prior to Wanda buying the place, the house and grounds had been a used tire lot. Wanda did a lot of work fixing the place up. It still has no formal sign out front as she and Miz Liz cannot agree as to the best type of sign to install. This dispute and subsequent inaction have now been going on for several years and at this point I'd say a sign is not necessary as Salon Wanda is already a well know Clinton institution. Miz Liz, Clinton's premier drag queen, actually runs the salon now that Wanda spends most of her time running her mortgage business. But Wanda is a hands-on owner and she and Miz Liz are always in the midst of some kind of epic battle.

Today, Miz Liz was not in and there were only a couple of stylists and three patrons in the shop. Wanda led us out to the brick patio in the back of the salon with its infamous David replica statue and water fountain. This copy of David was purchased by Wanda, who then had Lexi create and attach a huge penis complete with a water pipe in it. So Clinton's David, pees all day long into his surrounding fountain through his porn star sized wiener. It's now made it onto YouTube and last I heard there was some film crew from Italy that apparently wants to come over and do a feature on Salon Wanda and the statue.

Today there was only one salon patron seated on the patio. She was decked out in a pink vinyl cape thing, reading a magazine and had foil and glop in her hair. Wanda seated us at a shady patio table and then went back inside to check the stock of wine coolers in the refrigerator. Inside she met up with Pete Davies who followed her back out to the patio table with a cold Coke from the Salon's refrigerator in his hand. Wanda naturally had gotten herself an icky sweet wine cooler. At first Wanda was acting all coy and tittering with Davies (she has a thing for him or maybe it is all men who wear uniforms who knows) but as soon as they parked it at the table and Wanda pulled out the lab reports, she was all business.

"So let me just get you up to speed Davies on our latest case." To that he smiled a bit and shook his head. Wanda then filled him in. I have to say as I listened to her outline things I thought it sounded bat shit crazy. Apparently I wasn't the only one.

"Let me get this straight Ms. Billings. You and Mr. Campbell found or actually stole these items you had tested from this director or whoever she is, from her home at Seaview? Your theory is this ah, Ms. LeFaye is it, is a senior citizen, serial killer? Her motive for killing is to get more listings and thus make more money down there in Seaview?" he asked giving Wanda a significant incredulous look.

Wanda took a pull on her cooler, "Oh, it's like that again is it DAVIES? You know just like the last times, you should be thanking our asses for helping you po-po out. Doing all your legwork for you and we ain't charging you nothing! But no, you gotta go all proper PD and take 'tude with us again. Okay, you need to lose the 'tude and now Pete 'cause this here is some serious shit. We got old people being killed down there and that's no lie."

Round and around these two went for about 15 minutes and to Wanda's credit, I could tell Davies was at least intrigued. "Well, Wanda even if every single thing you think or say is true, and I highly doubt it, I don't have any authority or jurisdiction in Seaview. And I can tell you the Seaview PD is tight, they do not like to mingle or share with us or other police departments or any of the Sheriffs for that matter. Seaview is its own complete scene. I am sure you are not going to get any of their officers to even remotely listen to you and especially if this LeFaye lady is the boss. They are not going to want to investigate their boss for murder, she controls their pensions and salaries."

Wanda vigorously nodded in agreement, "And that is my point Pete! Old sugar lady down there has got it all under her thumb and she's knocking them off to make her bank, knowing nobody is gonna question her. I agree the Seaview po-po most likely ain't gonna listen to me or Alex here for one minute. See, that's where you come in."

Davies nodded no, "Oh no, I don't come in anywhere in this--"

"Like hell you don't. Now you owe us after the last breaks we have given you and you know that's true. What we need to do is figure out how to get Beverly to confess or catch her in the act of killing these folks. We need someone like you there with us, an official but unofficial eye witness who can back up our story when we break it."

This even made my mouth hang open. Did she really think she was going to get him to tag along unofficially to later back up our findings? Yes, she did and she kept going around with Davies for at least another 10 minutes. He didn't budge but he did offer this, "You could tape her, get her to confess and record it. That most likely won't stand up in court as real evidence since it is covertly done but it could help somewhat in getting her out of there, stopping the killing if that is what she is doing which again I highly doubt. This is all so farfetched; I really think you need to quit watching so many murder mysteries Wanda. But you could get it on tape and there would be some circumstantial evidence. Sounds like there is no body or physical evidence as everyone is cremated down there. There is no indication of foul play so no crime scene protocol has been followed. That's really the only advice I can give you, try and catch her on tape. But what I really recommend is for you two to go back to your day jobs or whatever it is you really do."

Wanda stood up, "Ahh, hum. Well thank you for coming over and drinking my Coke and calling me crazy to my face Davies. We'll keep you posted once we break this case and honey when you see me on the TV smiling at the reporters, you'll know I'm smiling cause I'm once again proving what a fool you are!"

299

*Oy!* Yes, she really just called a cop a fool to his face. Fortunately, he took it in stride, thanked her for the soda, nodded at me, laughed at the big dick water statue, and left.

Wanda was dialing her phone, "Percy it's me. Listen, you gonna be home, okay then me and Alex is heading over. We got some technical needs to discuss. Sounds good baby, see you soon!" She looked over at me, "What? Don't give me no what-the-hell-is-she-doing-calling-up-Percy-and-inviting-us-over, look. We need to go see if he has some recording equipment that you and me can use. You heard Davies, we gotta get the bitch on tape and even then it's not like we are really gonna be legal but at least it will be enough to get her to stop the killing. Don't stand there catching flies with your mouth open, let's go, we'll take my car."

And we did. She had us pulling up to the curb outside of Percy's house in record time. "Humpf, damn shame what them ladies is doing there next door at Serenity's old house. Would you look at that Alex? They got tire thangs and what's that over there some rusted out machine something, on her front stoop no less! That rusted crap look like something Lexi would use in one of her sculptures, ain't that the truth?"

Up the walk we went to Percy's designer abode, literally. It has been featured in at least two national design magazines. His front door is actually on the side of his house at the back. There he was waiting, he has some freaky sixth sense as to when people are at his door. No wait, he doesn't. He has enough surveillance equipment rigged up at his house to put a fucking mall security outfit to shame. And all this crap he set up so he could spy on a hot neighbor, what a perv. Doubtful he's doing much spying these days with Ronnie and Darla, the baby elephants, living next door. (see Volume Two)

"Ohhh, my two favorite people here at last! Alex I'm not going to let you leave this time! Do come in and let's refresh. Make sure you take off your shoes." He called out as he led us into his home. My bare feet felt great on his cool black marble flooring. Percy was wearing what appeared to be a man muumuu or what Wanda calls her at-home dress. Both of them apparently prefer to wear oversized dresses made of garish printed fabric. Percy's muumuu was an African like print in eggplant and white and it had slits up the sides, so you could see his very pale and plump legs poking out as he walked, eeeww!

Into his kitchen we went with its lacquered, white custom cabinetry and royal blue, some kind of stone or something, countertops. In the open living room, his dog Hadley, a Corgi, jumped off of the white sofa and bolted over to Wanda, who immediately smothered him with attention. However, he was too small to do the infamous dance she and Clyde always do when they greet one another. Percy's show pony house was still magazine perfect. Spotless furniture covered in white material, mirrored end tables, a large custom needlepoint rug with royal blue that matches the kitchen counters and white. The rug probably belongs on a wall as an art piece and not on the floor. He could put it next to his oversized Frank Stella painting that hangs over his fireplace. "I already made us a nice batch of slushies and they are on the tray so lets' go out to the patio and enjoy." The end of his living room opens right out onto a nice polished concrete courtyard area with pristine white, outdoor furniture. A soothing waterfall is the back-drop and there are stone steps that lead up to the second story outdoor level where he has an endless lap pool. It is surrounded by a nice size view deck and there is a ramp that goes directly to his bedroom, which he is always trying to get me and probably 100 other men to enter.

We chit-chatted a bit while drinking the strong slushies and nibbling on some family heirloom recipe of for lemon biscuit something anothers. All I know is they were not sicky sweet, they had subtle undertones of vanilla and some other spice and I actually liked them. Wanda then filled Percy in on the day's events. I get the feeling these two talk every night and most likely for hours on end. I used to feel a bit jealous of their budding friendship, now I think it is kind of a relief.

Percy popped another lemon thing in his mouth, "Oh my, you two have had quite the day! At least you got to see that hunky Detective Davies in person. Well, I still have my surveillance cameras all set up, not that there is anything remotely hunky to spy on mind you. Alex, you think you might be able to get those two back woods trash makers next door to list and get out of here before they destroy the whole neighborhood's value?"

How do I as a realtor have any control over his white trash neighbors listing their house for sale or not? Always fun when they start to assume we agents have some kind of super powers with listings and who lives where.

"Anyway, I don't think you two need a camera Wanda. Sounds like the policeman wants you to just tape the conversation and get Beverly to admit to her killings. Oh this is just too rich, I can't believe that old lady would be doing all of this and she's so---"

I interrupted, "Yes, we know it's a mind bender. So Percy, do you have a tape recorder we can use? Mind you, I think this is all completely stupid but Wanda here has her mind set on doing this, so away we go I suppose."

Wanda glared at me, "Don't listen to him Percy. So yeah, you got a mini microphone or something that we can use to snare the Seaview Slayer with her own words?"

Percy adjusted his dress, I mean man muumuu, "Offhand ladies, I really don't have much to offer you in the way of hidden microphones and recording devices. My specialty here has always been cameras and video surveillance. But let me think, your cell phone! Isn't there some kind of recorder on it?" Oddly enough with all the crap they include on those phones there was no recorder.

"Hells bells, this is silly. No recorder. Well, let me go check in my little office upstairs. I used to have one of those mini hand held recorders with a mini cassette tape in it. I used to use that to take notes when visiting clients, to remind me of things. It clipped right on my shirt or jacket's lapel. But that really didn't work so well for me and I was back to taking hand written notes in no time. I should still have that little recorder in my desk somewhere. I'll be right back, have some more drinks." And he bustled off inside to go check his desk.

Wanda filled the time by texting back someone and I just stared at the mesmerizing water fall. Percy popped out, "Got it and it still works! So here, hide that in your pocket book or really you could hide it in your hand if you are careful. It's got a great recording radius."

Wanda tested it out and we spent another hour at Percy's babbling about all kinds of crap and finally left. Wanda drove me back to my car at Salon Wanda. "Okay, so why don't you call that Beverly up tonight and tell her you and me would like to meet up with her, we got something to discuss, keep it vague. See if you can get her to meet us tomorrow out there in the afternoon. I'm going to call Ethel back and fill her in, she's left me a couple of messages. I don't think we need her there when we do this. Sound like a plan?"

A plan might be a stretch but I nodded yes and told her I'd be in touch once I spoke with Beverly.

# 38

Thursday came soon enough and I had left two messages for Beverly but received no return calls. That was definitely odd behavior on her part as I'm sure she has some kind of, "a lady always promptly returns her phone calls" rule or some shit like that. I checked in with Wanda around lunch time and we decided to pop down to Seaview and meet up with her unannounced. I set Clyde up in the back yard and Wanda picked me up. On the back seat was an enormous yellow pocket book. "That's one of my larger ones back there." Looks just as big as the others to me. "I thought I'd bring old yeller 'cause I can easily fit the evidence inside of her. I took a peek and sure enough, the small cardboard box with vials and syringes and the red file were inside. Wanda filled me in on what Ethel had reported which was essentially nothing. Seaview was moving along as if there hadn't been a B and E on Saturday or a fire alarm incident.

Our man Dave, Mr. Rigid, met us at the gate and once again did his whole full-tilt, entry drill. For the love of god, you would think he would know us by now but it was all still strictly by the book, running our i.d.s and all. Wanda told him we were there to see Ethel and that got us a Tower's parking pass. Once parked, we went inside and all was serene and clean. A musical serenade called *In a Mountain Greenery* was filling the airways. Pamela was all smiles at the front desk and welcomed us back, asked me how the Malloy co-listing was going. We told her we were there to see Beverly but had not be able to reach her today, so we were unsure where to find her. "Oh well that certainly isn't a problem. Mrs. LeFaye just left here about 10 minutes ago. She said she was heading out to the overlook picnic area and she planned to relax out there a bit and for me to hold all of her calls." I let Pamela know that we were unfamiliar with the lookout picnic area. "Wow, all these times you have been to Seaview and you haven't seen the famous lookout point? Well it is way out there and most residents never visit it but it is my personal favorite spot!" She then pulled out a Seaview map and showed us where it is. It was located to the west of the ninth hole on the golf course on a bluff that juts out over Warner Sound. "It's amazing. There are some fairly steep steps there that you have to walk up to get to the picnic tables and overlook part. I guess that is why most of our residents never visit it but you two can easily handle them. If you go over to the golf course pro shop, I'll call ahead and tell Charlie to give you all a cart. That way you can just zip out there. Otherwise you are looking at a 40 minute or more walk over there. By then, I'm sure Mrs. LeFaye will have left." So that is what we did.

Wanda lugged her huge yellow pocket book and the Seaview map that Pamela gave us over to the golf shop. There Charlie put us in a two-seater golf cart in Seaview green and off we went. I had to mind a few players on the course but after about the fourth hole the entire course was deserted. Wanda pointed the way commenting, "The course is empty because it is mid day and that's when all the geezers take their naps. I bet you though, this golf course is jammed packed first thing in the morning and late in the afternoon, that's prime geezer golf time. We made it to the ninth hole and found a side cart path that led west to the overlook picnic area. There were some dense trees and so it was cooler and so shady it was almost dark. We wound around the path and then there was a small paved area with Beverly's cart neatly parked in it. We pulled up alongside, and found some old stone steps that went up a pretty steep hill. There was a temporary sign posted that stated the picnic area was closed for renovations, which we ignored. Wanda had to use the wooden railing a few times to keep her yellow pocket book from pulling her down. At the top, was regular grass, and right out in the sunshine were three picnic tables. The one in the middle closest to the edge was where Beverly was seated. She was wearing a pale green dress, large white sunglasses and her helmeted hair was not moving one bit in the mild wind, because the sheer lilac scarf she had tied over her hair helped to keep it immobile. She was staring out at the vast sound and the view was incredible. You could see north to the city, and all down the south water line, a small island or two off to the west. We were getting a terrific aerial view of things, this has to be one of the highest lookout points on the sound in the area. We could actually look down at the Bluffs far to our north. My realtor mind was quickly trying to figure out how I could get some great shots of Clinton from up here and maybe some at night to show off the city's waterfront skyline. But then Beverly spied us.

"Oh my, it's you two! Alex I have been meaning to return your calls dear but I have just been so busy. It has been a madhouse. Why ah, oh you see I am just out here enjoying the view and I thought I'd have a little tea. I have someone who is supposed to meet me here any minute now. Is there anything urgent I can help you two with?" This she said as she stood up from the picnic table. A table she certainly had set up for tea. It was covered in a white Seaview table cloth. On top was a proper picnic basket, two Seaview china cups and saucers, a silver tea serving set, with a sugar bowl and tongs, green, cloth napkins, and a plate of dainty cookies at the ready. Just a simple picnic tea, Beverly style. She noticed us staring at the table, "Oh, as I mentioned I'm expecting company any minute now. Of course I would ask you all to join me but I'm afraid this is a private meeting and I do not have any extra cups or supplies to accommodate you. How did you know to find me way out here anyway?"

Wanda explained Pamela had directed us. Beverly's frosted pink lips turned down a bit, "Well, Pamela is really having some serious problems of late I'm afraid. I no sooner have her back on track with her five S's and then she goes and directs unexpected guests to my private meeting! Not that I'm not just thrilled to see you both but as I've mentioned this is a private tea I am having."

We walked over to the table and Wanda commented, "Damn, this view is the bomb Beverly and I mean it! You can see everything from way up here and the water and rocks are so far down below it don't even look real! Say why don't they have no fence or railing up here? This table sure is awfully close to the edge."

Beverly smiled, "Oh yes Wanda this certainly is our little secret view here. Why the railing has been taken down temporarily. It needed to be reinforced and with my outdoor music installation project underway, I just had them go ahead and lay the music cable line up the hill to here. The speaker boxes are going to be incorporated into the new safety railing. Soon enough we'll have lovely music piped in here just like on the course down below. So you two do mind that edge now! Anyway, is there something I can help you with because as I said, I am expecting company any minute now." With that she cocked her head to the side just a bit, sort of like Ralph does, and gave us a semi frigid, frosty pink smile. Wanda moved the plate of cookies and plopped her yellow bag down and said, "Beverly, Alex and I need to talk with you and it is very important. It might be best if you sit down." Wanda took a seat at the picnic table's bench, her back to the sound and I came around and sat next to her. Beverly looked simultaneously peeved and curious. She quickly glanced behind her and then sat down with her back to the stone steps and trees.

Wanda had already turned the recorder on and it was clipped to the side of her purse, hidden from Beverly's vantage point. Out of her pocket book she pulled the small cardboard box and opened the top. Beverly let out a loud gasp. "Where did you find that? How do you have that? Do you realize that box was stolen from my office on Saturday night?"

Wanda put her hand up, "It's okay lady. Now look the fact is we have this here box and you can clearly see what's in it. Vials, needles. What's more important is you just stated this was stolen from your office, is that right Mrs. Beverly LeFaye, of Seaview, that is your legal name right?"

Wanda was clearly overdoing her Perry Mason routine, hoping to get Beverly to admit to everything on tape. Beverly pulled her white sun glasses off and her pale blue eyes were steely and had that gleam in them. "Well! I sure never would have thought that you two would break into my lovely home, riffle through my belongings and steal my personal items. This is just too much! You two should just be ashamed of yourselves. Do you realize how much trouble you two are going to be in? Alex! I am especially disappointed with you, although with your endless clothing mishaps and all the help I have had to provide you regarding the way you present yourself to the world, well I have to say I should not be too surprised. Slovenly dressing habits are a sure indication of a predisposition for crime. And on top of these crimes, do you realize that you broke two priceless French figurines? I can tell you that you two are going to pay for those!"

Wanda put her hand back up, "Save it all for the judge lady, 'cause we both know what you have been doing here at Seaview. See we had these vials tested by a professional lab and guess what? They all came back positive for a list of poisons. Poisons you outlined on a sheet of paper in your own handwriting in your unlabeled red file. Remember that file Beverly? We got that too, right here in my pocket book. So we got proof you investigated poisons that can kill people and not leave a trace. Things that makes people stop breathing and cause heart attacks, gee like old geezers often die of naturally. Seems you have been offing people here and then as luck would have it, you end up with all those listings. Making some serious bank ain't ya killer?" With that Wanda leaned in closely to Beverly's face which was aghast.

"Oh NO! You can't mean that, you can't mean that you think, that I? You think that I was poisoning Seaviewers? You two are in way over your heads. I'm afraid you have no idea how sordid this all is.

I have been trying to save everyone! Those vials and poisons, those are NOT mine. They came from…"

Before she could finish Wanda and I simultaneously noticed that Beverly's tea date had arrived. "Go on Bev Ann, explain to your company here where those poisons came from. We are all just DYING to know, aren't we folks?" This from Ellen's mouth as she clamped her hands down on Beverly's shoulders from behind. Beverly let out a startled cry.

Ellen took her hands off of Beverly's shoulders and let out a loud laugh, "So you two found this crap here in my SISTER's apartment right? Isn't that rich Bev, you with all this poison and oh look, there are some syringes in here. There's even the new vial of thallium powder with the red cap here. The one I left on your desk that you claimed you never saw. Well, seems you might not have been lying after all, looks like these two got it before you saw it. Silly me, I thought you were playing another one of your cat and mouse games Bev! Trying to psych me into thinking you didn't receive my not so subtle reminder that you better pay up and soon or else we'd have us another round of thallium fun on our hands.

What a tidy little box you've put together Bev! Must say I'm not surprised, what with how you do everything so organized and perfect. Aww, look at the tea you set up and for little ol' me Bev? You didn't say you were inviting these two when I agreed to meet you here. Did you two crash Beverly's little tea party? Tsk, tsk, you KNOW that's a big check minus mark in her little book, now don't you?" With that Ellen used her arm and swept the picnic basket and tea service off the table, the sugar bowl actually bounced and fell over the cliff. "So much for your perfect little tea party!"

Beverly was shocked, "Why ELLEN HANSEN, the full tea service, on the ground! The sugar bowl just went over the side. You'll have to pay for this Ellen, there are no two ways about it. Just look at the mess you have made here!"

Wanda picked up the small cardboard box and placed it back inside her pocket book. Ellen walked around to our side of the table, "Oh, putting away your little tea party show and tell and so soon? Ha! We got lots to cover, ain't that right Bev Ann? Oh and what's this on the side of your purse missy? Why look Bev, this bitch is recording you! They are setting you up Bev! Can you believe it?" Ellen then went into a wild manic cackle while hoisting Wanda's purse up from the table and hanging it off of her left shoulder, flipping her long braided pony tail out of the way. I started to get up but Ellen cut me off, "NO, don't get up! When you are around me, you don't need to go through all of that stand-for-a-lady shit that Beverly insists on. SIT! See I'm good at that command because I used to be a veterinarian, worked with animals, ain't that right Bev? Yep, had me one of the best vet practices in all of Clinton, dogs and cats and farm animals too. But you two already know that don't you? Guess who I ran into the other day at the Clinton Co-op Bev? You know that grubby little hippie grocery store that you think is just *too nasty* for words? Turns out these two have been talking with old Doc Baxter! Yep, they had some lame horse to unload and you and me came up in their conversation Beverly. Ain't that rich, your friends here know I used to be a vet! You don't

312

like anyone to know about that now do you Bev? You know, I think you two need to stand up now after all and stretch out your legs. Don't you agree with me Bev?"

Wanda's eyes bugged out and then I looked more closely and knew why. Ellen had pulled out a sizable switchblade. "Yes, you two get up nice and slow, step back from the table's bench and stretch out those legs. Tell 'em Bev, proper stretching is just oh, so essential to ensure one's perfect health, or some sunshiny bullshit like that, right Bevvy?"

We got up and Beverly was sputtering, "Now Ellen, Ellen dear! Let's just have a nice sit down here and we'll get this all sorted out like we always do. I'm sure all four of us can make this a win-win for everyone."

Ellen snickered, "Shut the FUCK up Bev."

Beverly shot back, "Ellen! There is no need for such vulgar language. Now you need to just calm down and..."

"Zip that plastic surgery face shut and just listen for once in your damn life. You miserable fucking CUNT! There, bet you just adore that word, huh Bev? You are NOT in charge of this Bev, we are playing by my book and rules from now on, you got it? We got us a problem here with these two. They are now in the know about our situation and I intend to solve it. You are always making it sound like you have done me such BIG FAVORS, ain't that right? Acting like I'm the worse piece of shit you ever stepped in. Bailing me out when they framed me and took away my vet license. Said you got me out of the psych hospital. Ain't that rich, YOU getting ME out of the loony bin.  YOU are the MENTAL bitch here Beverly!  YOU!  Little miss fucking perfect, you could never stop could you?  Telling me how you've helped me with legal bills, living expenses and how I should eternally KISS your ass for getting me this fucking bedpan job here at Seaview.  Yes, all hail Beverly LeFaye, the queen of Seaview!  You are rotten to the core Bev, and you know it!  It's true you might have helped me out of a jam or two and lent me money, I will grant you that.  But miss high and holy here has such a fit when she suspects I'm offing these rich assholes here.  I don't see you having problems with the money from all the vacant listings, huh BEV?  You just want it all done on the down low, all peachy and sweet just like you, right Bev Ann?

Little do these people here or elsewhere know about the REAL Beverly LeFaye.  They don't, DO they BEV?"  Ellen was now as red as a beet and she was waving her knife in the air with each word.  Beverly slowly rose from the table and started walking around the side towards Ellen with that gleam in her eyes.

"You just shut your mouth right now Ellen Hansen!  I have a good mind to wash it out with some of the poison in these vials.  You are awful!  I have done nothing but try to help you, your whole life!  You are ungrateful and you ARE mental Ellen.  Mother should have had you put away a long time ago!  You were always such a nasty little sister, jealous of every single thing I ever did and mama just coddled you and encouraged your un-lady like behavior.  Then you took off with all those grubby little hippies, you were gonna be *one with nature*, wasn't that it Ellen?  Disgusting!  Nothing but a bunch of unwashed,

314

disease ridden, drug addled, naked, sex perverts! Disgraceful! Well I helped to pull you out of that abyss and you are still nothing but a completely ungrateful, spiteful little bitch! I knew you were sick when you killed my little kitty Fluffy, just snapped her poor little neck in front of me as if it were nothing and then straight faced lied about it to mama! Mama never did want to see the truth about you Ellen. The truth is, you belong in the insane asylum and you always have!"

Ellen was boiling, "It's too damn bad I didn't just snap your fucking little neck instead of your damn little prissy cat's! I should have gotten rid of you a long time ago when I had the chance. But you see, that's where I have manners you bitch! I let you live, I politely put up with all of your bullshit. Yeah, you only see the one side of things, the Bev side! Well there's two sides to each coin Bev Ann, now ain't there? I bet you haven't told our little friends here about your bad doings now have you Bev? See folks, since we are all here today for a full confessional ladies tea, let's put Beverly's dirty knickers on the laundry line, huh? You wanna tell 'em Bev? It's all out now how you are the great protector of me, how you covered up my little pokes and potions, but that ain't the whole story now is it Bev?" She pulled the pocket book up higher on her shoulder, "Want to make sure this all gets on their tape recorder. See Beverly here has some dark skeletons of her own, skeletons no one but me ever knew about. Ain't that right Bev?

When Beverly doesn't get what she wants, well I'm sure you and the rest of Seaview knows what that is like, right? Well way back when, old sweetness here wanted to be a movie star. Thought she was on her way with that Miss America Pageant. Prim and proper there

315

even fucked two of the pageant judges but that still didn't get her a win, now did it Beverly? So she came back to Clinton with her tail between her legs but soon enough she met herself a local TV producer, didn't you Bev? She schemed her way right into his marital bed and then onto his ladies show. Poor Leon didn't have a clue what a conniving cunt you are! Old Beverly here knew what I did for kicks and she came to me and asked me for help with getting rid of Mary Anne Devail. That's what we did, we off-ed her; she too enjoyed some thallium tea. It was much easier to do way back when, even as a high schooler I easily figured it out. I just purchased the rat poison at Lawson's Hardware and helped older sister here make it work! Of course that being the first time, it took a bit of work and trial and error to make it work. You gotta account for that margin of error when you are young and just coming out of the gate. And there were more jobs I helped her out with over the years, right Bev? The final one was when your stupid fucking show got cancelled for good and you couldn't take having Leon around anymore because he was no longer useful. So I helped you arrange for that heart attack, didn't I Bev?

Beverly has always been a pro at using and manipulating what she can in others and with me she had her natural born killer close by, at the ready, and in the family!"

With that Beverly snapped, she literally snarled like a wild cat and lunged at Ellen, slamming right into her gut. The knife flew out of Ellen's hand and she fell back onto her ass and then flipped right over the side of the cliff. We could hear her screaming and then nothing.

## NO REST

Beverly was lying face down in the grass, her head almost touching the edge of the cliff.

Well, so much for a lovely lady afternoon tea.

# 39

Wanda helped Beverly get up while I ran down and used the radio in Beverly's golf cart to call the Seaview police. Beverly was quite upset about Ellen and kept trying to go over to the edge of the cliff and look for her, see if she was okay. Wanda sat her down on the picnic bench facing the steps. I told her help was on the way. Help meaning your sister is certainly dead and washing away far below in Warner Sound as I speak. Beverly started to calm down a bit and collect herself. "Oh, this is just too awful! I certainly hope you two did not believe what Ellen said for a minute. I tried so hard all of these years to help her. Too awful. I am sorry you had to be privy to her insanity. I've tried to get her on medication for years but she just won't listen. Oh, this is terrible! Oh! My, would you look at me? My hose is ripped and I have grass stains on my lovely dress. I bet my face and hair are a fright! Wanda do you have a compact handy, I hate to look such a mess when my security people arrive it sets such a bad example."

Wanda looked around for old yeller and then gave me a look, "Well Beverly it seems my pocket book is not here now. I don't have a compact on me. Why don't we just go and sit in your golf cart and wait for the police there. You don't need to worry about your hair and face, I'm sure they are going to realize you have just been through a lot."

We escorted Beverly down the steep steps and when we reached the carts, the Seaview security and police were just pulling up. From there the rest of the afternoon was a blur. They interviewed

Wanda and me at the scene and then again at the Seaview Police Station individually. We both told them exactly what had taken place, that the sisters were arguing over suspected foul play evidence we had uncovered and at one point Beverly lunged at Ellen and that was all she wrote. They said they were taking statements from Beverly and if they needed anything more from us they would be in touch. Right now they were focusing on recovering the body and considered this incident to be an accident. We left and then realized Wanda's pocket book contained her life. We had no keys to her car, her cell phone was gone, all of the evidence over the cliff as well. So we walked to the Towers and had Pamela ring Ethel and she told us to come right up.

Ethel made us some coffee; well she boiled water for the coffee crystals. And we filled her in on everything that had taken place. We sat out on her balcony and watched as the search and rescue helicopter flew back and forth just off of the lookout point. Farther out in the sound were the local news helicopters circling like vultures at their allowed distance. Eventually we went inside and Ethel decided we could all use something stronger than coffee. So she got out her bottle of Manischewitz Concord Grape Wine and started pouring. Meanwhile Wanda called Percy and he agreed to pick up her spare car key at her house and then bring it to us. Then she called Miz Lyla and let her know to meet up with Percy at her house, so he could get the car key.

Ethel asked me to turn on the TV and Channel Four's Katie Katori was manically babbling away about the "Breaking news at Seaview!" According to Katie, speculation was there had been a suicide, murder or accident at Seaview's prominent lookout point. Amazing how they could deduce those three possible scenarios, such ace reporting. However, I am surprised they didn't factor in a possible alien abduction. They kept cutting to their helicopter reporter and we could see an aerial view of where Ellen had fallen over and there were all sorts of search and rescue boats down below in the water. Wanda took a sip of her wine, "Humpf! I guess it's not too likely I'm gonna be getting old yeller back is it? And damn, you know all of our evidence every bit of it, is now down there sinking to the bottom of the sound. I have to say, I did not see this one coming, old sugar getting that Ellen to do her dirty work. No sir that was a shocker for me. Them bitches double blackmailed each other all these years. With all the evidence now floating away, Ellen dead, and all the victims nothing but ashes, old Beverly LeFaye is a free lady! Ain't that a shame."

It was a shame but that's the way life is sometimes. The next two weeks were filled with the usual real estate hoo-ha. Mushy and Joocey's situation got sorted and what I predicted happened. Mommy and daddy Amanzo took title of the condo and planned to quit claim it to Precious once the bench warrant for her arrest had been cleaned up. I even got an e-vite to attend a "Rocking Hot Tub & Pool Kegger at Courtney's New Bitchin' Pad!" which I had to politely decline. I can only imagine whose idea that event was, who created the e-vite, what kind of mother/daughter swimsuits would be on hand, and who was actually going to enjoy it more. I'm betting Mushy.

According to Wanda, via Ethel, they held a brief memorial service for Ellen at Seaview and Beverly cancelled that week's Saturday night show. But, Beverly was back on the air the following week and Wanda invited me over to her house so we could check her out on the local cable access channel. I arrived at 7:45 with Clyde and a box with a coconut cake from Sasser's. Percy had wanted to attend but apparently he had met some "hot" guy online and they were supposed to have a date. I for one was all for it being a great date as Percy could then direct his pervy intentions on someone else, someone who appreciates them. Ralph greeted Clyde and me by breaking out into a very loud squawking repertoire with some choice expletives thrown in for flavor. Wanda turned on her TV, which sits in her kitchen and we sat down on her kitchen island bar stools, slurped our slushies and watched *What's Happening Seaview!*

Beverly was decked out in an extremely bright butter cup yellow sequin dress with matching feather boa. She looked like Big Bird's human cousin. Pinned on her flowing gown near her neckline was a simple black ribbon. "I'm so happy we can be together again friends, this means so much to me after my recent tragedy. I'm so sorry I had to miss last week's show but I believe you all understand that grief is a timely and multi-stage process and I am now at the acceptance stage and moving gaily forward! It's so important not to dwell on life's little unpleasantries. I'm sure you all know that my dear sister, Ellen Hansen, recently passed away unexpectedly and so tonight, in her honor, I am wearing this black ribbon. When we go to break in just a minute, I have asked The Seatones and our very own Marvin Tuttle to provide a little tribute to Ellen, some of her favorite songs. Anyhow, now let's get right down to business and let me tell you what's in store for tonight's show...." It was a real doozie of a line up: her special guest was author, Cindy Swanson, there to discuss her book, <u>Grieving in 7 Easy Days</u> who Beverly described as the Evelyn Wood of the grieving world; Sequin-ing with Sandy in the craft segment; today's special recipe was Pot Roast Supreme and Marshmallow Surprise; and their newest resident, former world champion ball room dancer, Juan Feuvos was there to teach everyone a "new" and fun dance called the *Macarena*. And then just before they broke for commercials, Marvin Tuttle sang his syrupy tribute to Ellen, which was compiled versions of Procol Harum's *A Whiter Shade of Pale*, Jefferson Airplane's *White Rabbit* and the Velvet Underground's *Heroin*.

"Damn, if that man's mash-up of those songs doesn't sound just like the shit you play in your ride Alex. Too bad old Ellen was a killer and died. Otherwise, you could've had yourself a nice hippie cougar mama to listen to records with in your spare time."

"Shut up! Like you are one to even talk, the one who sings into her hairbrush late at night to Barry White."

The rest of the show and evening at Wanda's continued on as above. I for one am deadly when it comes to coconut cake or pie, so we completely killed the coconut cake.

The following Monday I received a call from Beverly. She said there was an offer on Harvey Malloy's place and since I was the co-listing agent we should meet and review it together. Like she gave a shit what I thought. Then her brilliant idea emerged, "Oh Alex, it's been quite a while since I saw both you and Wanda and it would be ever so nice, help the healing process, if we all met and created some

322

closure to that unfortunate incident two weeks ago. Why don't you see if you can bring Wanda along and gosh, we can have lunch together! Now that does sound pleasant, doesn't it? Say around noon today? I'll host us in my apartment and—"

When hell freezes over am I eating anything that sugar witch might whip up in her kitchen! One because I've seen her nasty TV recipes and no they are not the *new* nasty. And two, what kind of poisons might she have tucked away in her kitchen cupboard? "Ah, Beverly, that is nice of you to ask us to your place but I think we'd prefer to meet up with you say out by the pool?"

"Oh, I get it! Why of course we should enjoy this pleasant sunshine while we have it, Indian Summer is almost over after all. What a delightful idea Alex! I'll meet you and Wanda at the Towers' poolside and we can have Seaview cater luncheon for us. See you soon!"

I called Wanda and she said she was going to cancel her existing lunch plans, "This is a must-be there, killer lady lunch." I picked her up at her office and we rolled through the front gate fairly quickly as Army Amy was on duty today and not Dave. While we walked out to the pool area, the speakers assaulted us with a prissy musical version of *Light My Fire* which featured a screechy violin and every now and then a sugary, whispering chorus of women would hiss, "Light my fire." Wanda looked back at me while holding the door to the pool area open and rolled her eyes, "Only fire I'd like to light around here would be one underneath old killer over there and these here fluffy white lady singers. Mmph!"

323

Outside, there was Beverly smiling pleasantly at a prime table near the wading pool. She was wearing a white straw sun hat with a lavender scarf tied around it and a pale blue dress. "Oh I am so happy you two could join me for luncheon today! As I told Alex, this could be one of the last sunny days where we can sit outside. My and look at you two! Wanda in your pumpkin dress again I see? Well this time is looks better on you but you know dear, it is important to rotate your clothing so you are not repeating a look too frequently. I have a great chart I devised that can help you with that. That dress *is* tad bright for this time of year but well, perhaps you are thinking pumpkins and that time of year is really almost here! Oh and Alex, well dear your shirt is tucked in and fairly flat but I'm still going to send you home with a can of my hairspray so you can tackle that fussy little cowlick of yours! It's just too sweet of you two to join me. Here is a copy of the offer for Mr. Malloy's place Alex. I'm sure you'll agree with me that we should just accept and let this new Seaview buyer start enjoying all the fun!" She kept all this pleasantry bullshit up while we ordered and then ate our lunches and then it was brass tacks.

"So, I just want to make sure we are all in agreement as to what a tragedy it is that Ellen slipped and fell from the lookout point. We have never had a chance to really speak since all of that unpleasantness and I feel it is best that we all move forward together on a happy note. And I want you both to know that I have forgiven you for breaking my priceless lady figurines. I have decided I am not going to have you pay for them. I am going to just let it be! Now I am assuming that today you do not have a tape recorder hidden anywhere?" She smiled as she gave both of us an up and down with that special gleam in her eye.

Wanda shook her head, "No we are not taping today. You know Beverly there is a good chance you might not be sitting out here with us today having lunch at all if things had not gone down like they did. Ellen had an interesting take on things. You don't know this but I always thought you were the killer, that you were doing it all. So I was very surprised when Ellen spilled the beans. But you still knew about it all, encouraged her, helped out even. And we don't have any of that evidence; it died with Ellen and went for a swim in the sound. So I'd say you are a lucky lady."

"Aww, why thank you Wanda. You know I do realize just how fortunate I am and as everyone knows, I sure have always tried to be a lady! Well this is just fine that you two realize things are what they are and we are all now just moving gaily forward."

"Lady, I'd still like to bust yo' ass. Don't get me wrong, you know that we know and that's really all that matters. So don't you get too comfy late at night thinking you got it made in the shade Miss LeFaye, 'cause honey someday karma gonna come along and whoop yo' ass!" With that Wanda stood up and so did I.

Beverly was sputtering a response of some kind when all of the old lady geezers around the pool started to scream and call out, "The Flasher! The flasher, he's back!" Sure enough, there he was next to the small wading pool in his black ski mask, wide open green rain coat, black army boots and his "little dingle" as Wanda so lovingly refers to it, wagging back and forth for all to see. Before I could blink, Wanda took off and just as the Flasher was turning she tackled him from the side, both of them going down in the wading pool with an enormous splash.

The Tower staff arrived, then security and Wanda was helped up off of the Flasher, who was lying spread eagle in the wading pool. Wanda was soaking wet from head to toe but as she stood up she pulled the ski mask off and...

"DAVE? Seriously it's Dave the gate Nazi! Dave the asshole guard is the FLASHER! Say what? I knew your little dingle was too young to be no old man's dingle! Damn this here Seaview is just beyond some serious old white folks crazy! DAVE?!"

Well, at least we got one "crime" solved and bagged the perp or however Wanda would phrase that.

**The following two chapters are from the forthcoming Alex Campbell Real Estate Mystery Novel, <u>No Reality</u>.**

# One

*atya Loki Luna!*

> *Or should I say Wise Crone? ☺ I was shopping at the Clinton Co-op today when my bladder let me know it was time to release. Upon exiting the restroom, I took time to look at the bulletin board. Wow, was Goddess guiding me when I discovered your flyer for your Wise Crone Wisdom Circle!*

> *You write about getting shivers when a Crone courageously steps forward, I too had shivers upon finding your flyer! How can I convey? It just spoke to me on so many levels! Each of your bullet points, connecting, respecting and leaning into all we do not know—just momentarily blew by charkas. We are so on the same wave length, I can feel it! I had to treat myself to a yummy bottle of organic, raw, Kombucha and re-center.*

> *Though I am not yet technically a Crone, I too yearn for the connection and wisdom that Goddess imparts upon us all at that sacred time. Soon too, my moon cycle will be no more and I will joyfully and with reverence bury my monthly cup in a special ceremony. I would love to have a Crone group, such as yours, in place and there with me to witness, honor and revere the ceremonial burial of my menses cup. Giving birth to my new and wiser womynhood, my Crone!*

> *When I got home I told my familiar, Ankh, that I'd found a new wisdom circle. Ankh perked right up and trust me, Ankh is very intuitive and knowing. Technically, Ankh is a Norway rat but anyone who meets her knows she is way wiser than the mere confines of body and stereotype.*

> *I would be honored to come and witness, learn, share and bask within your circle of Crone Wisdom. I notice in your group photograph, the ceremonial walking*

1

*sticks or are they Goddess wisdom wands? So creative and festive! I too am very*
*creative and one of my passions is crafting custom Goddess gowns from found,*
*reclaimed materials and repurposing with natural, organic dyes. Perhaps I could*
*bring some of my gown creations to share with Circle?*

*On a more mundane note, I note that your flyer only provides this post*
*office box as a means of reaching out to you. I imagine this too is part of Crone*
*Wisdom at work, here; i.e. no email or phone number, just an anonymous snail*
*mail box. Sort of a test perhaps to see who is truly motivated to come and learn and*
*grow with the Circle. Who is willing to write a letter, place it in an envelope,*
*address it and affix postage to it—a real commitment and time drain in our modern*
*word, n'est-ce pas?*

*Anyway, if you too feel this connection, the energy here in this moment,*
*please feel free to connect and let me know more. If not, no worries, all in the hands*
*of Goddess! I too am providing a post office box for response, as I feel this line of*
*communication is part of the journey to enter the Wise Crone Wisdom Circle!*
*Mahalo,*
*Raven's Dawn*

"Now you tell me what the fuck all that is, huh?" Wanda said
while her potty mouth parrot reiterated, "What the fuck, what the fuck,
what the fuck…squawk!"

I shook my head looking down at the letter on light blue
stationary written in purple ink, "Ahh, sounds like some group for
former seventh grade loser girls who have turned into aging spinsters
and like to spend time with each other playing dress up power games
while reassuring each other they are indeed very special."

Wanda nodded, "Ahhum, I hear that and it could be. Also, could be a big group of some no man love, aging lezzies getting' their groove on with each other under the moonlight."

"Wanda, really?"

"Don't start up with me Alex. You, Mr. Bisexual, but I ain't had none from either side of the fence in…, how long is it now? So I'm thinking that like makes you a nosexual. Kind of harsh but hey, you called these crones the loser girls or whatever. Just sayin' them loser girls could also be lezzies. I don't have to explain all this or defend it, with you especially! I'm not sayin' it's a bad thang if them loser girls as *you* called them is out there all up in each other's business under the moonlight, just stating my take on it. So what the hell is this Raven bird lady sending me letters for at my post office box? I ain't no Crone lady or whatever they call themselves. Shit, my va-jay jay has got a lot of life left in her! I ain't no withering, dried up old lady downstairs!"

"Too much information, thank you very much. Okay, well I would say this nut found some flyer on the Clinton Co-op bulletin board and she either sent it to the wrong post office box or the flyer has a misprint and lists your box by mistake."

Wanda agreed while motioning me to plug in the blender, "You probably right. Damn this here is sure some fucked up crazy for sure! Gonna put this one right up here on the refrigerator." She said while taping it onto her glass door refrigerator and then filling the blender canister with ice. Glass door, as in Wanda insisted on purchasing (at a huge sleeping-with-the-salesman discount) this expensive glass door

3

refrigerator, she claimed it would make her eat healthier because she'd see the contents of her refrigerator all the time. She later realized the glass front shows how sloppy her refrigerator is inside and so she had curtains made. These are now hanging inside the refrigerator to hide her mess. Go figure. I told her from day one I though the glass front refrigerator was a dumb move, but deaf ears.

Wanda added rum to the ice, threw in limes and juice and started up the blender. "Here, another batch of perfect slushy and none too soon after this week, huh?" The week she was referring to had been another slow one and in the business of providing home loans and selling houses (our respective professions) a slow week is much worse than a busy week. Living on commission is akin to walking a tight rope and never really getting off. When the market is hot and you are making sales (money) it is great but you never know when that faucet of good fortune might be slowing down or turning off, so you are constantly trying to squirrel money away so that you can survive the lean times. And these times had become lean indeed. In harsh times when the real estate market tanks, the industry gets cleaned out.

However, contrary to what common sense might say many of those who are cleaned out are actually good, competent, and ethical people. Many of those left are the unethical sleaze balls that must have some eternal deal with the devil going on and others are independently wealthy and play real estate agent/lender when it suits them. Nothing wrong with that but unfortunately far too many of those are grossly incompetent and have all the attitude that deep pockets can buy. The rest of us, like Wanda and me, try to keep above water, do the right thing for our clients and hope that someday the public or universe will wake up to these con artists and support us. It's very hard to not get bitter or jaded in this business when you watch the rip-off artists, manipulators and psychos take the bulk of the biz. However, they know how to spin and tell their clients, the public, exactly what they want to hear. They know how to appeal to the client's inner greed, even if their inner greed is actually shooting them in the foot in their transaction. Yes, it's a good thing Wanda was hosting a slushy night because rants like these in my mind were becoming far too frequent. "Cheers Wanda! To a better week, may we be busy."

"Truth to that baby! Here let's sit in the window and relax our minds a spell." She said guiding us from the kitchen island over to her open dining room with its original 1900s art and crafts style paneling and box beam ceiling and now with a large cage in it for Ralph her newly inherited parrot. (see Volume Three) The dining room has a terrific bay window and built-in bench seat with comfy, colorful cushions. There is a nice view of the downtown (which lies just below the huge hill which is Wanda's neighborhood, the Highmont) and beyond the downtown, views of Warner Sound, its water sparkling in the moonlight. "It's definitely time for us to get out there and stir the pot, shake some trees and all that. But tonight is meant for slushies and I thought I'd fry us up some chicken, then maybe we'll see what's what!"

# Two

W hat's what, went on until about 1:00 a.m. and once home to my little ranch, I had to take Clyde out back so he could water the grass and check out every corner to make sure no squirrels were out late at night partying. The rest of the weekend went by in a haze, just the usual house work, paying bills—the whole chop wood, carry water bullshit that we all do. Unfortunately Monday came too soon and for once I had to go into the office. We had a mandatory meeting or as mandatory a brokerage can make a meeting, i.e. the agents are technically independent contractors and labor laws do not allow them to impose too many strings on us, thank god!

This meeting promised to be interesting, I suppose. It was suddenly called last week and the email stated we all must attend and if not to provide a legitimate excuse for not being there. Yes, all sorts of rumors were flying at my brokerage, Winterfrost Real Estate, as to what this meeting would be about. Some claimed they were raising monthly fees which I doubt because they are too ball-less to want to do that face to face and in person. Others thought they were going to try and start re-implementing weekly meetings, god forbid! The weekly meeting bullshit used to be somewhat necessary back in the day prior to agents having unlimited access to the multiple listing service. The meetings back then had a purpose to provide agents with news, new listings, etc.... That all faded away and the weekly meetings had become just a bad habit. Agents reluctantly coming in once a week to hear news they'd already seen online, to hear about another agent's new listing, which who gives a shit because if you have a client that is looking for something like that then you will know about it immediately when it posts on the multiple listing database, or you should if you are actually working for your clients. The meetings were just a lot of crowing and back stabbing and a bore. So many brokerages have now done away with them, some altogether. This meeting was not something anyone was expecting, hence all the rampant speculation as to what it was going to be about.

I made sure my shirt was tucked in, I was wearing a belt and that I looked fairly business like and hopped in my two door aging blue Volvo. I headed over to Winterfrost Real Estate, leaving my in between the tracks unknown neighborhood south of downtown behind. The Winterfrost parking lot was almost full and all of the assorted luxury cars *de jour* were crammed in the narrow spaces. I saw Stinky (a.k.a. Share Shelton's) hulking black Mercedes SUV with its SOLD vanity plate and next to it was Tiger Conley's two door cherry red Mercedes with leopard skin seats and her vanity plate, GROWL3. I guess my plate should say IT RUNS. No sooner was I out of the car then fucking Kenny Vance came bopping up.

"Hey there stranger! Alex you are never here, we don't ever get to see you!" he said all perky and jolly as he attempted to hug me. This I skillfully turned into a hand shake. What is it with all this hugging shit these days and especially from the likes of Kenny? Kenny is a 30-something, pomaded Beiber hairdo, and oh so proud to be gay, asshole. He reminds me of an updated, gay Eddie Haskel from *Leave it to Beaver.* He joined our office a while back and is the phoniest, fake

7

happy, butt kisser I've come across in a long while. He enjoys handing out candy bars and trying to become best friends with everyone in our office. What he hopes to gain from all of this is beyond me. Apparently he hasn't gotten over his former corporate life's brainwashing yet and doesn't realize that in this business kissing ass with your so called co-workers is not to your advantage. They are not going to promote you or give you a bonus or raise. So if you are butt kisser, why waste your time?

"Yeah, hi Kenny. Parking lot sure is full today."

"Yes it certainly is! I could barely slip my little 320i in here and it's brand new so I don't want any scratches on my baby! Isn't this meeting too exciting? I was up all last night on the phone and online just chatting with *everyone* about what this could all be about. You know I heard it might be they are going to do away with having a receptionist. I for one think we really need Nayina and you know this is a lot of the reason I chose to brand myself with the Winterfrost name and …."

Yes, and blah, blah, blah to you too. Jesus.

Inside, the Viper Pit was a complete frenzy. I haven't seen it this cluster fucked in ages, since we used to have the obnoxious weekly meetings which Todd Blund, our manager, thankfully did away with. All the assorted agents were there and on display. Display being the right word as they remind me of turkeys strutting around and displaying their feathers when they are in mating season. Everyone was all sunshine smiles, and ha, ha, ha, while oh so busy texting and talking on their cells, diddling their iPads. I guess hiding your insecurity behind fake smiles and technology is the preferred tactic these days. Meanwhile, it didn't take a psychic to see they were also busy shooting daggers of envy, jealousy, anger at their real and presumed nemeses and employing enough passive aggressive techniques to fill a pop shrink book. Speaking of, the latest pop shrink book I am reading (which I force myself to do with some regularity in order to tell myself I'm not completely jaded and cynical) would go over well with this group, <u>Lean On Me and Thrive: Learning to Always Have Your Bro's Back in Challenging Times</u>.

Nayina was putting out more metal fold out chairs, guess that puts an end to Kenny and company's no receptionist theory. I took a crappy metal chair that was in the last row and closest to the back door and waited for the Winterfrost circus to begin. And begin it did.

"HI THERE! I'M SUZIE HORTON!" This from a very pert, lean, woman in her 60s with a short, touched up, brown hairdo. She was dressed in an immaculate black pant suit with razor sharp pant leg creases, and a crisp burgundy blouse peaking out. Her suit's jacket sported a gold name badge, she wore sensible flat black shoes and simple gold earrings. Her voice was extremely loud and reminded me of Lucy from *Peanuts* when she yells or talks over the other characters. "WELL, I SAID, HELLO THERE, I'M SUZIE HORTON! AND THAT FOLKS IS WHEN YOU SAY, *HI SUZIE* BACK TO ME! GO ON LET'S GIVE THAT TRY, I'LL DO IT WITH YOU...READY...."

Hi suzie.

## CHARLES CHAPLIN

"OH NO, I AM SURE WINTERFROST REAL ESTATE CAN DO MUCH BETTER THAN THAT! NOW COME ON SAY IT LIKE THE NUMBER ONE OFFICE YOU ARE…READY…."

"HI Suzie."

"WELL THAT IS BETTER BUT WE'LL PRACTICE. THAT'S ONE OF THE CORE COMPONENTS OF TEAM WORK, PRACTICE! Alright now that I have your attention, let me introduce myself. I'm Suzie Horton and I've been selling real estate for over 40 years. I've been in a management capacity going on 20 years and was most recently with Dale Brown Real Estate in Denver where I headed up their national outreach division. So why am I here today in Clinton, in your office talking to you? Well, I AM YOUR NEW MANAGER AND WE ARE GOING TO TAKE YOUR BUSINESS TO THE NEXT LEVEL! SAY THAT WITH ME, ALL TOGETHER, NEXT LEVEL…READY…"

"Next level."

"Oh, we have a lot to work on here! Right off the bat I want to put this new mantra in your head and I want each and every one of you to say this in your mirror out loud when you first get up in the morning, in your car's rear view mirror every time you glance at it, all day long I want this mantra playing! This gem is going to be the foundation upon which you are going to grow your business. ACT ENTHUSIASTIC AND YOU'LL BE ENTHUSISATIC! TOGEHER NOW, READY…"

"Act enthusiastic and you'll be enthusiastic." This shit went on for several more rounds until butt munches like Kenny were practically

10

doing somersaults to say it louder and jump for Suzie's proverbial carrot on the stick. Gee stupid mule, in this case there is no carrot and guess what fuck-tard, they ain't gonna give you a carrot, i.e. a buyer or listing.

"OKAY GOOD START THERE TEAM! And KENNY, that's your name? You were the most enthusiastic! I want everyone to note how he jumped up out of his chair and put his whole body into it. That's what we are going to do each Monday morning when we meet. Let's give Kenny a hand!" Which we all did with zero enthusiasm but Kenny didn't miss the chance to stand up and smile really big and take a bow which just made Suzie's nipples hard I'm sure.

"I like to start every meeting off with the enthusiasm huddle as I call it and then at the end of today's meeting you'll see how we end. This creates great synergy. So, I know you all are wondering what am I doing here, where's Todd? Well, Todd is tying up some loose ends and will be away for a while. When he returns, Winterfrost will figure out his new role. I just want us to focus on our future here together and growing this office and of course YOUR business! I'll be doing things differently from Todd and we'll all be adapting but that's the key to life and business right, ADAPTING! I think you caught the first change here. We are going to go back to the old ways and will be having a mandatory Monday morning meeting here every Monday at 9:00 a.m. sharp. I expect each and everyone one of you to be here, no excuses." To this there were quite a few loud groans and a round of low level chatter.

# CHARLES CHAPLIN

"NOW QUIET DOWN! You'll be getting a revised office policy and procedures manual in your boxes today, Nayina is busy at work printing them. I know a lot of you are all into your emails and remote officing but we are not going to do that anymore. It's live and center here every MONDAY! I can promise you that you will learn something at each of our meetings, our HOUR OF POWER as I call it and you all are going to grow your business like never before! I'm going to personally make sure of that. Many of you might think you are at the top of your game now but I can assure you that I'm going to take you out of your personal comfort zones and up to the next level, to the mountain's peak and HIGHER!"

Higher than the peak, what would that be the steep fall back down to the valley? I scouted the room to check out the reaction. Everyone was squirming a bit, many whispering to each other, some texting. Stinky was scowling but I couldn't tell if that's just her normal look or if this was setting her off. Tiger was picking her teeth with her index finger's stick-on nail and Kenny gazed up adoringly at Suzie as if he were about to turn straight on the spot.

"Now, I've got name badges for each of you, just like mine, in my office. I want each of you to stop by and pick yours up. New policy here, you've got to wear your Winterfrost name badge every day, especially when you are out in the field, no excuses! We want everyone to know that YOU ARE A REAL ESTATE PROFESSIONAL! Say that with me, ready… I AM A REAL ESTATE PROFESSIONAL! LOUDER, I CAN'T HEAR YOU!"

# NO REALITY

Suzie finally ended this bullshit with her meeting "closing." I would call it a prayer. We were all now apparently worshipping at the Winterfrost Church of Real Estate with Pastor Suzie but she called it the closing, "My non-denominational, non-religious meditation that I like to end all my Monday Motivations with! DEAR JOYUS ENERGY...," I guess it isn't a prayer since she's yelling. "...WE ARE ALL HERE TODAY TO FILL OURSELVES WITH YOUR BRILLIANT ENERGY AND ENTHUSIASM AND TO GROW OUR BUSINESS! WITH YOUR AWESOME POWER, ANYTHING IS POSSIBLE SO LONG AS I BELIEVE IT AND LIVE IT. HELP US THIS WEEK TO SELL MORE AND GO TEAM WINTEFROST!"

With that she quickly snapped on a boom box next to her podium and proceeded to blast us with Calloway's *I Wanna Be Rich.* "HEAR THIS MUSIC FOLKS! Feel that snappy energy! We'll talk more about how you too can pump yourselves up with some funky party music!"

Should I vomit now or try and hold it? And the perky music to lift your mood? I know a sugary bitch Suzie needs to meet. (see Volume Three)

With that the meeting adjourned and everyone was talking all at once while Tiger started to dance to the music and naturally this encouraged Kenny to join in. Gag me. Tiger Conley is a naturally busty, bottle blond, Farah Fawcett hairstyle, 50-something, plump agent who always wears animal print clothing to go with her name. Her tagline is "Tiger Leads the Pack," apparently she hasn't figured out that felines travel in prides not packs. She recently moved to Clinton and joined our office and she and Stinky are new arch enemies. Tiger had on a loose purple and black cheetah print blouse which her double D girls practically fell out of as she moved all around and started twerking with Kenny. I'm seriously going to be sick now.

Stinky. Her real name is Share Shelton (pronounced Sharee) and I call her "Stinky" because she always wears the most noxious perfume that leaves a vapor trail coming and going for at least a full 30 minutes. Yes, the awesome stench of freesia, rose, musk and some unknown spice was wafting through the whole office. Share is somewhere over 60 and barely clears five feet without shoes. But she always wears pointy stiletto bitch boots that add a foot or so to her height. To give her credit, her bitch boots and inch long stick-on nails always perfectly match her camel toe tight pant suits. Today's suit was a vivid purple with a wide silver metallic belt at the waist. Her blouse was undone sufficiently to give her tanned and freckled tit valley and plumped up girls some air. Nestled in the valley today was a chunky gold and purple stone necklace. She had been wearing silver sunglasses which were now removed and she was yakking away with some other agents while stroking her dyed, spiky red and orange streaked hair or what Tiger calls her Annie Lennox look. Her lips were turned down, of course, and slathered in two shades of lavender to match her outfit. She was looking over towards Suzie's office and glaring while holding court with several agents.

I thought I could just zip out the door. Wrong. "Alex! Alex, over here." Stinky said, motioning me over. Shit. "Say you aren't trying to get out of here are you? Don't you want to hear the dirt? And can you believe this new Suzie person? I was just telling the gang here that as Winterfrost's premier agent I am having a real problem with this. Who the hell found this Suzie from Denver bitch? I want to know. I am going to be talking with upper management about this! I guess we all should fill Alex here in on Todd's sudden departure, we all know Alex never comes in the office. But I guess you are always busy with the dead bodies at your listings and the latest round of hell down there in Seaview, right Alex? (see Volume Three) You know that bitch Beverly tried to take me down on my bungalow listing at Seaview but I sold it before she could get me. See that's the thing when you are a premier agent, you get things sold quickly and you out maneuver old bags like Beverly LeFaye. Isn't that true Alex? Oh wait, I forgot she trumped you but good, took his little listing down there away from him and made herself the main listing agent, stuck him with co-lister status. What's the scoop on that little place Alex, think it is ever going to sell? Anyway, just so you are clued into reality here Alex, I wanted you to know that Todd was arrested again for driving drunk. This time the Winterfrost lawyers couldn't help. He's got to do mandatory rehab time. They are sending him to some place in Arizona to dry out and then he has all of these community service hours to do. It's a real pity, I personally always liked Todd Blund and now we see what is shaking around here with this new woman."

Yes, I'm sure Stinky did like Todd. All he ever did was fall over backwards to accommodate her, placate her and bend every possible rule he could to suit her whims. Nothing like a double standard manager to molly coddle his premier asshole, I mean agent. "Well this is news to me Share and it does appear there are some changes brewing here. Oh, the listing you mentioned actually closed last week, so I'm out of Seaview now, thankfully."

Share nodded, "Good for you, getting out of that senior living nightmare down south! I'll let you and everyone here know what I find out from upper management about all this Suzie shit. I for one, do not have the time to attend a weekly meeting and even those who aren't busy like you Alex, well I'm sure you have better things to do with your empty hours. Anyhow, I've got to move it. I'm due in the Beaumont right now! Harry and Cynthia Widener have asked me to stop by and list their stunning home. So I've got an awesome new listing coming on very soon!"

As she turned to make her grand exit, who did she bump right into? "Aggh, Tiger! You startled me. Look I have to go, get out of my way, I'm late for a very important listing appointment in the Beaumont!"

Tiger giggled, "Whoa, calm down there sexy lady! I was just coming on over here to say my howdies to you and all these other folks in the house today. Say are you off to the Widener's house in the Beaumont? I was just there yesterday showing them how a tiger leads the pack. Why look at you Share, looking sharp today! My shirt matches your pant suit, ain't that something. I keep telling you that we gotta get us some girl time shoppin' in. You ain't never power shopped till you've Tiger shopped!"

16

Stinky was now really glaring, "Wha—ugh! Get out of the way, some of us have business to get to! We don't have time for some ex-cheerleader's Monday morning pep rally complete with Kenny the gay go-go dancer and his white woman *Soul Train* wanna be!"

Tiger smiled wider, "Ooooh, now you are on it tooo-day and how! You go out there and git 'em Share! Word is that big time agent from King Arthur Realty is also stopping by for a listing presentation at the Widener's house. Well, we'll all have to wait and see who gets the prey in this one, now won't we? Best of luck Share, I know you'll dazzle them with your *preeee-mere* agent charms!"

Stinky stormed off and I, took off for the side door exit. Once outside, I stopped to breathe in some non-perfumed air and then take in what I just heard. Looks like I wasn't the only agent Harry and Cynthia Widener had contacted to come out and give a listing presentation. Oh this should just be ducky, but what do I care? If they want a would be tiger or a woman who smells like a whore house or whoever this top agent from King whatever real estate is, well then so be it.

## About the Author

Charles Chaplin (no relation) lives on planet earth (for now) and works in residential real estate (for better or worse).

To receive an e-mail notification when <u>No Reality</u>, the fourth Alex Campbell Real Estate Mystery Novel, is available for purchase, please e-mail charles@lifeinseattle.com and write "notify me" in the subject header.

Friend Alex at:

Facebook.com/Alex Campbell